Praise for
The Daughter's Walk

"Jane Kirkpatrick is a wonderful writer who creates a story full of strong, admirable characters with human flaws. Clara and Helga come to life with dimension and depth, pulling us into their world. I walked across the country with them, experienced their triumph and disappointment, and faced the shattered, angry family when they returned. Jane has given readers a wonderful story of a family schism that comes full circle to love and grace, and of the importance of family, especially when one has been an outcast. I highly recommend *The Daughter's Walk*!"

—FRANCINE RIVERS, best-selling author

"Jane embraces the finest qualities of the human spirit in all her writing. One of America's favorite storytellers."

—SANDRA DALLAS, author of *Prayers for Sale*

"Jane Kirkpatrick brings immense integrity to historical imagination, using her consummate skills as a historian sleuth and psychologist. A compelling portrait of Clara's own bold entrepreneurial spirit gives readers believable insight on how a mother and daughter's love survives financial hardship, a courageous thirty-five-hundred-mile walk, family tragedy, and estrangement. Bravo!"

—LINDA L. HUNT, award-winning author of *Bold Spirit: Helga Estby's Forgotten Walk Across Victorian America*

"Jane Kirkpatrick gives us inspiring stories of women who accomplish amazing feats. She has done it again with the poignant story of Clara Estby, who walked with her mother from Spokane to New York in a desperate bid to save the family farm from foreclosure. What was left for this daughter when her connection to family was severed? Jane brings Clara's story to life."

—DEON STONEHOUSE, Sunriver Books and Music

"Jane Kirkpatrick's attention to detail and ability to craft living, breathing characters immerses the reader into her story world. I come away entranced, enlightened, and enriched after losing myself in one of her novels."

—KIM VOGEL SAWYER, best-selling author
of *My Heart Remembers*

"*The Daughter's Walk* brings to mind another much-loved book, *Mama's Bank Account* by Kathryn Forbes, which became the Broadway play and movie *I Remember Mama*. Jane's Norwegian characters captivated me in much the same way. Uplifting and heartbreaking by turns, this is a wonderful story, superbly written."

—IRENE BENNETT BROWN, author of *Where Gable Slept*
and the award-winning young-adult novel *Before the Lark*

The Daughter's Walk

Other Books by Jane Kirkpatrick

NOVELS

Portraits of the Heart Historical Series
*A Flickering Light**
An Absence So Great

Change and Cherish Historical Series
*A Clearing in the Wild**
*A Tendering in the Storm**
A Mending at the Edge

*A Land of Sheltered Promise**

Tender Ties Historical Series
*A Name of Her Own**
Every Fixed Star
Hold Tight the Thread

Kinship and Courage Historical Series
*All Together in One Place**
No Eye Can See
What Once We Loved

Dreamcatcher Collection
*A Sweetness to the Soul**
Love to Water My Soul
A Gathering of Finches
Mystic Sweet Communion

NONFICTION

A Simple Gift of Comfort
Homestead: A Memoir of Modern Pioneers Pursuing the Edge of Possibility
*Aurora: An American Experience in Quilt, Community, and Craft**

*finalist and award-winning works

The Daughter's Walk

A NOVEL

JANE KIRKPATRICK

WATERBROOK
PRESS

THE DAUGHTER'S WALK
PUBLISHED BY WATERBROOK PRESS
12265 Oracle Boulevard, Suite 200
Colorado Springs, Colorado 80921

This book is a work of historical fiction based closely on real people and real events.
Details that cannot be historically verified are purely products of the author's
imagination.

ISBN 978-1-61129-673-0

Cover design by Mark Ford; photography by Jim Celuch

Published in the United States by WaterBrook Multnomah, an imprint of the Crown
Publishing Group, a division of Random House Inc., New York.

WATERBROOK and its deer colophon are registered trademarks of Random House Inc.

Printed in the United States of America

To strong and transforming women of all generations.

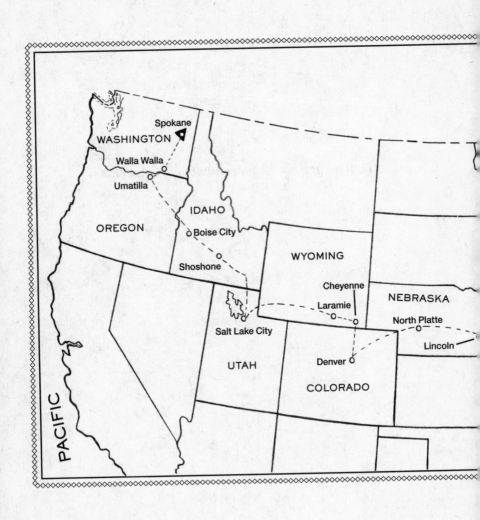

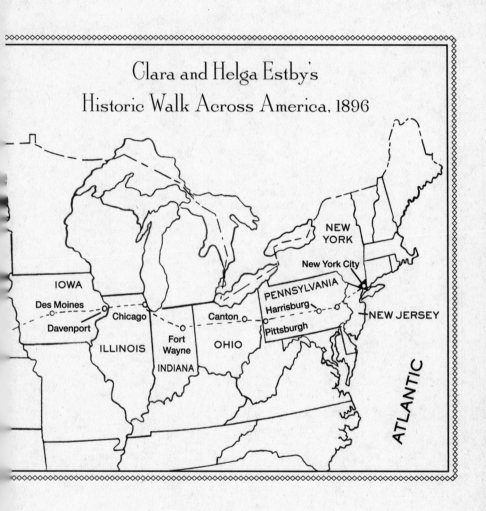

Clara and Helga Estby's
Historic Walk Across America, 1896

NEW YORK

New York City

PENNSYLVANIA

Harrisburg

NEW JERSEY

IOWA

Des Moines

Chicago

Canton

Pittsburgh

Davenport

Fort
Wayne

OHIO

ILLINOIS

INDIANA

ATLANTIC

Cast of Characters

Clara Estby	daughter of Helga
Helga Estby	wife of Ole and mother of Clara, Ole, Olaf, Ida, Bertha, Henry, Arthur, Johnny, William (Billy), Lillian
Ole Estby	husband of Helga
Hannah Estby	aunt of Clara's; sister to Ole
*Forest Stapleton	son of Clara's employer
the Rutters	employers of Bertha and Olaf
Martin Siverson	friend of Ole
Chauncey Depew	railroad magnate and philanthropist
Olea Stone Ammundsen	New York furrier
Louise Gubner	New York furrier
*Franklin Doré	agent of Olea and Louise
*John Doré	lumberman in Manistee, Michigan

*Characters designated with an asterisk are not based on actual historical figures and are fully imagined by the author.

Whether you turn to the right or to the left, your ears will hear a voice behind you, saying, "This is the way; walk in it."

ISAIAH 30:21

Nothing strengthens the judgment and quickens the conscience like individual responsibility.

ELIZABETH CADY STANTON, 1848

God is love. Love is the proof of God, and forgiveness is the proof of love.

DALE CRAMER IN *Levi's Will*

Prologue

"Go back! Just go back!" The woman glared at the dog, who stopped, his tail down, ears tipped forward in confusion.

"You can't come with me," she said. "I'm not part of this family anymore." Her voice cracked at the truth that now defined her life. Heavy, wet snow fell on the solemn pair. The dog failed to obey. Even in this she was powerless. She looked at the window, hoping her mother or sister might wave. No one. She returned to the dog.

"Go back. Please." She pointed, her voice breaking. "Go, Sailor. Go home." The dog curled his bushy tail between his legs and then turned, walking toward the farmhouse now shrouded in snow. He looked back once, but she pointed and he continued back to the family as she'd ordered.

The woman bit her lip to avoid crying, then stuffed the packet close to her chest to keep the papers dry. She pulled her fur coat around her.

Maybe she shouldn't have worn it; maybe her success offended them and that's why they'd refused.

The wind shifted, drove pelting snow into her face. She'd forgotten her umbrella at the house. It mattered little; she'd left so much more behind. She trudged toward the railroad tracks, taking her first steps into exile.

PART ONE

Family

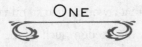

ONE

Decision

My name is Clara Estby, and for my own good, my mother whisked me away. Well, for the good of our *family* too, she insisted. Trying to stop her proved useless, because when an idea formed in her Norwegian head, she was like a rock crib anchoring a fence: strong and sturdy and unmovable once it's set. I tried to tell her, I did. We all did. But in the end, we succumbed to her will and I suppose to her hopefulness, never dreaming it would lead where it did. I certainly never imagined I'd walk a path so distant from the place where I began.

But I'm getting ahead of myself, telling stories out of sequence, something a steady and careful woman like me should never do.

It began on an April morning in 1896, inside our Mica Creek farmhouse at the edge of the rolling Palouse Hills of eastern Washington State, when my mother informed me that we would be walking from Spokane to New York City. Walking, mind you, when there were perfectly good trains a person could take. Walking—thirty-five hundred miles to earn ten thousand dollars that would save our farm from fore-closure. Also to prove that a woman had stamina. Also to wear the new reform dress and show the freedom such garments offered busy, active, sturdy women.

Freedom. The only merit I saw in the shorter skirts and absence of corsets was that we could run faster from people chasing us for being foolish enough to embark on such a trek across the country, two women, alone.

We were also making this journey to keep me "from making a ter-rible mistake," Mama told me. I was eighteen years old and able to make my own decisions, or so I thought. But not this one.

Mama stood stiff as a wagon tongue, her back to my father and me, drinking a cup of coffee that steamed the window. I could see my brother Olaf outside, moving the sheep to another field with the help of Sailor, our dog, dots of white like swirling cotton fluffs bounding over an ocean of green. Such a bucolic scene about to reveal hidden rocks beneath it.

"We are going to walk to New York City, Clara, you and I."

"What?" I'd entered the kitchen, home for a weekend from my work as a domestic in Spokane. My mother had walked four hundred miles a few years earlier to visit her parents in a time of trial. We'd all missed her, and no one liked taking over her many duties that kept the family going. But walk to New York City?

"Why would we walk, and why are we going at all?" I had plans for the year ahead, and I figured it would take us a year to make such a trek.

My father grunted. "She listens to no one, your mother, when ideas she gets into her head."

"Mama, you haven't thought this through," I said.

My mother turned to face us, her blue eyes intense. "It's not possible to work out every detail in life, but one has to be bold. Did we know you'd find work in Spokane when we left Minnesota? No. Did we think we'd ever own our own farm? No. These are good things that happened because we took a chance and God allowed it."

"We didn't expect me to become injured, to mortgage the farm because we needed money to plant and live on," my father said. It sounded like they'd had this argument more than once but never in front of me. "Bad things can happen, and this…this is a bad thing, I tell you."

"There is nothing certain in this life," she said to both of us. "We must grab what is given. 'Occupy until I come,' Scripture tells us. 'Multiply' is what that word *occupy* means. Here is our chance to do that, to save this farm, and all it requires is using what God gave us, our feet and our perseverance, our effort and a little inconvenience."

"A little inconvenience?" I said. "I have plans for the summer, and I'm going to go to college in the fall and work part-time. I can't leave my job."

"I, I, I… Always it is about you," my mother said. "You won't have money for school if we lose this farm. You'll have to work full-time to help this family. You see your father. He can't do carpenter work as he did before. One must risk for family. We must trust in the goodness of human nature and God's guidance."

"But who would pay us for such a thing? Do you have a contract?" The wealthy Spokane people I served often spoke of contracts and lawyers and securities as I dipped squash soup into their Spode china bowls or brushed crumbs from their tables into the silver collectors before bringing chocolate mousse for dessert. These were businesspeople who would never try to *multiply* by walking cross-country without a written contract.

"These are trustworthy people. They have the *New York World* behind them and the entire fashion industry too."

What Mama proposed frightened me. "If we make it, how do we know they'll pay us?"

"If we make it? Of course we'll make it," she said.

My father sagged onto the chair at the table, held his head with his hands while my mother flicked at the crumbs of a *sandbakkel* cookie collected on the oilcloth. I wondered if she thought of my little brother Henry. He'd loved those cookies.

"Who says these sponsors are reliable?" I said. I was as tall as my mother but had a rounder face than either of my parents. My mother and I shared slender frames, but her earth-colored hair twisted into a thick topknot while my soft curls lay limp as brown yarn. My mother set her narrow jaw. She didn't take any sassing.

"Never you mind." She brushed at her apron. "They're honest. They've made an investment too. They'll pay for the bicycle skirts once we reach Salt Lake City, and they'll pay for the portraits. They've promised five dollars cash to send us on our way. The rest we'll earn. Can't you see? It's our way out."

"So you say," my father said. He ran fingers through his yellow hair, and I noticed a touch of white.

"But why do I have to go?" I wailed. "Take Olaf. A man would be safer for you."

"It's about women's stamina, not about a man escorting a woman. And you... You're filled with wedding thoughts you have no business thinking."

My face burned. "I'm not," I said. "He's... I work for his family, Mama."

How she knew I harbored thoughts of a life with Forest Stapleton

I'd never know. I was sure I'd never mentioned him. Well, maybe to my sister Ida once, in passing.

"I know about employers' sons," Mama said. My father lifted his head as though to speak, but my mother continued. "Besides, family comes first. You can go to college next year, when we have the money. What we need now is that ten thousand dollars so we can repay the mortgage and not lose this farm. It could go to foreclosure if we don't do this." My father dropped his eyes at the mention of that shameful word. "Ole, God has opened a door for us, and we would slight Him if we turned this down," she pleaded.

"How can you leave your babies?" my father said then, his voice nearly a whisper. "How can you be away from Lillian and Johnny and Billy and Arthur and Bertha and Ida and Olaf—"

"I know the names of my children," my mother said, her words like stings.

"*Ja*, well then, how can you leave them?"

"It is only for a short time, seven months, Ole." She sat next to him at the table, patted his slumped shoulder. "They will be in good hands with you and Ida and Olaf to look after them. It is a mark of my trust and confidence in you that I can even think about doing this thing." She looked at me now. "When I walked before, that four hundred miles in Minnesota, you did well, all of you. It made you stronger. And I came back." She patted my father's hand. "I'll come back. We will, Clara and I. Everything will be as it was before but with the mortgage made. The entire farm paid off, money for each of my children to go on to college when they want. No more worries about the future." She took his silence as agreement. "Good. We go into Spokane later this week for our portrait," my mother said to me, relief in her voice. "These will be sent to the New York papers and the *Spokesman-Review*."

My father winced.

"People in Spokane will read about this?" I said. The thought humiliated. What would Forest think? What would our neighbors think?

"People across the country will know of it," my mother said. She almost glowed, her eyes sparkling with anticipation.

"American women listen to their husbands," my father said in Norwegian. "Or they should." He rose from the table, shoved the chair against it, and stomped out.

I wanted my father to forbid her to go so I wouldn't have to leave either. I didn't dare defy her; I never had. We always did what she wanted. I was stuck.

"He'll come around," my mother said more to herself than to me. "He'll see the wisdom of this. It'll work. When we succeed, then, well, he'll be grateful I did this for him, for the whole family."

"Maybe he will," I said. "But don't expect me to ever be."

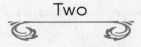

Two

The Plan

wo days later, on April 26, we stood in city hall "to receive the blessing of the mayor of Spokane," Mama said.

"Mayor Belt," I said, curtsying to the rotund man standing before us in his walnut-paneled office.

"My daughter Clara," my mother said after she'd introduced herself. She wore a small hat with a single feather that topped off a dress with wide sleeves, a high neck, and a velvet throat ribbon. She had sewed everything herself. She had made my dress as well, and we looked like fine ladies worthy of a meeting with the mayor of Spokane even though I didn't feel we were. "She'll be making the trek with me. I can't thank you enough for your support."

"And how do you feel about this extraordinary if not dangerous journey, Miss Estby?"

I hesitated.

"Well, answer him, Clara."

I wanted to say I felt awful. I wanted to say: *My life is coming to an end with this ridiculous scheme. My father is upset. My brothers and sisters will be when they find out, especially Ida, who will be left to cook and clean and tend the youngsters we're abandoning. I think the whole thing is foolish, without any real certainty we can survive the trip let alone receive the elusive money at the end of it that my mother puts such hope in. I can think of dozens of things that could go wrong. I don't want to be separated from my family for so long or from my own budding life to satisfy my mother's plan to rescue the farm. There must be another way.*

That's what I wanted to say.

"We're very grateful for your support," I said instead.

"Hmm. Not exactly an answer," Mayor Belt said. "But then, young ladies aren't expected to be articulate." My face burned and my mother frowned. "You should thank my wife for this," he said then, holding an envelope marked *For Mrs. H. Estby.* "She's found the…romance in this entire thing. Two women, walking their way across the country to prove their stamina."

"And promote the new reform dress," my mother added.

"Yes, indeed." He looked at our ankles, well covered with our long skirts, and I imagined him visualizing risqué hemlines raised above the tops of our shoes, the leggings we'd have to wear, waistlines without corsets. I scratched the back of my leg with my foot and he looked away.

"Until a woman is in charge of her ankles, she'll never be in charge of her brain," my mother said in her cheeriest voice.

He smiled. "I suspect easterners don't understand the strength of the western woman," the mayor said. "Why, my mother walked the trail carrying me, worked side by side with my father to clear fields, helped build a house and barn, planted fields, handled mules. She once outran a wheat fire started by dry lightning. Remarkable woman. She grabbed my hand and—"

"Did what was necessary for her family," my mother interrupted.

Everyone knew of the mayor's tendency to go on and on telling stories. "Is that the letter of introduction?" He still held the envelope.

"Yes. Indeed." He withheld it from her. "How did they happen to pick you, Mrs. Estby?"

I wondered that myself. It amazed me that I often found out important details affecting my life by listening to my mother talk to someone else. "On behalf of the sponsors who are in the fashion field, the newspaper asked for essays, statements of why I thought I could make the walk and why I must succeed to save our family's farm. I was chosen for this from many entries, I was told."

She told them of the pending foreclosure.

"It'll bring fine fame to Spokane if you do it," he said. "And if you don't, well, what can one expect from a woman?" He grinned. "You really have nothing to lose and everything to gain. A perfect wager." He handed her the envelope, and she thanked him again without looking at what he might have written.

We made our good-byes and began the walk to the portrait studio where our picture would be made and sent to the *New York World,* compliments of "the sponsors."

"May I read what he wrote?" I asked.

She handed me the letter. I stumbled while opening it and she grabbed my elbow. I was forever tripping, the clumsy one in a family of light-footed souls. "Wait until we're at the studio, Clara. You don't want to be like me and fall and break your pelvis."

"Mother!"

"There's no shame in the word, Clara. If the city had kept their streets repaired, I wouldn't have fallen and there wouldn't have been the lawsuit."

"Which told everyone of your...female problems."

"Yes, but I won, and the money allowed us to buy our farm. Besides,

I located a good doctor because of it and had the surgery and met a fellow suffragette in the process. It all worked out. Out of bad came good. Remember that."

"Then maybe if we…couldn't pay the mortgage, if we lost the farm, something good could come of that too."

My mother stopped as though struck by lightning. Her shoulders stiffened and she looked like she might slap me, something she'd never done. "Clara. How you talk. Nothing could be worse than a foreclosure. Nothing. Give me that letter."

She read it then. "Please, sirs, give kindly considerations to Mrs. H. Estby, who has been a resident of this city and surrounding area for nine years and is a lady of good character and reputation."

"Why does he call you Mrs. H. Estby? Shouldn't you use Papa's name?"

"A woman has a name of her own, Clara." She looked at the letter and nodded. "It'll be enough. We have to get the signatures of dignitaries when we visit a state capital or large city, to verify that we've actually been there."

I looked at her, aghast. "The sponsors won't sign a contract, but they expect us to show that we've done our part? Mama."

"We have signed a contract." To my surprised gaze she added, "Well, I do listen to you." She nudged me with her hip. "We have seven months to make the trek. We start out with five dollars and must earn the rest as we go. We can accept no rides but must walk the entire way. And we can accept meals and lodging from friendly supporters but not beg for it or money."

"Beg? We might be so destitute we'd need to beg?" I could hardly swallow, the bow at my throat as tight as a noose.

She waved her hand to dismiss my worry. "I expect we'll sleep most nights at the railroad stations, at least until our journey makes the newspapers and people are curious to meet us. They'll discover we're ordinary women doing something extraordinary. We might like a bed in their haymow or their attics. There's even a provision in the contract to make time adjustments if one of us becomes ill. So you see, it's not such a big risk."

"And the money?"

"They'll provide ten thousand dollars if we arrive on time and have met the conditions. Oh, Clara." She grasped my gloved hand. "It will be the trip of a lifetime. You'll see."

"If we die, it'll be the last trip of our lifetime."

"Nonsense. Where's that Estby spirit of accomplishment?"

She said nothing to my scowl.

The spring breeze lifted the soft curls at my face. I hoped we could wear our hats in the photograph, as I hadn't brought my curling iron along to spruce up, and a hat turned my hair flat as a deer's bed lying in the meadow.

My mother hummed as we walked along. "Remember the story I told you, Clara, about when I was a young student in Oslo? In religion class they told of Jonah swallowed by the whale, and then I went to science class and learned the whale has a narrow throat? Too narrow for a man. So I—"

"Challenged the religious teacher the next day," I said. I'd heard the story numerous times.

"Yes, and he said to me, 'Don't you know, Helga, that with God all things are possible?' So you see. We will pass through the narrow throat of uncertainty. We'll succeed, get the money, and pay off the mortgage."

"With the mayor's letter?"

"With all of us doing our part. That's what families do, Clara. They sacrifice and serve, and then all will be well."

I wished I could share her enthusiasm, but it wasn't in my nature.

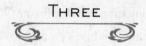

THREE

Letting Go

MAY 1896

I entered the servants' quarters at the Stapleton household. It would be my last day working for this fine family. Giving a two-week notice would have been the professional thing to do, increasing the likelihood of reclaiming my position once we returned, but my mother hadn't granted me the luxury of an organized departure.

I'd first worked for another family, the Rutters. When Bertha, my now fourteen-year-old sister, was ready to serve at age twelve, she took my place there and I joined the Stapleton family household. (My mother would correct me if I said "joined the Stapleton family." She'd remind me that I merely worked in it.) Olaf tended the Rutters' yards and gardens weekly. During our trip, Bertha would continue working out; Olaf would return to the farm to help my father.

I donned my cap and white apron and entered the drawing room to ask Mrs. Stapleton if I might have a word with her.

"Of course, dear," she said. The *Spokesman-Review* lay on the table. She looked at her lapel watch. "Come back in, say, thirty minutes? I'm sure the upstairs linens need tending. It's Monday after all." She was a stately woman who dismissed me by adjusting her glasses and returning to the newspaper.

They'd had houseguests over the weekend, and that meant changing the linens on all the beds in the five upstairs bedrooms. I didn't mind the work, but it wasn't what I intended for my life. What I wanted was to be a wife and mother, to support a husband's efforts at managing money as he cared for his family. I was good with numbers and once even imagined becoming a banker myself, but it wasn't an occupation for a woman—or at least I knew no women who were. I'd be a fine mistress of a grand house and generous because my husband would be kind and generous to me. And we'd never worry over money or do ridiculous things like expose an unfortunate personal situation to the world because of money.

Mr. Stapleton was a banker and his son, Forest, would be one day. I sighed, thinking of Forest as I worked and nearly burned my hand on the hot iron while pressing the sheets left for me.

When I came downstairs, Mrs. Stapleton was standing in front of the fireplace, her arms crossed over her chest, and she tapped her foot though I wasn't late at all. Lilac scent wafted in from the open window but didn't sweeten Mrs. Stapleton's disposition.

"I know what you have to tell me," she said. "Or does your mother have another daughter she intends to take across the continent on this ridiculous scheme?" She nodded toward the *Spokesman-Review*. " 'Walk to New York,' it says. 'Hoping to meet a wager and save the family farm,' it says. 'Wearing the new reformed dress.' " She scoffed and picked up the newspaper, jabbed at it with her finger. "What on earth is your mother thinking? Aside from the fact that it's terribly dangerous, it's… it's…an affront to womanhood. Traveling across town unescorted is uncivilized enough, but across the country? And to publicly announce your family's financial position? Well, I… And the dresses you're to wear! Absolutely provocative showing so much ankle. You'll be assaulted and understandably so."

"We'll carry a pepper-box gun," I offered. "My mother will have a revolver too, and she does know how to use it."

"What western woman doesn't? But that's beside the point," she said. "It's your reputation, Clara. You're tarnishing it with this foolishness. You're old enough to make your own decisions now. Refuse to go. Save your mother from further humiliation."

I agreed with her, but I had no choice that I could see. An Estby did what was required for family. "It won't be foolish if we succeed," I said, my eyes downcast. "It's a…business decision. We're…advertising the new reform dress for the sponsors, and they'll pay us when we arrive."

"Surely you don't think they'll actually pay that kind of money for advertising. Ten thousand dollars? Clara, that's…preposterous. I thought you were a much brighter thinker than that."

"My mother says there's a huge push for suffrage nationally, and the sponsors are people who know that women are capable, able to do more, be fuller members of society. They're investing in the future through this walk." I had to defend my mother.

"We women rock the cradle and rule the roost. Gaining the vote won't change that. It'll put women into the mess of politics with men. Unsavory at best." She sat down, fanned herself with her fingers, clutched at her long beaded necklace with the other hand. She acted almost frightened.

"Clara, Clara." She scanned the article again. "Who will look after your brothers and sisters? Don't you have a baby sister?"

"Lillian," I said. "She's two."

"A baby! How can your mother consider leaving a baby behind? Your father agrees to this?"

"He…he understands the importance of saving the farm," I said. "He was injured, and the support we receive from the carpenters' union isn't enough." My hands grew moist with this intimate disclosure. My father would be appalled if he knew I had spoken of the payments.

Mrs. Stapleton shivered, then stood. "I'll pay up your wages through today. I'm sure I can find a replacement, even with this short notice." She shook her head. "Don't expect to have a place when you return. I can't have…your kind of person in my employ. I assume that's what you wished to discuss with me?"

"I regret the short notice, ma'am." I curtsied, drying my hands on my apron.

"Finish up with your day, then you may leave. I imagine you need the money."

If I didn't say it now, I never would. "I wonder if I might wait… until Master Forest returns from school," I said. "I'd like to say good-bye to him as well. I'll wait outside, of course."

Mrs. Stapleton stared at me, and then she narrowed her eyes and said in a low seethe, "Absolutely not. My son takes no notice of the help, and I'm certain he won't want to be bothered by a schoolgirl's silly *au revoir* as he's returning from his studies. That's foolish thinking, Clara. Foolish. Perhaps you should just leave now."

"Yes ma'am." I backed out, tears stinging from her rebuke and my lost wages.

My future in Spokane was over. I might never get another job in the finer households here. And all because of my mother's warped way of taking care of her family.

Four

Wedding Thoughts

On the Saturday when my mother planned to tell my brothers and sisters of her plan (she was of the opinion not to give them too much time to cry or protest), I helped fix breakfast while the little ones slept. Even Bertha and Ida were given time to sleep past dawn in our shared room upstairs. I guessed it was because I wouldn't be frying bacon or grating potatoes in this kitchen for a while and Mama wanted to give them all a rest before she told them what was happening. While we worked I told her that I'd defied Mrs. Stapleton and waited to speak with Forest. She shook her head in disgust at me.

"I told you he was driving you," mother said, "and how damaging that can be."

"He's not driving me." I'd blame the old onion for my pinched tears instead of her embarrassing words from the old country about men pursuing young women.

"But you wish he was. I see it in your eyes and that's a danger. You're *hun gå i giftetanke.*"

"I'm not going in wedding thoughts, Mama," I lied. "We've done nothing." I didn't tell her that last January, when I couldn't sleep and neither could Forest, I'd prepared warm milk for him in the kitchen and we'd had a conversation about school and life almost as though we were equals. I'd even told him of how much I missed my brother, Henry, who'd died that month. For comfort, Forest kissed my cheek as I stood between the copper pans and herb pots. It was then that my wedding thoughts began, and I wondered if I'd turned my face, if he would have kissed my lips instead. I would have let him, lived with the guilt of finding joy in the midst of grief, dreaming of a future as Mrs. Stapleton, wife of a banker.

"Trust me in this, Clara. A mother knows what can happen between the servants and the men of the house."

"How does a mother know such a thing?" I asked.

She didn't speak, kneaded the bread a little harder, pushing out the scent of yeast. "We know. It is a mother's duty to anticipate."

"He does like me, Mama, but he's a gentleman and would never do anything—"

"You don't know."

"All I did was wait for Forest so I could tell him good-bye. I hope that was all right with you," I snapped and chopped the onions smaller. She said nothing, leaving me to savor my last moments in memory.

I'd waited beneath the large elm tree near the corner of the lot, out of sight from the house. Forest's face lit up when he saw me, I know it did. He removed his hat, set his briefcase down. "Clara," he said. "Are you off to the store for my mother?" He stood taller than I by two inches, and a section of his blond hair hung straight over his right eye, so it always looked as though he was peeking at me from behind a golden drape. His slender fingers and perfectly filed nails lifted the strand of hair to free both his eyes. His smile was butter to my bread.

"No," I croaked. Clearing my voice I said, "I'm...I'm leaving. On a trip. I won't be here for a time. Maybe never again." I hoped he'd look sad at my parting.

"Nonsense," he said. He looked behind me, toward the Stapleton home. I turned to look too, leaning out from behind the tree. Leafed out, the branches blocked a view of the window that his mother might look through if she still ruled in the parlor. He moved closer, smiled, and I pressed my back against the tree trunk, the bark scratchy and firm against my thin jacket. He checked the house again, then stared into my eyes. He leaned an arm over me, resting it on the tree, and with his other hand, he lifted my chin. So very close. "You'll be back. Trips don't last forever."

"This one will take seven months at least," I said. I swallowed, relishing his closeness, fearing it. He touched the back of his finger to my cheek, stroking gently, then to my neck, where blood pounded. His touch felt like lightning crackling in a summer storm. He left his hand there, my veins disclosing the secrets of my heart. "Your mother will fill you in, I'm certain of that," I said. I wanted him to move his hand, and yet I didn't. "She thinks the trip a foolish one. So do I."

"Don't let Mother frighten you," he said. "I've read about it, your journey. You're…brave, Clara. I wish I'd known of your adventurous streak."

I hadn't thought of bravery or being adventurous, only that I was obedient. His gaze caused my mouth to dry up like creeks in autumn.

He leaned away then, removed his fingers from my throat, empty cool air replacing them.

"Well, I shall miss our little chats," he said.

"I could write," I whispered. "Send a postcard."

He shook his head. "Mother always checks the mail first."

"Maybe I could send letters to one of your friend's addresses?"

He smiled, touched my soft curls as though they might break, wrapped one around his finger. "Write and keep them, and when you return, perhaps you can hand them to me in person. We can...have lunch together."

"All right," I said. *He invited me to lunch.* "They'll be my diary." He returned his hat, picked up his case. "You could write to me," I said. "The newspapers along the way will receive our mail and—"

"It wouldn't be wise for a Stapleton to send messages to a newspaper," he said. "Possible publicity, you know. Bad for my father's bank."

"I suppose...not." I lowered my eyes. I'd embarrassed myself with such a suggestion.

"You write things down, Clara." He sounded like one of my teachers indulging my enthusiasm for a subject unrelated to their classes. He stood in front of me, both hands on his briefcase. I no longer needed to lean back into the tree. "You can tell me all about it when you return." He moved toward my face then and I thought that, yes, he might kiss me. Instead, he simply whispered, "Good-bye, dear Clara. I wish you well."

He'd stepped around me, leaving confusion and the scent of his cologne in his wake.

I wiped my eyes of the onions. I didn't tell Mama that part, only that Forest Stapleton was a gentleman and I'd be writing to him instead of keeping a journal. She took that to be that I had wedding thoughts, for heaven's sake.

"There'll be little time for writing and such," my mother informed me. "We must make twenty-nine miles a day to finish on time."

I gasped. "That's walking from Spokane to Rockford. Every day."

"Every day. Oh, don't look so glum. A woman can do anything for a day."

"Hurry Ida and the children along," Mama said. "No sense eating these cold." She started to sing a Norwegian festival song. I didn't have the heart to tell her that she sang out of tune.

My siblings' timing proved impeccable. Ida joined us in the kitchen first. My father and Olaf entered from the barn, taking cooled milk from the icebox and replacing it with fresh warm liquid. The middle-age children, Arthur and Bertha, rumbled down the stairs and gathered round the table that Ida and I finished setting. My brothers filled in the bench where Henry once sat, but they couldn't fill in the space he left in our hearts.

Bertha wiped her eyes with her fingers as she sat, waiting for the signal to begin. She'd been called home from the Rutters' for this week-end. She scanned the table with the stack of pancakes, little dishes of jams and jellies, fresh-baked rolls promising to be soft and chewy. "It feels like a birthday party with Mama singing. All we need is a cake."

"Do you remember when I made that cake for your birthday?" Ida asked Bertha.

"When Mama visited her mother? In Wisconsin?"

Ida nodded. "I was your mother for then."

Actually, I'd taken care of the children while Mama was gone those two months, walking across Minnesota and Wisconsin. I didn't need to steal Ida's thunder; she'd be drenched by the end of this meal anyway.

"We had a big cake, Clara. Papa rode to Mica Creek, to Schwartz's store, but they had no soda, so he had to ride all the way to Rockford to get it so Ida could make my cake."

"She knows the story," Olaf told her. He arched one of his seventeen-year-old lanky legs over the back of the chair and sat down, reaching for a slice of the bacon our mother set on the table. Ida rolled her eyes as he said, "We all know the story."

I knew it but still felt left out. At the time I'd been working on a neighboring farm while they all shared this pleasure.

"Now I make cakes for the Rutters," Bertha said and she wrinkled her nose at her brother. Bertha reached for a potato pancake.

"You wait for grace," I cautioned.

"You weren't here for the party. And neither was Mama," Bertha said, "so I have to tell you the story." Her blond hair hung in braids and she smiled.

"Hedvig, fill your plate," my mother said as she poured the milk. "But wait to say grace."

"My name is Bertha, Mama. It's more American."

"Nothing wrong with Norwegian," Ida said. She refilled our brothers' coffee cups, brought a small amount of sugar, and set it in front of Papa.

"Silence," Papa said. "We pray over the food, then you eat your *potet* without chatter."

We all sat now, except for the little children, who still slept. All bowed our heads in silence while Papa prayed in English. Then the sounds of forks on ironstone interrupted while the occasional "please pass" and *mange takk,* a Norwegian thank-you, punctuated the rest of the meal.

As we finished, the younger children skipped downstairs in their nightclothes, and Ida and I assisted with their dressing. Even though it was May 1, the air felt chilly and I imagine the stove was a welcome comfort to their birdlike legs and slender little bodies. They sat at the table while I served them hot *rommergrot,* pouring milk on the creamy porridge I'd begun to prepare as soon as I heard their feet on the floor above us. Johnny, William—Billy, we called him—and Lillian ate silently as Mama stood at the end of the table.

She looked at me and a shiver went through me. What she was about to tell the little ones would change their lives forever. Mine too.

"You older children know we are facing a difficult time," Mama began. "Your papa's injury makes it difficult for him to work, and the world now makes it hard for people to find jobs doing carpenter work even if he could do more. No one builds in either Rockford or Spokane. The farm feeds us, and that is why Olaf comes home so often. Now he works two places, Spokane and for the family."

"He got sick," Bertha piped up. "He came home so you could make him well."

"Yes. He had diphtheria but now he's better. He is a big help on this farm, and the farm is very important. So important that we must find a way to pay what is due. This year, even the ten percent interest on our loan is playing hide-and-seek with us. So it is very important that we keep the farm from foreclosure. Very important."

"What's four closure?" eight-year-old Johnny asked. "Is there a five closure?"

"It means we need to pay back money we don't have," I told him. I touched his blond hair with my hand. "They will take the farm instead of money."

His eyes were big and round, but I only spoke the truth.

"Where would we go if we lost the farm?" Bertha asked.

"It will work out," Papa said. "It always has. What your mother proposes is not necessary. We could live with my sister if needed."

The boys looked at each other. Our parents were disagreeing in front of them, an event as rare as snow in July.

"Not this time," Mama said.

I looked at my father. His eyes drooped. It must be difficult for him to have his wife talking about finances, something a Norwegian man usually took care of, saw it as his duty, not his wife's.

"Without the farm we cannot sustain our family," my mother insisted. "I've found the help." She spoke to the children now, turning her back on my father. "Sponsors, wealthy women, will pay us ten thousand dollars if we can walk from Spokane to New York within a certain time."

"*Ti tusen dollar*," Ida whispered. She was shorter than I, slender, with perfect gold hair braided in a crown at the top of her head. She sank back into her chair.

"Why would anyone pay that?" Bertha asked.

"Where is New York?" Arthur asked. "Can I walk there too?"

"No. It's too far away and you're too young. And to answer Bertha: for a fashion campaign, to show off the new reform skirts that women can wear when we bicycle or go on a picnic, without having to wear corsets." Olaf raised his blond eyebrows at our mother. She said, "Nothing risqué. Goodness, no. Legs all covered by stockings or boots or skirt. But it will show that women are strong, that we are more capable than men give us credit for. Imagine, earning our way across the continent."

"If you finish the walk," my father said. "Unharmed. The danger does not go away because you tell us so." The little ones had stopped eating their *rommergrot* and watched, heads turning back and forth as each parent spoke.

"We've been given this great opportunity. God will be with us in the danger, and walking thirty-five hundred miles will prove a woman's endurance."

"But not so much her sound judgment," my father said.

I agreed with him, for all the good it did either of us.

"I'm so sorry, Ida," I said. My sister sobbed as we slopped the pigs in the pig shed, their grunting and squealing loud enough that we had to raise our voices even to share a confidence. "I wouldn't go at all except that Mama needs a companion."

"If you refused, maybe she wouldn't go," Ida cried.

"Mama never changes her mind. You know that. She'd go on alone or get someone else to go with her, and none of us would know what was happening."

"I hated it when she went to Wisconsin to help *Bestemor* when *Bestefar* died," Ida said.

"Her mother needed her."

"*Ja,* I remember," she said, then mocked Mama. "'You had your father here and Clara and each other, much more than *Bestemor* had in her time of grief.'" Anger seasoned Ida's tone. "What if one of the children gets sick?" Ida said. She set the bucket down and turned to me. "What'll I do if—?"

"Papa is here. You're not alone," I said. She was more frightened than angry; I could see it in her face. "The big medicine book is in the kitchen. Neighbors will help." But I knew what she feared. Accidents happened. Diphtheria sneaked into a household and ravaged it. Fires burned houses down. "You'll be proud that you kept the family fed." I didn't tell her how the days dragged like a weighted iron attached to my foot when Mama had been gone before. There'd been another feeling then too: emptiness. No, *empty* wasn't the right word either. My mother was our anchor, and when she left, even for short periods, I felt adrift.

"What is it about her that makes Mama go like that?" Ida said.

"Why can't she be a good wife like Olga Siverson or Nora Olson? They never go anywhere. Do we make Mama want to leave us?"

"No," I said, though uncertain. "No. This is Mama's way of being a good mother. We have to be good children and do our part."

Ida wiped her face with her apron. "Aren't you afraid of walking that far?"

"Yes, I am. But I'm more…mad, that I have to leave my job and maybe…" I decided not to tell her about Forest.

Ida's lips quivered. "I'm really scared she won't come back this time."

"No. Don't worry about that. I'll bring her back. There's no sense putting your worries in a wheelbarrow," I said.

"It's heavy enough as it is," Ida said with me. We both smiled at one of Mama's sayings. Ida sighed. "I guess it's going to happen and there's nothing I can do about it."

"At least I won't have to wear a corset after Salt Lake City," I said.

"You're so like Mama," she said, "finding the good in a bad."

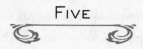

FIVE

Mighty Fortress

According to the contract that I never did get to see, we had to start from Spokane. So on May 5, 1896, we rode the Oregon Railroad and Navigation Company line to the Spokane terminal, walked to the *Spokane Daily Chronicle* to verify our presence, and then walked the twenty-eight miles from Spokane, home to the farm on Mica Creek. We spent our first night of the journey in our own beds. I dreaded the good-byes in the morning.

I walked out onto the porch with my parents there, Mama saying, "We cannot lose the farm, Ole. We can't."

"A man is the head," he said lamely.

"Maybe in Norway. But we are here now. We decide together."

He snorted at that, and I made a noise to alert them to my presence.

Mama turned but didn't acknowledge me. Instead she left the porch, walking toward Olaf. My brother brought the horses from the barn, and as she patted the animals' rumps, a puff of dust rose up. I followed her out. She told Olaf how good they looked as he brought them up beside the pig shed. Olaf hugged Mama with one arm, holding the harness in the other. "Godspeed, Mama," he said. "Write to us."

"You know I will," she said. She brushed the blond hair from his forehead. "You're well," she said. "You are."

He nodded. "I'm strong as an ox." He flexed the muscles of one arm. "I'll look after Papa, make sure he doesn't reinjure himself."

"That's good. Take care of yourself too, my son." Olaf nodded, checked a ring on the harness. I thought he avoided her eyes so that she might not see his tears or maybe how her kind words affected him.

"Don't go driving anyone while we're gone," I teased. He smiled. I wasn't sure he'd ever courted a girl, though he had lagged behind with Mary Larsen while walking back from church once or twice. "The little ones will tattle on you."

"Don't you either," he said.

"Tattle? Or drive with someone?"

"Both." He grinned. I hugged him. We had our secrets, the two of us, trouble we'd gotten into as children, wasting precious time in the fields telling stories instead of working, things we thought about farming and our futures. We looked as different as night from day, he so blond and muscular, me so dark and lean. The horses stomped their impatience and Olaf took the signal to nod to Mama, then spoke to the horses and flicked the reins across their rumps. He jerked behind them with the harness trailing until they reached the field and could hitch up the plow.

Bertha ran out of the house as we moved back toward it. She carried two hard-boiled eggs. "For your lunch, Mama," she said. "And yours, Clara."

"A good idea!" Mama said as we returned to the porch where our leather grips sat waiting. "You're so thoughtful, Bertha."

"It was Arthur's idea. He said we should boil them." Arthur stood off to the side patting the dog's head. Sailor panted. I wished that dog was going with us.

"Then we thank you both." Mama pulled Arthur forward, kissed his face, Bertha's forehead. I took the eggs and put them in my grip.

Johnny pushed his head between his siblings and wrapped his arms around Mama's neck. Then he came to hug me and whispered, "Bring me back a New York frog. It will jump higher than Arthur's from Mica Creek."

"I'll look for the very best," I whispered back.

"You be a good boy for Ida and your papa, all right?" Mama said, tapping him on the shoulder. Johnny nodded. His lower lip quivered. She pulled him into her skirts, held his arms as he lowered his head into her side. The two stood rocking side to side until four-year-old Billy cuddled close.

Mama started to lift him, but Billy said, "I'm too big for you to carry."

"So I can't put you into my little case and take you with me?"

I winced at her mistake.

His eyes grew large. "Yes, take me! I'll climb right inside!" He wiggled free, pulled at her grip, which weighed less than he had at birth.

She opened the bag, snapped the frame and handle back, and it stood open, wide like a jaw. He peered inside as she squatted beside him. "You are too big, son," she said. "See?"

"You need the lantern," he agreed. "If I go, you won't have room for light."

"That's right. And we need the light very much."

"All right," he said and stepped back. "I'll stay here."

Lillian waddled over and wove her sticky fingers into Mama's hair.

In the seven months we'd be gone, Lillian would change the most. Lillian's blond hair, soft as peach fuzz, glistened in the sunrise.

"Mama go?"

"Soon." Mama kissed her head, squeezed her, then handed the baby to me, her eyes moist.

The smell of Lillian's hair and the smoothness of her face against my cheek closed my throat. *How can she leave them? How can I leave them?*

"I have a surprise for you, Lillian," Mama said. She sniffed, then handed my sister a piece of Hardanger lace shaped like a heart, one Mama had stitched herself. She pulled a small pair of scissors from her pocket and cut the heart in two. "You keep this half of my heart. Keep it safe for everyone to have now and then. Put it under your pillow, then maybe Johnny's, then the rest. A different pillow each night."

Lillian nodded, though I knew Ida would have to sort out who got that piece of Mama's heart and when. I looked at their faces, my brothers' and sisters', aching with such longing.

"Mama," I offered. "Why don't you cut a little piece of your heart now for everyone to have?"

Bertha piped up, "Oh yes! Please do that."

Mama looked at me. "All right. Lillian, can Mama have it back for a minute?"

Lillian hesitated but, by nature a generous child, she handed it to Mama, who cut off sections and then placed these in the open palm of each of my siblings, their pink skin showing beneath the squares and diamond shapes made by threads pulled back so carefully by my mother's hands over many hours.

"Do you have a small piece for me?" I asked as she gave Lillian back a little square.

"You're going with me, Clara. You certainly won't need one," she said.

I thought my heart would break.

She cut her own half heart in two and shared this with Papa. He looked at it, didn't speak. Then she took Lillian's pudgy hand and rubbed it across the piece Mama would take with her. "I'll keep this one with me." She held it to her breast with the child's hand. "My heart will be complete only when I come home again and all of you put your pieces together with mine. All the while I'm gone my heart will be smaller because I've left so much of it with you."

Noses sniffled. Silent weeping shook Arthur's shoulders, Billy's too, though Arthur tried not to show it. He clapped his hands, and the dog romped to stand beside him. He petted him, pulling comfort from Sailor's presence.

One more good-bye and that was to Ida. Mama saved the hardest for last.

"Come here, daughter." Ida slouched forward, a scowl marking her face. She'd stuffed her lace piece into her apron pocket. "I know this isn't what you want," Mama said. "You are making a great sacrifice, and I will never forget that. You take my place now. Look after the little ones. Make sure Papa has his morning coffee. Read my letters when they come, out loud. You're a fine reader with good eyes, better than Hedvig's. Make sure Johnny eats his greens. He doesn't like them very much, does he?" Ida nodded. The scowl had lessened. "Good. Know that every night I will say prayers for you and every morning your well-being will be the first thing I think about, the first prayer I pray. I love you all so very much." She hugged Ida, who clung to her. They rocked, with Mama's chin on Ida's head.

At that moment, I envied them all hearing Mama's clear expression of her care for them. I missed the intensity of their good-byes, the assurances she gave of her love, her confidence in their ability to endure the next months. I longed for that assurance. I wanted to fit in with those blond heads lined up, those boys and girls who would have experiences very different from the ones we embarked upon.

After a moment, Mama peeled Ida free, pulled her daughter to her side, then opened her other arm to her flock. They dived toward her.

I stood off, closer to my father than my mother. He said nothing.

"I'm sorry, Papa," I said, though I wasn't sure why I apologized. This was none of my doing, none of it.

My father reached over then and thumbed away the tears against my cheek. His tenderness surprised me; he so rarely touched me.

"Keep her safe, Clara," he said. "Headstrong woman that she is."

I nodded. I wished he would call me *daughter,* but he never had, never even introduced me to others as his daughter. I was always just Clara Estby.

"Well," my mother said, "a handsome crowd you all are. We do this for each other." Mama seemed to be memorizing their faces, moving from one set of blue eyes to another. "Come along then, Clara."

Lillian's lower lip pooched out, and my heart pounded, and I watched as tears pooled in my mother's eyes and my own ache threatened my composure.

I said, "Let's all of you walk with us to the field, where we can say good-bye to Olaf."

"I've already—"

"Arthur and Bertha, you set the pace. Everyone else behind. Mama and Papa and I bring up the caboose. Do you have one more piece of lace Ida can save for Olaf?"

"Yes, indeed," Mama said and cut another piece from what remained. Ida took it with one nod.

They started out then with us following them. My father remained on the porch. "March to the music," I shouted and began to sing, "A mighty fortress is our God." The children finished with the second line: "A bulwark never failing."

"I never thought of that hymn as a marching song," Mama said. She wiped her eyes with her handkerchief.

"It may become ours," I said and motioned for us to slip away toward the rails while they sang.

We were abandoning them. That's how it felt to me, without a piece of Mama's heart to hold and call my own.

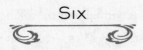

Six

The First Secret

We walked quickly. I didn't want the dog to follow or the children to come running after. Still, I couldn't get our farewell out of my mind. Was it a premonition, this desire to memorize them? Olaf, so handsome and kind. Ida, brittle—no, fragile in her fear. Bertha, happy and giving. Arthur, animal-man with his dog beside him. Johnny, playful. Billy, a lover of music, always tender to another's sorrow. Lillian, the baby who smiled through everything because she didn't know there were things that might make her sad.

And my father. His slender frame, sloped shoulders, the pale mustache that twitched beside my cheek as I hugged him even though he didn't hug me back. I wished I'd told them all those little things I loved about each one of them, but I wasn't good with words. At least not when the eyes of those I loved stared straight at me.

"Let's say good-bye to Henry too," I said as we started up the first hill.

"Go by the cemetery? All right," Mama agreed and we headed up the dirt road.

The landscape, so vast and emerald, scooped me in its arms from the hilltop. Spring wheat thrived over the rolling hills and disappeared into the shallow swales. At the Mica Creek cemetery, wind whipped us as we stood over Henry's grave. Rheumatic fever, the doctor said, had caused my brother's death. Mama pulled at weeds around the stone, lost in thought.

"He wrote the sweetest letters to me when I was gone to Wisconsin," Mama said. "I'm so glad I saved them. Glad we have his picture too. I wish I had a picture of Ole."

"You have one of Papa," I said. "Didn't you bring it?"

She looked confused, then looked at me. "No, I meant Ole. Our first son. He's buried in Minnesota."

"I had a brother who died? Another brother?" Her words were like stones thrown into a still pond, disturbing in all directions.

"It was a long time ago," she said. "Before you. Our firstborn. Son. I wish I had a photograph," she said. She patted my shoulder.

"But you never said—never spoke of a brother. Older than I? Does Olaf know? Do the others?"

"No," Mama said. "No need to tell you either, I suppose. But we have seven months to face together, so I imagine secrets will come out."

In an instant I had a fleeting memory of an infant crying in our sod house in Minnesota, fuzzy lantern lights casting strange shadows on the earth walls, Mama crying too, hands to her mouth and a man holding an infant. Could that have been Ole? No, Ole was older, Mama said. The crying child must have been Olaf, sixteen months younger than I. Yes, it must have been Olaf I remembered crying, my now-big, scrappy brother. I had no memory of Ole, who'd come before me.

"What happened?"

"The sod house. So very cold. Pneumonia. It was why I wanted us to leave there, come here. That and the cyclones that lit the sky like fireworks with booms and crackles. I hated them." She shivered. "And the prairie fires. And the harsh winters with their snowdrifts." She sighed. "Little Ole wasn't with us very long, but I still miss him. So," she said in her changing-the-subject voice, "let's stop at the store and pick up a hard candy to help us commemorate our walk."

I'd have to catch her in a thoughtful time to find out more.

Mama hesitated at Schwartz's store in Mica Creek.

"That's Martin Siverson's horse. Your father's best friend thinks I should listen to my husband and not take this walk."

"Let's not go in then."

The door opened as we turned to leave.

"I suppose you're off then, Mrs. Estby," Martin said. He motioned to our bags. Mama paused and turned. "Such a crazy scheme. Shameful."

"It's for good," Mama said.

"So you say," Martin said. "And Clara. You can't talk sense into your mother, then? Are you stubborn like she is?" He shook his head and crossed the street.

My face burned. His expression reminded me of Mrs. Stapleton's. Shameful. My mother's wish to save the farm brought shame to our family. Would success even wash it away?

"Let them say what they will," Mama said. "I will prove them wrong. Don't you worry about a thing."

Since I was going with her against my will, the least she could have said was "we."

SEVEN

Walking

So much for God smiling on our venture. We walked through days of pouring rain. Mama said once we reached LaCrosse Junction, a Norwegian town in southern Washington, we wouldn't have to sleep on the hard benches in the train stations because people there were like family. We'd speak Norwegian and be treated with hospitality.

"Don't be ridiculous," one woman said as we approached her house, drenched to the bone. "You should have stayed home with your children where a good Norwegian wife should be!" She slammed the door in our faces, so we slept on the benches again, only ninety-five miles from Spokane.

"I thought you said we'd be welcomed," I complained.

"They don't understand," Mama told me. "As we move east, we'll have a better reception." We munched on hardtack in the depot and took turns watching the door so we could squeeze rain from our woolen coats by holding them in front of the potbellied stove. "At least we have a roof over our heads," Mama said, putting the bag under her head as a pillow. I slept that night wondering at my mother's ability to look for the good in things.

We decided early on not to stop to eat according to the sun—which we hadn't seen much of—but rather to be guided by our stomachs. Eggs were cheap and filling and could be eaten at any meal. Often when I ate them, I recalled Martin Siverson's comments, or the women who closed doors in our faces, and the food coated my stomach with new uncertainty. Rain greeted us in Walla Walla, Washington, but the *Walla Walla Union* ran a long article about our journey, mentioning Mayor Belt's endorsement and saying we were headed on to Boise City. We sold several photographs to sympathizing women and replenished our reserves, buying hard rolls and even a pat of butter because Mama said we needed fat to keep going. A family offered us a sweet-smelling bed above the horses in their barn. The sun came out one day and steamed our wet wool clothes. We slept mostly in the railroad stations, which were about nine miles apart. It was how we kept track of our daily distance. Well, that and the maps of the railroads we carried with us.

My feet scraped along the Union Pacific outside of Umatilla, Oregon, and I remembered reading *Astoria,* a history book written by Washington Irving about the Astor fur-trading expedition coming this way, the first big cross-country expedition west after Lewis and Clark returned. There'd been one woman in that party, a Madam Dorion, and she'd walked or ridden a horse from St. Louis, Missouri, all this way, heading to the Pacific. At least Madam Dorion had the luxury of traveling with her husband and sixty men. She'd also brought her two young boys with her instead of leaving them behind.

Red willows bushed up beside the Umatilla River, which ran right through the Umatilla Indian reservation. Those Indians had been friendly in the book I'd read, had helped Madam Dorion when she got into trouble. Nevertheless, I hoped we wouldn't encounter any and said as much to Mama.

"Me either," she said, for the first time not minimizing my concern.

We both heard the clatter of rocks at the same time. "What's that?" she said. I saw the tramp first and pointed.

He was shorter than both my mother and I but much stockier. He wore baggy pants with holes in the knees. His pockets bulged, and an old tweed jacket covered what looked like two shirts. The coat was stained with spots big enough to be seen even though he was a good twenty yards from us. He must have been sleeping in the bushes as we walked by. Our chattering probably woke him up. Clumps of mud hung on his pants, but mud hung on us as well. I didn't know if he was a *stygging*, a nasty man, or one like us, walking the rails.

Mama put the grip in front of her and dug into her stride, saying, "Keep walking. Faster."

The tramp began a singsong cry of, "La-a-a-dies. Let's have lu-u-u-nch. La-a-a-dies, let's have lu-u-u-nch." I twisted to look. He appeared frazzled more than dangerous.

"Ignore him," Mama said, urging me along with her hands when I turned.

A stone inside my shoe rubbed against my heel. I nearly twisted my ankle turning to see how fast he approached. I picked up my long skirt, wishing we had the reform dresses to wear right now.

"Leave us be or I'll shoot," Mama said. I could tell by the direction of her voice that she'd stopped. *Does she have her Smith & Wesson out?*

"Don't...don't..."

I heard the gunshot, smelled the powder, watched the man fall.

"You shot him," I screamed. "Mama! You shot him!"

"I gave him fair warning."

"Maybe he was hungry," I said, running past her to him.

"Then he should have said so."

"He said he wanted lunch."

Mama joined me. He lay on his side, still. A light rain drizzled. I leaned over to touch him. One eye came open. I jerked back.

"You...you shot me," he said. "My leg."

"A mere flesh wound," Mama said, but she sounded relieved.

He moaned loudly. "Meant you no harm," he said. "Haven't eaten in two days. My leg!"

"Are you armed?" Mama asked.

"No," he said. I could see blood through one of the holes in his pants. "If I had a gun, I'd have traded it for chicken. Just wanted a little food. Thought you were tramps too."

"Do we look like tramps?" Mama asked. She pulled on her jacket, straightened her shoulders. Actually, I thought we did, mud all over us, hats as flat as grinding stones. Mama didn't wait for his answer. "Come along, Clara. We'll bandage him up. He can't do any harm hobbling."

His mouth dribbled hardtack Mama gave him. I tore up one of his shirts to use as a bandage. It was a flesh wound, but I was sure it hurt. "Don't you know it's dangerous for two women alone out here?"

"You can see we can handle ourselves," I said. I hated defending my mother's actions.

At the river I found a stick that would work to help him hobble along to the next town. Having injured him, we felt obligated to take care of him, even though his wobbly ways delayed us. At the next train station, he said he'd wait and see if he couldn't get one of the other tramps who rode the rails to give him a lift. Mama left him an egg.

"I don't think we should be so hasty in the future," I said as we walked away.

"What? Why not? He'll tell the other tramps that the two women walkers aren't to be toyed with. He could have been trouble. You must do whatever is necessary to protect your family, Clara. This trip should prove that to you if nothing else."

I knew my mother was strong, brave even. She'd sued the city of Spokane over an injury. I'd taken care of her and my brothers and sisters while she healed. But shooting the tramp wasn't brave; it was...impulsive, just like this trip. It had cost us precious time, caused the man pain, and we'd likely sleep under a willow, drenched in the rain, because of Mama's hasty action. One needed to think things through. That's what this trip would prove to me.

We stepped aside for trains rumbling along the tracks. I held my hand to my hat and turned my face away from the black smoke that billowed as engines chugged past. Passengers sped by us, blobs of color in the windows. Surprised looks washed over faces flashing by. A man in the caboose waved. Strangers, all of them. Yet we were dependent on strangers to see us through. That's what Mama said. We couldn't live on hardtack and eggs forever. Everyone we'd encounter would be a stranger. Perhaps even my mother.

EIGHT

Sunflowers in Boise

JUNE 1896

Soggy sunflowers hung their heads over a fence outside of Boise City. Rain poured down as it had all but five days since we'd left. It's good when God gives us great beginnings, because soon after come the downpours of discouragement. One needs the memory of good starts to carry on, and we'd had that one good, dry day. Since then, we'd crossed flooded streams, stood beneath leaky storefront porches in cowboy towns like Pendleton, hoping the rains would ease. Dirt paths became streams and I fell more than once, mud caking on my skirt and building up on the soles of my shoes. "At least we don't lack for wash water," Mama said, holding her hands out to the rainy heavens.

We'd come only four hundred fifty miles in six weeks of walking. It was taking us too long. The leather bags weighted us. The mud, rain, snow in the Blue Mountains, tramps, and need to earn our meals by washing dishes or laundry had all slowed us. So much for my mother's planning. The only good thing so far was the ample time I had to daydream about Forest.

Boise City ended at a railroad stub line, and trains backed into the city, then headed out and south, so following the rails meant we'd have to backtrack part of this road. But we had to go into the town, find work, and get new shoes, carpetbags to replace the leather. Boise was our first capital city, so we needed a governor's signature too.

Calf-high water covered the only road, giving us no choice but to slosh our way through it. Wet leather chafed my ankles. We'd sold all but one of the portrait pictures, so they needed replacing too. Our buyers had been startled ranchers out with their cattle or sheep, a few housewives who thought our adventure grand. A lot more looked at us with disgust and sent us on our way. I looked at our mud-laden skirts and snorted. "A fine picture we make."

"Hopefully the *Union* article preceded us," Mama said. "We'll need new shoes here. I should have realized how badly the cinder packing the ties would cut the leather soles."

"Maybe a few other things we should have thought about too," I snarled. My ankle ached from walking awkwardly outside the tracks on the rough and uneven ground. It made walking slow and messy. "We're far from averaging twenty-nine miles a day."

"Clara, look on the bright side. A woman gave us dried cherries. Such a luxury. We had a day we made forty miles. Or more."

"And I cut my foot on those empty bottles tossed out."

"You have to pick up your feet, that's all."

No sympathy came from her. It was all work. Do. Persist.

Conductors on the trains emptied their wash water and human refuse right onto the tracks, and if we weren't careful, we stepped in it, our long skirts picking up the mess as well as the stench. My mother, always so clean and tidy. *Papa should see her now,* I thought. Mrs. Stapleton would have fainted.

"Pretty flowers," Mama said.

"If they weren't so wet."

"The Norwegian Feminist Society recently adopted the sunflower as their special flower because it follows the sun, claims light and air, and reaches for more."

I rolled my eyes. "That can't be so."

"It is. I learned of it before we left. My suffragette friends certainly know that's what a sunflower stands for."

"So anytime we see a sunflower we can stop and perhaps be invited in by a kindred spirit to spend the night? In a bed perhaps? That would be pleasant."

"Sarcasm does not become you," Mama said. "I'm not saying that sunflowers are so…significant. Even though their faces are wet and gray, they turn toward the west, as though they know the sun will set there and dry them out."

"What sun?" I said.

My mother sighed. "Let's stop first at the statehouse. We'll find the governor and get his signature. We'll take that to the newspaper, and that'll help us find work."

"And what if he won't sign it?" I said. "Look at us."

"Don't put trouble in your wheelbarrow. It's heavy enough as it is."

"My feet hurt. I'm cold and tired and wet. I'd like to rest tonight in a real bed."

"You've been irritable all day. Are you starting your monthlies?"

"Mother. Please."

"Nothing wrong with a woman discussing her feminine needs. I know you have rags with you because I put them in your grip, but I hope you'll be able to work."

"I'll do what I must. Right, Mother?" I didn't like myself as a grumpy woman, but I wasn't having any luck letting go of blaming my mother for how miserable I felt.

Once in Boise City, I noticed streetcar tracks. "Can we ride to the capitol?"

"No. The streetcars are not free, so we can't take them. We have to walk. Those are the conditions. They may have spies watching to see that we don't cheat."

"No one is going to come all this way to watch us. And certainly not in the middle of a flood."

"The cars won't run with the high water, and if a reporter saw us riding even on the back of a farmer's wagon, the contract could be invalidated."

"*Fandem!*" I said.

"Don't bring up the devil, Clara. His ears are too good, and if you invite him, who knows what can happen?"

"I'm so…tired, Mama." I couldn't think of a deeper, bigger, more expansive word than *tired*. I was an elephant weighted with stones. My fingers ached; my hair hurt. I could barely feel my feet.

"Oh, look. There's the capitol. We've walked down the right street. Isn't that fortunate?"

I rolled my eyes at her enthusiasm.

Once inside the building, our feet clicked on the marble floors, and Mama asked directions to the ladies' powder room. I sank onto a settee with a high wooden back and a stuffed brocade pillow seat. I ran my hands over the fine fabric. "If I weren't so exhausted, I might find this pleasant," I said.

"Well, that's an improvement in your disposition."

Mama washed her face in the fresh water pitcher and used the gold-framed mirror to set her hat straight and brush mud from her skirt and light jacket. The stains beneath her arms barely showed on the damp wool. "Come along," she said. "I'll brush your skirt off in back and you brush mine. Get the hem good."

"I can't stand up," I said.

"Yes, you can."

I brushed off my own skirt, and then we left the room and climbed up to the second floor. "He was a senator first," Mama said. "I think he and the mayor are friends."

She acted…excited. As bedraggled as we looked, her eyes sparkled as though she was about to enter as the belle of the ball. Was it rubbing shoulders with a governor that intrigued her? Was it reaching this first big goal, collecting the first signature, that gave her energy? I didn't have a drop of her enthusiasm in my blood; was I even her daughter?

A door that reached to a fourteen-foot ceiling took up the wide hall. Gold eagles flew over the opening. The doorknob looked gold. Through the glass window that lined one side, a chandelier of great proportion glittered from the high ceiling inside. I gazed up at it.

"Is this mining country?" I said swirling around. "There's so much gold."

"Gold and silver. Don't look so awed, Clara. We have every right to be here. It's a public building. It belongs to the people."

"The people of Idaho."

"All of us," she said. "This is America."

She pulled open the heavy door, and I met the eyes of a woman older than Mama, looking out through thick glasses. "May I help you?"

Mama stepped up and handed her a portrait. "We're the two women walking from Spokane to New York City," she said. "You may have heard of us? We were written up in the *New York World*."

"Did you say walking to New York City? There's a train that goes there," she said. "It would be much faster. Well, after the waters recede."

"I know. But this walk isn't about speed; it's about endurance," Mama said. "We're walking for a contract of ten thousand dollars."

I cringed. Every time she mentioned the money I felt like I'd stepped in dung, and it stuck on my feet.

"Goodness! That's a tidy sum."

"It is," Mama agreed. "But we have to receive signatures of dignitaries, especially the governor's, if we are in a capital city. Here's a letter of introduction from Spokane's Mayor Belt."

The woman took the letter, looked back at Mama over her glasses. "I'll ask His Honor if he's free," she said. She lowered her voice then and added, "He's usually available to meet with pretty women, even if they can't vote."

"One day we will," Mama said as the woman left us.

Pretty women? Does the woman have poor eyesight? We look like swimming cats.

The governor stepped out then and bowed at the waist. He handed the letter back to Mama. "Am I to understand from Miss Simmons here that you fine gentlewomen are walking to New York City? Whatever could you want there that can't be had in Idaho?"

"The completion of a wager," Mama said. "And I'll be showing your signature along with those of other dignitaries when we reach our destination." Mama took the signature book from her bag. The governor signed with a flourish. His dark beard framed a pleasant enough face, and he smiled when he said, "Is there anything else I can do for you?"

"Recommend a portrait studio, if you will," Mama said. "And perhaps someone who might be in need of a washerwoman or ironer for the day, perhaps a servant for a fine event. My daughter has served in the finest homes of Spokane."

He scratched at his chin. "I doubt there's much partying planned with this river situation. Miss Simmons here can recommend a portrait studio."

"And a place to sleep tonight?" I said, elbowing my mother. "Someplace warm. And dry."

"Clara. The governor is much too busy to worry about where we globe trekkers might sleep." My mother batted her eyelashes. *Is she flirting?*

"I'm afraid I can only recommend the Grove Hotel. I wish you well, dear ladies. Send me a post from New York." He returned to his office, and Miss Simmons handed Mama a piece of paper.

"The Grove's address," she said. She looked more closely at our clothing caked with mud. "And a portrait studio." She tapped her lips with her finger. "Do you sell these portraits?" She still held the one Mama had showed her.

"Yes. We need to get more made and hope to spend only a week here. We're to make it to New York by the end of November."

"I'll buy one. Put it in my scrapbook. Not many women walkers come this way. And my sister might use a washerwoman this week," she said. "The Grove could need extra serving girls with people stuck here because of the flood. Lots of miners in town too. You must be exhausted."

"Oh no, we're doing fine," Mama chirped.

"We need a place to sleep," I said. "Can anyone think of a place to sleep?"

"My daughter is tired," Mama said, apology in her voice.

"What about the ladies' preparation room downstairs?" I said.

"Clara," Mama said.

"You told me this building belongs to us, the people," I said.

Miss Simmons brightened. "Why, I can't imagine anyone would mind if they did notice," she said. "It's nearly closing time. You could… wash out your things there and hang them. Lock the door. No one will bother you. Tomorrow I'll see if my sister might have a couple beds to spare. She runs a boardinghouse."

The mere thought of a warm, dry place to sleep on a brocade settee slipped fatigue from my shoulders. In the powder room, I collapsed onto the couch. "This belongs to us," I said.

"We Americans are one big family," Mama said plopping into the chair across from me. "The sunflowers brought us to good things. I'm sure grateful the governor signed that paper."

"But you sounded so certain he would," I said. She looked away, and I realized that some of her bravado was an act to convince not only me but herself.

She looked more tired than I felt now. "Here," I said. "You take the settee. I'll sleep in the chair. That way I can curl my feet up beneath me and get them warm for the first time in days."

"Thank you, daughter." She sank onto the settee and fell immediately to sleep.

The growling of my stomach didn't keep me from joining my mother's rest, and I hoped for sweet dreams and dry weather for tomorrow.

NINE

Shortcut

In the morning, we met with a reporter who did a fine story about the governor's endorsement and referred us to jobs. With Miss Simmons's sister's boardinghouse, we located warm beds for five days. Refreshed and replenished at the end of the week, a warm sun greeted us as it dried the landscape and the river receded.

"Why are we going this way?" I asked. I'd thought we'd head back out the spur track to pick up the Union rail line again. Instead we followed a pack train more east than south.

"There's an old immigrant trail this way," Mama said. "It intersects with the railroad and will save us several days."

"We don't have a map for it," I said. My stomach clenched at this risky change. "We should follow the rails."

"We have a compass. I spoke with a miner who takes the road to his claim. He gave me landmarks to look for," Mama said. "We can go with him to his claim and even pan for a little gold."

"Mother."

"Nothing wrong with trying that," she said. "He's safe enough and we lost time, Clara, through all the mud and having to work. This will help us."

"He might lead us out to a forsaken place and—"

"Don't fill that wheelbarrow," she said. "Miss Simmons knows him. He's a common man, a working soul. They can be trusted."

Like the tramp you shot because you didn't consider other possibilities.

We walked southeast, and the sun beat down hotter than anything we'd experienced in the summers in Washington State. I wanted to unbutton my jacket but couldn't because the man and his pack mule traveled with us. The desert trail revealed pools of water surrounded by chalky dust. We made camp earlier than usual, beside a little stream, the miner sharing our fire. We couldn't walk the streets of Spokane for fear of strangers; yet now we planned to bed down beside one. I wondered at my mother's choices.

When she pulled out a frying pan, my jaw dropped. She scorned my curling iron for being too heavy, but she carried an iron pan? Worse, I soon learned it wasn't for cooking.

The miner showed Mama how it was done—the swirl of stone and water around the edge, over and over, panning for gold. She was like a schoolgirl, giggling, her skirts hiked up into her belt, her shoes on the side of the stream. She looked...young to me. Happy.

"You can use any old pan," he told her. "None with grease. Got to be clean to capture gold."

She called out for me to join her, but I refused. Such a waste. I wrote to Forest instead, describing the beauty of the landscape and that we'd stopped to pan for gold. I made it sound like we were having fun. Maybe I was like her, pretending.

"How could you spend money on a pan?" I hissed when we bedded down.

"I got you a gift too," she said.

"I don't want a pan or that speck of glitter no larger than a pimple he said is gold."

"Nothing like that," Mama said. "I was keeping it a surprise, but you've been so disheartened of late." She rose and reached into her grip. "A sketchbook and pencils. You can record those things that interest you, to keep them in your memory. Here. Take them."

"I… We won't have time," I said. Her frivolity worried me even though the pad and pencils were a rare present from my mother, impractical. There had been moments when I wished I could draw, though. That sea of sunflowers dipping their heads to the west, a cattleman moving his herd through the sage. Accepting the book would make it seem like I accepted her impulsive buying and this shortcut too.

"I still don't know why you wasted money on that pan," I said, deciding to keep the pad.

"We can cook in it if nothing else. I'll carry it, for heaven's sake. In the morning, you look for sunflowers to sketch. They always seek the light instead of dwelling on the dark."

The miner said south of Shoshone, go left, take the settlers' trail. We did that.

"Mama, we passed by this rock outcropping before," I said many hours later. "See, those are our tracks."

"I'm using the compass," Mama snapped. "We can't go through these…monoliths. We have to go around."

We'd entered a dark maze of lava rocks that bit into the sky yet rolled like the folds of a giant caterpillar, slick and baked in sun. We'd been wandering most of the day, our second in this desolate place. In going around the sharp lava rocks, passing by black and red formations that shot up like chimneys after a house fire, we'd gotten turned around. These chimneys were all that remained from volcanoes exploding years and years before, and now they threatened to be the grave markers for Mama and me.

Mama repeated. "The old miner said, 'Beyond them hills there, you can see the flat plain where you'll meet up with the railroad. Shouldn't be no trouble at all to make up time.'"

Make up time.

"I told you we shouldn't have come this way," I croaked with a parched mouth. Both of our canteens were down by half. No shade. Nothing green to even consider eating, and no living thing roamed except snakes. The lava cut our shoes, and I'd stumbled and jammed the palms of my hands against long strips of rock that looked like turkey talons. They stretched for miles, making walking uneven and our energy spent. I'd thought we were exhausted through the rains, but this ache sucked at my bones; the heat of the day weighted our chests, stole our breaths. My face burned from the sun despite wearing a hat, and Mama…Mama's eyes had a frantic look that unsettled me more than the snakes we watched out for.

We rested on a rock so barren it didn't even host a lichen. "We'll try traveling at night," she said, wiping her brow. "It won't be so hot, and we'll use the lantern to watch the compass."

"I can barely walk in the daylight without falling," I said. But I complied. What else could I do?

Coyotes yipped in the distance. We didn't make it far before Mama fell too in the dark, and she agreed we needed to stop and pray that the daylight would bring us new clarity about where we should go. Every sound startled my attempts to sleep. Was that a rattler? Was that a coyote closing in? Were there scorpions out here?

I did pray. Oh, how I prayed! *Please, please, please. Don't let anything happen to Mama. Please, forgive us for being foolish.* I'd never take the word of a stranger, not ever again! I'd never take a wager like this. Money needed to be earned, not received for wild schemes. I prayed for my brothers and sisters, thinking, *What will they do if we die here?* They'd never even know. We'd be two lost clusters of bones found one day by strangers, and they'd make up a story about what happened to us. I started to laugh.

"Clara. What's the matter with you?" Mama asked, shaking me as I leaned against a rock that looked like a statue of flowing water.

"What will they find of us?" I said. "My curling iron. Your frying pan. How will they ever explain that?"

"Don't," Mama said. "Don't think that. We have to get out of here. We have to."

I started to cry then. The fear, the hunger, the realization that we were lost set in.

"Please, show us the path and we'll walk in it. Please, save my child if not me," Mama whispered into the still night. I could feel her rocking beside me.

The night was a grave, time disappearing into darkness.

I slept, awoke in a start. "Mama? Is Papa here to take us home? Over there? By the lantern." My face felt like I had my head in an oven, checking on the brown rolls. "Are you talking to him?"

"No, no," Mama said. "You're… I'm so sorry. Let me hold you. I'm praying, child. That's what you hear. Hush now. The crying won't help us, and it robs you of strength. Try to rest."

She held my hands, rubbed at my fingers, smoothing over the rough edges. I didn't remember her ever holding my hand. I must have been a little child.

"Your nails, they're all torn," she said then.

In the morning, Mama held the compass. She directed us to the northwest, saying we'd walk back the way we came, back to Boise City. I lagged behind. Thirsty. Rocks looked like soft pillows I could just lie down on. I sat in a crevice between rocks as big as buckboards.

Mama shook my shoulders. She looked blurry and fuzzy as a rabbit. I wished I had a rabbit to hold.

"Listen to me, Clara."

I couldn't.

She struck my face. I blinked, touched my cheek.

"We're going to take one step, then another, then another."

"I hear you. Everyone hears you, Mama." I sloughed Mama's hands from my shoulder. "Everyone hears what you say. That's why we're here. Hold tight," I told her. Mama looked confused, but I only needed her to hold my hand again, to keep me from floating like a bubble from the washtub up, up into the air and far away into blue sky.

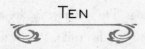

TEN

Desert Starlight

Night. Darkness. Whisperings. "If you must take us, please let Clara die first, Lord, so she won't have to die alone without her mother tending her."

A rumble far away. A storm brewing. Whispered words continue. The thunder.

"Clara! Do you hear that? A storm! We'll have water."

I hear her scrambling in the night.

"Where is that frying pan? We'll collect water. It'll rescue us, that old pan!"

She sounds happy. Mama is happy. I look up. No moon. No rain. Only pinpricks of stars. I close my eyes.

"Clara. Listen to me. I need to tell you something. Listen now. Clara?"

"My ears aren't tired. Only my eyes." I keep them closed. There's nothing to see but darkness. I sleep maybe. I dream of *julekaga*, Mama's Christmas bread, so sweet, so filling. One slice and I am full from all the love that goes into that bread for Christmas morning. Smells fill the kitchen. Am I dreaming? "Do you have *julekaga*, Mama?"

"Clara. Listen. It's not Christmas. I must tell you a secret thing." She holds me in her arms. I'm little, like Lillian. She rocks me. "There's something I hoped I would never have to tell you, but you should know this. If something happens to me—"

"Are you going away again?"

"No. No. But if I… If you get back to Boise but I don't, you should know…" Thunder rolling, closer this time and steady, rolling and rolling through the still night air. She sits up, pushes me up too.

"A secret, Mama? Another secret?"

"Clara," her voice changes. "Clara, I don't think that's thunder." Joy in her voice then. "Clara! Oh, Clara, look!"

It's too dark. I can see nothing but a tiny star moving across the low horizon far in the distance.

"A star."

"Not a star at all," Mama says.

"Lightning in the storm. Rain will come."

"No. No storm, Clara. It's a train! God has sent us a train!" She stands. She leaves me. "Where is that compass?" She clatters over the rocks, finds her grip. I can hear her, then see her in the lantern light. "Yes! That's the direction we will follow in the morning. We know where we're going! Oh, Clara, we're saved. We're truly saved."

Is she going to tell me another secret? How many does she keep?

ELEVEN

Changing Clothes

Weak as a kitten, I followed her in the morning. She put everything into one grip and carried it. I had to carry only myself. I imagined *lefse* soaked in butter and rolled up around fresh blackberry preserves, or *sandbakkels* shaking sugar from their crispy shapes, and my licking the crystals from my mouth. I imagined cream porridge served with milk and eating mounds of boiled potatoes, saving the water for the next day to use for making bread, fresh brown buns, straight from the oven, soft and smelling of yeast. I could see the *julekaga*. I could see tables spread and a chicken steaming, its oyster-flavored stuffing spilling out onto the plate. I saw pools of water Mama said weren't there.

"Clara. Sheep!" She pointed and held up the empty canteen, shouting to them. "Water! May we have water?"

Sheep will give us water?

Two Basque sheepherders halted, then walked out of the desert heat toward us. They spoke no English, but it wasn't necessary. We looked so gaunt and ravenous, and we received the gift of water and biscuits like communion as in our Norwegian Lutheran church back home. Two hours later we were at the railroad tracks. I bent down to touch them.

"Praise God," Mama said.

"Don't ever leave these again, Mama. This is the path. We follow the rails. Promise me?"

Mama nodded, tears in her eyes. She dropped to her knees too and said, "Thank You, thank You."

Mama changed after that. She was as determined, but a part of her seemed…humbled, maybe a little more open to my thinking. When I suggested that the eggs we were given might contain more fuel for our bodies than the venison jerky pressed onto us by a rancher's wife outside of Battle Creek, Utah, for example, my mother agreed. When she mentioned politics and how much she admired William Jennings Bryan, she didn't try to cut me off when I said I preferred William McKinley. Once, she even agreed with me when I told her that Bryan supported segregation, and that didn't seem like the actions of a man who worked for the downtrodden, as my mother claimed he always had. She accepted that we had differing views and didn't push to make me think like her.

But when I tried to have her talk a bit more about what she'd almost told me in the lava beds, she said it was of no consequence. "You were nearly delirious, Clara. It wasn't anything so important." She changed the subject then, telling me a story of a pair of red shoes she'd brought with her from Norway, beautifully embroidered. "They'd never have survived this trip," she said.

My mother, the avoider.

The July day felt balmy with white-capped mountain peaks looking down on us as we approached the Mormon town in Utah. We could walk side by side here instead of having to traverse narrow trails that kept me behind Mama and made conversation difficult.

"We might have people stare and point at us in Salt Lake City," Mama said, "once we put on the reform clothing."

"I know. The Rescue League of Washington thinks wearing such clothing is the work of the devil," I said. "But then I suppose they think the devil rides the bicycle too."

Mama laughed. "I can't tell you how many of my women friends said every part of this trip would be of the devil, but we've already proved them wrong in that. The light of a train when I felt most lost came not from him, I'm certain of that. God answers in His own time, but He always answers."

I didn't want to contradict Mama, but bad things still happened: I'd been dragged on this trip, for one.

"He can answer in ways we don't want, though," I said.

"Yes. But that's another way of telling us to wait, that He has chosen the path, and at the crossroads we are to look to Him to say right or left, rather than look to ourselves."

It seemed to me that often Mama didn't wait to hear the direction; she set off on her own.

"The sponsors were to ship the clothing to the train station. We'll change there, walk to the nearest newspaper to affirm that we've made it this far and are now clothed in what some call our Weary Waggles wear."

"Leaving behind this skirt won't cause me any crying," I said and I meant it. I brushed at the Victorian skirt I'd been wearing since home, a chipped nail catching on the stitching over a tear made by the volcanic rocks. "I'm amazed you were able to stitch up these tears," I said.

"A needle and thread are a woman's lifeblood," Mama said.

But it was my curling iron that satisfied a group of Indians who stopped us outside of Salt Lake City. Sea gulls screamed in the distance. The men, half-clothed, surrounded us and grabbed at the bag I held on to.

"Give it to them," Mama whispered, what sounded like fear shaking her voice.

There were five of them. They snatched the bag and dumped it out, compass and maps and curling iron falling beside the tracks. Mama had the revolver in her pocket; the pepper-box pistol rested in mine. The apparent leader picked up the curling iron, pressed it open and closed, then held it, curiosity in his eyes. Maybe they thought it was a gun.

"It's for my hair," I said. My voice shook. "Here, I'll show you." I put my hand out and he gave it to me. Without being heated it wouldn't do much, but I demonstrated a fire by holding it over the lantern, then removed my hat and rolled my hair around the tube. It left a limp curl.

They chattered to each other, eyes marveling, handing it around. One touched my flat curl, gazed as though it was precious. I motioned to use one of his long strands, and it left just the slightest twist. They laughed together and took it, chattering as they walked away, leaving behind our guns.

It's surprising what people claim as treasure.

The elevator cage jerked as we rode deeper into the throat of the silver mine outside of Park City, Utah. Cool air rose as we descended, but the lower we went, the more the earth warmed. I could feel it from the open sides of the cage. Danger lurked here. I didn't think I had prognostication as a talent, but I was positive Mama didn't; here we were, choosing risky, taking precious walking time to do it.

A male escorted each of us, "Because even some of the men get woozy and could misstep," our guide said. I didn't mind the escort; it was the wasted day that mattered. We'd already lost extra days working in Salt Lake City and altering the new clothes we had to wear.

The skirts were shorter than our regular dress, with a two-inch embroidered trim about a foot up from the hem. My waist was much smaller than when we'd left Mica Creek, and Mama wanted pockets, so she sewed a patch for each skirt. We wore wide belts to cover the waistline. Those we had to buy.

"The skirts will be easier to walk in but much more controversial," she told me. We wore them for our trip into the mines. The men escorting us had frowned, but Mama disarmed them with her charm.

"I'll tell people about your mining work and the union's efforts here," she told him, "when I speak in Denver."

She has a speaking engagement in Denver?

"Who's invited you to speak?" I whispered as our escorts talked to the miners, who wore dark hats like ours with little lights to show their way.

"I sent a letter ahead to the Denver paper hoping they'll buy an article about the journey and perhaps book me into an auditorium. We're quite a novelty, you know. We can wear the reform dress when we walk but a long skirt and jacket for the events."

"But won't the sponsors think that's cheating?" I said.

She actually looked thoughtful. "I believe you're right, but using a traditional outfit suggests we can make decisions depending on the occasion. We aren't likely to pick up phthisis on the hemlines in the performance halls. I can mention how much healthier the reform dress is. And we'll prove it when we arrive healthy in New York."

If we ever get to New York for all the side trips Mama chooses.

Our escorts returned to point out silver veins. Mama asked questions. I hated the closed-in feeling and earth's hot breath on our faces.

After what seemed like hours but was likely only one, we stepped back into the cage, listened as the cables groaned us upward and then stopped with a jerk at a wood landing. Had this sinking into earth's depths really been necessary to save the family farm?

A few days later, at Silver Creek Canyon, we attempted to climb down the sides of a nearly perpendicular rock as a way to avoid walking around the land formation the way the railroad did. We had to climb back up, and a rock gouged out from beneath my foot, leaving me perilous. I was no mountain goat like one we'd spied a few days before.

"Hold tight, Clara!" Mama yelled. "Don't let go!"

It was my anger at her for taking this trail that pushed me upward and over the ledge we never should have gone down in the first place.

"Stay with the tracks," I said, panting, my hands on my knees as I leaned over. "Do it systematically. One foot after the other. Stop these 'adventures,' Mama. Stop them. We lose time." A good businessman would never think like she did. No wonder my parents couldn't pay the mortgage.

The thought was sacrilege, blaming them when it was the poor economy, Papa's accident, so many other things that made our situation precarious. But I wouldn't have been scared to death if Mama hadn't taken me on this trek.

"The rest of the country is flat. We can make forty miles a day, easy. Besides, I'll have things to write about," Mama said. "And you'll have interesting illustrations to make instead of simply railroad tracks to draw."

"I'll make an illustration of me tying my mother to my grip so she doesn't take a spur track into a dreaded canyon again," I said.

Mama laughed, but I hadn't meant it to be funny.

In the Red Desert, food was scarce but mountain lions weren't. One night we sat up with guns in hand on the far side of large fire we built to keep the big cats at bay. I could feel eyes watching, and this time Mama didn't dismiss my worries. "I feel him too," she said. "They don't attack from behind, so we'll keep our fire bright and make sure we're ahead of him when we walk out tomorrow."

We walked through coal-mining country and, in small towns, felt if not saw the tensions between Chinese workers and local miners. Federal troops walked about, armed. "We may be safer out on the desert than in these towns," I said.

"Remember that wheelbarrow," Mama cautioned, but she picked up the pace.

One day we found a jar of water like a lily pad blooming in the desert beside the railroad tracks. We stood and looked at each other.

"Do you think it's safe to drink?" I asked.

"It looks perfectly good." But we didn't pick that jar up. Several miles down the tracks we encountered another jar of water with dried cherries in a paper cone beside it. "They're looking out for us, those railroad men. They know we're walking their rails." Mama lifted the jar and drank, then ate a cherry. She offered me a few and I took them.

"Maybe it's not the railroad men, Mama. Maybe it's these Wyoming people, the ranchers and such who have read the articles. Maybe they're looking after us."

"I believe you could be right, Clara. After all, those men gave women of Wyoming the vote. They know a thing or two about how to treat a gentlewoman."

"Don't turn everything into politics," I said. I took a swig of the water now too.

"But this is about politics," she said. "We've come through four sparsely populated states and been unharmed, treated with respect. We've had no threats." I raised my eyebrow. "Well, that one, but he was hungry. In many ways, we've been taken care of. We've only slept out seven nights since we left the lava craters. We've been given shelter, which speaks to the character of this country's people."

"Now you're talking Bryan again." I wagged my finger at my mother.

"Everyone's talking politics, my daughter. The campaign begins soon."

"Why is it so important to you—getting the vote, knowing about the elections and all of that?"

"You have to pay attention, Clara. Otherwise laws get passed that come to haunt you. Maybe interest rates on mortgage loans are raised without you knowing. Wages. We women get paid so little, yet we work so hard! I think of Hedvig having to work out; you and Olaf, all so young for poor wages. Crop prices, those are all part of public life. Unions." She had found her footing on this subject, and she kicked up dirt as we walked. "If it weren't for the union, we would have starved after your father's accident. This isn't about government and politics, Clara. It's about family and knowing what you have to do to take care of them."

"I know. It's what Estbys do," I said.

"Yes," she said. "It's what Estbys do. And you as well."

I had no idea what she meant and was too startled to ask.

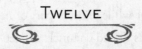

TWELVE

Crossing the Bridge

We tried to walk side by side, but our strides varied. We didn't say much to each other even when we were so very close, our now brown hands bumping each other beneath the hot sun, the only connection we might have for hours at a time. Mama walked faster than I, so I found my pace behind her. I walked silently in her footsteps.

It might have been the beef stew with potatoes and carrots that looked to me as though it had a scum on it. But Mama ate it too when we were offered it before Laramie by a friendly woman hanging clothes on her line.

"Maybe it was the cream pie," Mama said. "You had a piece but I didn't."

"What could make me sick from that?" I groaned. "Wait, don't tell me." I buried my head in a bucket and threw up, then set it down outside the outhouse door while another part of my body took my attention. My entire innards ripped channels as deep as those silver mines.

"You've got to get fluid back into you, Clara. Here, sip a little water now."

"I…I can't hold anything down," I said.

I wanted to die, to be left alone to die.

Mama pointed out that at least we had the graciousness of a widowed grandma here in Percy, Wyoming. Living on the outskirts of town, she'd shown us comfort, offered her outhouse. I groaned again. Mama rose. "I'm going to ask her where the doctor is and see about finding a little work while you're down."

"No, don't leave me," I said. The thought of sitting alone in the disgust of my own aroma gave me chills. I started to shake.

"I have to go, Clara. I'll be back as soon as I can."

I imagined this was what my sisters felt when we left Mica Creek: wanting to believe she'd be back but feeling like they'd die while she was gone.

I tried sipping water again, watched a spider make its way up the side of the door, then spin a web. Bees hovered on the hollyhock branches; the sun moved across the sky.

"Here we are." Mama's cheery voice reached through my agony. "The doctor said water then a little rice, if you can hold it down. The lady of the house has dried apples we can mash later. And tea, he told me tea will help." She handed me the bowl, but another wave of cramping coursed through me. I was grateful this hadn't happened in the wide-open spaces. Thunder rumbled in the distance and lightning crackled in the foothills. At least I had a roof over my head. And Mama was taking care of me and didn't seem upset with me even though this delay was bad. We weren't even halfway to New York yet.

"I'll contact the sponsors," Mama said later that evening. "Get an extension. They said we could do that for illnesses, and the doctor will surely verify that you've been sick. I've got a laundry job for tomorrow. And here, I replaced your curling iron."

I lay on a cot in a guest room of the kindly woman. My hair was as dirty and flat as old leaves. I didn't need a curling iron.

"Don't fret, Clara. You should have at least one delay on this trip with your name on it," she teased. "You don't need to remind me that all the others have been mine."

Sun pierced the darkness of the mile-high Wyoming mountains, casting heavy shadows against stone. I was recovered from my bout with "not quite botulism," as the doctor called it, and we'd walked several more days, including up a twisting mountain climb the locals called Rattlesnake Pass Road. I didn't need my mother squeezing my shoulder and forcing me awake with her cheery, "It's time, Clara." I knew what time it was: time for yet another of her challenges, time for me to once again wonder what I was doing here. My fear of heights competed with my dread of uncertainty. This day threatened both, and there was nothing I could do about it but keep walking.

"Susan B. Anthony was stuck here twenty years ago," my mother said. She stood, her angular face in profile. "Snow kept their train here four days, but they had plenty of coal and the railroad served them crackers and dried fish. They made an adventure of it. We're lucky we're here in the summertime."

I put my jacket on, rubbed my arms, warming myself. "I could use hot tea."

"On the other side," my mother said, "we'll look for a spot out of the wind to build a fire, make tea. No time to lose here." She handed me a circle of hardtack, our regular morning breakfast.

My back ached and my throat felt scratchy as old socks. I drank from the canteen as I walked to the opening of the snow shelter, gazing up at patches of dirty snow hugging dips in the granite crevices. I stared at the narrow train trestle. I rounded my shoulders in an effort to relax them, pushed them forward and back, took deeper breaths. The thin air made me feel dizzy. This whole adventure, as my mother called it, made me feel dizzy.

"Nothing to be afraid of, Clara," my mother said. She put her arm around my waist, gentled her head to mine. "We've walked farther than that. It's what, maybe three hundred feet across?"

"More like four hundred fifty," I said. "And the canyon's at least a hundred and fifty feet deep."

"You are the better judge of distances." My mother patted my waist, turned back to put items into her carpetbag. She grabbed my curling iron and stuffed it inside. "It doesn't matter. We've got to cross here, and the sooner the better."

"It looks sturdy enough," I ventured. "It's…the height. I'll have to look down to step on the ties, but then I'll see…how deep it is." I swallowed. "It'll make me dizzy and then—"

"I suppose we could backtrack to that old wagon road through the canyon. But there are snakes down there, no doubt. We'd have to climb like mountaineers to get up the other side. We don't have that kind of time."

"That's not my fault, Mama," I said.

"I know. I know. Something you ate, though I still don't know why I didn't get sick."

It hadn't been only my recent illness that delayed us, but I kept my tongue. No sense having an argument when we might die within the next moments. "The trestle's the only way. But should a train come…"

"We've not met any trains this early in the morning," my mother said. "I checked at the Laramie station. One arrives at 7:00 a.m. and stops for passengers to eat. Then it makes the long climb up Sherman Hill. We'll be long across Dale Creek trestle by then. No trains are expected this early from Cheyenne either. We'll scamper across like rabbits and be done with it before the sun can peek over that ridge." She pointed to the rocky promontory in the distance. I shivered. "This is how Estbys deal with fear, Clara. Fears or disappointments or betrayals: we face them early on with a strong jaw forward, a refreshing drink of water, and a prayer."

I walked to the opening of the snow shelter, lifted my skirts to relieve myself, then rubbed my hands clean in the pebbled dirt beside the tracks. We were saving precious water. Returning, I took the items my mother handed me and stuffed them into the light grip, making sure everything balanced well. I pushed my worn straw hat onto my head, held the grip at my side.

I'd heard stories that the winds could be so fierce that railroad cars had toppled off the Dale Creek trestle, plunging into the hundred-fifty-foot depths below. Both my mother and I together weighed less than one good stout man, so who knew what the wind could do to us if it took a mind to.

"What is it, five o'clock?" I yawned, couldn't get a good, deep breath.

"We do not walk in darkness," my mother chirped, and I knew it was as much a statement of reality as a reference to Scripture.

The wind came at us in blustery gusts. In between them, the world fell silent as snow.

The thin soles of my leather shoes—my fourth pair since the

journey began—gave rise to little pebbles pressed against my feet. Maybe that was good, to feel the ground so closely. It would keep me bound to earth and forbid my missteps. I could see myself dropping a leg between the railroad ties or, worse, losing my balance and tumbling to certain death. My feet attuned to earthly things might notice the vibration of a distant train, feel it strong enough and early so I'd know before we stepped onto the first railroad tie that we should wait, that there wasn't enough time before a train came smoking around that distant bend and the engineer faced the horrified looks of two women about to meet their deaths. Could my feet save us both?

A hawk screamed overhead. Or was that a distant train whistle?

No, the wind. It seared through the iron monolith, pushing against the guy wires that reminded me of tiny threads futilely hoisting a ship's sail. Still, I had to believe it was secure.

At the trestle's edge, my mother halted, looked ahead, then turned. "Keep your eyes on the ties, not between them. We'll make this. We have to."

I set my carpetbag down, bent to flatten my hands onto the iron track, willing myself to feel even the tiniest vibration. My breaths came short, rapid. The steel felt cold and silent as a dagger. My fingers scraped the iron spikes holding the rail to the ties.

"Come along," my mother shouted, swinging her arm forward. She didn't look back.

My head buzzed as I stood. The world spun.

I took the first tentative step onto the railroad tie, thin soles making me aware of the ax marks struck by a Chinese worker who labored in building this trestle. The essence of another human having touched that tie gave me courage. Others had made their way on foot across here; so could I. I set the grip in front of me, took another step. Through the ties, I saw a tiny dark snake of a creek wind its way beneath me. I felt lightheaded again. *Am I going to be ill?* I shook my head, took the third step, then another. I got my rhythm: a step, then move the grip forward, eyes on my mother's slender back, eyes down to the next tie, then step, grip forward. I refused to see what lay beneath us, what the sun wouldn't hit for hours. I focused on the solid ties and my mother's frame as we two met yet one more challenge.

I heard the shout, stunned by my mother's body jerking forward and her, "Whoa!"

"Mama?"

My mother dropped to the rails. Before I knew what was happening, the blast of wind that lowered her struck me. I felt myself shifting, threw my arms out like a tightrope walker I'd once seen in a circus. I'd be cast aside without a net. My heart pounded in my temples. "Ooh!" I shouted. The wind pushed me down, and I squatted and gripped the sides of the tracks with my face buried in the carpetbag on the tie in front of me, sucking up air. At least it hadn't been blown away. Tears of fear and outrage pressed against my nose. *What am I doing here?* Cool sweat threatened my rib cage beneath thin wool. I was frozen in place.

If I got across this trestle alive, I vowed I'd never put a member of my family in such a position; I'd never do such a foolish thing. Anger spurred me to crawl. Being on my knees made praying easier.

" 'This is the way, walk ye in it.' " I repeated the verse from Isaiah.

"You can do it!" Mama called out. I looked up. She was already across. "Swallow your fears. Keep coming."

I crept and finally looked up to my mother's hand reaching out to me.

"We did it, Clara." She hugged me. "Come, we'll fix that tea I promised."

"No one should be in that kind of danger," I said. "No one." I wanted to cry in relief. "This is all because you didn't think this through." I shivered both from outrage and fear.

"Clara. We're here. You have to let go of what got us here and take one step at a time. It's the Estby way."

"Maybe I'm not an Estby then," I said.

She softened. "You're truly frightened."

I started to cry. "I thought I'd die," I said. "And you too. Why did you bring me? What did I do to make you want me along?"

"Oh, Clara, I would never knowingly do anything to hurt you. Never." She pulled me to her. "I...I hoped you'd like the time with me on this journey. You're a wise young woman. You add respectability to the wager. I enjoy your companionship. This could be such an education for you. I... You can't let things frighten you. We must be bold. We must be."

"But I was scared."

"Come, let's have that tea," she said then. "And a little conversation."

I drank the tea, inhaled the mint of it. My mother stared at me in a thoughtful mood.

"What makes you think you're not an Estby?"

"You tell me often enough that Estbys aren't fearful; they keep going."

"Oh, we're fearful all right. But it doesn't put us in shackles. It shouldn't you either."

I sipped my tea. My hands still shook.

"I'm different, I guess," I said. "I mean, I can *see* that I'm different. I have a different shape, hair color, eyes. I don't see things like Ida or Papa do. Or you. I think things are either right or wrong, and the rest of you think, well, things are either good or bad."

She stayed quiet, replenished my tea. "Clara. There's something you should know. If something were to happen to me on this trip—not that I think it will, but, well, the lava craters and this dangerous trestle… It's possible."

Her words sent fear through me. "Don't, Mama. Don't you dare die and leave me alone in the middle of nowhere."

"Not my plan. However"—she cleared her throat—"perhaps it's time you knew."

THIRTEEN

The Spoils of Achievement

A moment of tingling, a premonition of something bad.

"When I was fifteen," she began, "I...became with child."

"Oh. But you were sixteen when you married, you always said."

"I...wasn't truthful about that." She didn't look at me. "It was by the son of a wealthy family I worked for. It... I thought... He wasn't much older than I. I wasn't sure how things even happened, but I knew I loved him. Or thought I did." She cleared her throat. "When my mother learned of it...they were...shamed. She had my stepfather speak to Ole, a friend of his from the old country. Ole was willing to cover the shame I brought to my parents." The wind whistled behind us, and I felt cold despite the warming tea. "We married and I gave birth to you."

I stared at her.

"You were born in Michigan. We moved right after to Yellow

Medicine, Minnesota. What I wrote in the Bible about your birthday was written to conceal my shame. Your grandparents moved with us, and we told everyone that you were big for your age. So there'd be no question about your legitimacy."

"So I'm—"

"You're actually nineteen, Clara. You'll be twenty in November."

I was shocked into silence. Then, "But if Papa isn't my..." *Is that why he hugs Ida, teases Bertha by tugging on her braids, holds Lillian laughing on his lap, but rarely if ever touches me?*

"He's your father in every way, Clara, save one."

"But if you didn't really love him..."

"It was best for the family. All of us."

"And the man, the one who is my real—?"

"There's no need to know more. He was in my life and then gone. I moved ahead. That's what Estbys do."

"Which I'm not," I said. My voice cracked. *I'm truly not.* "What am I?"

"You're an Estby. That's that."

"And baby Ole?"

"He came after you, not before. And yes, he died."

"What was his name, my father?"

She shook her head, packed up, quick to move on now, leaving me to wonder about my mother's secrets and the man she'd fallen in love with, a man with no name whom I might be more like than anyone in my so-called family.

"You were ashamed for having me," I said as we walked the rails again. I padded beside her, trying to keep up.

"No. You made it all worthwhile. My shame was in believing in the words of a man, a boy, who had no good intentions. This is why your Forest—"

"I don't know if he's *my* Forest."

"You wish he would be," she said. "It's one reason why I wanted you to go with me on this journey. I didn't want the same to happen to you."

"You don't know that Forest might not be a good man," I said. "I'm not fifteen, a girl. I'm eighteen years… Nineteen, I guess."

"Nineteen."

"Didn't Papa know?"

"Of course he knew." Mama stopped and took the grip from me. She held my hand, brown and scratched. She stared at my stubby fingers. I still gnawed at the nails. Her fingers were slender as asparagus. She looked up, chewing the side of her cheek.

"At the lava craters, I wanted to tell you, in case… Ole would never tell you. It was mine to tell, he always said, but he didn't see the point of it. It didn't seem right that I might die still holding the truth. It was time you knew, but that's that now. Nothing more needs to be said. That boy who fathered you…he isn't family. Ole is."

We walked in silence for a long time, and I finally dropped behind, hung my head like the soggy sunflower, trying to piece together who I was.

What was he like? What was his name? It became my new internal conversation. After acquiring a signature I'd wonder, *Could my father have been like this mayor or that governor?* Once we scared off a herd of curious pronghorns, and I wondered if my true father ever hunted or if he had crossed the Mississippi River. A world of otherness opened to me, a way to make sense of why I was the only one in the family not a towhead, why I was nearly as tall as Papa. Who would my father vote for in the upcoming election? My mother gave out no new information. I feared I had all I was meant to get, at least for now.

Cooler weather gave us renewed spirit. In Greeley, Colorado, we bought yet another pair of shoes and welcomed September. A news reporter wrote about us, "They wear the beat look of a pedestrian stomp." It was the first time we experienced disdain in the newspaper before leaving town. The article ended with, "The fakes left this city for Denver."

A part of me did feel like a fake: I'd been masquerading as an Estby.

"What was his name?" I asked. We rested for the night in a shared bed in the house of a suffragette.

"There's no reason for you to know that, Clara. He was young. I was young. I did what was best for him and for my parents, who had dreamed I'd go on to school. They'd sent me to private school in Norway. All that investment, lost."

"But—"

"Not all questions need answering."

"Will you write to Papa and tell him you've told me?"

She sighed. "Better left until we get back," Mama said. "Besides, I fill the letters with so many details of what we've seen, the people who have befriended us, our adventures, that such intimate things can wait, *ja*? Wait until we have a *sandbakkel* to dip in our coffee and I am baking the Christmas bread for us all. We can sigh together about how God has been so good to us. We are your family, Clara. This"—she tapped her heart—"this is who you belong to and always will."

Not far from Denver, a man approached as though he had news, hailing us. "Women walkers," he said. We stopped to greet him, and before Mama could show him a photograph to sell, he grabbed the grip that held our money and possessions, save the pepper-box pistol I kept in my pocket.

"Give that back!" she shouted.

"Stupid women," he snarled. "Tramps. You're asking for this."

His need to condemn us before running gave me time to get my pistol out. I stepped forward and pulled the trigger, purposefully shooting past his head.

He screamed and Mama grabbed for the grip, swung it from him.

My heart pounded, but I'd acted, done what was necessary. We couldn't afford to lose our grip. My letters to Forest were in there, all the signatures. Evidence of our accomplishment, which the sponsors would want.

"Now skedaddle," Mama said. "Perhaps learn to avoid attacking women." She had her revolver out now. "You'll walk before us into Denver, and we'll drop you off at the police station or maybe the governor's mansion when we get His Honor Mr. McIntire's signature."

But as we approached the rail house, we lost our robber when he dodged behind a rail car. I was too tired to chase after him; Mama didn't either.

"You did well to scare him, Clara, and you'll notice I didn't shoot him. It would have delayed us. And for the record, it was your quick thinking and our teamwork that caught him," Mama said. "Not any well-laid plan."

In Denver, Mama was granted her speaking engagement. She spoke at a large hall filled with big-hatted women, a few wearing reform dresses like the ones we wore, but most dressed in long skirts with light summer jackets for the late-afternoon heat. Feathers shifted with round fans bearing advertisements for products like Coca-Cola and politicians like William Jennings Bryan. At the auditorium door, I sold pictures of us, which kept us out of the laundry houses to earn our next dollars. It also kept me out of the limelight, something I truly wanted to avoid.

Mama looked magnificent on that stage, burgundy curtains behind her. She told her stories of the mines, of crossing the trestle, and included the latest adventure with the would-be robber. She wove in local stories such as the upcoming elections and chastised Colorado women, who had given up their right to vote a few years ago, urging them to get it back. She acted out the events and made people laugh and cheer and applaud. I'd never seen this side of her. I was nothing like her, nothing. She was magnificent.

She ended by speaking of our family, how she was walking not just to prove a woman's strength but to keep her family together, acting out in her way what every woman in America did by cooking, cleaning, taking in wash, putting in gardens, canning peaches and pears—all the little things that go unnoticed, she said, but were critical for life, for family. All for family.

Women had tears in their eyes and I did too. She hadn't mentioned the money, and I was glad of that. And proud of her performing. I liked how happy she looked.

"My family is my compass," she said, "giving me direction, telling me how to find my way home."

A man in the back yelled out, "Your husband should have kept that compass for himself and kept you home with it!"

A murmur rose from the women and the few other men as necks craned to see who had spoken. My mother's face grew pink.

"Only a strong man would not be threatened by a strong wife," I said loud enough for my mother to hear from the stage.

"My daughter," my mother said, and the crowd began to applaud, drowning out the heckler's retort.

We walked back to our hotel, each of us in thought.

"Clara?"

"Yes, Mama?"

"Oh, never mind. Just Clara." She held my hand, swinging it as though we were children playing. "I'm so glad you came with me on this journey. Every good adventure deserves to be shared. Aren't you a little bit pleased we've come this far?"

"I guess," I said and realized I meant it. For the first time in a long time, I didn't feel put-upon. I felt hopeful.

Coming down the steps the next morning from our hotel room, which had been provided by one of the suffragettes of Denver, I stumbled and fell. Pain seared through my ankle like an ice pick pierced into bone.

"You didn't break it, did you?" Mama asked. She squatted down.

"No." I gasped, taking in the sharp stabs that radiated all around my right foot.

"Let's get you into the room and take that shoe off," Mama said. "I'll get ice to keep the swelling down."

"I'm sorry, Mama. I just—"

"Not your fault. I think I see a loose carpet tack. It tripped you up. I'll have words with the management."

"No, I—"

"Let's get you up on the bed." She helped me hobble upstairs, then pulled out pillows, which I gingerly set my foot on. My ankle throbbed with my toes pointed upward. Oh, how it hurt!

She unhooked the shoe quickly, tugged at it gently, but the movement still brought tears to my eyes. I sat up on my elbows to look. It already swelled, as big as a bedpost.

I flopped back on the bed. I should never let myself be happy or hopeful. There was always another shoe to drop, and it most likely would drop on me.

FOURTEEN

Negotiations

I'll telegraph the sponsors," Mama said. "We've got to get an extension. They gave us one for your sickness. Surely a sprained ankle qualifies. You need time to heal. I'll speak to the hotel manager too."

"Please, Mama. No talk of lawsuits. We don't have time."

"*Ja,* you're right about that, but they're negligent. That carpet wasn't tacked down."

"Don't...don't bring attention, please."

Mama looked at me, a frown on her face. "I'll simply tell the manager that I'll need work, as we must remain. Any meals or other accoutrements their fine establishment cares to offer will be mentioned when I speak to the newspaper."

"You have to go to the newspaper about this?"

"Clara. We are here. Now. On this journey. We do what we must and adapt. That's what an Estby—"

"—does. But I'm not."

She sighed. "I've work to find."

Mama did go to the newspaper to advertise another presentation. She added to her performance the benefits of walking, how she'd been strengthened despite her accident four years previous.

"You talked about your broken pelvis?" I couldn't believe it when she rehashed the evening. I couldn't attend. I spent my time writing letters and making sketches from memory, and I worked on a design of my own.

"No. I wasn't specific. You wouldn't have been embarrassed." She held the quarter heart of Hardanger lace in her hands, moving it between her graceful fingers. "But there are proposed laws in states east of here to prevent women's 'walking exhibitions.' I might not be able to speak about what we're doing. I just learned that. The intention is to protect us women. But in truth, they don't want people to hear about women who are not wasting away, not weak, who don't constantly need a helping hand. People need to see that we are enduring souls willing and able to step up both mentally and physically to help our families." She might have given her lecture right there, but she noticed the object in my hands. "What have you made there?"

"It's…something I've designed," I said. "Since my monthlies have stopped—"

"They'll come back as soon as we're not walking so much," she assured me. "Dr. Latham said that might happen."

"I used the rags to make a binder for my…breasts." My face felt hot. "Since we've been without the corsets, I… My chest…"

She held up the strips of cloth I'd sewn together. "How does it work?"

I put it on over my blouse, showed her how the straps formed a crisscross over my shoulders and wrapped beneath my breast. "It offers support," I said.

"Why, that's inventive," she said. "What good thinking, Clara. Can you make one for me too?"

I lay awake as she slept. Despite my worries over arriving on time, I secretly liked my mother's company. I enjoyed her descriptions of the women in the audiences, her encounters with the wealthy, her presentation of herself as an equal. She wasn't a scared child waiting to deliver an unplanned baby; she wasn't a tired mother looking after her children and husband in the big farm kitchen; she was formidable, a woman making her way. Despite the risky wager, I found I admired her tenacity, her refusal to be a shamed woman for the rest of her life though she hadn't married for love. I liked, too, that she admired something I'd made, an idea that would ease both of us as we walked. This was an educational journey.

After two weeks, we began again and followed the Burlington rails through the unending horizon heading for Lincoln, Nebraska, where my mother walked right up to the porch of William Jennings Bryan's home, hoping for his signature. Sadly, he was off campaigning to become the president of the United States. His wife, Mary, though, bought several pictures and signed her name to the signature book, the only woman who had. "In Cambridge," Mary Bryan told us, "they voted not to give women university degrees even though they attend classes, and then they hung a woman in effigy, on a bicycle, wearing a bifurcated skirt, right from the top of Cambridge Hall."

"Appalling," Mama said when Mary showed us the photograph in the *New York Times*.

That picture jogged my complacent fear. Mama had said in the

East we'd have sisters. But Cambridge represented civilization, didn't it? Our bold adventure might not be so welcomed.

Out of Omaha, we followed the Rock Island Railroad lines. In Des Moines, Mama gave two interviews, one with *Decorah-Posten,* the Norwegian paper, which gave us one sentence. With the English paper, she emphasized the wager again, and the reporter suggested we were "greedy," trying to take hard-earned money from businesspeople, the sponsors, for our own gain. He said we were women of questionable morals for walking the rails unescorted and fraternizing with men all across the country.

My face burned with the charge that seemed half right.

The weather changed as we trudged toward Chicago, cold stings of snow hitting our faces and melting on our straw hats and shoulders though it was only October. Nothing looked worthy of sketching, so I didn't. I complained that my legs were cold despite the woolen socks, and my ankle ached by day's end. The chilly wind roared up our shorter reform dresses. "I never thought I'd miss our long skirts," Mama said, "but I do." It was the closest she came to a complaint.

We stepped out behind the curtain onto a stage inside a Chicago department store to stares and scattered applause. Modeling the reform clothes available in the store helped us to earn funds, publicity for our photographs, and advertisements for Mama's speeches. Best of all, the store had heat. We needed warm jackets, which we'd get as part of our modeling pay. I looked with envy at the women in their fur stoles and muffs. A few sniffed at us, and one even covered her daughter's face with her gloved hands, she thought we were so provocative.

Mama was her performing self, quoting the *Chicago Tribune* in an article advocating reform clothes, decrying the suffering of tight corsets and the filth that long skirts picked up. She wove a good story, that was certain, embellishing what I would have reported as just facts.

"One hundred and ninety-five dollars so far," I said that evening. We splurged after our modeling job and stayed at a hotel. Mama asked for an accounting of our expenses.

"We'll get that all back once we reach New York and pick up our prize money," she said.

"You did get the extension, didn't you, Mama?" My ankle ached as I stood to dab a wet cloth on stains on our dresses.

"Nothing to worry about." Mama put the accounting book back in the grip. She didn't look at me.

"You got them to go to January 1, didn't you?" By my calculations, we'd need every bit of that time to make even that date. We couldn't possibly make December 13, the date she'd negotiated when I got sick from the stew.

She turned to me, took a deep breath. "December 13. They wouldn't accept your ankle injury as an illness."

"Mama!"

"I argued. I did my best. I don't get to talk to the sponsors, though. Everything goes through the editor at *New York World,* and men don't understand. If I could talk to them… It'll all work out," she said patting my shoulder. "We'll make it. Have a little faith."

"Taking this detour is not right, Mama." After walking for nearly a month more, we traveled yet another side trip, which took us close to Canton, Ohio. "Can't you see our problem, Mama? We have to keep going east."

"Sometimes you have to put goodness over rightness," she told me. "We're visiting a cottage. You'll like it. It's only a few miles out of our way. And we don't have to get signatures anymore in these more urban areas. But this one will be worth it. It'll be our last."

This distraction bothered me more than the silver mine episode or the time we spent talking to Wyoming ranchers or Nebraska wheat farmers and their wives. All that talking took time from walking, and that was what mattered most. I couldn't imagine what made Mama so certain we'd be successful when the facts didn't support it.

The "cottage" turned out to be a large Victorian home with a picket fence and bare elm branches framing the charming white house. "It's the president-elect's home," Mama said.

"President McKinley?"

"Don't look so surprised. Surely you didn't think I'd pass up an attempt to let you meet your hero."

"And get that one last famous signature."

"It will add to the story," she said, bumping my hip.

"You can't just walk up to the door and knock. Maybe he won't be here," I said. I hoped he wouldn't be. My hair looked a fright. And yet when William McKinley came to the door and Mama introduced me and herself, I could barely say his name. Mama congratulated him, said she hoped he'd remember the women's vote one day, and then showed him our picture and a newspaper article we'd brought with us, the most recent one from the *Ohio State Journal* of November 24. "I'd like your signature, for the sponsors," Mama said.

"Certainly. Come in," he said. "If you'll wait in the parlor." He pointed after he signed Mama's book. "I'll wheel my wife in to join us and ask Lotty to set up for tea."

A satin flowered settee, the pictures of a young girl and an infant, frames with gold flourishes, mirrors (which revealed the decrepit state of my hair), a coal stove, and a grand piano marked the parlor of a home both modest yet elegant. Distinguished, orderly, not too opulent, and pleasant—the way life ought to be, I thought, just the way McKinley had campaigned.

"Mrs. McKinley has fainting spells," Mama whispered. She fingered the fringe on the lamp. "They're devoted to each other. That's why he didn't campaign away from home very much and answers his own door. Both of their children died; so tragic. The story is that they met when Mrs. McKinley worked as a financial manager and ran the bank when her father traveled. The president-elect had his accounts there."

The mention of banks made me think of Forest. I wondered what he was doing now. Might I one day live in such an elegant home, loved by a devoted husband like Forest?

"A woman as a financial manager? You mean like a banker?" I said.

"Like a banker."

"Who would never be caught less than three weeks away from a deadline that's nearly five hundred miles ahead."

"Clara," Mama sighed. "It's your birthday present, meeting him. You'll please me if you simply accept it."

My birthday. I'd forgotten. I'd lost a year of my life on this trip. I thought I'd be turning nineteen, but instead I'd be turning twenty, with my mother giving me the only birthday present I could remember that she hadn't sewn herself, at least not with thread.

Thirty-five miles a day, walking to make up time, legs aching, feet wet and cold. Chapped cheeks, no fur mufflers to keep my neck warm, though we'd bought warm hats after Chicago. No fat on our bones, so the wind played against our narrow backs as though we were xylophones.

Through Pennsylvania we accepted warm meals from the Amish, whom Mama described as the true heart of America. I could have bunked with them for the winter, they acted so welcoming.

Energized, we made forty miles one day. In Pittsburgh we rode a trolley, acceptable because it was a free ride, Mama said, apparently no longer worried over spies turning us in as contract breakers. Maybe because there wasn't any way we'd fulfill the contract. But like a child who hopes for dessert even when the plate is empty, I prayed we would prevail. Maybe it was Jonah and the whale that inspired, despite the narrowness of that whale's throat.

News of our arrival now preceded us with greater interest, so in Reading, when we stayed at a hotel, we had requests from visitors who'd read the news reports of our trek. Mama entertained the reporters and society people with her stories. I even joined in at one point by saying, "McKinley well deserved to win. He's steady and conscientious and understands finances. Mr. Bryan makes a good speech, but his interest in returning to the silver standard from the gold I think not very wise at all."

"Everyone's entitled to her opinion," Mama chirped. "I know I have mine!"

"A woman who doesn't is dead," one of the suffragettes said to laughter.

One reporter described us both as "intelligent and well-spoken even as they disagreed" and said he was "charmed" by the "bronzed western women none the worse for wear." Maybe Mama could charm the sponsors. Maybe I could too.

On December 10, with us slogging our way through New Jersey, I knew we could not make the deadline and all we had left was charm. This entire trip would be for nothing. We'd spent two hundred dollars and had one hundred remaining. We'd been seven months away from family, pushed our bodies to such leanness, and all for nothing. Anger and disappointment, futility and regret, churned through my day.

"It'll work out," Mama said. "God provides."

December 13 found us still miles from the New York skyline, and I couldn't keep the terseness from my tone as Mama chatted gaily with a tramp warming his hands over a metal tub near the tracks. I stomped my frozen feet. "We have to keep moving," I said. Why couldn't she see the consequences?

"Don't be so glum. With the publicity of our arrival—we're only a few days away, Clara—the sponsors will change their minds. They wouldn't want bad press, now, would they?"

"If they didn't allow an extension for my ankle on a walking trip, why would they give up ten thousand dollars when we didn't meet the conditions of the contract? In business, even bad publicity can be a good thing, so they likely won't mind at all. The facts do not support your view, Mama."

She said nothing, then in a firm whisper, "God will provide."

In New Jersey God did *not* provide. We walked forty-five miles in the wrong direction, then a blizzard rolled in as we headed back, forcing us to huddle for a full day in a rail station lacking coal. I think it was my lowest point.

We limped into New York City December 23 while a big clock clanged 1:00 p.m. I looked up at the tall buildings, the seat of power and influence. We were almost two weeks late.

I'd been right, and it wasn't good.

FIFTEEN

A Business Decision

ailed?" Mama said. She actually sounded like it was a surprise, yet she repeated the *World* editor's words. "We've failed?"

"You're ten days past the adjusted date," he said. He tapped a pencil on his desk, didn't look right at us.

"Because they didn't account for my daughter's ankle sprain, which is ridiculous. We made it within ten days, for heaven's sake. The press across the country touted our walk and the reform dresses. That's what they wanted. The time we had to stop and work to earn the money we needed to support ourselves equaled two months. We're here, with proof." She showed him the signatures. "We demonstrated a woman's stamina."

"But not on time," he repeated. "Not on time."

"Come along, Mama," I said taking her elbow. "There's nothing more we can do here."

"But—"

"We'll write about your arrival," the editor said. "Maybe you can sell more photographs and get speaking engagements, though during the holidays it's difficult to draw a crowd. I…" He fiddled in his pocket, took out his wallet. He put a five-dollar bill on the desk, slid it toward us.

"We don't need your money," Mama said then, standing. "We certainly won't take charity. We earned that ten thousand dollars. If I could please talk—"

"Mama," I urged, "take it."

"The truth is, a couple of the sponsors are out of the country," the editor said. "And those who are here don't feel they can make any adjustments without the vote of everyone. I'll make certain they see these signatures," he added.

"When might they all be here?" I asked.

"Oh, not until the summer," the editor said.

"The summer," Mama whispered. "We have to be home before then."

"I'm sorry." He pushed the bill closer to Mama.

I snatched it up.

"Do you suppose they're having lingonberry sauce and sour cream pudding at home?" I said. We'd rented a room at a Manhattan hotel. "Or maybe *lefse* and *lutefisk*. Or the almond cookies that Bertha makes. And do you think Ida could make the *julekaga*?"

"Not the bread, but the other. I'm sure she could do that," Mama said. She pored over the newspaper clippings. In the two days since we'd arrived, there'd been several articles about our walking "success" and our business "failure." Letters to the editors supported us receiving the award, but that had little merit. The sponsors didn't.

I hated being right. I did.

"I wish we were there with them," I said. Thoughts of family made me wonder about my father again, whoever and wherever he might be. I thought of Ole too, how he must have taken the news that the wire service sent to the Spokane papers too.

The Estbys would spend Christmas Eve together around the fire. They'd probably exchange few presents with money so tight, but they'd have the pleasure of each other. They'd play games and maybe reread letters sent by Mama and me. I'd written postcards addressed to Lillian, but the newsy ones came from Mama.

My brothers and sisters… No, half brothers and sisters. That's how I would need to think of them now. I was not only a year older on this trip; my family had changed too. I'd lost them as full brothers and sisters. Any children my natural father might have would be only half to me too.

I was all alone.

"We have to go back to the newspaper offices," Mama said, standing. "Bring all of these clippings to verify where we were and that we accomplished this goal. If we hadn't had to work to make expenses— why, a cat could have made the journey if it didn't have to beat rugs for a meal."

"And if I hadn't sprained my ankle or gotten sick so much."

"The time is less significant than that we did it. Walking all the way but for one little wagon ride near Walla Walla and the electric car in Pennsylvania, both allowed. They were free. It's scandalous that they'd withhold the money because of a few days' time. It's not right."

"But those were the conditions," I said. "Maybe they never intended to pay, thinking it so unlikely we'd succeed."

"Don't talk dumb," Mama said. She stuffed notes and photographs in the grip, put her purse inside along with my curling iron, all our goods.

"What are you doing?"

"We don't know how safe the hotel is," Mama said. "We take everything with us. We'll go back. Get the editor to wire the sponsors, wherever they are. The *New York Times* even ran a story this morning, Clara. They love the signatures we gathered. Come along. We need to return and finish this contract so we can buy train tickets and go home."

She was wasting our time talking to the editor. Maybe after January she could make some presentations and we'd collect enough for the journey. One had to face facts; Mama wouldn't.

"We need to find a charitable society who might be willing to fund our train ticket home," I said.

"What, beg? Never. That's immoral."

"It's simply accepting money," I said. "It's no different from Papa receiving union payments for his injury."

"It's every bit different from that." I thought I saw fear in her eyes, maybe for the first time on this entire trip except in the lava craters. "He earned that pension, as we earned our walk. We do not beg, Clara. An Estby does not beg. We will find a way to complete the contract and get home."

"We have to cut our losses," I said.

"Where do you hear such talk?"

"At the Stapletons', the Rutters' before that. It's business, Mama."

"How can you be so cold, Clara?"

"Cold? I'm not cold at all. These are the facts, Mama. We made a contract; we didn't keep it. It's no different from what will happen if you can't make the mortgage payment."

She slapped my face then, the sting shaped like her fingers staying with me even as I added through stinging tears, "It's business, Mama. We misjudged our sponsors and our abilities, and we failed. I want to get home however we can." She stared at me, and I couldn't tell if my words or her action distressed her more. "It's the day after Christmas, Mama. The editor may not be in. He may be spending time with his family. Like I wish we were."

"You can come with me or stay," she said.

Against my better judgment, I followed her, wishing later that I'd stayed right where I was. And yet I told myself, wrongly, it couldn't get worse.

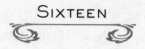

SIXTEEN

Nothing Left

We pressed against people crowding the city's streets. "I'll buy you that ceramic pot when we return," Mama said. She pointed to a piece of pottery with a sunflower shiny beneath the glaze in the window of a store that sold only dishes. The piece was marked down, an after-season sale.

"Before or after we buy the train tickets?" I said.

"I didn't have a present to give you for Christmas." Her emotions simmered like a custard getting ready to jell.

"It would be nice," I said. "It would remind me to keep looking up for the light. But don't waste any money on it. Not now."

"It will be a reminder of our success."

"Mama—"

The man came out of nowhere, grabbed at the grip, knocking Mama down.

"What…?" she groaned.

"Stop! Stop that man!" I shouted while I tried to lift her up.

"Go after him, Clara!"

"I can't leave you."

"I'm fine. Just go!"

I pushed my way through the throngs of people dressed in their furs and finery, my heart pounding. He carried away everything we owned: the letters to Forest, our clippings, my sketches, our story, even what money we had left! I brushed people aside, bumping, shouting, "Stop! Stop him!"

But people opened for him, then turned to look at him run, closing behind him, making me throw them aside. Off balance now, my ankle throbbing, all taking time—no time, we were out of time.

He dipped past buildings and people and corners and the cars he ran in front of. I couldn't gain on him. He disappeared the way a rock sinks to the bottom in a murky pond; one can't see it even though it's there. I bent over, hands on knees, gasping for breath. It was over. All of it. People nudged past me. No one stopped to ask why I cried. Everyone had a place to be. I guess I did too: back to my mother's side.

"Did you find him?" Mama had a gash on her head, but someone had placed a handkerchief against it. Two women knelt beside her and helped her lean against the brick building. They moved away as I approached, and Mama thanked them. Dizzily, she reached for my hands. "Did you find him?" Her eyes searched mine like a lost child's looking for hope.

Couldn't she see? My hands were empty.

"I didn't, Mama. He... The crowd closed around him. I did the best I could."

"Of course you did. Of course." She dropped my hands. "What will we do?"

"Go to the charity house and ask for fare home, Mama. We have to go home."

"We'll run a story of the robbery," the editor of the *World* said when we arrived and Mama hurried out the story about the robbery. She held the handkerchief to her forehead. It had a good effect, though I knew that wasn't why she did it. "Maybe the thief will take the money and dump your diary and personal things. Perhaps a good New Yorker will turn them in."

"Tell them to keep the money. It's the notes in my pocketbook that I need."

"Mama."

"Well, it is." She turned to me. "We'll have the sponsors' award soon, but those notes, the clippings, your sketches. They're all gone."

The editor frowned. He had a face like a ferret, I noticed now: lean, eyes narrow and hard. "I wish you well with your search for the lost items," he said, then saw us to the door.

We visited other newspaper offices to tell them our story, and the *Herald* editor said they'd run a sketch of the criminal as well. "Someone might have seen you and this robber on the street." He waved for a young man to join us. The artist worked quickly, making us out to be caricatures of strong western women. He put a gun in my hand and knife in my mother's, making myth of our effort. "We didn't carry a knife," I pointed out.

"It's part of the romance," Mama whispered.

"Life isn't about romance," I said when we got outside. The cold wind snapped at our cheeks as we hurried back to our room. "It's about making good decisions based on facts, not fantasy."

"Not always," Mama said. "You have to have things to dream about."

"This dream is a nightmare."

We'd paid in advance for a week at No. 6 Rivington Street, Manhattan, so we had a bed to sleep in for a few nights while we tried to figure out what to do. The futility of the last months weighed like a stone on my chest as I stared at the water stains on the ceiling. My life had been defined by money: working for enough of it, saving for college, then using it instead for family needs. Neither Olaf nor I would be able to go on to the new state university at Pullman. The last months of my life on this trip, we'd earned money for the next pair of shoes, a warmer hat. Money. One night I even dreamed about it, old coins rolling away through the grates that covered holes in the streets of New York. Then I tumbled into one myself.

"We need to go to the charity house and request money for the train ticket," I repeated to Mama the next evening. We'd washed dishes in a sweaty restaurant and earned enough for a meal. We'd taken the tea leaves with us, reusing them for the cups that now steamed in our hands.

"I know I could convince the sponsors to make at least a partial payment. I've conversed with the president-elect, yet I can't talk to the sponsors? If only I could meet them."

"We simply need enough to get us home."

"We'll look for cleaning work, or laundry or sewing." She brightened. "I'll write articles. Perhaps one of the reporters knows of a publisher who might be interested in portions of our story." She set the cup down. "Clara, that's it! We'll write a book about the journey. I've sent hundreds of pages home to your father, and we can add to it from memory."

"He's not my father," I said, not sure why I needed to make the distinction. Maybe I wanted Mama to start living the truth of everything, including who I really was. "Did you ask him to keep what you sent?" I added before she could protest what I'd said about Papa.

"Of course he's kept them. We'll go back to the sponsors and ask if the money might still be available if I write a book. We could share proceeds from the sales. That should sweeten the pot for them."

"They'll want you to pay them," I said. "Writing a book for money is just like the scheme that got us here in the first place. It's almost as risky a wager as what we already made."

Mama raised one eyebrow in protest. "At least writing won't require a new pair of shoes." She sat beside me on the bed. "I know you're discouraged, Clara, but things could be worse. We mustn't let the darkness overwhelm us. Think of Jonah's whale. Think of that sunflower. Keep your eyes toward light." She spread her hand across the air as though declaiming. *She's making a presentation.* "There's no sense in dwelling on the negative. Our minds have to think of something; it may as well be something good. 'Occupy,' Scripture tells us. Multiply what God gives you. That's what we'll do."

"I guess I could try to sketch a few places. The trestle. That will be memorable...for what happened afterward."

"That your fears didn't materialize?"

"It's when I learned about my... That I'm not an Estby," I said. "How could you forget that?" I chewed at my nails.

"I would have thought the lava rocks were more memorable. We nearly died there," Mama said. She stood up. "You can draw whatever you like, Clara. We'll get the sponsors to bring you back by train so you can carry the manuscript to New York. It'll be grand. You'll continue the adventure. Later this summer. It'll work, it will! We just have to convince them! You can start now."

"I don't have any paper."

"Clara. There will always be obstacles. It's your duty to overcome them in service to another. Go to the market; ask for a sheet of butcher paper. Draw on that. We'll take it as a sample for the editor. We'll do this, Clara. First thing tomorrow."

I let her hope fill my empty stomach.

"Remember when I read to you?"

It was the middle of the night, but neither of us slept well in the narrow bed. The sounds of mice or rats scratched in the walls. A cold wind rattled the window.

"Yes, Mama," I said.

"I read *The Lamplighter,* maybe *Uncle Tom's Cabin.* I loved that book."

"Our stomachs would be full, and you'd bring dried apples out to make up a perfect pie and whipped cream for the topping."

"Yes, yes." She silenced my talk of food. "Those stories, they were about persevering, Clara. Keeping on despite the sorrow. Justice. Family. It's all about doing what we must for family."

"Yes, Mama, I know."

She stroked my arm. I pulled away.

The *World* editor agreed to confer with the sponsors in New York about our latest idea, and while we waited on their reply, we worked. At night, Mama wrote an article. It was in response to a letter to the editor in the *New York Times* about labor issues and mining. "It'll show that I can write," she told me when I raised an eyebrow at how she spent her time. "I might get invitations to speak," she pointed out. "Raise our own funds. Maybe they'll pay me."

Another of her fantasies.

The *Times* didn't use her piece, but it appeared instead in a Norwegian paper. There was no payment and we received no invitations. Then Mama sent a letter (she had to ask a stranger for a stamp) to the woman in Spokane who had helped initially make contact with the sponsors. Mama asked if she could intervene on our behalf, especially since we'd been robbed and now had no money to return home, though we'd accomplished all that had been asked. "I told her but for the sprained ankle, we'd have made it and that we hoped to write a book now."

Mama asked her to telegraph her response, which the woman did. She had no influence, she said, and told us she didn't want to jeopardize whatever negotiations we might yet work out by sending money.

"There is no agreement; nothing's being negotiated," I told Mama. "You shouldn't have told her about the book. That's a dream."

"No, Clara, listen. If she doesn't want to break the agreement that we not beg, then that means there is still hope that the sponsors will come through. Yes. Meanwhile, we'll support ourselves here. We can do this. But we will have to walk."

"To the charity offices? Please?"

"No, to Brooklyn. Manhattan is too expensive."

SEVENTEEN

For the Love of Money

1897

I'll remember Brooklyn for the pans I scrubbed while we lived there and maybe for the little flowers that grew in the window boxes. These were watered by the wet clothes we hung to dry on lines that crisscrossed between the tenement houses, where I could hear languages from a dozen different countries spoken between mothers and their children, between husbands and wives. Families, working things out together—though from the arguments we heard in the evenings, not always successfully.

I wished I could have been cheery like the other working girls, who stopped asking me if I wanted to join them after we finished our duties for a soda or a walk in the park. I didn't recognize their offers of friendship; I worked to save every penny for tickets home. Besides, my ankle ached after standing for the day, and I found little joy in the daily grind of the labor that split my fingernails and gave me red, harsh-looking knuckles. I remembered with fondness my domestic duties in comfortable Spokane homes. The only advantage to this daily grunge was that the work required no great thoughts. I was free to daydream, to imagine a life with Forest when I got home, to speculate about my mother's life before she married. I also had time to be frustrated and angry at the sponsors, at my mother for trusting them, at myself for getting sick and spraining my ankle. Any lessons I had to learn had occurred on the journey. New York City had nothing new to teach me, or so I thought.

Spring came to the city with no word from the sponsors about the book. Mama and I walked by the windows of the finer stores naming things we thought Bertha or Arthur or Ida might like, wishing we could buy that wooden horse for Johnny or the doll with a china face for Lillian.

"Seeing you again will be their present, Mama." She nodded. We stopped in front of shops with elegant jewels and furs, grateful the weather no longer required the worn coats and winter hats we'd bought in Chicago.

"I wish we'd splurged and bought new clothes the day we arrived," Mama lamented. "At least then the thief would have less of our money and we'd have nice things to show for our trip."

Sometimes we walked through Central Park, invisible to all but each other in the sea of strangers. I didn't mind the anonymity, but I think Mama did. I think she missed the applause of her programs about our journey, the attention from the reporters, and reading about ourselves the next day in the paper. At night, she wrote. She seemed content to work and save money for the tickets, believing we remained under the original obligation not to request help but to work for our needs.

We didn't receive many letters from home, or at least Mama didn't say we had. She'd taken piecework so could stay in the room with her needles and thread while I found employment scrubbing pans in a restaurant at half the wages of men who did the same task. So she was the one at home when the postal bell rang and everything changed.

"Ole's written!" Mama shouted. She waved the letter as I came through the door. Outside, April buds woke up spring, and even Brooklyn freshened up with the smell of blossoms. "I hope it's all good news, nothing about the mortgage." She put the letter on the table, then stepped back, staring at it as though it might jump out at her and bite.

"Well, open it," I said. "Maybe Papa's sent money so we can go home."

"Not likely," Mama said. She still stared. Her smile looked pasted. "Everyone's in bad straights. Even the Brooklyn papers are filled with stories of property worth five thousand dollars sold for three thousand at auction because the original owner owed two hundred in taxes. One bank disgorged a family and allowed another to purchase the house for a pittance because they fell behind on their payments back in '93." She picked the letter up, put it back down. "The Brooklyn Bridegrooms hope to put their losing season behind them," Mama said. "I read that in the paper too."

"Well, I'd like to put our losing season behind us too," I said. "Now open it."

Mama sighed, turned the letter over and over in her hand.

"Maybe there'll be a little drawing from Lillian," I said. "She turned three last month. And Bertha is fifteen now. Those two get to celebrate birthdays every March 12 together."

"I've missed a year's worth of their celebrations," Mama said as though the thought just occurred to her.

I did quick figuring remembering each of my brothers' and sisters' birthdays. "Three March birthdays in our family. June must have been a...special month for you and papa. Olaf was born in March too."

"Ach," Mama said. "How you talk." She actually blushed a little. "All right." She took a deep breath and opened the letter.

She began to read.

I would not have believed a person's countenance and demeanor, attitude and hope, could change so profoundly by the reading of another's words.

Color drained from her face. A slow moan grew as her hands shook, and tears coursed down her cheeks.

"What is it, Mama? What's happened?"

Mama handed me the letter then lay her arms on the table, covering them with her face as she wept.

"Diphtheria," I read. Diphtheria had entered our home while we worked away, window-shopped, dreamed of a future. Diphtheria had claimed Bertha.

"Alone," Mama wailed, holding her stomach as she rocked. "He had to bury her alone, make her casket by himself. Oh, my God, my God. They were quarantined. I wasn't there! I wasn't there."

Bertha. Hedvig. My sister. Gone. And Ida, left behind to care for the little ones. Papa, tending to Bertha. Would he have sent Ida and the others somewhere safe? I looked at the date. It was written April 8. Bertha had died on the sixth.

"Mama." I put my arms around her as she rocked and cried. "Mama." I kept my composure. I'd cry later. "We must go to the charities commission. We must find a way to get home."

"No, no begging." She looked at me as though I'd suggested she take poison for her pain. "That won't be good. The sponsors—"

"We have to, Mama. It's the right thing to do now. It's what the family needs."

Those were the words that cut through to her.

"*Ja, ja.* You're right," she said. "You're right." She wiped at her eyes. "We'll go now." The task would help her set aside her grief for the moment. "We'll tell the newspapers. They'll cover the story maybe, put pressure on the charities commissioner or on the sponsors. Yes, that's what we'll do."

"Let's ask for help, Mama. And accept it."

"He would send us to the almshouses, Commissioner Brute would," Mama told the reporters. We'd met with the commissioner but had no success. Neither my mother's desperation nor charm moved him. "He must be a Swede," Mama said. "They're so stubborn and unimaginative." I hoped the reporter wouldn't quote that. "I told him we had no time to be housed and fed at the almshouse," she continued. "We'd be taking food from poor immigrants. We have jobs; we can pay a loan back, but we need it now. We need money for the tickets home. I am good for a loan. I can pay back the commissioner," she insisted. "Or anyone. But he sent us to the Bureau of Charities on Schermerhorn Street. They cannot help us either. I tell them of all our past trials, all we've endured, and that I am a woman good for her word."

"May I include some of those past trials in the story?" the reporter from the *Sun* asked her.

"Yes, yes. Say anything. Let them know I will repay. I must go home; my daughter and I must go back. Diphtheria entered my house."

Diphtheria could even now be slithering through the barn boards, seeping its way into the throats of my brothers and sisters, choking out more lives. Something sharp forced down the child's throat could break the membrane that cut off air. I wondered if Papa had thought of that.

Of course he would have! They all knew what to do. There'd been that terrible epidemic in Minnesota. Mama's cleanliness, exceptional house-keeping, keeping food in good condition—those were things that kept diphtheria at bay.

But we weren't there to do that this time.

At the *New-York Tribune* office, I told the story. I sounded firm but not desperate, though I'd never felt more powerless in my life. The night before, Mama hadn't slept at all. She'd scrubbed the floor instead, scraping with the rough brush over and over. I fell asleep to the grating sounds of grief.

When it was published, the *Sun* article spoke of our "intelligence and perseverance" and suggested that we would be good for a loan.

But no one contacted the paper to offer one.

Especially not the sponsors.

EIGHTEEN

The Right Thing to Do

My teeth chattered less from the cold than from the shock of the past three days. We stood in the entry room of the offices of Chauncey Depew, president of the New York Central and Hudson River Railroad. He'd contacted us, inviting us to come. Mama looked gaunt and wild-eyed at the same time. She'd spilled all our family details of loss and accident and deaths to reporters, so the world now knew of our journey from poor to destitute. There'd be no happy ending even if the sponsors came through, what with dear Bertha gone forever. Since the letter, I never knew what state I'd find Mama in: one moment scurrying about, raving about sponsors or her failure to be there for her family; the next moment sobbing and still as a cemetery on a hot summer's day.

Could there be anything more pitiful than to be paupers in the offices of a railroad magnate? Wealth shone elegantly in the brass ashtrays on the shiny wood tables that graced the reception room and reflected large pots of ferns. Chandeliers flickered golden light on us as we waited, sunken into the posh leather seats. Glass cases with slender brass labels announced "President Abraham Lincoln's coffee cup" and "General Ulysses S. Grant's ivory toothpick." People collected and touted the strangest things when they had little to do with their money. I used to love such opulence, but now it made me angry. Here we sat, prepared to beg to get us home to our desperate family instead of being able to take care of ourselves.

"Mr. Depew will see you now," his assistant said. The slender man wearing a tidy suit had kind eyes filled with pity as he showed us into Mr. Depew's office, then he stepped back and closed the door.

"Please sit," the railroad president, who was also a lawyer, said. "Would you like tea? I have cakes here." His oak desk took up a quarter of the massive room. Another glass case displayed what purported to be a "Letter from Shakespeare to His Publisher."

Mama declined the tea and I did too. I gazed around the room, saw plaques that read "state senator" and a framed diploma from Yale. Another photograph showed Mr. Depew standing in front of a podium. He sported a bow tie like the one he wore now beneath his chubby chin, and I remembered Mama telling me Mr. Depew gave after-dinner speeches as Mama did to raise influence and political supporters.

"I have read with interest your plight, dear lady. Ladies," Mr. Depew said, nodding to me. He furrowed his brow. We still had no funds to replace my stolen curling iron, and I must have looked the way I felt: pathetic. "I admire the scrappy way you've tried to do all you can to save your farm," he continued, smiling then at Mama. "Your journey for a man would be remarkable; but for two women, I must say it was a truly amazing feat."

This was the moment when Mama would have waxed eloquently about the escapades, the people we'd encountered, the beauty of the landscapes we'd crossed. She would tell stories that brought gasps to people or made them laugh. My mother the showwoman, raving about the adequacies of women.

But that woman didn't show up.

Mama sat silent, her hands clasped in her lap, her eyes blinking back tears. We had nothing to offer, nothing to trade. What would he ask for? Would he grant us the loan?

I'd have to speak, be the one to beg.

"We're desperate," I said. "But we are respectable women who keep their commitments. We will repay you if you grant us a loan. Can you help us?"

"I believe I can," he said. "The newspaper provided the details of your plight. My offer is to provide you with a pass on my rail line to Chicago. It is not a loan but a gift. You'll have to make your way from Chicago to Minneapolis; walk, I imagine. But I've arranged for a ticket from Minneapolis on to your home in Spokane." He tugged at his bow tie. "Hopefully you can garner publicity between Chicago and Minneapolis, as you did before."

"For what purpose?" I asked.

"Oh, to let the world know of your amazing feat. And perhaps of a New Yorker's assistance in your return home." He smiled. "One never knows what the future may bring. New York did host the first convention for women's suffrage, in Seneca Falls, all those years ago. The fairer sex will appreciate a man who supports the remarkable feats of women. Perhaps you'll come back and help campaign for such a thing."

"*Mange takk.* Thank you," Mama said.

"One more thing," Mr. Depew concluded. "I would like a signed copy of the book you must write about your journey. It would please so many to hear of your exploits and all you did and saw."

"You think there'd be interest?" I asked.

"I do. Both in Europe and in these United States. What you did was beyond belief for many, and it's a story that ought not to be forgotten."

"First, we must go home," I said. "Thanks to you, now we can."

Mr. Depew pulled a bell cord, and the male assistant who had shown us into the room returned with an envelope in his hand. He gave it to the railroad president. "Will you have trouble earning your way between Chicago and Minneapolis?"

"We'll work and walk," I said. "It's only four hundred miles."

The hopeful Mama reappeared at the news office. "In addition to Mr. Depew's generosity, I have the first sale for my book," Mama told the editor of the *World* after relaying the gift of tickets and thanking him for running the story. "Mr. Depew wants a signed copy. There is interest in this story." She took a deep breath. "I can write it and promote it too. You've seen that. Clara will illustrate. I've already written to newspapers that covered our journey along the way. To get their clippings. They'll help re-create the walk. I'm sure we can generate good publicity for the book. Why, three papers here in New York covered our terrible need this week alone. Of course, I'll want the clippings from the *World*," Mama said. "How could I tell the story without mentioning you? You printed the first photographs nearly a year ago. I hope you'll consider reviewing the book when it comes out."

"We have been in on this story from the beginning," the editor said. "I did notice that the *Times* urged financial help for you. And the *Sun*. They're such rags," he sneered. He tapped his pencil.

"Did the sponsors ever respond to the suggestion of a book when we spoke of it earlier?"

"Let me make a phone call," he said. "Could you wait a moment? I know you're anxious to leave."

We waited. Mama tapped her fingers on her lap, looked up at the wall clock. This was what persistence looked like. I was anxious to be on the train, but coming to the *World* to report on Mr. Depew's generosity, Mama said, was a small price to pay for the tickets. "And if at the last minute we're able to pull off financial assistance from the sponsors, then it wouldn't all be for naught. We gain for Bertha." Her breath caught. "A small portion of our loss might be redeemed with the book and money."

"All right," the editor said, returning. "You write the book. Clara illustrates it. She gets a ride back on the railroad this fall, repeating your trip to make the illustrations authentic, but this time she comes by rail. The book gets published and you get ten thousand dollars, and we split everything else the book might earn."

Mama reached to clasp my arm. "They changed their minds," she whispered.

"It appears...they've adapted to this new possibility."

"Is there a contract?" I asked.

"Shush," Mama said.

"No contract, but I have the sponsors' word."

"The sponsors' word isn't reliable," I said.

"Clara, please—"

"They didn't break the contract," the editor said, his eyes shining with a hint of condescension. "You did, by not making it here on time. It'll all be up to you with the book. You don't get the money until the book is published."

"And the train ticket for Clara, for illustration purposes?"

"Contact me when the manuscript is finished and you're ready to retrace your steps to develop illustrations, Miss Estby. I'll see that things are arranged. By the way, the sponsors aren't requiring that you walk back home now," he added. "But the condition of earning your expenses along the way continues, though you may accept the train tickets, given the passing of your child. The sponsors aren't heartless. I'm authorized to give you the five dollars you started out with to help you depart as soon as possible, under the circumstances."

Mama nodded. "I thank you, I thank you," she said. "Isn't that wonderful, Clara?"

Outrage knotted my stomach. *Not heartless. May accept the tickets. How dare they!* But I had to think clearly.

"When we arrived here last December, before our robbery, my mother gave you the signatures of all the dignitaries we'd met and who verified our arrival in their towns. We'd like them back."

"We would?" Mama said.

"You would?" the editor said.

"We'll need them to help with the writing, and since the original contract was voided—by my sprained ankle—those signatures really do belong to us."

"Clara—"

"No, no," the editor said. "She has a point." He pulled at is earlobe. "I see no harm in that. I'll get them for you now."

We left the offices, signatures in hand. "I wouldn't have thought to ask," Mama said.

"We'll ask each one of them to promote the book. We could plan a trip when it comes out, stopping back at all those places. I'm sure the papers in Boise City and Lincoln and Canton would cover it. President McKinley—"

"That's brilliant, Clara."

The admiration on her face was almost as satisfying as eating a piece of *julekaga*.

Mama looked almost peaceful when we boarded the train. We'd decided not to look for a frog for Johnny but to pick one up in Washington State, as the creature would never survive the train trip home. Mama had written to Papa to tell him that when we left Minneapolis, we'd send a telegram so he would know when to expect us.

"I told him to bring everyone to meet us," Mama said. "I'm certain they'll be waiting for good news given the year we've all had."

"At last we have some," I said, thinking of the tickets home. Of all the skills I lacked, however, predicting the future was chief among them.

NINETEEN

The Empty Hole of Why

The trouble with a train ride is all the time one has to think. We rumbled through New York City and the Amish farms where we'd been treated with such care, through coal country, and out through Pittsburgh across its triple rivers, wide and swift. Everything looked different rushing by. Everything had changed since we'd dusted the earth with our footsteps.

Bertha's death wasn't real to me yet. I held her in my heart as I'd done during the entire trip east, as I had held all my brothers and sisters. Bertha was still there, right where she belonged. It didn't seem possible that she wouldn't be waiting for us when we arrived.

"Is Bertha with Henry now?" I asked as black smoke drifted back from the engine.

"It's what we Lutherans believe," Mama said. "We will see them again, these baptized babies. Bertha knew her catechism, and she had the heart of Christ, loving and giving. It seems not right, I know, that young people like Bertha and Henry and young Ole should pass away from this land while Ole and I still trek along as though we contribute to God's plan at our age."

"Why is that?" I asked. "Why did I live but not little Ole or Henry and now Bertha too?" Mama winced, and I wondered if she said things to herself about how Bertha might have lived if she'd been there to keep the house clean of the disease, if she'd been there to comfort Bertha and nurse her through. What if I'd insisted that Olaf make the trip with her or if I'd refused to go at all? Maybe Mama would have stayed too; she might have kept Bertha alive.

"Ours isn't to question the why of things, Clara. It takes up too much time and energy without any promise of answers. 'Why Bertha? Why Henry? Why not me?' No answers in those questions. None."

Mama stared out the window as farmland blended with industry. "A better question," Mama continued, "must be, 'What next? What now does God have in store for me?' These will take you to a new place, moving forward on one's way rather than hovering over the empty hole of *why*, where you can only tumble down."

In Chicago, we left the train and walked past buildings that had been part of the World's Columbian Exposition of 1893, where reform-length skirts had first been introduced. At the *Tribune*, Mama asked for a clipping of the article written when we'd passed through before. It included a picture of the two of us, and Mama left our Spokane address so they could send a copy of any articles they wrote as a result of this visit.

"The walk will be good for us," Mama said as we began the next four hundred miles. "Sitting on a train weakens the body. We need the benefit of physical exertion to calm thoughts that ride on sorrow."

The walk north through the rolling hills of southern Wisconsin was nothing like the route we'd taken across the country the year before. Yes, cornfields lined our dusty trails, and little clusters of trees marked farmhouses, but we also walked past long miles of oak and maple forests. The hill climbs were steeper than in Iowa, and the humidity limped my hair straight as a horse's tail even when I used the curling iron Mama bought for me with a portion of the editor's five dollars.

"When will you write the book, Mama?" I asked. Southern Wisconsin was awash with fresh green and birdsong and little pools of rainwater where yellow butterflies danced about.

"I've been writing it. The letters I sent to Ole are like chapters in my mind. I'll be busy at home, yes, but there is always early morning before the sun comes. Writing our story brings me comfort. I find new ways of thinking about things. It's as though I went on to school myself with the experience of the walk, and now writing about it is another education: what to put in, what to leave out, how I felt at various times. It's easier to…write than speak about how I feel."

"People won't want to know how you felt, Mama. They'll want to know what we did and how we did it, what we saw, who we met."

"When I read, I want my feelings touched," she said. "I want the writer's imagination and his facts. But they're different things, the walk and writing about it. Each gives me…peace. Its publication will bring honor to Bertha. We'll save the farm with it." She switched the grip to her other hand. "I'll dedicate it to her. You won't mind, will you?"

Dedicating the book to Bertha meant everyone would know that my sister had died while we lived in Brooklyn, separated from our family, victims of the sponsors' withdrawal.

"Must there be a dedication?" I said.

"Of course."

"Dedicate it to the entire family. We couldn't have made it without them staying faithful at home."

"You're absolutely right." She turned around and walked backward as she said, "They supported us. They'll support us too with the writing and your sketching. You'll see. It'll work, Clara. It has to. I'll save the farm yet."

My mother made her own facts. I remembered the looks on the faces of my brothers and sisters when we'd left them. If I'd learned anything from this journey, it was that to take care of one's family, everyone needed to tell the truth and not make up facts when evidence was lacking.

In Winona, Minnesota, we visited the *Daily Republican* newspaper but got no coverage. Two women walking home had less appeal than brazen western adventurers walking east. At a park bench where we sat to eat an egg and biscuit, I picked up a copy of an old newspaper lying near the trash basket. I read the headline aloud. " 'Two St. Paul Women Fined.' They lifted their dresses too high as they crossed a muddy road, or so says a peculiar policeman."

"The paper called the policeman peculiar?" Mama asked.

"No. They said he was 'keen-eyed' and that if 'the simple-minded females had but joined a vaudeville troupe doing barnstorming work around the country or become members of the grand opera company exhibiting in Paris or Chicago, they might have lifted their skirts a good deal higher without incurring official censure.' Mother, are we going to be arrested in St. Paul? Maybe we shouldn't wear our reform skirts there."

"Nonsense. Our ankles are covered with the shoes, and besides, hemlines will be coming up before long; I'm sure of it. Didn't you get the feel of that back in New York with all the talk of women's suffrage?"

"I was too busy working, Mother," I said.

"How does the article end?"

" 'St. Paul must be set down as one of the rural villages in the country in questions of female dress—or undress.' "

"There, you see?" Mama said. "The newspapers know that change is coming, and they'd like to push St. Paul along toward a more open view of female outfitting. We'll be inspiration in St. Paul."

In Minneapolis, we posed at the Anderson Studio on Washington Avenue, wearing our reform skirts so we'd have new photographs to sell. A row of buttons at the top of the side seam added interest to the waistline of the linen skirts. Blousy shoulders with narrow sleeves to the wrist gave a respectable appearance from the waist up. While on the train, Mama had embroidered delicate stitching down the shirtwaist fronts. In the photographic pose, Mama sat revealing the tops of the leather shoes while I leaned on a prop, a tree stump, with my skirt a good eight inches from the floor and my shoe, topped with a canvas overshoe, showing. We gave one print to the reporter at the *Times* and another to the reporter at the *Tribune*. Reporters from both newspapers showed up at the Scandia-Excelsior Hotel, where we sat in the kitchen telling stories to the staff.

Complimentary and thorough articles appeared in both papers the next day. "They liked us, didn't they?" Mama asked.

"I believe so," I said. I spit on my finger, then tapped the curling iron heating on the coal stove in our room. "It's hot," I said.

Mama stood and rolled lengths of my fine hair around the narrow rod, holding it until the hair nearly steamed, then untwisting it and gathering up two more strands before placing it back on the stovetop to reheat. She got better results with that iron than I did.

The articles raved about our feat and wrote that we would receive the ten thousand dollars after we published the book. The reporters praised the future story of a woman's unusual perspective in this time of the "woman question." "'A settlement has been reached between the two pedestrians and private parties in New York,'" I read. "I wish I shared their certainty. Your certainty."

"Set your sights, Clara. No one thought we could make the walk except the sponsors and me. And eventually you. But if we hadn't determined to go, we surely wouldn't have been successful. We went for a good cause, and God blessed our walk. It will all work out."

I stared at her. How could it all work out? Bertha was dead.

"Mama. It says here that one reason we made the walk was because of your consumption, and your wanting to prove that with good exercise like walking, you could get your health back. When you said that last night, it surprised me. I didn't know you were 'threatened' with consumption."

"I suppose that was too strong of a word, *threatened,* but I did want the trip to prove to myself that I could get my strength back, especially after my female surgery, and I didn't really want to talk about that in the paper."

"We might not want Papa to see this comment." I pointed. "'Both are enthusiastic over their work and adventures and are satisfied in their own minds, at least, that man is not much the superior of woman after all.'"

"*Ja,* well, that one we might not." She winked at me.

The old Mama was back.

TWENTY

Another Trestle

I spread out drawing paper on the table in the train's dining room car. Mama slept at her seat, and so I'd slipped away. Since we'd boarded, she'd slept, and when she woke, her face at first wore a haunted look. I stared out the window thinking I could sketch the skyline along this prairie land, but this route took us much farther north and didn't look like the landscapes where we'd walked the previous year. Remembering the lonely train station of Nebraska, I started to draw, capturing as I could the rails coming together where land met sky. I drew a few more lines, thinking of how to create the sense of an endless horizon. I thought of the Dale Creek trestle instead.

Taking out another sheet of paper, I set to work sketching from memory the sheer rock walls, the canyon's depth, the intricate buttresses of tall, straight, and crossed sticks that held up the railroad tracks.

"Dale Creek, is it?" A woman slightly older than Mama spoke to me as she leaned over my sketch. She dressed as someone comfortable in New York's society gatherings, with an ermine collar on a stylish jacket and a long linen skirt that accented her slender frame. Porters had lit the gaslights and prepared the meal for dinner, which sent wafts of good smells into the car. The table light warmed even further the silver fur piece that gave dignity and beauty to her wide-brimmed hat. "The Dale Creek trestle, yes?" The woman had a Norwegian accent.

"Yes," I said. "We walked across it."

"You mean you took the train. There's no walking across that place."

I smiled. The woman had the blunt way of stating things common to Norwegians. My aunt Hannah spoke like that.

"No," I corrected her. "We walked. My mother and I, on our way from Spokane to New York to publicize the reform dress. And to prove that women could endure such a journey." I didn't mention our financial reasons.

The woman gasped, put her gloved hand to her mouth. She stepped back and I wondered if her actions were in response to the reform dress or the very idea of women walking across the country.

"You're them," she said. "The globe trekkers. I...read about you in the *Minneapolis Tribune*."

"Yes. We're them." I studied my pencil, tapped it on the table, then set it down, not sure what else to say.

The woman fingered the small set of binoculars that hung around her neck. "I'd love to hear about your journey. May I?" She motioned that she'd like to sit down and I nodded. I wasn't sure what Mama would say, but I suspected it would be fine. A stranger interested in our walk would soon be a friend of my mother's. This stranger would hear the story first from me. Few did.

"I'm O. S. Ammundsen." She reached out to shake my hand the

way a man might. Many women who attended Mama's lectures did the same. I put my hand out. The woman's gloved hand gave two strong shakes, the small set of binoculars bouncing on her bodice.

"And you are?"

"I'm Miss Estby, Clara Estby."

"You're headed for Spokane?" Miss Ammundsen said.

"Yes. Home at last."

"That's my home too, or it may be soon. I'm from Norway. Well, New York most recently. I've been visiting my sister in St. Paul."

"My mother too, a long time ago. Near Oslo. Christiania it's called now. I forgot."

"One day they'll change the name back to Oslo, I suspect," she said. "Much easier to spell and takes up less space, so more efficient. We Norwegians are obsessed with efficiency." She laughed.

"My...stepfather, my mother's husband. He grew up there."

It was the first time I'd described him as anything other than Papa. Our relationship too would change, I realized. Unveiling secrets opens doors whether we're ready for what's on the other side or not.

"So," Miss Ammundsen said, "tell me about crossing the trestle at Dale."

I found I could make the woman's eyes grow large with anxiety then crinkle with laughter at my descriptions of our crossing and how I made light of my fears. I didn't tell her that I'd learned on that same day about my Michigan birth or my mother's trials and decisions as a young woman. Instead, I could sense a bit of what Mama enjoyed being up on stage, holding an audience's interest, though mine was an audience of one. I embellished the feel of the wind, the cry of a hawk flying beneath us as we crossed.

"When I was there," the woman said, "it was winter and dreadful.

We were in a train car, of course. I thought the wind would push us over like a wheat shock, but we survived. I have to say, I haven't been back since and didn't leave anything there I have to go back for."

I laughed. "What takes you to Spokane?" I asked, a question I often overheard at the Stapletons' while serving at parties.

"Business," she said. "I prefer to travel for pleasure, but this time it's business bringing us here." She didn't elaborate on the "us."

"When we left, there wasn't much building going on in Spokane," I said. "The city is still coming out of the depression."

"Often that's the best time to invest," she said.

"Maybe the situation has improved while we were gone." I hoped my stepfather was stronger and could take on construction work again. That would help us stave off the mortgage man.

"What kind of business?" I said.

"Furs," she said, the word spoken as though filled with magic. She rubbed the binoculars absently. "Wasn't there a wager attached to your journey?"

I nodded. "But because of my ankle sprain, the sponsors wouldn't extend our deadline. We arrived ten days past, on December 23, I'm sad to say."

"Have you considered a legal suit?"

Her words surprised. I couldn't go into detail with this stranger about the great humiliation, as I'd begun to think of it. We didn't even know whom to sue. How foolish would that sound? "It was a business risk," I heard myself say, a phrase spoken by Forest's father when men discussed their stocks and bonds. "I gained the equivalent of a college degree from the experience, and my mother improved her health. So we achieved something without earning the wager." I wasn't sure I believed this, but it sounded wise and Miss Ammundsen nodded her head sagely. Then before I could stop myself I added, "Now the sponsors have offered a new incentive for us: we'll still receive the award money, but first my mother has to write a book. I'm to illustrate it." I made my voice sound light, the way Mama had bantered with the reporters from the Minneapolis papers. I could perform too.

"Yes. The article mentioned that. Well, I'll look forward to reading your book," she said.

A porter leaned at the waist and offered service. "Would you join us?" she said. "I'll go get my cousin, and you could invite your mother."

"Oh, we have our basket for supper," I said.

"Another time then. My cousin, Ms. Gubner, will be wondering where I've gone off to anyway." She looked thoughtful, lifted her binoculars, then let them rest. "New adventures await you, Miss Estby, you and your mother. What a pleasant time you must have had on this journey together." Then the woman removed a calling card from the reticule hanging at her wrist. "Here," she said. "Perhaps we'll have a little more time to talk on the train, but if we don't and you'd like to meet in Spokane, you can reach me at this postal address of the friend we're staying with. I'm always interested in the future of young Norwegian women who show such promise." I felt my face grow warm.

Miss Ammundsen turned away, then stopped and looked back. "I think you should call me Olea when we meet again," she said. "And if I may, I'll call you Clara. We're reform women, yes?" I smiled. "It's been such a pleasure to meet you, Clara."

"Likewise, Olea."

I watched her walk away with a twinge of envy and no anticipation that one day she'd be back into my life. But I hoped for the financial security to travel, dress well, and consider real business risks as she did—well-studied risks, nothing foolish, decisions that didn't put my family in jeopardy or change their lives forever.

TWENTY-ONE

Homecoming

The train arrived earlier than expected, so no one was there to meet us at the stop near Mica Creek.

"Well, I guess we walk up to the house," Mama said.

"They'll come greet us, surely," I said. "This gives us time to find the frog."

"That's right! Johnny would never forgive us if we forgot his frog."

We stepped across the tracks, headed toward the banks of Mica Creek, then set our bags down. The air smelled of new-mown hay, and the sky was as blue as Mama's eyes. The landscape seemed to open its arms to us, welcoming. I squatted beside the little creek that rushed across leaves and swirled broken willow boughs around. I could see where the water had been higher with spring rains before time tamed it.

"Here's one," I shouted. I shivered at the feel of its skin, all rippled and wet, and it leaped from my hand.

"I've got one too," Mama said. "Well, I guess I don't," she added when the frog disappeared from her palm. We hollered back and forth, laughing as our prey departed, and then I found another.

"Here, put it in my grip," Mama said.

"No, it'll mess up your papers. Take off my hat," I said. "Plop him in here. Johnny will be so surprised and he'll never guess we didn't bring it from New York. I wonder where they are? You don't suppose they're still—"

"In quarantine," Mama gasped. Color drained from her face. "I should have thought."

We heard Sailor barking as we left the road and walked up the lane to the house. The sign "Quarantined" hung on the gate like a pox. Mama hesitated, inhaled deeply, gearing up for what lay ahead. I patted her back. In a strange way, I felt stronger at that moment, perhaps because I had lost a sister while she had lost a part of her flesh and her heart.

The farmhouse sat in a dimple of green, the pig shed and barn beyond, and I heard my heart pounding against my temple. We stood for a moment, Mama and me as we'd been for over a year, just the two of us. Now all that would change. Sailor nosed up and I bent to hug him. "Where is everyone?" I said scratching at his ears. He leaned into me, sniffing at my closed hat.

"Hello!" Mama shouted. "Ole, children, we're home."

The sound of muffled talking reached us as my brothers and sisters came out of the house, their slender forms straight as arrows, eyes hollow. Arthur and Billy stepped out first, followed by Ida holding Lillian's hand, with my stepfather and Olaf walking—no, standing behind them. I didn't want to look at the space that Bertha would have filled beside Ida.

For my mother's sake, I wanted my stepfather to give a nod or smile. He wasn't the kind of man to take Mama in his arms, at least not in front of us children, but it would be good if they could weep together for their lost child. I wanted them to be glad we were home, and I hoped they'd be happy once Mama told them about the book, that good had still come from the walk.

Arthur stepped forward then, the first. "Mama," he said before Ida grabbed at his shoulder and pulled him back. He waved a small hand but didn't approach again.

"Hi, Mama. Hi, Clara." Billy followed with his own greetings, but he didn't push ahead either. "We're quan-tined," he said, his five-year-old tongue stumbling on the word.

We'd be now too.

Ida had picked Lillian up, held her on her hip. The child lay her head on Ida's shoulder, looked warily at us. *She doesn't recognize us. She doesn't know who Mama is.*

Olaf was the only one to actually smile. "Welcome home," he said. "Though this isn't much of a homecoming."

"They shouldn't expect a party," Ida said.

Mama looked at Ida, and I felt or maybe even saw a wave of revulsion roll between them, daughter riding on hostility so thick and powerful that Mama actually stepped back. Something more was wrong, more than Lillian acting cautious, more than Bertha missing and my stepfather not giving even a nod of greeting to his wife, whom he'd not seen for more than a year.

Mama dropped the grip she'd held in her hand. She let her arms fall to her sides.

The hair at the back of my neck prickled.

"Where's Johnny?" Mama whispered to the hedge of eyes and anger before us. "We brought along a frog for Johnny. Where is my son?"

"He's dead," Ida said. "Just like Bertha. And you weren't here to save them."

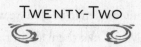

TWENTY-TWO

The Siblings of Sorrow

Lillian jerked her head up from my sister's shoulder, Ida's words like gunshots slamming into my heart.

I looked at Mama, ached for her.

She covered her mouth with her hands. I dropped my hat, stepped back to reach for her, caught in a crossfire. The frog jumped out and the dog gave chase.

"When?" Mama wailed. She dropped to her knees. "How?"

My stepfather came forward but didn't reach to comfort. He lifted Lillian from Ida, who looked like she'd explode with rage. "What do you think?" she growled. "What do you think killed him?"

"Diphtheria," Olaf said. "Four days after Bertha. We did what we could, but…"

"But the children were quarantined, weren't they? You kept everything clean, sterile?"

Mama, grabbing at straws.

"I did what was needed," my stepfather defended, his first words to

Mama. "As soon as we know Johnny is ill, Olaf carries him from the pig barn, where Ida keeps the children when Bertha becomes ill. We had to do it without the help of a mother here to do her part."

"I did everything I could," Ida said. "Everything. But we were in the shed! The pig shed."

It was a well-built barn with a loft entered from a ladder on the outside and a small stove inside for heating when the pigs birthed. But she wouldn't appreciate my observations. Ida would have had to clean it, maybe with Olaf and the boys' help. Cooking would have been complicated, and keeping the children entertained would have demanded much of her.

"It was so cold," Ida said. "Papa couldn't even bring blankets to us for fear they carried the disease. He left food on the porch and I picked it up. We ate cold things. Poor Johnny." Ida started to cry now. "Arthur and William and Lillian, we cried over Johnny, and there was no one to cry over us."

"It wasn't your fault," Mama said softly through her own tears.

"I know that!" Ida snapped. The braids crowning the top of her sixteen-year-old head weren't neatly done up the way she was known for. They shook now with the vehemence of her words. "I didn't kill Bertha and Johnny."

"But I did," Mama whispered.

"No, Mama," I said. Had we been here, the grieving would have been different, but there was no evidence that either Mama or I could have kept the children alive. I looked at the man I'd called Papa my entire life. I pleaded with him to come to Mama and help her up, lift her in her anguish. But he stood rooted to the porch.

Mama sank forward as in a deep prayer, her head nearly on the ground, and she cried out the names of her lost children.

"Olaf," I said. "Come help her." My sweet brother came around from the back of the hedge of sisters and brothers and squatted beside Mama. "I'm not sure I should touch you," he whispered. "I might carry—"

She leaned against him, and he put his arms around her. "I'm so sorry you had to hear it like this, Mother. So sorry."

"Where was she when we needed comforting?" Ida said. My sister had been harboring this anger for months, covering her own pain and grief, and now she had Mama to vent it on. She was a child; I could forgive this. But my stepfather should stop this disrespect of Mama, this pounding of nails into a coffin of grief. Where was his kind nature; what held him back? Couldn't he see that Mama was sick with sorrow? Someone had to defend and diffuse.

"Ida," I said quietly. "That's not fair."

"You know nothing of fairness," Ida spit the words at me.

Lillian fussed now to be let down from my stepfather's arms, and she trotted over to Mama before Ida could haul her back. "Lillian, you come here this instant!"

But Lillian reached Mama and patted her on the shoulder. "You stand up?" she asked. "Are you sick?"

Sick at heart, I thought. *She's sick at heart.*

"Mama needs to rest a little longer," Olaf told his youngest sister. When he looked at me again, his eyes held pity.

Both Arthur and Billy moved in a little closer but looked warily in Ida's direction. They stood on either side of me and let me put my arms on their shoulders and pull them to me. Lillian with her wide gait found me too, and I bent to pick her up.

"She doesn't want you to hold her," Ida snapped.

"Oh, well, it looked like she wouldn't mind."

"You don't know her," Ida said. "She doesn't know you in those ridiculous costumes." She ran her eyes up and down my reform dress and snorted. "You have no idea what she's been through, and all for what?" She scoffed.

"She's my sister," I said and patted the child's back as the girl leaned into me, seeking comfort. They all needed comforting.

"Mama grieves deeply for your children, Ole," I said. I heard Ida gasp with my use of his name. "And for what you must have all gone through with our not being here."

I saw a flicker in my stepfather's eyes, acknowledgment a change between us. "She will grieve a long time before she catches up with us," he said.

"But at least we're all together again," I said. "We can help each other."

My words fell like rocks into deep water.

Mama looked beaten, an old rug with no luster. I helped her into the house, helped her undress, removed her shoes, pulled a light sheet up to her neck, browned from our walking in the summer sun. "Rest now, Mama," I said. "Rest."

Grief has many siblings. Anger, isolation, sadness, guilt, and, yes, distraction, avoidance, pretense. I met them all in the weeks that followed. So did our family.

"I should have sent you away once we saw the quarantine sign," Mama told me a few weeks later when she felt a little stronger and we'd disinfected the rooms yet again to be sure no new diphtheria would steal into the house. "You weren't exposed. You could have gone on to find work until you return to New York." She poured generous amounts of the Labarraque's solution the doctor had brought out. We had manganese peroxide to mix with muriatic acid to create chlorine gas.

"Be careful not to breathe the fumes," the doctor said. "Leave the room and close the door." Mama had Olaf show us where he and my stepfather had buried the body fluid of Bertha and Johnny so we could put additional lime on top. Then we resteamed all the sheets and clothing, the hot water boiling on a July day, creating a penance I hoped would bring Mama relief. She sank further into despair.

Glimmers of light reached me unsuspecting. If Ida was outside or the boys weren't around, Lillian might let Mama hold her, and more than once I watched as Mama wept into the sweet clover smell in the girl's hair or the taste of earthy salt at the back of her neck. The younger boys acted sullen around us, but Arthur was eleven, and that was a hard age for a boy anyway. They didn't openly sass Mama or me. Olaf worked long hours in the fields, and while he didn't say much over the meals, neither did his eyes send barbs sharp enough to cut.

But any mention of the trip brought stark silence, and then, more boldly, my stepfather announced over a quiet meal: "There will be no talk of the trip, no words about that time when you deserted us, when you did not listen to your husband and bad things resulted."

"But if we write the book," I said while everyone sat silent at the table after his announcement, "we can at least receive the money we earned."

"There will be no book."

"But we—"

"Enough of this reform," my stepfather shouted. "That money is dirty money now. I am the head of this family, and I say no more talk of this terrible thing."

"But—"

"Clara, please," my mother whispered. She shook her head. She had nothing left to fight him.

If I thoughtlessly spoke of a Basque sheepherder in Idaho or a window in New York City, I was silenced by any or all of them, though not nearly as harshly as if Mama forgot and spoke. Everything that went wrong was Mama's fault.

Ida was the keeper of the guilt. Too much salt in the stew? Mama had been away from cooking for too long. The garden wasn't producing right? "We should have gotten the garden in by April, but of course, we had other things to do, not that you'd understand." Ida insisted that Mama and I go with her to the pig shed, where they'd had to stay during the weeks of Bertha's and Johnny's illness. Ida wanted to point out where they'd been isolated from the sick children. "Papa built a fine barn for pigs; it was never meant for his children," Ida said. "If you had been here…"

"I will never forgive myself for my absence," Mama told her. "Never."

"Guilt cuddles up next to me and steals my sleep," she told me when we walked in the field together, both of us safe with each other. "I wish I had died in their stead." I worried that she might die of a broken heart, of the despair that was deeper than the Dale Creek Canyon with no bridge for crossing. She waned like the moon, her light going out.

There was nothing I could do. Neither of us belonged anymore; we were both outcasts from our family.

"I need to find work, Mama," I said when the quarantine was finally lifted in August. I hoped it would mean that the neighbors would come by now, that seeing friends might brighten Mama's eyes. We pulled weeds in the garden, something she seemed willing to do. Ida did most of the cooking these days, and Mama let her. "I... There's no reason to tell a future employer that I might be heading east on the train, making illustrations, is there?"

She shook her head.

The loss of the book's possibility hurt more than I'd expected. Worse, I had hoped her writing of the journey would give her relief. In New York she'd told me writing eased her pain. "What if I tried to write it? I could make the trip. I could do it on my own."

"Ole sees the trip as the cause of all this trouble and our silence as small price to pay for my having done it."

"But you were behind on the payments before we left," I insisted.

"It goes further back for him. My surgery. His accidents. All of that cost money, all contributed to my desire to earn the ten thousand dollars. I believe he feels he's failed, and our journey without the money rubs salt into that wound."

"But it's still about money." I remembered Mr. Depew's office, the opulence. "Being safe and secure from the hands of the banks, that's what all of this is about, why we went at all, isn't it?"

"No, Clara. It's about family. Doing all one can for our family and respecting what they need now to heal."

"Your family turned on you and made another foolish choice, to let the book contract disappear."

"Another foolish choice? So you still think our going was foolish too."

I hesitated. What good would it do to tell her of my concerns now proven to be true? "I think...not having a better way to adjust the contract for the unexpected was imprudent, not properly thought out." I pointed to my ankle. "I don't want you to compound it now by letting the book contract go."

We sat in silence, and I wondered at my arguing for the very thing I'd once called another foolish act. "What if we told the sponsors that the book was ready and we needed the train ticket east? That way we'd know if they intend to keep their word, and I could use your notes and my own to write it like a long travel article, without mention of how it affected us, nothing personal."

Mama reached across and brushed my soft curls. "Clara, if they did send the ticket and you wrote it, then your father would never speak to either of us again. The money would mean less to him than that I disobeyed his wishes. I can't have that. I can't live without my children, and I want no animosity between you and your father. And if they didn't send the ticket, then we'd be where we are now, but we'd know for certain of their intentions."

"So we're victims. They exploited us; they got their promotion for reform dresses, and we got nothing."

"Nothing can take away the journey, Clara." She sighed. She was always so tired now. "Or what we gained as two women. We are simply asked never to speak of it again." Her voice caught. "It is important for our family to remain together."

"You may think it's about family, Mama. But from where I sit, it's still all about money and maybe power too."

"Oh, Clara." She patted my back. Then, "Where's Lillian?" Mama stood, looking to the barn, the house, back toward the fields. "Where is she?" A frantic look filled her face.

"She was right here, Mama. I'm sure she's all right." Mama started toward the barn, turned back toward the house. "There, Mama. In the barn shadow. Looking for eggs maybe. She's fine."

"*Ja, ja,* okay. Good. You're right. She's fine."

"It wasn't your fault, Mama. It wasn't."

Mama sighed. "I didn't listen to God's guidance," she said then. "That's my fault. I didn't listen for His voice telling me right or left, walk this way. I prayed for wisdom, but only after I accepted the wager. I thought He opened the door to save our farm, but He didn't. I never should have left. Remember that, Clara. Listen for His voice; don't trust your own."

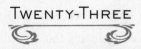

Twenty-Three

The Way of Wounds

S wallowing my pride, I approached the Stapleton residence. It was futile, I knew, but I hoped I'd find Forest at home for the summer and maybe move our relationship along. Absence made the heart grow fonder, didn't it? I wouldn't be as foolish as my mother had been, forced into a marriage without love. With a year passed, Mrs. Stapleton might relent and consider hiring me again, opening a door the trip had closed.

She had not and did not. Nor would she give me a letter of reference. "Your choice will have long and far-reaching consequences," she told me. "No one in Spokane will hire you as a domestic. That latest news article, about your writing a book about that ridiculous trip? Nonsense. Your father must be mortified to have a wife and daughter who are so public about your financials."

I wondered how mortified he would be when our farm went into foreclosure.

But her hostility toward me forewarned. I was refused interviews, not hired at the one or two I was given. No suffragette women sought a domestic, apparently. It would take time for our story to be forgotten. Until then, I daydreamed again, but this time about how I might make contact with Forest to have that luncheon he once promised.

The newspaper carried the story in the spring of 1898 announcing the engagement of Forest Stapleton to a local girl. Forest worked in his father's bank, and the newlyweds would make their home in Spokane.

I stuffed the letters I'd written to him since the theft into a packet, along with the clippings and the signatures and my sketches. I couldn't bring myself to throw them out.

I found the scissors and cut my hair. It would be easier to care for while working in the fields.

The farm became my refuge. I relieved Olaf so he could find work that paid, as his reputation hadn't been sullied. I plowed the fields, harvested grain, milked cows. I stopped dreaming about Forest or even going on to school anymore. The one chance I had for acquiring a large sum of money meant writing the book and hoping the sponsors would honor their commitment, but that was a lost dream too. To attempt it would put Mama at risk and probably myself as well. I could move away to another city and try to write the story. But I was no author. I knew that. Even to call myself an artist was questionable. No, I was good with numbers and figures, with solving problems that weren't a part of a family's journey. I could design a breast supporter that I didn't need now that we weren't walking, walking. I hadn't worn it since we'd come home.

No Estby would speak of our trek again. Our efforts would keep up the farm, but it was clear: there'd be no miracle of rescue. A fore-closure notice would be posted soon.

In the next two years, Ida mellowed. With no mention of the trip and Mama's fading, her quiet sewing, her allowing Ida to discipline the little ones, Ida assumed a position of authority in the family as though she were the oldest sister. Ida no longer needed to send angry barbs at either Mama or me. Only if one of us forgot and spoke of the trek would she say, "Now, Mama, we'll have none of that." My mother clammed up as though slapped. Even Arthur spoke those words if we talked about any-thing that could be associated with the walk. Once, when I recalled the Chicago exposition, Billy said, "Now, none of that, Clara." He sounded like my stepfather.

But otherwise, the family appeared to accept—or perhaps ignore—us.

My mother and I were passive participants in this family reconstel-lating. I felt powerless to change our status and so took solace in the fields, in watching the grain come up, in pulling at weeds, in feeling the heads between my fingers with the wish for a good harvest. I hoped for food to eat and maybe enough leftover to pay down the debt. The com-panionship of the landscape also kept me from watching my mother disappear into a woman I no longer recognized.

When everyone was asleep, I'd often pull out the old sketches I'd made and reread the news clippings as a reminder that once I'd done something unusual and brave, that I wasn't always this woman who waited for her life to begin, who couldn't hear the voice tell her to go this way, walk this path. I suppose it was a reminder of how a life can change. What we'd done had been remarkable by some standards, but foolish too. Perhaps the path to wisdom required making mistakes.

Our weekly routine included trading eggs for staples, and butter and milk for boots or coats for the growing children. At Christmastime, Ida made the *julekaga*. Mama slept, and when awake, she sighed. She was as fragile as a *sandbakkel*. Even the children singing in the Christmas choir didn't brighten her eyes. Nothing seemed to interest her except conversations about saving the farm.

"We will keep this farm," she said when my father counted out the money available to pay the interest on the loan. "They won't foreclose. God will see to that."

She carries a fantasy again, I thought. But then, we'd been back nearly three years, and still we hung on to the property. Maybe there was a guardian angel looking out for us.

In our Little Norway, as our neighbors described the Mica Creek valley, we lived inside an aquarium where everyone could see how we fared. They acted as though we were still under quarantine. Ole played cards with his friends, but few came to visit with Mama. I swam around in the same routine. My companions were family and the dog. And I was totally dependent on others for my survival.

I awoke in the night with hot sweats, fears of living my entire life this way, a wakeful nightmare.

The new century found us in the same straights as we'd been in before, and I almost hoped the foreclosure would happen so we could move on. Instead, my stepfather's health improved. He felt up to working in the fields a little more, his back stronger than it had been in years. He told me he'd be managing the farm from now on. My help was no longer needed.

"Haven't I done well with it?" I said.

"It's a man's job," he told me. "Now I'm good enough. I can do it. You can find work in Spokane."

"Doing what?" I said. I guess my mother hadn't told him about my blacklisting by the Stapletons. Had he thought I'd chosen to stay on the farm of my own accord?

"What you did before," he said. "Service. It's what good Norwegian girls do."

"I'm an American girl," I said.

"Then find something American."

I lay awake that night annoyed that I'd become a pawn. Maybe Mama's desire to make the walk had been more about escaping her daily routine than about serving the family. No, she'd wanted to save the farm and have an adventure at the same time. She'd been encouraged by Spokane's reform women. There must be one or two out there who would give me a serving job. I tried to remember the name of the surgeon, the woman who'd helped Mama after her injury and the failed lawsuit.

Mary Latham. I sat up in bed. I'd pulled the name out of the air. I took it as a sign.

What I wanted from Dr. Latham wasn't sympathy for my travails but her ability to open doors. She hadn't wanted to interfere with our "book deal" by giving us assistance when we'd asked for help while in New York, but perhaps now she might help me find work. She was a reform woman who had railed against Washington State's decision when it transitioned from a territory to a state to take away the woman's vote. Dr. Latham had assumed a profession specializing in female problems and wasn't the least shy about it. She'd even requisitioned a patented device to help in women's surgeries. She would be an ally, I was sure. Why hadn't I thought of her before?

I took the train to Spokane, where Dr. Latham invited me in, a woman wide where I was thin. She asked after my mother's health and then, when I told her of my need for work, sat thoughtfully. "It's not a domestic job, but rather a secretary or bookkeeper."

"I'm good with figures, though I've had no training," I said.

"I suspect they'd train you. Let me see what I can do," she said. "Do you have a card to leave me?" I shook my head. "That's a must," she told me. "Domestics don't need cards, but professional women do, and Clara, you will one day be a professional woman. Of that I have no doubt. You come from good stock in your mother."

And perhaps even from my father, though that I'd never know.

The idea that she saw possibilities in me buoyed my spirits. I needed to be around people who looked forward and not always back, or worse, attempted to stay the same.

So it was that a week later I received a letter asking me to come apply for a position of secretary to a small business. The owner and interviewer was Olea S. Ammundsen.

I didn't need to look for her card. I remembered her: the woman on the train.

I dressed as carefully as I could, grateful that the corset I wore again still fit. My hair had grown out enough to pull into a chignon that fit under my hat. I'd miss the privacy of the fields, I decided, and the satisfaction of hands in earth, the smells of horses as they nuzzled me with their velvet noses. But this is what I'd prayed for, a chance to be on my own, more than a servant, on a path to a career. I'd paid my dues for the family these past three years. The new century would be my new beginning too.

I walked from the station toward the address given, past the rushing Spokane River falls that raged through the center of downtown. I hopped across a streetcar track as the vehicle came around the corner.

A pleasant house on Sixth Avenue bore the address I looked for. The well-built home had a wide front porch and was painted white with soft green trim. A cedar tree took up much of the front yard and offered shade. I rang the bell, my heart fluttering.

"Come in, please," a rather short, plump woman said. "You must have walked so far. We should have given you tokens for the streetcar."

"I'm used to walking."

"Well, of course you are."

I wondered if this woman was the domestic, but she wasn't dressed as one. She wore no apron, and she moved through the house as one who owned it. She showed me into a finely furnished room. Elegant vases holding peacock feathers stood beside divans with smooth lines and fur throws over the back. In fact, almost all of the furniture had some accessory of fur. "I'm Miss Louise Gubner," she said, then suggested I sit in a high-back chair. I sank onto a throw of silver fur, adjusting it against my back. "I believe you've met my associate and cousin, Miss O. S. Ammundsen."

"Olea to my friends," Olea said as she entered the room. Tall and elegant, she put out her hand and I stood. "Welcome, Clara. I hoped we'd meet again. You remember meeting on the train? Yes, I knew you would. Louise and I returned to New York after that trip. But earlier this year we decided to make the move permanent, manage our business from the West. Rather exciting, we decided. And we have need of a bookkeeper. We hoped you'd wish to assist? Mary Latham is a friend of ours. She suggested you. Please, sit."

"I'm good with numbers, but I have no training, none at all as a bookkeeper."

"Something to remedy. You'll be attending Blair Business College when the session begins in the fall. We're sure you'll qualify. You qualified for the university some years back, I understand."

"Yes. But…" My mind spun with the goodness of what was offered. "I'll pay you back, I will."

"You'll keep our books, maybe assist in the household duties."

"I'm a fair cook," I offered.

"I rather like doing that myself," Louise said. "I hope you have a good appetite. You look a little puny if you don't mind my saying so."

"Puny? I like to eat."

"Well then, we'll work out your wages. We're hoping you can start immediately," Olea said. "We'll need to go to the college and get you enrolled. Then you can return home at the weekend and pick up your trunks."

"I only have the one," I said.

They were a whirlwind, and I was at the center.

It occurred to me that I ought to put on a business head and negotiate for wages. But I was too excited by the possibilities ahead to quibble over details. I wondered if that same anticipation had affected my mother when she first agreed to that wager so long ago, hopefulness blinding her to truth.

TWENTY-FOUR

Moving Forward

I think it would have been better if I'd gotten the job," Ida said when I returned on the weekend for my trunk.

"It's not a domestic job, right, Clara?" This was Olaf. "It's book-keeping."

"A little domestic work," I said. "But Louise, I mean Miss Gubner, likes to do the cooking and cleaning. She's round as a pumpkin and really sweet. Miss Ammundsen is always looking at birds through these little binoculars she wears like a necklace. But she's the one with a good business sense. She's a good teacher too. I'll learn more at Blair College."

"You're going on to school?" Ida said. "No, that doesn't seem fair."

"You're needed here, Ida," my stepfather said.

Ida nodded agreement, and part of me envied her for being told she was needed, that she had a place to belong. Now I would too.

Mama sighed. "Maybe I can do more of the cooking, resume my duties," she offered. "Then you could work in the city, Ida."

"Nonsense," Ida said. "You need care."

"Have you met the instructors?" Olaf asked me.

"Yes. There's only one female, for English. The typewriting and shorthand and penmanship classes and commercial law instructors are all men."

"*Ja,* as it should be," my stepfather said. "Men know how to lead."

I caught my mother's gaze; then we looked away. The meal was completed in silent chewing, only Olaf enthusiastic about my good fortune.

Mama and I walked to the pig shed, where I slopped the hogs for the last time, at least for a while. She leaned over the half door, as slender as a child. Her hair had begun to turn white at the temples.

"I'll visit," I said. She looked so sad. I set the bucket down.

"I can never be near this shed without thinking of..."

"Maybe you should ask Ole to tear it down," I said.

"Oh, I already asked, but Ida insisted it remain. A memorial, I suppose."

"Or a way of hanging on to her outrage," I said.

"She did the best she could," Mama said. "I forgive her."

"She hasn't forgiven you, I don't think."

"In time," Mama said. It would be good for me to be away, so good.

After breakfast in the morning, I said good-bye to my family, and Olaf carried my trunk to the train and waited with me. "This is right for you, Clara," he said. "You need this chance."

"I'm glad for it. I plan to earn enough to send home but also put a little aside for your schooling. You need a chance too."

He shrugged. "I may be one of the Norwegian bachelor farmers like Papa says were in the old country. Like he almost was before he fell in love with Mama."

I wondered if I should tell Olaf. I'd told no one of what Mama shared at Dale Creek about my place in the family.

"Olaf, if I tell you a secret, will you promise not to tell anyone?"

"I can keep a secret."

"Papa didn't exactly fall in love with Mama. *Bestefar* introduced them, and they married quickly because...because...Mama was with child. With me. It was for the good of her family that she married him."

"Ah, no," Olaf said. He frowned. "That can't be."

"It is. And they had a child right after me, before you, one who didn't live long, Mama told me. I'm actually a year older than everyone thinks."

"But then...who is your father?"

"I don't know his name. Mama wouldn't tell me. Someone in Michigan. Mama worked for his family. But it explains why I'm... different."

"You're not."

"I am. All the Estbys have white-blond hair, and here I am, a dirty blond. You all have such thick, strong hair, and mine is as limp and stringy as Sailor's tail without my curling iron."

Olaf shook his head. "So that's why you called Papa 'Ole' that time." He brushed aside a curl that had escaped from beneath my hat. "You're different because you're smarter than the rest of us," Olaf said, "if you're different at all."

"I'm not." I bumped his shoulder, pleased by the compliment.

"You'll always be my big sister," he said. "The rest doesn't matter. I'm glad for you. When one of us makes his way, it gives the rest of us hope that we'll make our way too."

"What do you think Mama will do if the farm is foreclosed on?" I said. I fanned my face with my straw hat.

"What will they do? I think it will be the best days of their lives once they get over the shock of it."

"Olaf!"

"It's true. The farm has consumed all of us. I know they love the land and it's fed us, but it devours too, taking every dime we'll give it but not in proportion to what it demands. There is more cost than just dollars, Clara. Once they got behind and borrowed with no way to repay it, then with Papa's injuries, trying to hang on to it has been like holding on to a cow's tail in a cyclone. You know you're going to get hurt and separated. It's just a matter of how much pain you'll endure before you let go. They'll hate it, the humiliation. But it will free them. All of us."

"Mama walked east for the farm," I said.

"And see what it cost her?" He pulled on a grass stem and chewed on it. In the distance we heard the train chugging. "I'll keep your secret," he said. "And you need to keep mine. They'd think me a traitor if I said good riddance, let the farm go. But that's how I feel. At least today." He smiled.

"We'll keep our secrets," I said. I hugged him and whispered, "I'll miss you most of all." I thought it was the truth.

The routine of Blair College and the presence of the two women filled my life in ways I'd never known. Days I spent in classes; evenings I assisted with laundry, the heavier work, as both Olea and Louise were in their fifties (or so I guessed) and were pleased by my strong arms and back. Then I studied while Louise plied me with cookies and cakes. On Saturdays, Olea introduced me to their ledgers. I took her training seri-

ously and saw it as the path that would help me move on to full independence, having a business of my own.

The women were frugal and careful managers. I found the book-
keeping well in hand and thought they used it more as an excuse for my
learning than because they truly needed an employee. The only real
office work I thought they lacked was a secretary to write the letters
Olea dictated. I liked the secretarial part, learning how to phrase words.
Their correspondence went to places like Romania and France, Italy
and Greece, to London and Oslo. Over supper they often told stories of
their trips there and of their lives in Norway before New York.

"We were schoolgirl friends in Christiania as well as cousins," Louise told me one day. "Olea was always smarter and faster than I."

"And Louise attracted every lost soul in the city," Olea said, "from
children to cats."

"We complement each other," Louise said as I served chicken and
dumplings for supper. Louise cooked, but I insisted on serving. At first,
I also declined to sit with them at their table.

"I'm a servant," I insisted. "It wouldn't be right to assume I was your
equal, eating with you side by side as though we were family."

I stood while Louise spoke grace before the meals. She offered not
the childhood prayers I'd learned in Norwegian, but original words
each day, asking for guidance, talking about the day's events. After
grace, I sat in the kitchen alone to pick at my food. When they were
finished and the table cleared, they'd drink their coffees and I'd join
them then.

"You treat food like life," Louise commented once. "Like you don't
deserve a full plate shared with friends."

I didn't think that was so, but I had no response to her either.

Olea often explored theological questions during the coffee time, posing thoughts like whether one ought to worship Jesus as a signpost or by following His direction. "If you see the sign saying 'Seventy Miles to Coulee City,' you don't stay there saying, 'Yes, this is what matters. I will worship the sign.' No, you follow the directions; you follow Him. That's true worship, by doing what He asks of us."

"Would Jesus want to go to Coulee City?" Louise said.

"He might," said Olea. They laughed and I joined them. Coulee City was a little town an hour's train ride west that had as many rabbits as people.

Once or twice the conversation turned to lost loves, men who had come into the women's lives and then departed. Olea had watched her future husband go off to the North Sea fishing and not return. Louise's love interest had married another.

"My only attraction was to the son of my employer," I said. "And my mother made sure by taking me on the walk to New York that I didn't violate any employer-employee rules."

"Did you meet any interesting young men on your trip?" Louise asked.

"She's a romantic," Olea explained.

"No. No one."

"Well, one day," Louise said. "You're a lovely young woman. A nice man to take care of you will be good."

"A woman ought to be able to take care of herself. I want to be financially independent one day." I didn't want to violate that employee barrier, but I added, "The two of you have done well without a man to take care of you."

"Yes. That's true," Olea said. "But one mustn't ignore the treasures God provides in companionship. We all need companionship," she said.

"An independent woman can push men away," Louise said. "Olea finds that true, don't you? She can be intimidating if you don't know her. Smart women have to think of that. And frankly, two independent women living together makes some men only worry they might have to support two women rather than just one." Her eyes blinked rapidly.

"Then three of us must scare them terribly," I said before I realized how the words might be interpreted, as though we were a set of three and not the two of them with me, an employee, sipping coffee with them at their pleasure. "Oh, I'm sorry. I didn't mean to suggest—"

"We know what you meant." Olea patted my hand. "Since you've joined us, we do think of us as three women making our way together. There's nothing wrong with that."

Olea's words warmed. Perhaps I could alter the employee-employer relationship in the same way that my mother altered dresses that no longer fit. These women were the sturdy dock I needed as I set sail on an unknown sea.

Through the summer of 1900, they taught me about the fur clothing business. Their agent, Franklin Doré, purchased pelts at auctions, then sent them for tanning and dressing in either Montreal or Europe. After the skins were prepared, they were sent to manufacturers. The best were in France and Italy, Olea insisted. Louise said New York was gaining fast. Finished coats and ermine capes or jackets with skunk-trimmed collars were then shipped to New York on Twenty-eighth Street. In the women's younger years, they often traveled to Europe, China, Russia, and the leather markets of Turkey and Greece. "But our agent does most of the traveling now. We leased our furrier shop in the city earlier this year, when we came here. But we're still active in the trade," Olea said, "taking on specific clients who want certain garments."

"Trends are important," Louise said as I rubbed my eyes from the hours of looking over the ledgers as the women explained them. "People are fickle about fashion. Sometimes they want silver fox, and sometimes they 'simply must have sable.'"

"Louise is partial to mink," Olea said and she smiled.

Louise noticed my impolite yawn, and she picked up the large ledger books I'd been looking at. "That's enough lessons for one night. It's your bedtime, Clara. We don't want to work you to death. It seems to me you do little but study and labor."

Working me to death. I smiled at that. I occupied my own bed in my own room. My labor brought no ache to my back, wasn't needed to keep cows from sliding on my instep while I milked. No feathers took me to a fit of sneezing while butchering chickens for a Fourth of July picnic. Once, when I had a sore throat, Louise treated it with mustard packs, as Mama would have. When my foot swelled, Louise put ice chips on it. What these women offered me in comfort was as warm as a winter quilt and as far from working me to death as a turkey feather was from sable.

Their kindness extended to more than just me. They gave contributions to the Lutheran church we attended in Spokane. They supported the Sons of Norway and the Norwegian Independence Day and insisted that I take time off May 17 to celebrate. Louise had a place in her heart for orphans; Olea gave to the carpenters' trade union, the fund that helped Mama when my stepfather was first hurt. Their generosity to that organization brought me even greater trust in these women.

I didn't go home for Christmas that year. We had heavy snows. Both Olea and Louise assured me I wasn't a bad daughter by not risking the possible delays and avoiding the drifts. "One day I might own an automobile," I told them. "It would make life so much easier." That holiday I ate Louise's *julekaga* with the white frosting swirled this way and that across the top of the heavy bread, attended Christmas Eve services with my two friends, and sent the gifts for my family by post on Thursday, the day after Christmas.

We three exchanged gifts. Louise and Olea gave me a jacket made of a Canada lynx's spotted belly fur. "It's very desirable," Louise told me.

I couldn't stop running my hands over its softness, its elegance, brown spots against the white fur. "It's too much," I said. I'd given them each a set of pillowcases I'd embroidered. They were paltry by comparison. "I only gave you—"

"What you had to give," Olea corrected me. "As did we, 'every man according to his ability.'"

"From the book of Acts," Louise said. "About people taking care of each other."

"I'm sure she knows," Olea said.

I might have, but I'd forgotten until Louise reminded me.

Queen Victoria's funeral took place in February. Louise, surprisingly, seemed saddened by this event so far away. "The death of someone famous always makes me think of other deaths," Louise said. "It always does."

"I'm not sure it needs to be a famous person's death," I said. My mind went to Henry and Bertha and Johnny and when I'd last seen them. I needed to make a trip to their graves. I wondered if those pieces of Mama's Hardanger lace heart had been buried with them.

"Did you ever meet her?" I asked.

"Oh, goodness no. We've met the Roosevelts, and of course there was that terrible loss he had in '84 with both his mother and wife dying on the same day. So tragic. But that's as close to fame as I've come."

"I met President McKinley and his wife," I ventured. I'd not talked of the journey in the months I'd been with them. A twinge of guilt caused me to pause, but there was no reason not to speak of it to these women. Speaking of the story couldn't hurt Mama from here.

"Yes, and Mary Bryan, I believe. And the governors of Idaho and Ohio," Louise said. "You met so many people on that trip."

I frowned. Had all of those names been mentioned in the newspaper accounts, if she'd even read them? And would Louise have remembered that? It was so long ago.

"Louise," Olea cautioned.

"Did I tell you that when we met on the train?" I asked Olea.

The two women were silent, looked at each other.

"It was in the papers," Olea said.

"That's it. I read those names in the papers," Louise agreed. She blinked rapidly, a habit I'd noticed came paired with some distress.

"But only the Minneapolis papers covered some signatures by name," I said. Had they been in my room, looking at my packet? Impossible—the packet was still at the farm, hidden behind the flour mill cabinet in the kitchen. "I'm sure of it."

"That must be where we saw it then, before we left for Spokane," Louise said. "Would you like a cookie? I baked extra today." She continued to blink as she handed me the Spode plate piled with sweets.

I took one, but it didn't answer what discomforted in the conversation.

Twenty-Five

A New Walk

Ida's letter arrived in March of 1901 saying our parents had received the final statement from the mortgage holder, and the loan had been called in. They either had to pay the full amount or our property would be foreclosed and sold. Mama and Ole planned to auction off as much as they could, hoping to keep the land and start again. I felt a clutch in my chest. After all this time, it was coming to pass. I didn't know whether to feel great sadness for Mama or to secretly share Olaf's sentiments about letting go of the cow's tail.

The auction was set for March 28. The sale of cattle and hogs might produce enough to meet the back taxes, but I couldn't imagine the family would have money left over to keep the land. Selling cows and horses meant even if Mama and Ole raised the payment, they'd have nothing left to farm with.

"If there is any way you could borrow the money from your rich employers, that would be a small thing you could do for this family after all that's happened," Ida wrote. "We only need one thousand dollars." She didn't even tell me how everyone was.

Ask my employers for that kind of money? I didn't see how. Still, if I could pay off the mortgage, perhaps then my stepfather might let Mama at last write about the story, for herself if for no one else. I was sure the sponsors no longer looked for the manuscript. That bridge had been blown apart.

But I didn't want to jeopardize my relationship with my employers. Though I knew of their investments and bank accounts, I was not free to ask for money I knew they had. That would violate a rule that Blair Business College professors spoke of. "The relationship between employer and employee has barriers that must not be crossed." I'd almost crossed it that one evening by suggesting we were three women living together like a family.

But I thought of Mama, how she had sacrificed for that farm, how much she'd risked. I had to risk too. I would ask for a loan to save the farm. I would find a way to keep it all strictly business.

"Of course we can talk," Louise said. We'd been shopping—Louise loved that activity—and I wore new clothes that the women had insisted I let them buy for me, telling me that I represented them now and must look the part of a successful associate furrier. I hung the Canada lynx coat and put away my ermine purse with a large black ring on the zippered handle. Both Louise and Olea removed fur coats. I hung these in the closet, then stoked the wood stove. The women wore long skirts over their Gibson corsets and long-sleeved linen blouses with a dozen pleats down the front that I had personally pressed before putting the irons to my own.

"So what can we do for you?" Olea asked.

"I have a business proposition," I said. Olea opened the windows, letting in the cold air. Louise shivered, causing Olea to think twice and close it. Louise sat, and the cat that she had recently adopted, Lucy, curled up on her lap. Blue jays argued outside where snow lingered on the lawn. "I'd like to borrow fifteen hundred dollars to repay my parents' mortgage," I said. I'd rehearsed a preface to my request, but my heart pounded so that I didn't remember how to sound professional and confident. I cleared my throat.

"What?" Louise said. "You want to borrow money from us?"

"I'd pay it back to you in monthly payments with interest you deem fair. I'll be out of school soon. I could get other work, pay you cash each week, and continue to do your books and domestic work to cover my room and board. I'm a hard worker, and my grades at Blair are very good." I caught my breath.

This isn't begging; it's business. For family.

The women glanced at each other, an exchange between relatives that excluded me.

"Do you remember," Olea said then, "the day Louise happened to mention the signatures of people you'd met on the walk east?" I nodded. "You've never talked about that trip much."

"I'm sorry, I guess I didn't phrase my question well. I don't want to talk about the trip. I...hope to borrow funds."

"On the train, you'd been so happy to discuss the journey with me. You described it as worthy of a college education," Olea said.

"It was that," I said softly. "I shouldn't have mentioned meeting the McKinleys that night. I was prideful." I dropped my eyes.

"Nonsense, you have a right to talk about your own experiences," Olea said. "They belong to you."

"It struck us as odd that it was the very first time you mentioned walking to New York," Louise said. She stroked the black and white cat with shiny fur. I could hear Lucy purring from across the room. "We thought maybe you disliked the new reform dresses after all. It's the coming thing in the apparel industry. With the death of Queen Victoria, there'll be changes. Her son Edward is already wearing a different kind of suit. Deaths of prominent people always bring a fashion change."

"It wasn't the dress. Nothing like that. Tragedy…happened. After we got back."

"The death of your sister," Louise nodded.

"And my brother," I said. "Then, after we returned our family, my father—my stepfather took our making the trip as an affront to him. He—and my brothers and sisters—blame my mother for not being there when the children got sick. She blames herself too. He forbade my mother ever to speak of the trip again. Any of us. I'm sorry. I shouldn't be telling you all these intimate details. You know we Norwegians aren't like that. We keep things to ourselves. Or should."

"The old Norwegian ways aren't always wise," Olea said. "It can be healing for the soul to share its stories."

"I'm not to speak or write about it either. Ever. Ole, he's not a mean man. It's… He thought our trip shamed him in our family and in Mica Creek. People acted like we were in quarantine long after the sign came down. We'd violated what they expected of a good mother and decent Norwegian women. Some might have even thought the deaths were punishment for our bringing attention to ourselves so publicly."

"Nonsense," Louise said. "That's not how God does things."

"Part of the reason why I need the loan," I said, glad for a path back to the subject, "is that if I could prevent the sale of the farm, maybe my stepfather would allow my mother to speak of the trip again. Maybe she wouldn't be so sad then, so…listless. She only undertook the trip to save the farm."

Olea inhaled deeply. She looked at Louise, who nodded her head. "The truth is, Clara," Olea began, "we know something about your trip and what happened when you reached New York."

"We didn't make it on time," I said. "I sprained my ankle and the sponsors wouldn't pay. That added to Ole's upset."

"We never thought that was fair," Louise said. "After all, a sprained ankle on a walking trip is certainly predictive of a consequence not unlike food poisoning, and we made an adjustment for that."

I frowned. Had the newspaper articles covered my food poisoning?

"So we felt we ought to tell you…" Louise looked to Olea. "We were going to in time, but your request gives us the opening."

"What?" I said. My heart started to pound, and my breath tried to disappear. "What do you have to tell me?"

"We, that is, we know about the sponsors, the 'parties' in New York. There were five sponsors," Olea said. "Each put up two thousand dollars to make the wager. We hoped to raise awareness of new trends in the fashion industry. It was an investment. We were…two of those investors."

My face burned at their betrayal. These very women had been the ones to victimize Mama and me? How could I have come to trust them, to think of them almost as family? I stood. I had to get out. "You…withheld the money? What kind of people would do that?"

"Please sit. Let us explain," Olea said.

"No! You made us beg to get back home. You didn't keep your part in the—"

"Please. Sit," Olea said.

In my confusion I sank onto the divan, shaking. I nipped at my nails, then clutched my hands in my lap.

"Louise and I were in Europe when you arrived, and the other sponsors didn't even advise us of the details until we returned in May, when the only thing in bargaining position by then was the book. We protested. It didn't seem fair at all, but we were outvoted by the other three, and even that was after the fact. You were on your way back to

Spokane, and there was this agreement about a book, which they said they wouldn't honor if we gave you some of the money ahead of time for having reached New York at all."

"There'd been a bit of a downturn in their resources," Louise said. "Well, ours too. They were looking for an honorable way out. It got very confused. And didn't feel right at all. We made the trip to Spokane that summer to get away from it, thinking a change of scenery would be good. And we knew Mary Latham, but she had no part in the decisions."

"They did urge Mr. Depew to advance the ticket," Olea said. "I'm sorry it took them so long to arrange for that."

"It was an ugly business," Louise said. "We consider it a gift that Olea met you and we saw what a fine young woman you are and that you had such hopes to finish the book. We hoped everything would work out, but then there was never any book."

"Because of my stepfather." I didn't add that my mother's sorrow might have prevented her from writing the book at all, but because of Ole, she wasn't even allowed to try. And neither was I. "But you… I…" I ought to leave, have nothing to do with them, and yet they had been so kind. I was as torn as an old bed sheet.

"So, no. You cannot have the loan for fifteen hundred dollars," Olea said.

I nodded. Of course not. These were wealthy people, and they played by their rules. I'd violated my own rule by trusting someone and then letting money become part of the equation. How foolish I'd been. Foolish and trusting, just like my mother.

I stood. "I'll pack my things and be gone in the morning," I said.

"What we will do is *give* you what we'd committed back then," Olea said. "We'll give you four thousand dollars, two thousand from each of us. You can give half to save the farm if that's what you'd like, and we hope you'll keep half for yourself to invest or to make your own start. No strings attached."

"You'll *give* it to me? But—" My words faltered. Such generosity was unheard of! Were there truly gifts without obligation?

"We won't loan it; it's yours. We'd consider it one of our best investments ever if you'd forgive us for the very long delay."

TWENTY-SIX

For Family

I took the train to Mica Creek the weekend before the auction. I thought about simply sending Mama a money order, but Ole would surely ask where she'd gotten the funds, and she'd have to say where it came from. Maybe he wouldn't mind knowing it came from reform women, though he'd be very upset if he knew the women had been part of the sponsors and that Mama and I had accepted funds from them. Besides, giving her the money and the mortgage wouldn't necessarily allow Ole to relieve Mama of his order that she never speak about the trip. What I wanted was a way for Mama to be freed from both the agony of the foreclosure and to speak again of her experiences. Olea was right. Our stories belonged to us. Mama ought to be able to speak about hers.

As the train clicked south, I thought it would be best if I spoke to my stepfather alone. I'd tell him I had the money to save the farm and the condition was that he must let Mama speak again of the journey. I'd been right to tell Olea that he wasn't a mean-spirited person. Only stubborn at times, seeing things in certain ways that no amount of evidence or even practicality could change. I'd have to be a superb negotiator.

I breathed a prayer of relief as I stepped off the train and saw my stepfather's wagon parked in front of Schwartz's store. Perfect timing. I opened my parasol against the cold drizzle. The scent of snow filled the air. I'd wait until he picked up whatever he'd come to town for and then ride home with him. On the way I'd put my proposition to him.

But when my stepfather came out, my mother was with him. Well, it might work fine to have them both together, so Mama could hear me fight for her, stand up to my stepfather the way she used to. And Ida and the others wouldn't be around to witness it.

Martin, my stepfather's friend, walked out with them, helped Mama into the wagon as I approached.

"Well, look who's here?" Martin said. "Your lovely daughter all dressed like a fine lady."

"*Ja.* She's grown up now," my stepfather said.

"Clara?" Mama said. I put my foot on the step, covered us with the umbrella.

"May I ride with you?"

"Must be doing pretty good, all that store-bought finery she's wearing," Martin said. "Your fine shoes will get muddy."

"I have a good job in town now, Mr. Siverson," I said.

"Maybe she'll attract a rich farmer and you can borrow his tractor after she goes in wedding thoughts," Martin said.

Norwegian men had no trouble speaking of money with each other or assuming where a woman's thoughts might go, wedding or naught. But women taking on financial matters, that was an affront.

"I'll get one of my own one of these days," my stepfather said.

"*Ja,* that would be good for your back and all. Make harvest easier."

His friend still held out hope that they wouldn't lose the farm, or Martin wouldn't have spoken quite so teasingly nor have ended with encouragement about a tractor. Yet everyone must know about the auction and its purpose.

"It's good to have girls to take care of you in your old age," Martin said. "Otherwise age only leads to worse things."

My stepfather laughed. "One generation plants the trees, the next one gets the shade."

Martin lifted my fabric bag into the back and pulled the canvas over it and the lumber loaded there. I held on to my fur purse. "What are you going to build?" I asked.

"Making repairs," Ole said. "Before the sale. It should go into the hands of someone new in best condition."

My mother winced.

He flicked the reins and we started off as Martin stepped back under the store porch and waved.

"That's the reason I came to talk to you," I said. "I have a proposition." I cleared my throat from its soreness. "Mama. Papa. I've come into money of late. You won't have to have the auction. I can pay the mortgage and the back taxes. You can start fresh."

"What are you saying?" Mama said. She twisted to look at me.

My stepfather pulled the wagon up short, clucked to the horses so they knew to relax. "What's this?"

"I have enough money to stop the foreclosure. That's why I came, to give it to you."

"Where would you get such funds?" he demanded.

"Does it matter?"

"From these women you work for," Mama said.

"Yes."

"They would loan money to a girl such as you? Why would they do that?"

"Maybe because they see promise in me," I said. "I'm not a girl any longer. Twenty-five in November."

"What do you do that they give you such money? *Betre tom pung enn rangt skaffa pengar,*" he added.

"Better an empty purse than wrongly got money?" I repeated in English. "It's not ill-gotten gain, Ole. In fact, it's a just reward for work accomplished. 'A woman doesn't have to be shy about asking for what she wants nor bow too low in gratitude for what she rightfully deserves,' " I quoted.

He snorted. "Suffragette talk."

"Yes, it is, but it's the truth."

"These women you work for are suffragettes."

"I am too," Mama said.

"None of that," my stepfather cautioned. "None of that now."

Mama lowered her eyes and looked away as though struck.

"They're businesswomen. They've earned their money through wise investment and business decisions. I'm learning from them."

"And you want to give me their money."

"Give to the family some of *my* money," I said. My heart pounded. "It's mama's money too. A portion of what we were to earn by making our walk to New York."

"*Fandem!* Those women are—"

"Not of the devil," I said. "They're good people, and they know we deserve payment for our incredible journey."

He leaned out around Mama, who sat between us. He lifted his hand as though to strike me, his eyes wild with outrage. I shrank back, held gloved fingers to my face. He had never struck me, nor anyone in the family that I knew of.

"Ole," Mama said. She tugged on his arm, pulled it down. "Let her talk."

"That...walk, that walk is not a subject allowed in my presence," he shouted at her.

"But I am in your presence, and it is my right to speak what matters to me," I said. "I offer you a way out, a way to save your family from the humiliation of foreclosure, from financial ruin. Money rightfully earned! Accept it. Don't let your pride keep you from doing what is right for your family, for your wife. Let her speak of an accomplishment. Let her know she helped keep the farm you both worked so hard for, we all worked so hard for."

"What do you know of swallowing pride?" His eyes glared at me, my mother between us. The horses stomped, aware of his intensity. His hands were in fists. I thought he might snap the reins and jolt them forward just to keep me silent. "Years ago I swallow my pride for your mother, for what John Doré did to her, tossing her aside. How does she repay me? She names you for his mother! I do nothing about this. I accept. I let her go, with you, on that stupid walk."

John Doré? This is my father?

"Ole, please. She didn't know—"

"I do for her because I...love her." He choked, didn't say Mama's name. "I...accept because I care for her. New York." He spit the words. "I allow her to come back after she disobeys me, has left behind me and her children. She takes John Doré's child with her. I let this happen because I love her. But no more!"

"You don't love my mother anymore?" I shook. "After all she's done for you?"

"No more doing what she wants!"

Grief like a train whistle coursed through his voice.

"No more going back on what I say. No one talks about that...
walk. No one who wants to be in this family takes money related to it.
No one. I have spoken. That is enough."

"But the farm?" Mama said. She grabbed his sleeve. "We could
save the farm."

"I do not want your dirty money." He seethed. "I do not want
people with dirty money to have any say in my life. No more. None."

"And me either, I guess?" I said.

"You either if it is through that dirty money."

"Ole, please." He shook off her hand.

"I will provide for my family. Not those women, not you, Clara,
nor you, my wife. It is over."

"Mama—"

"It. Is. Finished." Spittle had gathered around the corners of his
mouth. His eyes blazed like a minister preaching that hellfire was
imminent.

I looked at my mother, caught between us. "It's the one thing I can
do for you," I said. "The one thing that would make it all worthwhile.
Take it." I shoved the purse toward her. "Take the money. We earned it,
you and me."

But my mother wasn't the woman who had defied her husband to
walk across the country. She wasn't that woman. She shook her head, no.

"I'll pay the mortgage myself, then. Pay it for you," I said. "Mama
doesn't have to be able to talk about the walk, but you could stay here,
on this land you both love. It's a business decision, nothing more. Turning down money..."

"Don't you listen?" He shook his finger in my face, eyes narrowed
in fury. "You do not pay our bills with dirty money. You hear me? If you
even speak of this to any of our family, I will send your mother out. She

will no longer be under my roof. You have made your choice, but you will not sour the rest of my family. If you were an Estby, you would give the money back. You would not work with those women who caused your brother and sister to die."

"It was a tragedy! Even if Mama had been here, she likely wouldn't have done any better than you did."

How can he say this in front of Mama, who already bears the weight of their deaths?

"You are nothing but a girl. How can you know the way of things? A daughter of mine would never touch such money."

"I'm not a daughter of yours."

"Never were. We are foreclosed. The auction is set. That is God's will." He snapped the reins, jerking me backward, forcing me to grab at the seat as we headed toward the house.

Bare trees without leaves blurred through my tears. The purse warmed my belly. I held a pocketful of money I couldn't use to save my family, while my mother…my mother sat broken in silence, tears streaming down her face.

TWENTY-SEVEN

Sacrifice

Well, aren't you the fancy one?" Ida said. We stood in the kitchen. I reached to give her a hug, and she accepted it. I took Mama's coat, hung it. She stood, uncertain, it seemed to me. She moved to the cupboard, opened the door, closed it, went to the icebox. Ida shooed her away. "I'll take care of that, Mama," she said. "You set the table."

Through the window, I watched as Arthur and Billy helped my stepfather unload the wagon, then bring my bag toward the house. I took off my fur jacket, removed my hat, and Ida said, "Lovely work," then set the hat on the table, tested the felt's thickness. "Those women must pay you well."

"I work for it, but they're very kind. The purse was part of their inventory when they leased their furrier shop." I didn't add where. "The coat was a Christmas present."

Ida raised an eyebrow.

"Are those blue things beads?" Seven-year-old Lillian pointed at the purse.

"They are. Imported from Spain." I tried to keep my voice steady and light while my heart ached for Mama. I could rescue them all; I couldn't. I wanted to be away, not watch this scene play out, but I didn't want to desert them.

"I'd like to work in a millinery that sells that kind of quality," Ida said.

"You should then."

"Not while I'm needed here."

"Working in a millinery would be a good job once you're in Spokane," I said. "Crescent's department store employs several."

"Can you whip the cream?" Ida asked me then. Mama had taken down the creamery bowl but seemed lost at what to do next.

I crossed the room to stand beside her, touched her slender back. *She is so thin.*

I removed the pitcher from the icebox and began to whip, turning my frustration and disappointment into spiky peaks of cream.

"You must take whatever you left here, Clara," Mama said then. "We can't move everything to Aunt Hannah's."

"It looks like you've already sold some things," I said.

"Papa's furniture gets a good price," Ida said. "He's very talented."

"I think the buyers purchase out of pity for us." Mama shook her head in shame. "I have my red slippers, the ones I brought from Norway when I was a little girl. I'll take those with me."

"Of course you will, Mama." *She sounds like a little girl.*

It makes no sense, their refusal of my help.

What would I want to take with me? *The packet!* I'd nearly forgotten it. Fortunately they hadn't sold the kitchen flour cupboard that hid it.

Ida motioned with her eyes and whispered. "Did you get my letter?"

Lillian dropped the hat at that moment and picked up the ermine purse with the black zipper ring.

"Will you stay in Spokane?" I said to Mama, ignoring Ida's question.

"Papa's trying to get back with the union for carpentry work," Ida said. Her eyes snapped at me. "He's been fixing things around here. It helps him not feel so bad about losing the farm. All he's worked for all these years."

"And all you've worked for. All of us," I said.

"If only you and I had been successful in New—"

"Mama. No," Ida said. She spoke as sternly as a mother telling her child to not even think about picking up that awful, dangerous black widow spider she stared at.

"*Ja,* I know." Mama sighed. She acted as though her tongue had outwitted her mind in letting her speak of such terrible truths. "So what kind of work do they have you doing, these women? What are their names again?" Mama asked. It was as though she pulled her interest out of a deep sack, the words flat and dusty.

I could hear the zipper pushed back and forth on my purse.

"Be careful now, Lillian. That's your sister's," Ida said.

"I'm being good," Lillian said as she moved the zipper.

The money the sponsors gave me is in there. Maybe if Ida knows, she'll convince Mama and Papa to take it.

I told them the women's names and described how kind they'd been, how interesting the fur industry was, how they got to travel but because they were women working in a man's world they had a man who actually signed their contracts. "I haven't met him, but his name is…" I stopped myself.

"What's his name?" Ida asked.

"His name is Franklin Doré."

Mama dropped the spoons she had in her hand. Her back stiffened and she turned, shook her head at me, her eyes wild with concern. *Speaking of a Doré doesn't violate a rule, does it?*

My stepfather had said my father's name was John Doré and his mother's name was Clara. I'd been so intimidated by his outrage that I hadn't realized I'd heard that last name before. *Doré.*

"What kind of fur is this?" Lillian said. She rubbed the gold-cast pelt of the purse, then put it to her face. "So soft." She ran the zipper back and forth again.

"It's ermine, from Russia. Maybe you should put that down and let's set the table," I said now that the cream stood stiff as frozen snow.

Ida said, "Clara, about my letter—"

Commotion followed the men and boys' arrival inside. Billy teased me about the mud on my shoes. The men sat down, and when they heard Sailor bark his old dog bark, Mama looked out the window and announced that Olaf was coming too. "Now I'll have all my children here. What could be better?" She sighed.

You could have the farm. Couldn't she see? Where was that independent spirit that had shot a tramp, walked right up to the president-elect's house, worked her way across the continent, keeping us safe, hoping to rescue this farm?

Olaf stepped inside then and hugged Mama, Ida, and me, tugged on Lillian's braid. He plopped his newspaper on the table. "Only two weeks old, this one," he said. Mama picked it up, set it aside. She thanked him for remembering. So news still kept her interest. Ida put plates on the table while I moved my hat to the daybed. Lillian set a plate or two, picked the purse back up.

"Arthur, put that umbrella away. Don't you know that opening an umbrella inside is bad luck?" Ida told him.

"Who believes in superstitions like that?" he said.

The pie was served then with dollops of whipped cream on top. I didn't look at my stepfather as he sat at the head of the table. For a moment, as people ate, the silence seemed normal, what it should be while hungry people received sustenance prepared by loving hands. I memorized the scene. It would be the last time I'd see my family in this kitchen, where so many sunrises had freshened the morning, so many conversations helped the evening wane. The farm would be gone. The sale would pierce my mother's heart yet again. How many more wounds could she accept without disappearing? How many little pieces of a lace heart could she leave behind? She had suffered enough.

There was nothing I could do about it.

I captured the faces of my family. Even in my stepfather's eyes I saw true sadness. He'd said I wasn't an Estby if I kept the dirty money, as he called it. But even before I'd received the money, I wasn't an Estby. That was the truth. Maybe that's why I could see the money objectively, as a means to an end, while my stepfather and mother gave it evil intent.

Life would change for all of them after today, me most of all.

I shook my head, remembering my brother's sage vision once shared in secret that the foreclosure would at last free them from a terrible debt that sucked them all dry. The thought gave me hope that maybe it would be all right for Mama without the farm. This amputation from the land might in time allow true healing to take place without the daily reminder of the losses suffered here.

"Do you want to go upstairs and see what's yours to take with you?" Mama said as we finished up.

"I think mostly I'd like…" I rose to the cabinet and pulled it out from the wall. The packet was still there tied with a dusty ribbon.

"What have you got there?" Ida said.

"My drawings. You remember," I said. I brushed off the packet. "And a few of Olaf's old newspapers." I hoped Ida wouldn't want to look inside. The clippings were there, the signatures of the famous people. It might challenge my stepfather if he saw that I'd kept evidence of our walk. I didn't want him to grab the packet and see what had been kept of the trip right under his nose.

"Ohhhh," Lillian said. "Look at all this!"

We all turned.

From the ermine purse, Lillian pulled one-hundred-dollar bills. They unfurled on the floor at my stepfather's feet like leaves falling from a windblown tree.

"Oops," Lillian said.

"Lillian," Ida said. "What are you doing getting into Clara's things?"

My mother gasped.

Lillian bent to pick up the bills, tried stuffing them back inside. Ida squatted to help her. She looked up. "Clara? There's so much money here."

Arthur stopped eating and looked at what his sister held. "There must be...thousands," he said.

"Maybe millions," Billy added.

Ida's face lit up. "You brought it for us!"

I looked at my stepfather. I pleaded with him to take this gift of accident, another chance that Lillian's curiosity had given. Under his breath I heard him say, *"Sjusket kvinne."*

"Who lives like a slattern?" Olaf asked.

"It isn't dirty money," I defended.

"Is it yours?" Ida said. "Are you giving it to us, to save the farm—"

"Yes, it's mine. And I would but—"

"You'll pay the mortgage? We won't have to move?" Arthur asked.

"No," I said. "Ole, Papa, has refused the money."

"Papa?" Ida said.

"It's money Mama and I earned by making the trip. The women I work for were two of the sponsors."

Ida gasped, dropped the money as though it held disease. "And you would take their money after what they did to us?" Her eyes flashed in outrage. "You worked for them, knowing this?"

"I didn't know when I started. It… The sponsorship… It was a business arrangement, with other people," I said. "They never intended for bad things to happen. Now they're hoping to make amends."

"Dirty money," my stepfather repeated.

"Papa," Ida said. "If it would save the farm…"

"No!" He banged his fist on the table, making the plates and forks jump. He shouted so loudly Lillian started to cry. That awakened Mama, who put her arms around her.

"We accept nothing touched by that time. Clara is foolish to want it. Or to work for them, to have anything to do with them."

For a moment, Ida teetered on our future, but she was driven by the past.

"Well," Ida said with no longer even a hint of an ally. "You have to quit working for them."

"They're the ones that wouldn't pay you and Mama?" Arthur asked. He looked confused.

Ida nodded. "Papa's right. It's a…betrayal to work for such women. Give the money back. Find another job. You need to be loyal to our family, Clara. How can you even consider taking it?"

"But it would save you. Us!" I pleaded. "It's only money."

"It has been decided," my stepfather said. "Ida is right; you must give it back. Get away from the influence of those women. You can live with us in Spokane. Help your family in an honorable way."

Help my family. Wasn't that what I'd always done? They refused my help. They couldn't see the merit of the money nor of allowing others to pay penance for a wrong.

I looked at my mother. She sat, a frozen sea within.

And then I chose.

"You said that an Estby wouldn't keep it, Papa. You're right. But I'm not an Estby, and you're not my papa. I guess that's the truth of things. This money is a tool; it's…it's not good or bad. Can't you see that? It would do what you wanted it to do. You're the ones who are foolish and betray the family by not accepting it."

"Clara. Stop now." My stepfather stood.

I could hardly hold back the tears. "I've done everything I could for this family. Everything. I made that trip even though I didn't want to. I grieved with Mama over Bertha's death, just the two of us alone. I ached with you over Johnny's. I gave up my own life to help save this farm, but it doesn't matter to you. If I have joy from my work, you say it's from dirty money. If I can't help in the way you think is good, then I can't help at all." My voice broke.

"Clara," my mother said.

"What?" I turned on her.

"Do what Ole asks."

"No. I'll get out of your way and make my own way." I pulled my hat onto my head, grabbed the purse.

"It's all right, Lillian," I said. The child shrank on the daybed, pulling her knees up as though all this emotion was her fault, begun by her opening my purse. But it had begun years before, perhaps when Mama chose to do what her family asked and marry my stepfather even though she didn't love him, denied herself to save her family. Always for the family.

"If you can't live with our rules, then you must live without us," my stepfather said.

The tears ran freely, and a sob escaped me.

"You're abandoning us," Ida said. She whispered as if in shock. "In our hour of greatest need."

"A need I can fix but not the way you want," I said. I hiccupped with sorrow. "Call it what you will. You're sending me out."

I thought Mama's eyes spoke to me as I pushed past her. I hesitated, to see if she'd reach up to stop me, keep me in this family. But her eyes had no message, at least none I could read through my tears. I touched Olaf on the shoulder as I passed behind him, grabbed my fur from the coat tree. I looked into the wide eyes of Arthur, Billy, and Ida, and then I stepped outside, struggling to catch my breath.

Sailor sat up on the porch, his tail hitting the boards in happy anticipation. I patted his head. I hoped someone would come outside and ask me back. I prayed that Olaf would say, "Let's think this over." But no one did.

Sailor padded with me down the lane until I stopped. "Go back, Sailor. Just go home." Snow fell like melting tears. "Turn around. You can't come with me."

The dog stopped, tail down, head cocked as though trying to understand what I told him. I pointed toward the house, and he turned around. "They need someone to take care of them," I said.

I wasn't certain if I spoke to him or to myself. It didn't matter. I was alone now, on my own, taking my first steps into exile.

PART TWO

Exile

TWENTY-EIGHT

Journey Outward, Journey Inward

For the love of family, I'd been sent away. At least that's how I saw it. While I waited at Schwartz's store for the afternoon train, I pulled my jacket tighter against the cold, as adrift as a snowflake tossed in the wind. The ride back to Spokane was long and lonely. A part of me wished I'd taken time to walk around the old farm before I left, to look in the barn and smell the hay, listen to the chickens cackling, scratch behind a horse's ear. Take one last cold drink at the pump. I'd never go back to that place even if it remained with the Estbys. I wasn't one of them anymore.

The train chugged along through the falling snow. I wasn't sure what to tell Olea and Louise. They'd want to hear how I heroically saved the family farm, rescued my mother from the shame of foreclosure, gave my parents a fresh start on a landscape they loved, used the money we'd rightfully earned for a good cause.

Would I tell them that my family thought their money was dirty? They'd both been so happy to help, when they hadn't done it before. My receiving the funds relieved them from a former guilt. Maybe they'd wash their hands of a family so foolish as to turn down good money. Maybe they'd wash their hands of me.

"Did the day go well?" Louise chirped when I came through the door. "Why, you're soaked. Where'd you leave your umbrella?"

"I left it at home. At the farm," I corrected. "One day I'll own a car," I said. "So I won't get so drenched."

"Well, get those wet things off and I'll heat up water for a tub." She took the fur jacket and hat, hung them in the hall while I peeled the packet of mementos out from under my blouse, where I'd kept it as dry as I could.

"I'll be fine." I shivered.

Olea came out of her room. "I thought I heard talking." She looked at her lapel watch. "Was there a train at this hour? We assumed you'd stay the weekend to finalize things."

I took a deep breath. "There was nothing to finalize. My stepfather, my mother, everyone… They…rejected the money."

"What?" Louise said.

"Indeed," Olea said. She sat down on the arm of a chair. Louise brought a fur wrap and put it around me. "They didn't want to pay off the mortgage?"

"They…didn't like the source of the funds," I said. I felt embarrassed for my family, shamed that they couldn't see the benefit of the money without the story behind it carrying more weight.

"But you earned it," Louise said. "You and your mother."

"Not in my stepfather's eyes. And Mama…she's too worn out to stand against him anymore. Saving the farm would have been a gift to her. She might have forgiven herself for not being home when Bertha and Johnny became ill. I wanted to do that for her. For them. But they…" The tears began again. "They want nothing to do with the walk or money from it. They think I've abandoned them because I came back here, because I want to continue to work for you. If you'll have me."

"Of course we'll have you." Louise put a teakettle on. "You must get out of those wet things. Go now," she urged.

I followed her advice, stripped the wet clothes, then put on a wrapper and rolled the fur around my shoulders again. Louise pointed to a chair and put slippers onto my feet when I sat. She brought me tea. My eyes pooled with tears at her care.

"The money is in my purse," I said. "Take it back."

Olea sipped her tea. "It's not our money anymore, Clara. It's yours. To do with as you see fit. You earned it. Invest it. Turn it into something your parents can be proud of."

"They'll never be proud of anything I do with it," I said. Nor would they ever be proud of me. I could see that now. Even Mama couldn't speak up for me anymore, though we'd shared a memory none of the rest of the family had. That might have been another reason why my brothers and sisters could so easily side with my stepfather against me, against their own best interests. They wanted to keep the farm too, but not if I gave the money.

"Then invest it for yourself. Make your own way," Olea said. "Prove that it isn't money but what you do with it that is the moral base of who you are. After all, God loved things. He made things every day for six days and said they were all good. It isn't having things that is the issue; it's the attitude. Make your own way; give back in your own way too."

I'd dreamed of having a career, a profession too, a life apart from working for my family. I could go on to college now. The world was open to me if I kept the money, so open that I was paralyzed to act.

"They'll feel better about it in a few days," Louise said. "Time is always a good healer. You plan to go back out there again. After they've had a little time to consider, they'll likely welcome your offer."

In that moment, Louise reminded me of my mother's once cheerful optimism about mishaps, and I knew it to be equally hopeless.

"They're not welcoming me back."

"Not want you?" Olea asked. "Surely that can't be right."

"I'm not an Estby anymore," I said.

My teeth chattered from the cold train ride back to Spokane. Or maybe from the possibilities that now lay before me with no one but myself to stand in my way.

I caught a cold. Its sneezing and sore throat kept me down for a week. I coughed and ran a fever and heard Louise say the word *diphtheria* followed by Olea's reassuring scoff. But as Mama had once tended me through food poisoning and my sprained ankle, so these two women looked after me, reassuring me that I'd be better soon with Louise's concoctions, prepared with what the doctor recommended.

Whatever it was the doctor had ordered to stop my cough put me to dreamless sleep, so I didn't feel up to taking the train back to Mica Creek on the day of the auction. Going would have been self-punishment. Even Louise didn't suggest it again after that first night.

I didn't know what I did want to do once I finished my classes at Blair College in a month, except for one thing.

"I've decided to change my name officially to Clara Ann Doré," I told Olea one morning close to my graduation.

"Doré? How odd. That's Franklin's name," Olea noted. "Our agent."

"I remember you told me that. I'm choosing it because one thing I did learn when I visited my family was who my father was. John Doré. Apparently his mother's name was Clara, and Mama named me for her."

"Indeed," Olea said.

"Maybe your mother wanted to maintain connection to him and chose his mother's name to honor him," Louise said. She put milk in a bowl for Lucy, who had now become an inside cat all the time, not just during cold winter nights.

I wondered if Mama might have named me as an act of defiance, the only action left to her with everyone else making the decisions that defined her life—leaving Michigan and arriving in Yellow Medicine, Minnesota, where no one knew her secret shame.

No one defined my life now.

"There's little use to speculate," Olea said.

"No, I suppose not," Louise said.

"Will I have to find a lawyer to change my name?"

"Oh, goodness no," Louise said. "I changed my name back in 1897 in New York. You go to the courthouse and fill out forms and stand before a judge. Like when you get married. I used to be Gulbrandson instead of Gubner. Gubner is so much easier to spell."

"You changed it because of the spelling?" I asked.

"As good a reason as any."

"We can get that started for you," Olea said. "I'll pick up forms when I'm at the courthouse later this week. So you're to be Clara Doré. And what will Clara Doré be doing with her time, once she's well, of course?"

"Do I still have a job?" I asked.

"Of course," they both said in unison.

"Then for now, I'll put the money in the bank."

"A wise choice," Olea said. "In the long run, I wouldn't invest in anything that doesn't stir your passions."

"Passions?" I said. What did passion have to do with money?

"Well, yes. Otherwise the work involved becomes a drudgery, something you're required to do each day to pay the bills. Meeting obligations is required, of course, but you don't want it to consume you. Our fur business has had good years and bad, but we've always loved the fashion part, the shows where new items are modeled, seeing happy looks on people's faces when they don the those coats. Passion allows you to see through the mists of disappointment or failures. Earn a little less but have work you enjoy. That's my motto. Money isn't the most fulfilling thing one can work for, Clara."

"Having money isn't the most fulfilling thing at all," Louise said. "But you'll discover that in time, now that you have it."

I let a few weeks pass before making a trip to the farm where Olaf worked. I was taking a chance, I knew. I didn't want to put Olaf in a difficult position, but I thought he might understand why I'd chosen to stay and work for the women rather than move with the family to Aunt Hannah's in Spokane. Maybe he'd understand that I owed the women, for putting me through school. He might accept the money and go to school himself. That was my hope when I approached him as he and several other men walked from the field toward the house. I'd arrived at lunchtime.

Olaf stopped short, frowned when he recognized me, and I wondered if he'd turn back. Could he really be displeased to see me? He didn't reach to hug me, but then, it was a public place. He soon smiled, enough encouragement. I stepped forward.

His fellow workers teased him when I approached, and they pretended not to believe him when he said, "She's my sister."

"Introduce me then," a large blond bloke of a man said.

Olaf hesitated, then said, "Clara Estby. Meet Erik Elstad. My boss's son."

"Miss Estby," he said. "Pleased to meet you." He had a grin that he knew charmed.

"Likewise," I curtsied, gave him a cool nod before turning to Olaf. "Is there somewhere we can talk?"

He took my elbow and we headed toward the haystacks, leaving Erik Elstad shouting, "You'll be back."

"He's pretty taken with himself," I said.

"And he's taken a fair number of girls too," Olaf said.

"So that's why you didn't want to introduce us."

"He sees women as conquests," he said. "You don't need to be one. You have to be careful, Clara. Men can be such dolts. I have my lunch," he said. "Care to share it?"

I let his words sink in. "I brought an apple along, thanks."

He swept an area with his foot so we could sit in the shade of the haystack. We sat side by side and leaned against it, the scratchy hay barely poking at my short jacket. I didn't remove my hat, knowing the humidity would have flattened my hair into a drenched-cat look.

"Was the foreclosure awful?" I said.

He shrugged. "The auction was worse. But it's done now, all over. Someone else bought the farm for a pittance."

"How's Mama?" I asked.

He shrugged. "She pretty much lets Aunt Hannah and Ida tell her what to do. I hope when Papa builds the house he wants and she gets her own home again that she'll be better."

"Papa is going to build a house?"

"He got a carpenter's job and he's doing well. I think they're all doing better without the weight of that farm, though I'd never say that in front of them."

"No," I agreed.

"Ida's got a job as a domestic. Arthur's looking for carpentry work too. With what I send them added to their income, they'll be able to build soon enough and move out of Aunt Hannah's house. How are you doing?"

"Good. I'm doing good," I said. I didn't tell him of the nights I cried myself to sleep feeling separate and alone. "Olaf, would you go to school if I paid your way?"

He looked startled. "Pay my way? Why don't you go yourself?"

"I finished my coursework at Blair and I have a job. The bookkeeping I do for the women is satisfying. I don't think having a degree would help me find a better job than the one I have." I pulled a strand of grass hay from the stack and chewed on it. "They wouldn't take the money back," I said. "I'm to invest it. And I want to invest in you."

Olaf stared off toward the fields, and the laughter of the other workers rose up now and then. He drank cold coffee from a jar, then set it next to him.

"I need to send money to Mama and Papa," he said. "They count on it."

"I could send it to you for them. They wouldn't even have to know it came from me."

"Clara…"

"Or that you were even in school. You could go to the university and—"

"If they ever found out, they wouldn't talk to me," he said. "I don't think I could… You're stronger than I am, Clara. Stronger than any of us. You'll do all right out there on your own, but me…"

"You work away from home now. You're hardly ever there. The university would give you a chance to do what you've always wanted to do—have a profession, not be tied to the seasons."

"There's nothing wrong with the seasons, Clara."

"Oh, I know that. I love the land as much as you do. I only meant you'd have a chance to operate a farm on your own if you wanted. I could even buy a ranch for you," I said. I hadn't thought of it before, but why not?

"I like working for other people, helping Mama and Papa when I can. Even if I marry one day, I can't see myself holding up under the pressure of being my own boss. I've seen what Mama and Papa went through. I'd rent."

His view was yet another indication of how different I really was from the Estby family.

"You have money now, Clara. Do something good with it."

"I'm trying to, but you won't take it."

He grinned. "Then do something you never imagined you'd be able to do."

"Help you. Help my family. That's all I ever wanted, and look where it's gotten me."

A terrible sadness crossed his face, and I knew he couldn't agree to anything I offered. The money was tainted by its history, by the consequences he'd endure if he accepted anything from his ostracized sister.

"I'm a coward, Clara. If I took the risk of having my own farm and failed, I'd have lost your money, and for what?"

"But what's the point of having a dream if you don't take a chance to accomplish it?"

He shrugged. "They'd never forgive me if they found out I let you talk me into something."

"I'm not trying to talk you into anything." I bristled. I didn't want to be angry with my brother, but I could feel the palms of my hands grow wet, heard my heart thumping louder in my chest. "I'm offering you a chance." Didn't he have an ounce of Mama's fighting blood in him—the blood that made her take a chance even though we failed in the end?

"I can't take it," he said. "It's too big a risk."

He'd chosen too.

I stood, brushed off my skirt, picked up my reticule, and wrapped the string around my wrist. I adjusted my hat.

"Maybe I can still write to you," I said. "Or will that be too risky?"

"Clara. Of course, write. Send it here. I'll let you know if I leave and take another job."

"I wouldn't want to get you in trouble with Mama and Papa," I said.

His eyes had the sad look of Sailor when I'd sent him home, wouldn't let him follow me.

"At least you talk to me," I said.

"Always," he said. "I always will."

I was connected to one member of my family. His would have to be the thread I hung on to.

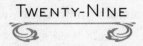
Exploration

I walked in a daze through the Blair College graduation ceremony, looked into the crowd for a familiar Estby face. None appeared. Olea and Louise applauded when I accepted my certificate, and we lunched at a nice restaurant in Spokane. The rest of the summer, I worked for the women, tried not to think of how alone I felt. Olaf was right about one thing: I wasn't doing anything differently than what I'd done before, even though I now had resources. Squashed dreams came in my size too. Was I as afraid to fail as Olaf was? Or worse, maybe I was in love with the idea of money, and now that I had some, I just wanted to keep it.

In September Olea announced: "You've moped around enough. We're going to make a trip."

"I love traveling," Louise said. She actually clapped her hands.

"There's nothing that requires our presence in Spokane, is there, Louise?"

"Where are we off to?" Louise asked.

"We've hardly been anywhere in Washington State," Olea said. "It's time we got more acquainted with where we live."

"You'll come along, Clara," Olea directed.

I could have resisted, agreed to remain behind, but for what? Hoping my family would contact me? Just to say that I'd decided on my own? "Why not?" I said. "We're a...team." I hesitated to use the word *family*. Our relationship was still very much that of employer and employee. Traveling with them might answer my daily question of what I should do with my life. I was, after all, Clara Doré trying to hear the words of Isaiah: "This is the way, walk ye in it."

We made preparations, closed up the house, hired a local man to rake the leaves. He'd build a fire to warm the house if it turned cold during the weeks we'd be gone. He'd also forward our mail to Seattle, where Olea said we'd spend a few weeks in that "marvelous city."

I packed my bank-books and a little cash, stuffing them into a waist purse I'd made so any cash I carried would be on my person. The belt felt tight but not restrictive. I wasn't going to risk a robbery again. My stomach knotted when I thought of how the money I had now would have helped us back then, and I wondered about Olea and Louise's part in all that. We'd have been home, and maybe Bertha and Johnny... No. If I thought of that, I'd have to reconsider my stepfather's words that the funds I had were dirty. Money was just money.

"Have you got Lucy?" Louise called out as the cab came to pick us up.

"In her basket," I shouted. "On my arm. Hurry along or we'll miss the train." Having the cat on this trip wasn't my idea, but I accommodated.

Louise waddled out, one hand holding her hat, the other my curling iron. "You forgot to pack this," she said, breathless. "It was still on the stove."

"Clara wouldn't want to be without that," Olea said. "She can't keep her hat on the entire trip."

"That I can't," I said.

They knew me well. I guess in time we reveal our most intimate selves even to assumed family members, whether we realize it or not.

We headed west, the train rumbling through little towns with names like Reardan and Wilbur, wheat-farming communities. I had time to think. The one thing I knew for sure is that I didn't want to undertake an investment scheme without safeguards in place. I wouldn't repeat my mother's mistake in not renegotiating the terms when things went sour with my ankle, then continuing to take side trips that delayed us further. Maybe she really did believe we could make it in time; maybe she trusted that, like Jonah and the whale, all things were possible.

What I needed to do was gather sound information and then honestly assess it and my own capabilities. I would look at the world through the eyes of an investor, not a flighty woman caught up in emotional demands of rescuing a farm. I wouldn't let that kind of emotion shade my thinking.

At Coulee City, a town about fifty miles west of Spokane, we spent the night at the Grand Hotel. In the morning, we hired a cab to visit the local attractions. The landscape was unlike any I'd ever seen, with high bare ridges. Beyond these were pools of water, shiny lakes really, reflecting white clouds in their mirrored surfaces. A local soul told us the lakes and landscape were the result of a huge prehistoric flood that gouged out this wide coulee. Olea scoffed at that and said there was no evidence of such an event. I didn't really care. I found the landscape exotic.

A single road worked its way east and west across the coulee, which ran from the Canadian provinces almost to Oregon. Through it, cattle were driven to high country pastures in the summer, then returned to winter in the wide, flat plain that looked to me like a riverbed. The railroad followed the same opening. Looking over the side of the high ridges reminded me of the Dale Creek trestle, though this canyon was much wider and deeper. I still had the dizzy feeling as I looked down.

"Isn't this an amazing sight?" Louise said.

"Such ruggedness only a few hours from the rolling Palouse Hills. You wouldn't even think they were in the same country, let alone the same state," I said.

I liked the dry heat of this coulee and thought the land would be rich and fertile with enough rainfall each year. It felt like a good place to me, but there weren't many people here, and most who were served the local ranchers. What was there to invest in?

The central part of the state cast a vast view of things. Fewer wooded areas flew past the train windows, and on the slow uphill grades, we watched vistas of deer and even elk herds disappear down deep ravines that bled into plateaus. Here, enterprising pioneers planted orchards. Farming. That's what people did in Washington State from east to west. It was likely my best bet.

I wanted to treat this trip as strictly business, but I found myself watching Olea and Louise as we traveled. Both seemed to enjoy meeting new people. Louise especially began conversations with strangers no matter where we were. I could have traveled the entire state without meeting anyone, my nose in a book or daydreaming through the windows or watching people from the corners of my eyes without presenting myself as interested in their doings. Louise, however, had other plans. It seemed she'd talk with any young man not attached to a female and then lead him to me for an introduction.

"I'll find my own fellow," I told her as we prepared for bed one night in our sleeping car. The train crawled slowly through the mountains, and the sway of it had calmed so I could brush my teeth without hanging on to the door to steady myself.

"I know that," Louise said. "But you're so shy. They have no way of knowing if you're interested."

"Because I'm not," I said.

"I can't understand why. You're what, twenty-four years old?"

"I'll be twenty-five," I corrected.

"The perfect age for marriage."

"Marriage is not an investment that's of interest to me," I said. Relationships couldn't be researched, checked for possible flaws and errors, and assessed for probable risk—all requirements of good investments if my Blair Business College professors were to be believed.

"Love can't be managed like a bank account, Clara," she told me.

"How else does it earn interest?" I said.

She looked at me, then smiled. "You're teasing me. But I'll tell you how love earns interest: two people have to make a deposit, pay attention, make adjustments over time. Then they see a return on what they've invested, a return that sustains them as they grow older. It might be closer to finance than you realize."

"You never married," I said.

"Not because I didn't want to," Louise said.

"Why not find another love?"

She looked thoughtful as she sat on the lower bunk, her head bent low. "If that door appeared, I'd open it. But I've been blessed with a great friendship in Olea…and now you. My Ladies Aid Society gives me reasons to knit baby booties for young mothers and hear about their children's lives and even help a little when I can. It's a full life, Clara. By God's grace that's been enough."

"Maybe it's enough for me too," I said, "being with the two of you, having work."

"No. There's an emptiness in you," she said. She wagged her finger at me. "I can see it in the way you hold back."

She was right, and her knowing me like that frightened me, until I realized she also didn't know what might fill me up. Until I knew, she'd keep trying by plying me with special cakes and cookies and introducing me to young men. I guess that was love too.

In view of Mount Rainier with its majestic white cap, we chugged into Seattle. The town bustled with its ferries, which were needed to get from here to there across saltwater sounds to freshwater lakes. It was a town anxious to become a city no longer defined only by timber but by other kinds of commerce, including ship building, a railroad terminus, fishing fleets, and service to the Klondike gold fields. "Maybe I could stake a prospector," I said as we watched a mule string board a boat headed north. We ate a leisurely lunch near a busy wharf on the harbor.

"That would be a low-risk investment," Olea mocked.

"But a romantic one," Louise added. "Nearly everyone in the gold fields are men. Well, except for...entertainers."

"I wouldn't go there myself," I said. "I'd have my own agent, like you have Franklin Doré."

"It's too bad we're here in the fall," Olea sighed. "The largest fur auction on the West Coast is held here in February. Seattle Fur Exchange. We don't usually buy through them, with our business primarily in the East. Franklin attends the auctions in Canada. But it would be fun to see how they operate here, what sorts of pelts predominate. I know they charge a four percent commission on lots of over a thousand dollars. Five percent on smaller lots."

"You've done well in the business," I commented.

"We've had our ups and downs, as you know," Olea agreed.

"But it isn't a business with much certainty," I said. "It's hard to know which pelts will be available, and fashion changes. You've told me yourself: people may not want mink one year; they want raccoon instead. Seems like a lot of unpredictability."

"We could do what the Finns are doing," Olea said. "They're ranching fur, have been since the nineties."

"Ranching?" I couldn't imagine.

"Well, it's a long shot, I'm sure; you know those Finns. But they're trying to breed silver foxes on their ranches and farms. That way they can control nutrition and create the best quality pelts."

"We could come back in February," Louise said, still with Olea's earlier comment about missing the auction.

"Yes, we could do that," Olea told her. "I suspect February here would be much milder than in Minnesota."

"Who would want to spend the winter in Minnesota?" I said. "I spent a fair number of them there when I was little, and I still remember the cold." I wiped my face with the linen napkin. The oyster soup was delicious. I hadn't had a bowl for years. It was usually a dish my aunt Hannah made for New Year's Eve.

"Well, I would," Olea said. "My sister lives in St. Paul, and while we're out and about with everything arranged at home, it's a good time to be with them. She's invited us all for the winter."

I wasn't tired of the travel, but neither was I looking forward to spending a winter in St. Paul. I would have said as much to Olea, but after all, I worked for them. They set the schedule. Still, I didn't like the idea of spending months with total strangers or my reticence in speaking up.

"Perhaps it would be best if I returned to Spokane," I said, building up my courage. "Let the two of you winter with family, where you'll be comfortable and can do as you please without my interruption. I can find my own place if you'd like." I pulled on my gloves and stood.

"Oh, Clara, don't pout," Olea said. She raised her binoculars to her eyes and pointed them toward a distant bird flying above the harbor. "Everything doesn't have to always go your way, does it? You can afford to be a little more accommodating."

"I wasn't proposing that things had to go my way," I said. "I…" I didn't confront people well, didn't have words to express how I felt. I rarely heard anyone in our family express disagreement with words that didn't hurt. Upset was often a stony silence, and I did feel upset by what she'd said.

"Sit down." Olea lowered the binoculars. "My sister included you when I told her we'd be traveling with our assistant. I wrote even before we left."

I sank onto the chair, brushed lint from my linen skirt.

Olea patted my gloved hand. "A little give-and-take never hurt anyone," she said, "and it promises that each of us can have a little, if not all of what we'd like. I think that's what life is all about."

I was about to find out.

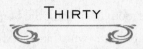
Looking for Answers

FEBRUARY 1902

Priscilla Bakke and her husband, Inger, had two children ages thirteen and fifteen, and they all lived in a large house in St. Paul. Servants were housed on the top floor, bedrooms on the second, and a large living room, parlor, and dining room on the first floor. The kitchen was in the basement. I was given my own room in the family wing rather than in the guest quarters. Inger was a banker, and I eavesdropped shamelessly as he and Olea discussed finance, taxes, and law.

Peder, the son, was treated like royalty, it seemed to me. He went ice-skating with his friends, set his own bedtime, ate what he wanted, and was rude to the serving staff, at least in my opinion.

Clarissa had more restrictions. She was the same age as Bertha had been when she died (and who had already been working as a servant for two years). Clarissa at least made her own bed. Peder did not.

I watched as Olea made suggestions to her niece that the child accepted, though the very same words spoken by her mother resulted in a haughty exit from the room. Her words did border on the edge of sass. She was the child in this family who, like me, didn't fit. I wondered if all families had one.

"You're like your grandmother," her mother told Clarissa when she crossed her arms and dropped onto the divan after being told, no, she could not go to the hayride with her friends because boys would be there. We women all sat in the living room, Louise and our hostess doing needlework, Hardanger lace like my mother's. Olea turned the pages of a colored bird book while I read Kipling's novel *Kim* about an East Indian orphan, my mind more tuned in to what these family members were saying than to anything in my book.

"Aunt Olea, you went on hayrides, didn't you? Tell Mama it's all right."

"I did," Olea said. "But my parents went with me. Chaperoned the ride."

"We could do that," Priscilla offered. She smiled at her daughter. "Would you like that, dear?"

"No. I wouldn't," Clarissa said and stomped out.

"Our parents never chaperoned a hayride," Priscilla told Olea. "You made that up."

"Maybe not one of yours, but they did mine."

"Mama was much stricter with me," Priscilla said. "I never even got to go on such events. You, she indulged."

"Every child suffers differently," Olea said. Her sister scoffed and returned to her needlework.

Through that winter, I spent long hours in my room reading the financial section of the *Minneapolis Tribune* and novels while thinking of what I wanted to do now. I was letting the women lead me, and I could feel their will sucking me under as if I were boots in a bog.

"So," Inger said to me one evening over dinner, "Olea tells me you're interested in investing in an up-and-coming industry. Do you have one in mind?"

I shook my head. "I've considered a number of things."

"I tell her she should find a suitable husband, invest in that," Louise told him.

"Well, you are of an age," he said, too polite to ask for specifics. "What do your parents do?"

"My stepfather felled trees in Michigan, then came here to Minnesota, near Canby, where they farmed before moving to Spokane. Now he's a carpenter."

"Ah, the trades," he said as though he'd eaten a pickle. "The bank is always the safest place to invest," he said.

"Spoken like a true banker," his wife chided.

"They pay so little interest," I said.

He grunted. "What sort of return are you expecting?"

"I want to be able to provide for myself. Perhaps make enough to assist my family, send my younger brothers and sisters on to school." I had only recently come to that thought, but in the face of Olaf's refusal to go, it seemed a wise one. Mama had insisted we all learn English as children, had even prohibited us from speaking Norwegian so my stepfather would learn English more quickly once we moved to Spokane. If I offered her money for Arthur and Billy and Lillian for schooling, would she refuse it because it came from me?

"Have you considered importing European furniture?" Priscilla asked.

Again her husband grunted. "It can be quite a lucrative business if the cost of furnishing this house is any indication."

"You'd get to travel," Louise piped up.

"Not a very tried-and-true business though," Inger said. "Too many unknowns. I'd suggest railroad shares. Transportation will grow mightily in the years ahead. Thank you, Else," he told the servant girl, who replaced his soup bowl with a clean plate and set the platter of meat in front of him. "Timber is still huge. And of course wheat. The Cargill Brothers built one of the world's largest grain-storage facilities right here in Minneapolis ten years ago, and the business has done nothing but grow. The hold stores grain from the Dakotas, Minnesota, Wisconsin, Iowa. I suspect the plains states will ship here as well if the cooperatives will stay out of it. Railroads are attached to that industry. Great potential."

"What have you invested in?" I asked.

He sat a little straighter. Whether flattered or offended, I couldn't tell. He cleared his throat. "I'm diversified," he said. He took a bite of beef. He chewed. "But coal is my main interest. I expect the demand to grow, and there's an unlimited supply. I'm certain there are mines in your region of the country, assuming you want to return there, of course. I hear you're headed to New York next? Be sure to visit the investment houses there," he said. "They'll have quite a number of options for you."

"New York?" I said. Olea combed her long blond hair with highlights of gray, the braids making kinky waves that flashed like gold in the gaslights of her room. I stood behind her, watching in the mirror. We wore wrappers, waiting to finish our undressing and put on nightclothes after the light was out. She had perfect skin, pale as milk, the spoils of a life of leisure.

"We're halfway to New York," she said. "It would be an opportunity for you to see the city in a different light than when you were there last. Louise and I can check on our interests, and we need to confer with Franklin as well."

"But we've already been gone nearly six months."

She shrugged. "What would you have done if you'd been in Spokane all this time?"

I'd have been Olea and Louise's secretary, which I continued to be; I'd have worried about encountering my family, half hoping I'd see them, half afraid I might not. I might have visited with Olaf again.

"I suppose I'd have spent time at the library or talked with my professors about what they thought would be a good investment for a young woman. Maybe I'd have gotten to know my banker better."

"So come with us to New York. See how the fur fashion industry really works. Personally, I think it has a better future than coal or railroads. People have to dress, and they have to stay warm all around the world, and fur provides for that. Designs change, so there's natural challenge but also the excitement of new seasons with young designers. As Louise would say, fur fashion is much more romantic than hard coal. Deal with soft, beautiful pelts, coats and muffs. There's your investment."

These women supported themselves well with fur and could afford to pay me and their agent, and live a good yet simple life.

"All right," I said. "Let's head to New York." And then I decided to exert a little independence. "But we'll make a side trip first to Michigan."

"Whatever for?"

"It's where my father's from. I want to see if I can find him."

THIRTY-ONE

Namesake

I began my investigation the afternoon I arrived in Manistee, Michigan, a small city on the state's western coast. I presented myself at the newspaper office as a woman of means researching a business connection rather than anything personal.

"What're you looking for? Maybe I can help," the editor said as he chewed on an unlit cigar.

"I'd like information about the Doré Lumber Company." I'd seen the sign with the announcement "position available" when I came into the town.

"Looking for work, are you?"

"To invest," I said. He smiled and shook his head as though such a thing would be impossible for a woman.

"Where are you from?" He cocked his head in curiosity.

"Spokane, Washington," I told him.

"Oh, well, that's big timber country. It'll be years before we harvest the replant here. It's been over thirty years since the big fire. Stick with the West," he said. "That's my advice. Don't waste your money here."

"I'll keep that in mind," I said, "though I suspect your local boosters wouldn't like to hear you say it." I turned to the newspaper piles he'd laid out for me, removing my white gloves so as not to rub the ink onto their tips.

I left two hours later with tired eyes, an address, and an obituary. The next morning, I'd make my move.

I was alone in the hotel in Manistee. The curling iron didn't sizzle. Not hot enough. Each time I waited for it to heat on the kitchen Monarch or over the small burners in the marbled train stations of the larger cities we'd traveled to, I thought of my mother. I recalled how she heated a curling iron in Idaho or Nebraska and even Pennsylvania, heated it over the lantern, then lifted a width of hair no wider than Lillian's palm and rolled the strands around the curling rod. She was ever careful not to burn my scalp, holding the iron and hair until she could feel the heat against her palm. Then she'd ease the strands free.

Once in Minneapolis, when Louise touched her fingers gently to my scalp, she said, "Oh, honey, you have the softest locks, like rabbit down." She kissed my temple as though I were a child, as my mother had, the memory so vivid that my eyes watered. Later that same day, Louise introduced me to hairpieces that gave lift and marked the styles of 1902. Extensions, she called them, though I think they had a more formal name. Imagine, wearing hair someone else grew then sold! But I still had to curl my own hair in order to wrap it into the extensions and look civilized. A daughter ought to look her best when meeting her father for the first time.

Through the Ramsdell Hotel window, I watched as the eastern sun slanted against the shingled roof of the North Pierhead Lighthouse on the Manistee River. If Olea and Louise had come with me, they'd have said the hotel could have been transported from London, with its carved stonework and Victorian design.

I made up the bed and imagined my mother working in this hotel before she went to work for the Doré family. I didn't know if she ever had, but it was possible. I could see her mending torn sheets or adding lace to the edges with her fine stitching skills, maybe laughing with other domestics, speaking Norwegian when they were alone and good English when addressing the American guests coming to broker lumber in this town. My mother was fifteen. What passion must have roiled inside her and how frightened she must have been to discover herself with child. Her own mother would have been devastated, having prepared for her a more sophisticated life only to have shame scrape away the luster of a hopeful future.

What might my mother's life have been like if she had not allowed this man to take advantage of her? Was she letting Ole take advantage of her now, silencing her?

For a moment I thought my search was foolish, not well thought out, with more potentially negative outcomes than positive ones. John Doré might have moved, left the name of his company behind. He might refuse to see me. It was a fluke I'd even learned his name, spoken in anger. And yet I wanted to see where I'd come from, to imagine what he might have given me that made me so different from my brothers and sisters, made me more Doré than Estby.

I finished with the curling iron, dressed, then slipped out of the suite, my gloved hand running smoothly over the glass doorknob. I walked down toward the shoreline where the Manistee River ran into the lake. The lighthouse sat on the north side of the river, and as I stood on the opposite shore, I thought of my mother waiting for me across the

Dale Creek trestle. I always seemed to be on the opposite shore waiting for someone to call me to them. I listened for an inner voice, heard nothing, so moved forward on my own.

John Doré's office nestled among trees, which struck me as fitting. Only one small window opened toward the street. Modest and quiet. I smoothed my skirt, pulled at threads, adjusted the collar of my linen jacket. For this occasion I'd worn my finest suit trimmed with female mink—light and soft pelts perfect for a spring morning in Michigan. Dignified, that's the impression I wanted to leave with this man. Dignified and sufficient unto myself. Well, almost all of myself. I wore those hair extensions.

I stood for a time as the cab pulled away. I'd rehearsed various phrases. "I'm your daughter." Much too direct, and yet that's the line that came to my head first, followed by, "Why did you abandon my mother?" But I also wanted to see what my mother might have seen in him. Was he a vain man and she'd overlooked it? Was he a charlatan who fooled her into thinking that he loved her? Was he even aware of her circumstance? Would he deny any involvement at all? My throat felt sore.

I planned to ask about the timber holdings, make it sound like I was interested in investing in a business rather than in history that could transform my future.

I opened a door made of clear cedar, not a knothole in sight.

"May I help you?" A young woman's voice came from behind a high desk. When she stood, I could see her head and bodice, but the wide plank counter still dwarfed her.

"I called earlier, to make an appointment to speak with Mr. John Doré," I said.

She looked at her appointment book. "Gubner. I have it written here. You called for a Mr. Gubner."

I'd borrowed Louise's name, thinking not to put Mr. Doré off by seeing the name Clara Doré.

"I must not have been clear," I said. "The appointment is for me."

"Oh well." She looked over her glasses at me. "Mr. Doré will be back shortly. He's having a meeting with the shingle-weavers' union." She gazed at me, her brow furrowed in puzzlement. "Do I know you?"

"No," I said. "I'm from Spokane, Washington."

"Spokane. Well, you look familiar. Must have one of those faces like a rubber ball, shaping as it goes."

"I guess I must," I said.

"I don't envy you your meeting time." She fussed with papers on her desk. "I doubt Mr. Doré will be in a good mood when he returns, just so you know. He finds the union taxing. You might want to come back another day so you won't have double stitches to unknot in him. He doesn't often meet with females."

"I'm only in town for a short time," I said taking a seat.

"These unions are a stick in Mr. Doré's eye."

I knew the shingle-weavers' union was one of the oldest in the country. My mother had talked of it as we walked the rails. Boys and girls worked side by side in the lumber mills, sorting the shingles as they came from the sawyer, bundling the roofing material so the roofers could lift them easily and place them wide end over narrow end as they worked to keep rainwater from seeping through roofs. Children worked twelve-and-a-half hours a day, until the union changed this in Muskegon in 1886.

Would my stepfather have been in a union here? Unions were never happily accepted by management, or so my mother reminded me as she cheered on William Jennings Bryan. John Doré would have likely voted with McKinley. If I could have voted, so would I, though for different reasons. I liked the unions that had rescued us when my father was injured.

The woman behind the wide counter offered me tea, which I took. I blew on it to cool it, my breath lifting the feather in my hat, the ends of the fur. My hands shook. I ought to have rehearsed more, arrived with a better sense of what I wanted. Otherwise, he'd control the interview. Maybe his secretary was right and I ought to come back later.

I stood. "I think maybe—"

A man I knew was my father opened the door. He rushed through, shouting an order at his secretary as he passed by me. My heart pounded like a woodpecker marking its territory on a tree. I was meeting him. A landowner, a corporate giant, my father.

"Your appointment, Mr. Doré," his secretary said, partially standing. "Mrs. Gubner."

"What?" He turned, glared.

He stood tall, over six feet. *Where I get my height from.* He had brown hair, blue eyes. His eyebrows, like mine, arched gracefully over the iris and narrowed toward his temple. His wide face—again like mine—wore a look of annoyance. His hair lay limp against his head. He pursed his full lips.

"Is your husband with you?" He looked beyond me.

"There is no Mr. Gubner," I said.

He frowned. "Well, let's get this over with. I'm a busy man."

I followed him into his office while his secretary pulled the door closed behind me whispering, "Good luck."

He took his place behind an oak desk, wider than the Mississippi. Paintings of landscapes and seascapes hung on the walls. His bookshelves were piled so full he'd begun placing tomes, spines out, in stacks in front of the shelved titles. Engineering books. One on architecture.

The Red Badge of Courage, a novel. A Tiffany lamp with stained glass graced the desk to his side.

"Are the paintings yours?" I asked.

He looked where I stood before a painting, surprised at my interest. "That one of the lighthouse. That's mine."

"It's very nice. It's good you sign them."

"Yes, well, I have so little time, Mrs.—"

"Do you know a Franklin Doré?" I asked as I faced him.

"Franklin Doré? No. Should I?"

"Not necessarily. I thought that with the name—"

"There are lots of Dorés around," he said. "As common as flies. But there's no Franklin in my family line that I'm aware of. Now, what can I do for you, Mrs. Gubner?" He motioned for me to sit.

"Actually, my name isn't Mrs. Gubner. It's Doré. Clara Doré." Blood throbbed at my temples. I hadn't asked him about his timber holdings, hadn't eased into this conversation at all.

"My mother's name," he said. "She passed on some years ago. But you said your name was—"

"And your son as well," I said. "He's passed too. I'm sorry for your loss. I read of it in the paper."

He squinted his eyes. "I thought you said your name was Gubner. Now you say it's Doré? Clara Doré?"

"My people came from here, well, after arriving from Norway," I said. "My grandparents were the Bings." I looked for recognition on his face, some reaction. "They lived here in '76, until moving to Yellow Medicine, Minnesota. My mother is Helga Bing."

A slight narrowing of his eyes was the only change in his facial expression. He would have talked with my grandfather and grandmother, wouldn't he? Maybe my mother never told him about me. Maybe her parents worked out the agreement to move to Yellow Medicine after I was born without ever giving him the chance to do right by my mother. Or perhaps his own parents intervened on his behalf. He looked to be about my mother's age. No, older. He would have been old enough to be responsible, to do the right thing. Would his family have offered her money? Would they have taken it? *Dirty money.* Did Ole take such funds?

His face paled. "Why have you used false pretenses to see me?" he said. His arms crossed over his chest. "Using the name of my deceased mother." The side of his lip quivered.

"I didn't think you'd see me if I used my real name, which *is* Clara Doré. Helga Bing isn't familiar?" I asked. "She might have gone by Helga Hauge. Bing was her stepfather's name. She was pretty, slender, a narrow face, strong hands. A woman of high spirit." My heart pounded like a farrier firming up a horseshoe nail, a hard yet steady throb. "What about Estby?" I asked. "Ole Estby. Surely that name is familiar. He rescued you."

"Rescued me? Hundreds of people work for me. What's this about?" He set his jaw and his face regained color. It turned red. "What do you want?"

I wasn't sure where my clipped words were coming from. My stomach swirled. I took a deep breath. I suppose it wasn't fair to spring this on him, but I'd committed to it now. "Ole Estby is my stepfather. He married my mother when she was quite young. My mother was fifteen. She was…with child."

"What's this got to do with me?"

"I'm Clara Doré," I repeated. "She named me for your mother."

He stared at me as though seeing me for the first time. "What did you say your mother's name was?"

"Helga," I said.

He sank into his high-back chair, his hands on the desk, knuckles white. "My family employed many domestics, you must understand."

"This domestic, you...bedded," I said. "And I'm the result."

I could tell by the look on his face that he accepted the possibility of it, but he said, "You've read of my son's death and you've come to what, make a claim on my family? You have no claim on Doré Lumber, no claim on me. I'll have the sheriff arrest you for...extortion."

"There is nothing you have that I want except your time," I said. "And you've already given that. I only wanted to meet the man who changed my mother's life and to see what I might have carried in my blood from him."

"I think you'd better go."

He moved around to the side of the desk, his hands rubbing at his chin. Being flummoxed must have been new for him.

I stood. Surely my mother was a better judge of character than to believe whatever this man might have promised her. Maybe we are all of us gullible at times. I would have to guard against it. "You don't remember her at all? Were there so many?"

A flicker of pain moved across his face.

I wanted my mother to be distinctive to this man, to feel there'd been something more than opportunity that passed between them, giving me my life.

"I really have nothing to tell you." His words came out softer, and he looked at me with greater intensity, as though seeing himself mirrored in my face or frame. "I'm sorry for any confusion you may have about your parentage," he added. "There are many Dorés, as I mentioned before."

"Only one in Manistee, Michigan, however," I said.

"I'll see you out," he said. At the door I hesitated, wanting to look once more straight into his eyes to see what I could see of myself reflected there, to imagine what my mother might have seen that drew her to him. He didn't look angry now, more preoccupied, as though remembering.

He said to his secretary, "Give her one of our...brochures. Have her leave her card. I'm sorry," he said. "I never..." The last thing I saw was the confused eyes of his secretary and the back of my father as he closed his office door in my face.

How would he have finished that sentence? I never knew of her plight? I never meant to hurt her? I never would have abandoned her had I known? Or maybe, I never wish to hear from you again.

THIRTY-TWO

Hunger

Let's stay here a few days. Weeks even," Louise said when I arrived back in Ludington, where I'd left the two of them while I investigated. *Investigated*. What had I gained? Nothing. All I'd done was waste my time and the time of the women with me as well.

"It's a lovely place," Louise insisted. "Perfect climate with lake breezes. Nice hotels—"

"It's time to move on," Olea said.

We ate supper in the hotel dining room in Ludington. They didn't pry, but I eventually told them what had happened. "I even found where my mother once lived," I said. The house was run-down now, but once it would have been considered modest with its wide porch sweeping around the front. An orchard groaned for attention in the back. It was a nicer place than what I remembered in Yellow Medicine. They'd left it all. Sacrifice. That's what family was about, doing what must be done despite the agony.

Tears welled up in my eyes. "It's...the time. Meeting him... It's been more difficult than I thought it would be."

"We don't always get what we're after," Olea said, not unkindly.

"I'm not at all sure I knew what I wanted."

"That's a problem too. If you don't know, then all those around you who do will likely get their hungers met, and you'll find yourself serving them while you starve. You'll be on your deathbed wondering where the time went and why you never got to Europe as you'd always planned or never spent an entire afternoon at the aquarium lazily watching fish."

It sounded like experience talking.

"I hoped he'd open his arms to you and say how much he longed to have done the right thing all those years ago and then sweep you into his chest." Louise wrapped her arms around herself and sighed. "I hoped he'd ask about your mother and say he would leave his entire estate to you, his only daughter."

"You read too many of those dime novels," Olea told her, patting her shoulder. "Family inheritance is never so easily given."

"I like your version of our meeting," I told Louise. "But Olea's right. It is pure fantasy." I looked at Olea. "Meeting him wasn't about an inheritance. I wanted to know…who I belonged to."

"Why, you belong to God, Clara, no matter where you set your feet," Louise told me.

"Will you keep his name?" Olea asked. She added extra sugar to her tea, as was her way. "Now that you've met him?"

"I always wondered why you kept the Stone name," Louise said to Olea.

"That's none of your affair," she said.

Louise dropped her eyes. "I'm sorry. I go too far." She glanced at me.

Olea's harsh response surprised me. I found important interest in my fingernail. I'd seen the "Stone and Bostwick" name as furriers on invoices, and then "Stone" in Detroit and "Bostwick" in St. Louis. The women did business with both. Olea's middle name was Stone. Perhaps there was a connection there, but both women had once said they'd never married.

Or had Olea only said she hadn't married the love who never returned from the sea?

"We're talking about Clara now," Olea continued. "Your name?"

"Yes," I said. "I'll keep the Doré name. I'm not an Estby anymore. My stepfather was clear about that."

"You could become Clara Gubner or Clara Ammundsen," Louise said. "We'd be honored, wouldn't we, Olea? You belong with us."

Olea nodded.

I hadn't told them I'd requisitioned *Gubner* for an hour or so. "It's a nice offer," I said. "We're sisters in spirit. But I think we can keep our separate names."

They could absorb me, these women who knew what they hungered for and acted on it: running a business, traveling as they wished, hiring and educating and gifting a young woman who could easily give in and let herself be shaped by their lives alone. I'd have to be clear about what I wanted.

I'm ashamed to say that I did once wonder if Louise and Olea were the kind of women whose companionship was questionable, women my mother pointed out to me at her presentations in New York, women more attached to each other than to men. The concept had left my mouth open in astonishment. Once, outside a lyceum presentation in Ohio, my mother and I had even been cursed as such, though my mother always introduced me as her daughter Clara, perhaps to make our relationship clear. People often thought we were of the same age, my mother looked so young and fit on that trip. We were women not afraid to live contrary to the dictates of custom, politics, or fashion, and that threatened. So I had wondered about these two women since I had come to care about them as more than my employers.

But though I looked for signs, nothing sensual ever passed between them, no lingering fingertips on fingertips, no eyes that invited falling into. I saw kindness blended with occasional irritation, the fitting of sisters—if not the cousins they were. I envied their shared history. It made me miss Bertha's laughter even more; long for days when Ida and I had walked barefoot, arms around each other's waists, to school or whispered during recess about whatever boy had caught our fancy even though they hid behind the outhouse and shouted "snake" as we entered.

This was family: people who shared griefs and joys and didn't let the love of money set the tone, people who accommodated each other, stepped aside at times without saying, "It's my way or no way at all." I didn't have a family now. John Doré promised nothing. I was at the end of *that* investigation. I looked across the table at these two women. I vowed to be myself but do what I must to limit any discord with them. I needed no more painful separations or rejections. I'd had enough of both.

That summer of 1902, Olea and Louise introduced me to the New York end of the furrier trade. I visited their leased shop. I stepped into the large cooler where people brought their furs during the hot months to be cleaned and stored. During winter months, the store window showcased brocaded gowns with fur trim, beaver hats and sable muffs, mink and ermine coats. We visited designers with drawings of future fashion clamped to boards that lined the walls.

"We can't take you to the dressers," Olea said.

"They keep the formula and procedures under lock and key," Louise whispered to me. "Much of the work is done in Europe. America is only now developing."

At the manufacturers', I recognized unique handwork as men cut through the buttery soft leather backs of the pelts to make strips, then sewed them back together, forcing the pelt to lie flat like fabric. Then they joined the pieces according to form and lined the garments with silk and satin, all stitched with flawless seams to make the finished work drape with perfection around elegant shoulders. I felt myself attentive to the smells and sounds and sights in new ways.

At the library I read about the fur business, ideas forming in my head.

The women provided more detail about Franklin Doré's role, about his lifting his tall hat at the fur auctions in Montreal or Copenhagen to indicate his bid, his exquisite evaluation of pelts that would one day warm the bodies of society men and women. He was nearly as good as the auction house graders, Olea announced. "If he buys a lot, we know we'll be getting the perfect pelts for that stole or that coat we have orders for. He always goes days early so he can check the pieces over at his own pace."

The women reminded me of his need to travel abroad to visit leather markets in Turkey, Italy, and Greece, furriers in Russia and China. More than once, he'd traveled with otter skins used for the oriental rituals that marked transitions into adulthood.

"People have to be warm," Louise repeated, touting the trade as we stepped from the streetcar and walked the short distance to the hotel. "It's a business that will last forever. What would we do without fur?"

"There's wool," I said. "That's competition."

"Yes, but wool will only keep you warm to about thirty degrees, and it has real trouble standing up to mud. Nothing keeps one as warm or wrapped in luxury as fur," Olea said. "Mud just dries up and flakes right off of it."

They were open and honest about the pitfalls and demands, but in my analysis of their business, I felt they missed something, a part they might have more control over than they did, a venture that would make any investment—my investment—show greater return.

The infamous Franklin Doré stood in the center of our hotel suite in New York City, bookended by the beaming Olea and Louise. The noises of Manhattan's drayage firms making daily deliveries and the occasional honk of one of those new Ford automobiles rose up to our seventh floor rooms through the open windows. I'd left this city with my mother five years before. This view of Central Park was a far cry from the scene she and I'd had from our small Brooklyn room. I didn't let myself think of that pain. Olea and Louise had been out of the country when all those choices were made.

"I'm pleased to meet you at last," I said to Franklin. I put out my hand to shake his.

"And you're the infamous Miss Doré," Franklin said. His eyes were the color of sable and just as warm. Instead of shaking my hand, he lifted it to his lips, soft as mink when they brushed my fingertips. His own hands remained gloved. "It's my pleasure to meet you after all this time. My women give you many compliments," he said, his voice slightly accented as though he'd spent time in the Canadian provinces. He dropped my hand and bent to kiss Louise, then Olea, on the cheek. He removed his fine camel coat, with the collar trimmed in the soft underhairs of skunk.

"I thought we were going out to lunch," Louise said.

"Oh, let's get acquainted here before I go out on the town with my women," Franklin said. He'd entered the room like a dancer, lithe and agile. I had expected Franklin Doré to be large, muscled, with dark hooded eyes squinting from years of trapping and blinking against frozen snows piled up along cold northern rivers. Surely he'd done all that before he graduated to brokering, bargaining, traveling with pelts to France, speaking foreign languages as he bowed over tea tables at auction houses in Hong Kong. I had not imagined he would turn heads with his good looks. I didn't think he'd turn mine.

Louise fluttered around us now, urging us to sit, taking Franklin's coat. Judging by the lines flowing out from his eyes and the hint of gray streaking the sable-colored bangs he brushed back with his fingers, he was a good fifteen years older than I.

"My women," Louise said. "How you talk." He tweaked her cheek and she grinned.

Olea said, "Proprietary men claiming they own women puts you out of touch with this modern time, Franklin."

He feigned shock. "Not possessive," Franklin said. "'My women' is a term of endearment, nothing more." He pulled tight leather gloves one finger at a time from his wide hands. They were red and marked with scars. Two fingers on his right hand, the ring and little finger, were shortened. "Frostbite," he said to me as he noticed my stare. Then returning to the subject of his women, he added, "Mere terms of endearment that allow me a smidgen of authority working for two women who are flames to my buttery soul."

"You see, Clara," Louise said. "You'll have to watch him; he's such a charmer." She giggled like a schoolgirl. I thought of my father and of Olaf's warning about Erik Elstad, and I wondered for a moment if there were safe men.

"Fortunately for us, he puts most of that charm to use with manufacturers, and thus he keeps us in coin," Olea said, "as well as in compliments."

"You're my family," he said.

"Clara wants to talk business," Louise said.

"Yes, but it's always best to separate family from finances if one can," Olea said. "Porous borders are weak ones."

"Never fear, Clara," Franklin said. "I may call you Clara, may I?" I nodded. "Good. You must never fear that what my women set their hearts on will come to be. One always wants to be on the side of their kind souls. If they're with you, I'm sure I will be."

Louise said, "Coffee now? Black?"

He jumped up to help her in the kitchen, behaving like a revered nephew to aging aunts rather than like the contracted employee he was. This was all a new world to me, and I wondered at Olea's comment about porous borders. It seemed to me that Franklin was warm water to their sieves.

Franklin carried the tray of *sandbakkels* Louise had made especially for this meeting. "So," Franklin said, "are we related? Doré isn't all that common a name. It's French in origin."

"I was under the impression it was as common as flies," I said.

He shrugged. "More in the provinces than here."

"There are Dorés in Spokane, at least there were. Clover Doré attended the same business school as I, but I...had a different name then. Where is your family from?"

"Connecticut," Franklin said. "Not all that far from Quebec. My father was a trapper there, my mother from the States."

"And you met Miss Ammundsen and Miss Gubner how?" I asked.

"In the guild," he said. "The furriers' union. They saw potential in me and made me the man I am today."

I hadn't thought women were allowed in the union unless they were widows of furriers.

"Well, they and John Stone."

Stillness followed. Louise halted, stared at Olea, who rose. "You've forgotten my sugar, Louise." She left the room.

"No, I didn't," Louise called after her. "It's right here." She pointed to the tray, then whispered, "Franklin, really, you mustn't."

"I'd forgotten how sensitive Olea is about Stone," Franklin said, his voice low. "I hadn't intended to. Clara here asked—"

"It's all right," Olea said, returning. "One day I'll fill Clara in. But for now, I suspect we ought to let Clara tell us what she wants to share with us. She waited until you could hear it."

Franklin turned his deep brown eyes on me once again. He leaned forward, elbows on his knees, moved closer to the edge of the settee. No one in my family or anywhere had ever looked so interested in something I had to say. I wasn't sure I deserved such attention. After all, I was a novice in the business world and wasn't certain I hungered enough to make my idea work.

But it was time to give life a try—a well-studied, investigated, and prepared-for try, of course. A Doré never did anything foolish.

THIRTY-THREE

Out of the Trap

I've spent a fair amount of time learning about the business," I told them. "I have great admiration for the way you've all conducted your affairs. You're honest and aboveboard. You use mostly cash, and when you've had to make advances, you've had assets to cover them. You're cautious but take informed risks. And you're generous. I see the donations you make to charities and church."

"We believe in passing on our good fortune," Olea said.

"Yes, I've been the beneficiary of that." I didn't know how much Franklin knew or needed to know. I cleared my throat. "However, I believe your operations miss an important part of the fur market. Franklin spends most of his time making purchases at auction houses, then ensuring that the pelts reach the European dressers and are manu-factured into those beautiful coats. He mostly goes to auctions in the East. The West Coast goes largely unnoticed."

"Nothing much has changed from when earlier trappers shipped goods back from the West, or sent them to the Orient by ship,"

Franklin said. "The population of buyers is here, in the East. Always has been. Astor hoped to establish a good West Coast market that would save time getting goods to the Orient. And of course, Hudson's Bay and the Northwest Company have done well out there. But Hudson's Bay is king in New York too."

"But what about pelts from the West? Why not trap on our own land and sell to Seattle?"

Both women looked at each other.

"You ought to be interested in the fashion end," Franklin said. "Not in the rugged part of it, trapping and all." Lucy took the moment to wake up, stretch, and move out of her basket to twist her way around Franklin's leg. He bent to stroke the purring cat.

I stood up now, to make my case firmer. "The finest fur-bearing animals in the country thrive in Washington State, in the Spokane area," I said. "Beaver, otter, mink, coyote, fisher, skunk, squirrel, muskrat, bobcat—even bigger animal hides, such as elk, for the leather markets. And bear for rugs and such. Raccoon skins make beautiful and warm coats, and we have thousands of them; they're almost like rabbits. Why depend on the auctions for pelts? Why not trap our own?"

"You want to move me from New York?" Franklin said. "Send me back out to the traps?" His face hardened, and I saw within the furrowed brows the steeliness that enabled him to buy at good prices. "Trapping is dangerous work, Miss Doré. And the West Coast harvests have declined."

"I understand that," I said. "I'll trap."

"Oh, Clara, no. That's much too hard a job," Louise said.

"Franklin could teach me. Then I'll provide choice prime pelts so you won't have to buy at auction. You'll still have to negotiate tanning and dressing, but we can bring the pelts right into Spokane for the sale...after we've kept the best ones for our own use."

"It's not a very large auction, the one in Spokane," Olea said. "We've attended."

"Then we'll use Seattle. But if we keep the prime pelts, Franklin could take them directly to the dressers and cut out the middleman completely. The rest we'd sell at the auctions in Seattle. They'll ship directly to New York or Hong Kong or even Russia. We'd make less than at the big auctions back east, but that would be compensated for by having quality pelts of our own for our orders. We can ask higher prices. After they're dressed, we'll have them sewn and manufactured and sold back to furriers in Spokane or San Francisco. 'West Coast Soft Gold,' we could call the line." I improvised.

"You've been studying," Louise said. She smiled like a proud parent.

"You should learn the fashion end of things," Franklin said again. "Trapping is only part of it. You'll have to learn grading for various coats and muffs and furs. It's not easily mastered. Consider design instead."

"He's right," Louise said. "You made that supporter for your...for when you don't wear a corset," she said.

"Louise," I protested. She'd seen my breast supporter one morning lying in my room and asked what it was. "That's—"

"Private, I know. But it is a good design. It tells me you could do that sort of thing."

"You could set new fashion trends from the West Coast if you're a good sketch artist," Franklin said. "Didn't I hear that you were illustrating a book once?"

"Design doesn't interest me," I said.

"To humor you: where would we trap?" Franklin asked. He wasn't scowling now. He looked more curious, surprised even.

"I'd buy land. The right kind of land, where I'd trap."

"It's not women's work. You're already thin as spaghetti," Louise said.

Franklin shook his head.

"Women's work is defined by women doing it," I said. "Indian women have handled pelts for decades, so it is women's work. Surely I can do it. The land is a good investment. Isn't that what you told me, Olea? There'll be timber I can sell. Trapping is seasonal, winter work. I could do it on my own."

"Franklin's right. You'd be better at the fashion end," Louise said. "You sketch well. Didn't you say your father was an artist?"

"Trapping..." Franklin said. He shook his head, his jaw flexing before he spoke. "It's cold, hard work. You'd have to live out there, it would be the only way, learn to boil the human scent from traps, plunge your hands into icy streams. Why, are you even strong enough to set a trap?" He looked at my arms.

"I've brought in loads of hay," I told him. "I'm sturdy. And I love the forests and studying the paths of beaver or muskrat. I love the cold air, a night sky filled with stars twinkling like lights on tall fir trees."

"You'd have to check the traps every day, regardless of the weather." Franklin wasn't interested in my romantic version of the work. "When you found the animals in the gripping traps, you'd have to look them in the eye and... Could you do that?"

"I've prepared my share of chickens for dinner," I said, "and helped butcher deer and elk and beef. I don't relish that part, it's true. But it comes with the territory. We're providing basic necessities for people to keep them warm and clothed. And who knows? In time, I may tire of it as you did, Franklin, and move on to warmer rooms."

"There's nothing all that warm about an auction house," Louise said. "The pelts are kept in cold storage and—"

"She knows that," Olea said. She'd been silent for some time.

"What do you think, Olea?" I asked.

"There are logistical problems." She sounded thoughtful. "Franklin's training you would put him out of schedule for this next season. You'd have to hire him separately. His schedule is arranged for this year." Her words ended in annoyance.

"All right. That's a concern I can address. I've looked at maps," I said. "There are public properties for sale with streams and tributaries that ought to have lots of good game and timber. I can buy a section or more."

"Where is this property?" Olea asked.

"Along the Spokane River," I said. "It's remote, yes. But we'll need that for—"

I stopped myself from going further. They were having enough trouble with the idea of my trapping. They'd never understand my interest in what the Finns were doing with their crossbreeding. "All places that support lynx or beaver are remote."

"Maybe you're telling us that you want to do this on your own. It doesn't sound like you really need us for this," Louise said.

"We'd live year-round…in Coulee City." Before they could protest too loudly, I said, "The *New York Times* touts Coulee City. The railroad goes through there, remember, and they sponsored an excursion to promote it. More importantly, they're talking about building a dam there, which would allow irrigation. Congress is considering a bill to reclaim the arid west. We'd be in on the ground floor. Land can be purchased fairly cheaply, good wheat-growing land. And the property for trapping that I've been looking into isn't so far away. You and Olea could live snugly in a house in Coulee City. The winters will be milder than in Spokane," I said. "That wide natural coulee offers that. It'll be easier farming than at Mica Creek too. I'd trap a few months a year and rejoin you."

"But you won't be farming," Louise said.

"I'd set traps in the fall until Christmas, farm wheat in the summers. The land will sustain us."

Franklin watched me as though I were a flower pushing through concrete, unexpected, worth noting. Then he stood. "Any more conversation about this ought to occur on a full stomach."

I wasn't hungry, but Franklin ruled the moment and Louise seized it.

"Oh, yes! Have you found a new restaurant for us?" Louise said. Lucy purred in her lap, and white cat hair drifted in the air as she petted the feline.

"We should eat at the Waldorf-Astoria Hotel," he said then, turning back to Louise. "It's more than fitting for a celebratory meal."

"I don't know that we're celebrating," Olea said.

Louise put Lucy in her basket, then hurried to get Franklin's camel coat. I really wanted to hear that they approved of my idea, but families defer, take on the pace of others in order to meet their needs at small sacrifice to themselves. I'd get resolution in their time rather than my own.

I met Olea in the small hallway outside our three bedrooms as Louise chatted with Franklin in the parlor. Olea checked her hat in the hall mirror, then turned to me. She readjusted my hatpin, one eighteen inches long with a sunflower at the tip. "I'm not sure your idea is a sound one, Clara."

"Didn't you say once that all new ideas are suspect because we tend to appreciate what already exists? Anything new doesn't carry that substance."

She nodded. "I said that about art and how artists diminish their own work at times because it isn't 'accepted' or isn't understood, which comes from our becoming familiar with it over time. New artists' endeavors seem to fall short, at least initially. I'm not sure that applies to this venture of yours."

"It's a way for me to become independent financially," I said. "And we can be in business together. If we control all aspects of it, we can't be exploited."

"We can't control every piece of a business, Clara. Or of living. It's naive to think that way. It's how one deals with the unexpected that marks a successful business."

"I've wandered around for almost a year," I said. "I need to be responsible for my fate."

She looked like she wanted to speak, shook her head, then added, "Our lives will change dramatically if we do this. You know that. A move is the least of it."

"I do."

"Elizabeth Cady Stanton used to say that 'Nothing strengthens the judgment and quickens the conscience like individual responsibility.' I can hear the quickening in your voice."

I nodded.

She brushed at my collar. "Coulee City. Goodness. I'd say you're avoiding Spokane."

"I'm not ready yet to bump into members of my family," I said. "That's true."

"Do you know when you might be?"

I thought for a moment, my fingers pressing down on the pewter sunflower of the hatpin. "When what they need is what I have to give and I have more hope that they'll accept it."

It had been a full afternoon and evening, much of it spent at Thompson and Dundy's amusement park. Franklin gave us little dolls he won throwing balls at bottles. I laughed more than I had in weeks. The lights flickered over the water, and the joy lingered on the Thompson-Culver ferry line that took us back to the hotel. Both Louise and Olea chastised us for coming back with them.

"You were having such a good time. We old folks surely didn't need to stand in your way," Louise said.

"You're not that old," I said. "And besides, we haven't come to a conclusion yet about my suggestions. Business is more important to me than pleasure."

"Pity," Franklin said. He didn't elaborate.

At our suite, Louise hustled about getting us hot water for tea while Franklin sipped at a glass of red wine. When they were all settled and before I could speak, Olea said, "I'm wondering why you bring this up now, Clara, this big plan to trap and travel and relegate us all to Coulee City."

"I… You and Louise, you have your business, and I can tell that you're slowing down while I'm just beginning. You've been a success. I haven't. I want this to be an operation that eventually I'll be able to manage on my own," I said, "after I've had good training."

"She's leaving us," Louise told Olea. "I mean you have every right to, but I thought…" Louise looked genuinely distressed.

"I'm not," I insisted. I wished my mother or even Ida had looked that unhappy at the idea of my going away.

"You and Olea can stay in Spokane if you want. I thought, well, if you lived with me in Coulee City, I'd have a place to come back to that wouldn't…"

"Put you where you'll see your family," Olea said. "You wouldn't see them in Seattle either, and that would be a much better place to settle in."

"It rains too much there," I said. "It's too far from property with streams. And we can't raise wheat there. We visited Seattle in the spring, and it's beautiful with rhododendron blooms the size of Lucy, but I know I'd suffer in the constant dreariness of winter mists and downpours."

I wondered whether to mention now the Finland fox-farming experiments but decided not to.

"I'd like to know that you were at home looking after things. I'd like to have a place to come home to that was well, my own."

"You want us to work for you?" Louise said.

"No. I'd own the house and you'd look after it and maybe even operate it as a boardinghouse." That thought had just occurred. "You love to cook and take care of people, Louise. When I'm not there, you'd have others to spoil besides Olea."

"I'd always have Olea," Louise said. "I guess it would make us money, having boarders."

"Assuming people want to come to Coulee City," Olea said.

"The dam," I said. "It'll bring in people. The *New York Times* says so. And there's good ranch land available now."

"You haven't even gotten to the expense of wheat seed and paying a manager to farm it."

"I'm going to contact my brother Olaf. He's a good farmer, and I hope he'll be open to working for us, farming the wheat on shares." He may not want land of his own, but he might be willing to work for me.

They sat silently while my own heart pounded. Summarizing it as I had did make it sound a lot more involved than what I had imagined. Maybe at first it would be, until I had things pieced together. Buying a house. Acquiring property to trap. Then the wheat land. Right now my vision wasn't something we could all see and understand.

But I could imagine it, I could. And for the first time, I felt excitement about moving forward in my exile.

We sat silent for a time, late-night-reveler sounds rising up from the streets to interrupt the teapot scream.

"I see what you're after," Franklin said. "But get someone locally to trap for you."

"I want to learn that part myself. If you won't teach me—"

"It doesn't make sense for me to do it," he said. "Find the men who have been trapping that land. Engage them."

Olea nodded in agreement.

I deferred to their wisdom. I'd find local help. Between Franklin's and the women's advice, I'd learn about pelts and their quality. We'd move, make a change. It would be one we chose, not one thrust upon us.

"Change is kind of like a prayer, isn't it?" Louise mused as she refilled our cups with hot water. "We present it and have faith it'll be received as intended, perhaps even better, trusting that one day it'll be answered in a way we hope is fruitful."

"Yes," I said. "Change is a bit like that." Risk too.

Once I learned the trade, had my own property, my own way of doing things, no one would be in a position to take advantage of me. I'd be financially secure. I'd have an independent business that could sustain me well into the future. If it served as a way to reconnect to my brother, then that was a bonus. Yes, moving intertwined Olea and Louise with me in new ways, but they were people I imagined would remain in my life. I wanted them to stay. Wasn't that the purpose in taking risks? Wasn't that why my mother had wagered everything to walk across the country, doing what she thought best for family and financial security too?

But I was making better choices than she had. I'd thought my plan through. I didn't hear any voice telling me not to pursue it.

THIRTY-FOUR

The Artistry of Risk

FALL 1902

After we returned to Washington, I purchased land from the government, short of three hundred twenty acres, a half section. An additional sixteen acres became available from the Department of the Interior, and not long after that another quarter section, all in the same region in the wide bend of the Spokane River west of Spokane. The sixteen acres had a little more open farmland that didn't need to be cleared at all and could support orchards. It was close to the LaPray Toll Bridge, so I had road access and could easily arrange for a wagon to pick me up and help get my pelts to storage. A couple named Welch had opened a small store/hotel and post office near the bridge, so I could keep Louise and Olea aware of my comings and goings. My property west of Spokane was so intertwined with timber and streams that when I bent beneath the branches and untangled my bifurcated skirts from the blackberry bushes, it was as though the land reached out with fingers, clutching me to it, and I knew this would be prime country for weasel and martin, otter and skunk, bobcat, beaver, and wolf.

That fall, after much ado, we found what we agreed was a suitable house in Coulee City. It had big bedrooms for the three of us and three more on the third floor to rent out to boarders, who could enter through an outside stairwell. Meeting each of our needs in selecting a home proved daunting, and I wondered how Olea had ever gotten Louise to move all the way from New York those years before.

Louise's concern had to do with the privy. She counted the steps between the back porch and the hollyhock-decorated house, wanting no more than one hundred between them even though the main home had a water closet with a flush pulled by a handle near the ceiling. The house even had indoor water, so we wouldn't have to go out to the pump in the winter. Louise didn't care all that much about the water in the house; it was the outhouse that concerned her, "Because all these newfangled things break down, and eventually we'll be glad we have the privy. I don't want to be walking that far in the dark," she insisted. "You never know what will slither across your path in the night."

She also wanted a bedroom close to the kitchen, "For late-nighters." She took a room on the second floor with a back stairway into the kitchen.

Olea had other needs. She desired a room where the sun wouldn't come up in her eyes but that wouldn't get too hot in the afternoons when she liked to take her nap. I suggested that she use the shades to keep the sunrise from bothering her, but she wanted her window open "a crack" at night in all weather and didn't want the breezes to rattle the shade. These preferences were unknown to me when we lived together in Spokane. Olea wanted a room on the first floor, so we turned what must have been a sewing room into a bedroom for her.

The house's features were not an issue for me. I'd slept in haymows and train stations, in lovely hotels in Minneapolis, and with my mother in a small bed in Brooklyn, and with Ida and Bertha until I went to work. What mattered to me was that my home be a place that no one could take from me, that it remained in my name so I would always have a roof without the fear of losing it, that it be free of a bank that had more leverage than I did.

Because the women had given me money and allowed me to invest it, I bought the house and the river properties outright. I could afford to be generous in meeting the needs of my good friends by selecting a house we could all appreciate.

A stray dog, a bushy-tailed mongrel with Newfoundland-like proportions and bearing one chewed-up ear, arrived at our porch, his fur matted with seeds and weeds. Louise took him under her wing. "He's lucky you found him," Olea teased.

"That'll be his name," Louise said. "Lucky." We all became attached to the dog, and even Lucy didn't object to his presence. He lay at Louise's feet while she knitted and Olea and I read by the evening light, awaiting the cold weather and my foray into trapping.

Coulee City held promise in its isolation, the very qualities I wanted. I was on my way to complete financial independence in the fur trade. My goal was to be successful by the time I turned forty, which would be in 1916. Years away. I set forth. This was my destiny now.

When I celebrated my birthday, the best present of all was that I had a path and still had money in the bank.

No letters had been forwarded to me from Olaf, and I received none in those first months back. After we moved, I took a chance and wrote to him care of the Elstad family, asking if he might want to work my farm.

If he was interested, he could even come and help me find the right property. The return address I marked simply as "Clara" and our box number in Coulee City. No need to rub salt in the wound by using the Doré name; no need to remind myself that I wasn't an Estby by using that name either.

Olaf wrote in October and said he was inclined to accept my offer. He'd winter in Spokane and contact me in the spring. "Don't write to Aunt Hannah's," he said. "Papa won't like it. I'll come help you look for land next year."

Arthur's birthday was in November, Johnny's too if he had lived. I thought about sending Arthur a card but didn't want to do anything that might upset the family. Still, if I sent a card and gave them my address, maybe they'd contact me one day, open a door of return. I had to give them a way.

With property purchased, papers signed, and winter approaching, the next steps meant trapping my own land—or at least learning how. A bit of the bravado I'd had in New York waned when the skies spit snow and temperatures dropped. Maybe Franklin and my friends were right about letting others do the trapping. But no, I'd sold them on this, and besides, if I was to eventually ranch fur-bearing animals, I'd have to begin by livetrapping wild game for my breeding stock. To compete with the Finns one day, I needed to know firsthand what I was doing.

I visited with the LaPrays, for whom the nearest road to the property was named. They told me of the Warrens, father and son, two men more intimate with the streams and timber than anyone who had actually owned it. They'd been trapping the government property for years. They truly read the land. "But they'll be wary of you," Joseph LaPray told me. "You being female and all and them being Indians."

The LaPrays said they'd put the word out, and one week when I finished work on the shack I'd built, two men appeared. They were from the Spokane reservation across the river. I wore men's pants I bought at the Coulee store, dressed with fur-lined boots and gloves and a fur hat. I looked like a man, I'm certain, and maybe that was good. The men remained silent to my questions, and finally I stopped asking, said that I needed their help. The elder Warren let a smile creep across his round, weathered face. "We know this," he said. "We wondered if you did."

Warily, they agreed to let me watch them set the traps that fall and winter. I assured them I wouldn't restrict their trapping on what was now my land, and I vowed to stay with them on the long treks in the snow, even sleeping out in the curl of the rocks at night if need be. "My grandmother knows the hides," the younger Warren told me, and I sent a prayer of gratitude to her for the spirit of acceptance she must have instilled in her descendants. The Warrens treated me as a daughter in need of guidance, with a nod to my femininity during my monthly flow. Those weeks through those winter months I remained in the hut and fleshed and prepared pelts so as not to attract coyotes or wolves to the trap line.

The Warrens showed me how to set the traps myself, explained what to look for in a tree crotch that, along with bait, might lure a weasel in. They demonstrated how to field dress and flesh the animals, stretch and cure beaver hides on circular frames. When I set and began checking my two trap lines, they commiserated with me as I told them a coyote took more than one animal, leaving just bits of fur behind. Like an indulgent grandparent, the elder Warren smiled when I described my delight at sleeping beneath twinkling stars when work along the trap line kept me from my shack. They nodded approval at the harness I made for Lucky, whom I used to pack the hides. They shook their heads at my clumsiness when my knife slipped through a pelt, ruining it. Franklin wouldn't like that either, and it took money from my hands. But I learned about desirable color, coverage, and other grading qualities from these two grisly men. They called me Miss. "Miss. Stick must be *inside* trap, not *outside*, or muskrat will trick you, go home another way." They snickered at the written logs I kept, writing down what was trapped where, how many skins I collected. I suspect they had years of oral listings they could tell me about, but paper and pencil did not appeal to them.

Still, they gave me wisdom. "Eat dark meat," the Younger told me. "Very good. Builds muscles for next time you set traps."

I also endured their grunts about my curling iron when they saw it, and I let them pick up my hair extension and shake their heads in wonder as they tossed it back and forth. These men were skilled, and I needed their wisdom to accomplish my plan. Even more, they were men who appreciated the passion of this intense dance in the wilderness, wits against animals, rivers and land, and the joy in the morning when my efforts proved fruitful and I said out loud my prayer of thanks.

After the first season, back in Coulee City, Olea, Louise, and I attended the Presbyterian church, meeting a few more of our neighbors. The

Lutheran church, with a pastor riding from Wilbur every other Sunday, was organized by the Danes. Olea suggested it was a good time, moving to Coulee City, to try out something new. As one could "never be certain about the Danes," we became Presbyterians. We took on boarders and attended meetings about the possible reclamation dam, and I waited for Olaf to contact me so we could look for that farm together. I'd been reconsidering grain, thinking a chicken farm instead so I'd have protein when I started my own fur-ranching, but I didn't know if Olaf would approve. I wanted to speak to him in person. Besides, I had plenty to keep me busy, just looking after the big house, continuing to be the bookkeeper for the women, and readying myself for the next season of trapping.

The women became more like sisters to me than partners in real estate or the fur business. I cared about them, but it wasn't in my nature to speak of inner thoughts with others; I'd had enough of rejection from people I loved. I'd put my risk in business, where the consequences of failure, I thought, wouldn't hurt as much.

We women moved into a routine that included a monthly shopping trip to Spokane, a trip we made by train, though I still threatened to buy an auto one day. On the April morning in 1903 that found us there, Olea followed up on her legal affairs while I stopped by the local furrier to see about having our furs cleaned and stored for the summer. Afterward I met Louise at Crescent's department store, where she toyed with bolts of material to find the perfect lavender for her bedroom curtains. I fussed over the *Godey's Lady's Book* the store kept in the ladies' lounge. I shouldn't have looked at that; I compared myself to the women with beautiful hair.

When Louise finally finished, we stepped from Crescent's at the same time as a couple entered, and we bumped into each other.

"I'm so sorry," I said, grabbing at my hat. I gasped.

It was my stepfather and Ida.

I caught my breath. "Ida. How—"

Ida's eyes grew large. She looked away.

My stepfather walked quickly down the steps, motioning for my sister, who then trailed along behind him. But she turned, hesitated for a moment. *Did she nod?*

"Who was that?" Louise said as the two hurried away.

"My stepfather and my sister," I said.

"They should have stopped and talked," Louise said.

"Did it look like Ida recognized me? Did you see her nod?"

"If she didn't, it's only because you've changed your hair with those extensions. You look quite sophisticated, Clara. I bet they didn't see it was really you."

I watched my family cross the street, then turn the corner without a backward glance.

I stood motionless, a fly caught in a spider web.

Then, "Let's get you a new dress, Louise," I said, taking her elbow and moving back inside Crescent's. "My treat. We'll pick out a purse for Olea too. Maybe shoes. A nice surprise for her when she comes back from the lawyer."

"But we finished. I thought you were…bored."

"Bored? No. Not ever. Only uncreative people are bored. Let's see if they have this style I saw in the magazine. It'll look good on you."

"A store-bought dress? They're so expensive, Clara."

"You deserve it," I said.

Inside I caught the attention of the clerk and showed her the dress

I had in mind. They had one in a pink as sweet as sunrise. It needed altering and it was expensive, but that was fine, I could do that for Louise. I picked out a leather purse with brass trim for Olea. A pair of shoes to go with it fit right into the shopping bag. Money could buy things for people, nice things. There was nothing wrong with spending money on friends.

"She'll love that," Louise said. "Won't you get a new frock for yourself?"

I shook my head. "Let's go back to the fabrics, Louise. Get a few more yards of material you'd really, really like."

I let Louise's chatter about fabric deaden the memory of the moments before. Except for Ida's faltering recognition, I might have been the striped pole outside the barbershop instead of an Estby relative. I wished I were that pole; I wouldn't have felt the piercing pain.

More determined than ever to move my plan forward, I wrote to Olaf again at the Elstad farm but heard nothing back. By June I let myself worry. Maybe my card to Arthur spurred a problem. Olaf might have said something to the family, and they might have told him not to get involved with me. Maybe Ida and Ole made comment about seeing me wearing the finery bought by "dirty money."

When July arrived without contact, images of my mother's pretending we'd make our walking deadline loomed. I admitted the truth to myself and decided Olaf wasn't going to follow his interest in farming with me. Maybe he'd decided working for the Elstads suited him fine. But he might have written and told me so.

I'd locate a farm without his help. That's what I'd do.

"It really isn't necessary, is it?" Olea said. "Extending yourself further by purchasing a farm? And you're upset now. Why not wait until you've had more time to think about this."

"It's an investment," I said. One day it might support a breeding farm like the Finns', only not with silver foxes but with mink. I didn't tell Olea that. She would have thought me daft. "I can find someone to perform the labor. It'll be a good place for Lucky to run. They're still talking about the reclaiming act, and when it passes, prices will only go up. It's better to buy now."

Louise actually found the farm I purchased. She'd taken the dog for a long walk and talked to the farmer out in his field. No stranger that she is, he was soon telling her of his daughter's wish that he and his wife would move to Seattle to live closer to her. Louise walked home, got me, and before the week was out, I owned a wheat farm of one hundred sixty acres. I could raise a passel of chickens on it too.

We rented the farmhouse to a young couple, and the husband agreed to work on shares. It was a perfect arrangement.

I didn't need my brother.

"At least he might have written to me," I complained. We'd bought peaches from a local farmer and were putting them up in Ball jars. "He said he'd always talk to me, and now he won't."

"Go see him again," Olea said. The heat of the day and our canning had left moisture above her lips. Birdsong married the air beyond the open window.

"No. He knows where I am. It's up to him. It's only right he contact me." I rubbed my forehead with my forearm. It was so very hot in the kitchen.

"But you're the one distressed. You can be right, Clara, but not be very happy about it."

"I wouldn't be happy begging him either," I said.

"You think it's begging to find out what might have gotten in the way of his contacting you again? He's surely not out to hurt you. It's in your best interest to believe he is doing the best he can. Maybe he's sick or had an accident and can't contact you."

I hadn't thought of that.

Still, he could ask someone to write to me. Maybe Erik Elstad. Or one of my brothers and sisters. He would find a way if he was really interested.

Obviously he wasn't. Like my fantasy involving my father, I'd created a story with Olaf in it. Both stories had the same real-life ending: neither wanted contact with me.

THIRTY-FIVE

Calculated Changes

FEBRUARY 1904

Franklin arrived for a visit, much to the delight of the women, and me too I guess. The snow was deep in the stream ravines, but he and I snowshoed a distance into the timber so he could see the land. Afterward, we sat in my little shack, the wood stove crackling. It was his first look at the land I'd been trapping.

He assessed my pelts, commented on their size, pointed out the cuts I'd made in the fisher hide when fleshing it. "You've reduced its value," he said. "You'll get the hang of it. Otherwise, they look good. We didn't see many beaver dams. Not as many tracks as I'd hoped for to indicate there'll be ample harvest in the future. Makes me wonder if it's overtrapped, or maybe disease has taken its toll and they haven't reproduced as we'd expect. Stress in the coats suggests that too."

"Are they good enough to sell on our own?" I asked.

"Some are. But we'd do better at the auction because you don't have that many quality pelts."

"Yet," I said, but his words stung. I'd messed up with my knife in my learning, reducing the pelt's value.

Franklin shrugged. He was like my brother Olaf in that way, not openly disagreeing but still expressing caution. "I've never been to an auction." I'd sold my first season's pelts in Spokane. "I guess now is the time."

We all decided to go to Seattle and make an adventure of it, as Louise said. She contacted a neighbor boy to look after Lucy, and Lucky went out to the farm for the few days we'd be gone.

At the Seattle auction, we women sat in the back while the male buyers lifted their hats or flicked a finger beside their noses to indicate the lot of furs they wished to buy. Excitement crackled in the air between those representing the trappers and the buyers hoping to get the best profit for their manufacturing firms.

Pampering ourselves, we stayed at a fine hotel in Seattle and ate at the best restaurants. The eyes of my friends, Olea and Louise, sparkled in recognition of a buyer from Quebec they hadn't seen for a while and the wife of a grader who sat with us after the auction.

"This is what I mean by passion," Olea told me that evening as we prepared for yet another party. Her eyes sparkled. "Isn't this grand?"

I did enjoy the hoopla and Franklin's attention as well. Mostly, I eavesdropped to hear anything I could about what the Finns were doing, how the industry was moving. If I mentioned their ranching program, people scoffed. "Oh, you know those Finns," they said. "I'll bet it's just rich gentlemen playing at a hobby. Why spend money gathering food for animals when the forests can do it for you?" A trapper's wife interjected that it would be nice to have her man at home in the winter with a ranching operation, and the other women nodded. The conversation moved on, the idea of farming furs something for those dreaming Finns. When the auction events were over, we walked with

Franklin to the train station. He'd head next to Montreal; we'd return to Coulee City. Louise and Olea had already boarded our train. I stood with Franklin, realizing I enjoyed his company and would miss it. Our friendship lacked pressure, carried the comfort of when I spent time with my brother, and had the added spark of bantering between two people who respected each other.

"I'll write more often if you'd like me to," Franklin said as we stood in the station.

"Do you think we need more information from you?" I said. He kept the women updated quite well, I thought.

"No," he smiled. "I'd like more response."

"Oh. Well, I can write reports more frequently," I said.

"Clara. It's you I'd like to hear from, not only the official correspondence of my women."

"About my trapping?"

"I'm interested in you more than in trapping. Will you allow me to write of other things? More importantly, will you write back?"

I was glad he couldn't hear my heartbeat. I liked the current arrangement. We were separated by miles, and I wasn't sure I wanted that distance shortened by his knowing me better or differently. The train whistle blew over any answer he might have heard if I'd had the voice to give one.

"I'll write back," I told him, but I didn't say about what.

By the next winter, I no longer felt baffled by the traps, though I still had much to learn about knowing where to set them. I still had two lines going now, both productive.

The Warrens were neighborly enough. At Christmas, they left me a wild turkey they'd shot. Once a salmon hung on a hook by my door. I set a packet of tobacco out for them, and it was gone by morning.

Louise worried out loud when I came home. She said that I seemed to grow taller but thinner and expressed concern about how hard I worked. Olea said more than once that she didn't think this whole "trapping thing" was the best use of my time. It was difficult, cold work, though Lucky made it less so. There were occasional disputes about my not appreciating the work the two women performed at home or my "apparent preference for furs over friends." The latter charge wasn't so, but I could see how they might think so. Franklin's letters spoke of designers he'd met with in Montreal and of bringing finished products back from Hong Kong to sell in the furrier shops of New York. He reminded me that design work was "much warmer than what you're about with those traps." He signed his letters, *Affectionately yours.*

The challenges made me more stubborn. No one was going to tell me what I couldn't do. I didn't take the time to listen for Isaiah's words about what way to walk. That season I didn't collect enough prime pelts, so I offered the Warrens good prices for theirs. I took all of the furs to the Spokane auction myself instead of having Franklin come west. No sense cracking muddy waters best left frozen. The pelts brought an average price, but I made little over what I'd paid the Warrens. My paltry contribution of my own pelts added a small profit, but I wasn't going to become financially independent this way. I'd have to consider livetrapping to begin fur ranching, and I needed to let Olea and Louise know what I had in mind for the farm.

The boardinghouse earned us additional funds, and we split it three ways. Olea furnished the rooms and Louise cooked and I provided the house, so it worked. I added my profits to a fund I had for buying land. In 1905 I found sixteen more acres along the Spokane River bordering my three hundred twenty. It had timber in addition to river frontage, and I thought it a good investment. It came with an apple orchard. My cash reserve grew smaller. With trepidation, I took out a small loan at the bank for wheat seed, a few apple starts, and twenty chickens.

"Don't overextend yourself," Olea warned.

"But you said one has to invest in order to get a return, right?"

"Yes, but caution is essential."

"I've studied yields and expenses. I'm diversifying," I said, remembering Olea's brother-in-law's advice. I didn't add that I thought her latest enterprise promised less return than my wheat fields. She and her sister, Priscilla, had begun importing European furniture into America. Olea used a few pieces to furnish the boarders' rooms and our living quarters; some she placed in the Spokane house she still owned, where she met monthly with society women looking for the perfect settee or that English burl elm Chippendale flattop desk (which she told everyone came from a royal estate). I was surprised by the prices people were willing to pay for secondhand items and wondered if they were moved to spend by the romance of the stories Olea spun.

Fortunately, we had bountiful rain that year. The grain harvest not only allowed me to repay my bank loan and interest, but it made all my expenses, the labor I hired, and feed and seed for the next season. We butchered several chickens and sold them in Spokane, but I knew that when I was ready for raising my fur-bearing animals, chickens or their eggs would meet the protein needs. I used a little of my small profit to buy Louise a new Monarch stove and Olea a signed first edition of Audubon's 1827 *The Birds of America,* published in France. If I could repeat my success each year, I'd have a nice little nest egg soon. I was doing what I'd set out to do, making my way with sound decisions that hurt no one else. I still wished I could tell Olaf of my success, but he'd made his choice. I'd made mine. Louise and Olea and even Franklin—at arm's length—were my family now.

"I wish you'd stop trapping," Louise said. I readied my kit for the months I'd be on my timberlands. "I worry about you there alone for so many weeks in the snow and cold."

"I have the Warrens," I assured her. "And Lucky." She handed me a pair of gloves, furry sides in. "It's not only danger that concerns me." She didn't look at me when she spoke, so I wasn't sure I heard what she said next. "I like your company. I miss you when you're gone."

"You miss Lucky," I teased. I couldn't recall anyone suggesting that my absence brought them even the smallest heartache. I assumed my brothers and sisters missed my mother while on our journey, but I'd already worked away from the Mica Creek farm for five years by the time Mama and I left for New York, so I didn't imagine they really missed me. I had already become more a memory than a presence to them. Louise offered a view of belonging that hadn't occurred to me before.

"No, I miss you," she insisted.

"I miss you too," I said. And I realized I did. The observation warmed before it alarmed.

I took plenty of food with me: hardtack biscuits, dried venison, and beef that I jerked from my Coulee City neighbor's stock. I added carrots and potatoes beginning to sprout eyes. I stored all this in the shack, along with fish pemmican the Warrens traded with me. I knew how to locate the best spots and set traps for the winter weasels, those ermine whose pelts were valued regardless of size. I could identify the slides the otters made on the stream banks, and beavers leave tracks even a child can find. I had the right bait (chicken parts Louise sent with me and, when my traps were full, scent glands from the animals). Lucky came too, and I welcomed not only his brawn but his fierce barks warning of wolves or bears. I understood that for my benefit, Louise had given up her own precious time with him, a clear sacrifice.

Lucky's tail wagged when I placed the usual animal innards in his dish one morning. Wood smoke from my stove made my throat sore, or so I'd thought until my cough turned into a seal's bark. Fatigue visited more quickly than I'd remembered, but I had to check the traps. As I trudged through the woods, Lucky trotted behind me on the narrow trail. Snow fell, sugaring the pine and firs and filling in my snowshoe tracks. Fur-lined boots kept my feet warm, but the coughing caused me to stop more than once, gloves on knees. I felt a buzzing in my head after each bout. "I should have fixed a mustard pack," I croaked to Lucky, who panted beside me.

For the first time, I was too weak to finish the trap lines. Instead, I took what I had and dragged it back to my shack, unloaded Lucky, and stood in the crisp air to flesh and stretch them. Despite my stupor, I ran my hands over the smooth fur, exerting energy to tie the edges to the circular frame and salt them. More hides waited, but I needed to eat. I rested for an hour before I fixed my supper of vegetable stew with pieces of beaver tail and fat floating on the top. I curled up beneath a fur blanket. I'd rest then finish. That was my plan.

When I awoke, it was morning, and my chest felt like an elephant sat on it. I knew I ought to remain where I was, fight the fever growing within me, but I needed to finish the line. Lucky licked my face, and I rose, stopping to cough, my lungs vibrating against my chest. Breath came with difficulty. I sat down on my cot to pull on my pants. I tried to stoke the fire, but now I shivered and dropped kindling. The ends of my fingers were white as bone, and when I caught my face in the mirror over the washbasin, my lips looked blue.

Even now, all these years later, when Ida gets up to stoke the fire, I remember how my hands trembled that day, lips and fingers numb, as close to giving in to final silence as any time in my life.

"I should eat," I mumbled to the dog.

I reached for a pan to heat water and watched the wood floor come up to smack my face.

THIRTY-SIX

Servicing

I wheezed in and out of memories. Once Ida flashed before my eyes, telling me how cold the hog house was and that Johnny was sick. Words wouldn't come for me to tell her I was so sorry that he was ill, that she was cold, that I was cold too, and that I wished it had been me instead of any of them, me instead of my mother having to ache and grieve the rest of her life. In dreams, words fail to express the heart, but the soul knows of the longing. Olaf swirled in my memory, flying up into a cyclone. I thought that dying would be good now, but someone wouldn't let me, lifted my head instead.

I opened my eyes to the brown face of Young Warren.

I smelled juniper, tasted bitter broth that Older Warren now spooned into my mouth. I lay back shivering. "Very sick, Miss," he said. "We stay."

And they did.

Lucky had been lucky for me. I'd let him outside, though I didn't remember doing it. He'd found the Warrens, urged them back to the shack. They'd put me to bed and stayed for four days watching over me.

When I felt well enough to sit up and take nourishment on my own, I remembered Louise's lament and agreed with her.

"I've asked the Warrens to do the trapping for me from now on," I told Olea and Louise when the Warrens returned me to Coulee City. I was weak and had lost weight. I pulled the fur hat with its ear flaps off, not caring how matted my hair must look. Getting a hot bath and my hair washed would feel like heaven.

"It's good to see you learn from experience," Olea chided, "even if it does take years."

"I'll buy pelts from them exclusively, for a fair price. Maybe my profit will be a little less but still enough. And I'll have them start live-trapping," I told my friends.

"Whatever for?" Olea said.

"To do what the Finns are doing, only with foxes here. I'll build pens out at the farm. We'll have chickens for protein. We have enough cold weather to bring us excellent pelts. I've investigated it," I said. "There's hardly any risk."

"Investigated? Have you been to Finland to see what's happening there? Have you talked with those who think ranching fur-bearing animals has merit? No, Clara. You haven't thought this through," Olea said.

It struck me that her words were the very ones I'd spoken to my mother all those years ago before we took our walk.

When we carried our fur garments to Spokane for summer cleaning and storage in April of 1906, I looked in the city directory. I hadn't done it before then, not wanting to see my family's names without mine included. Ida worked as a domestic. My mother, Ole, Arthur, William, and Lillian lived at 1528 Mallon Avenue. Aunt Hannah wasn't listed there, or anywhere. I wondered if she'd passed on. I'd last seen my brother Olaf in 1901. He wasn't mentioned, so I assumed he worked outside of Spokane, maybe still at the Elstads' farm. That he still hadn't written to me stung.

I also looked up the Doré name, and there were Dorés listed. An Elsie, John, and Mitchell appeared, the latter a conductor on the Northern Pacific Railway. Seeing their names affirmed for me what my father had once said, that there were many Dorés. It was a name like Olson or Johnson, with a hundred branches on every family tree.

On my own, I took the streetcar to the Mallon address. I'm not sure what I thought I'd do there, but I wanted to see where they lived so I could picture where they carried on lives without me. I stood across the street from a fine-looking two-story home with dormers on the top floor and a lovely porch to grace the front. Lilac scent wafted from the yard. My stepfather had detailed the area above the porch with an intricate framed design that added interest, made it unique. A bay window brought in extra light. If he'd built the house as Olaf said he planned to, he'd done a fine job of it. Without the dirty money, they apparently lived comfortably.

My heart leaped as two girls came out of the house, onto the porch. They were about twelve. *Lillian?* They sat on the stone steps holding little books in their laps. *Diaries.* They giggled together. The one I thought was Lillian suddenly looked my way, as though she was aware that I stared.

When I waved, she waved back. My heart pounded. I looked for traffic, thinking to cross the street, when I heard Ida's voice. "It's time Marcia went home," Ida said. "Lillian, come help Mama get the duster down."

The girls whispered to each other, then separated. Lillian, lithe and blond, ran inside. The other girl walked off down the street. The emptiness I felt surprised me.

I took the streetcar back toward the Fairview house Olea owned and where we stayed when we came to Spokane. Instead of going all the way to the house, I got off and walked into a beauty shop and asked for a pompadour frame and spent the afternoon having my hair built up around it. "You'll have to save the hair from your brushing," the woman told me, "to fill in these thin places. Your hair is so soft!"

"Yes, I know," I said.

"A little color can give it body. Would you like to try blond?"

I nodded.

"I love adventurous women!" she said and poured warm water from a pitcher over my head.

My hair still had no body, lay weak and limp. And I'd just spent as much as a fur muff on a style that outmoded my hat. I stopped at Crescent's to buy a new hat and bought one each for Olea and Louise. They met me at the front door of the house.

"Why Clara, you've…"

"Colored your hair," Olea finished for Louise. "It certainly is… yellow."

"But it's so…big," Louise said, gazing up. "That pompadour."

"It is too big, isn't it?" I had to duck to get through the door with the hat on. "I don't know what I was thinking." The flurry of hair activity had made me feel better, and I didn't need to tell my friends about the goings-on on Mallon Avenue or that I couldn't plug the hole I felt in my heart.

"It must weigh as much as Lucy," Louise said.

"The cat might have added more style," I said, and they both giggled. I did too, the three of us removing the hat and the frame, laughing at the idea of the cat, all balm to my aching heart. This was what friends were for.

The message at the First Presbyterian Church in Coulee City that next Sunday morning spoke of exile. "Being banished, expelled, sent out, is one of the deepest kinds of human suffering," the pastor noted. "Imagine the Israelites wandering in the desert. It is not of our doing that we are freed from such bondage. God gives 'the desolate a home to dwell in.'" He quoted a Psalm.

Olea leaned over and said, "In Hebrew the verse is translated, 'God sets the lonely in families.'"

"What an odd verse," I said. I wondered how she knew the Hebrew version, but Olea rarely shared her history. She was who she was now, a semiretired furrier, a woman interested in European furniture and birds, and apparently a student in Hebrew.

Olea shrugged and whispered, "In Exodus, when the midwives disobeyed the pharaoh, faced their fears, and did what God commanded, it says God gave them 'families of their own.' Family is apparently pretty important to the health of the soul."

I looked at her, wondered if she knew she spoke wisdom as though it were a morning greeting, gracious and simple and deep. She'd already turned back, paying attention to the pastor.

I thought of my mother being expelled from the farm through an unnecessary foreclosure, how lonely she looked the day I left, even surrounded by her children. I thought of her family not letting her speak of one of her greatest accomplishments, how they were held captive by the past, how she was exiled from herself in that way.

Maybe I was as well.

Our lives took on a languid pace, no real ups or downs. Boarders came and went. We hardly noticed them with the separate outside entrance. Most worked for the railroad and were gone for several days at a time. Louise collected the rent from our boarders, who took the rooms and ate one meal with us. Louise complained about her bunions, so took fewer walks with Lucky. I noticed she'd make trips to her room, come out and say, "Now what did I go in there for?" then return. She might do it two or three times before remembering. Maybe she'd always been that way and I only noticed because I was around her more now, listening harder, because that's what families did for each other.

Olea had her eyes checked and got spectacles. She said I should get my eyes checked too, that I might need glasses. I didn't like the tiny lenses. They looked…froglike. "You'd squint less if you had them," she told me.

"I don't need them yet," I said and found a magnifying glass I pulled out whenever Franklin's letters arrived. Franklin and I corresponded with no declarations of anything but *Affectionately yours.*

These were days of servicing, I called it, doing menial things to keep the system running, like oiling the plow each fall to deter rust. I lived a life without drama or trial and should have been gleeful.

The *New York Times* arrived weekly and gave us things to discuss through the week. When I saw the article about experiments in Finland, my malaise took a name. I showed it to Olea.

She scoffed. "I thought you'd put that idea out of your mind," she said. "You haven't spoken to the Warrens about livetrapping. You haven't arranged to travel to see things first hand."

"I've been waiting for the right time. The Warrens haven't been too encouraging about livetrapping for me. I either have to get someone else or try it myself. Look, it says in the *Times* that it's working."

Olea looked over my shoulder.

"With foxes maybe. You ought to pay attention to Franklin's wish for you to design."

Had she been reading my mail?

"What if it was a dream I had," I told her, "to do something new and innovative?" I thought about Olaf reminding me that I hadn't pursued any of my dreams. But I had. I owned property. I hired seasonal workers to harvest my fruit. We farmed wheat on shares, took chickens to markets that included Spokane restaurants. By all measures I was successful. So what was this longing that made me hungry even after one of Louise's big meals if not the desire to do something more, something bold, the way my mother and I had walked across the country?

Olaf might not be interested in farming on shares, but maybe I could inspire him with my idea of fur ranching. We could do it on the acres near the Spokane River or on the wheat farm. Olea was right, I finally agreed. This separation between Olaf and me needed to be addressed. I took the train to Spokane and walked the four miles to the Elstad farm east of town.

"I'm a sister to a man I hope still works for you," I told the woman who came to the farmhouse door. She was younger than I and wiped her hands on a yellow apron. "His name is Olaf Estby."

She shook her head. Sheep bleated in the background, and I heard a dog bark behind the barn. A recent rain added freshness to the air. I looked around hoping to see Olaf come out from the field, but he didn't. I wasn't sure the woman spoke English, so I started to repeat my request in Norwegian when I heard a man call out, "Who is it?" He was inside the house. I hadn't been invited in.

I handed her my card and she called back, "Clara Doré."

"I'm Olaf Estby's sister," I said loud enough for him to hear, and shortly, as I'd hoped, Erik Elstad appeared.

"Miss Doré." He grinned, looked at my card, dismissed the woman, and she disappeared. He stepped outside and directed me to a swing on the wide porch. "Would you like water? I can have Beatrice bring it." I shook my head. "What brings you here?"

"I'm trying to track down my brother. He's a terrible letter writer." I smiled.

He looked puzzled, and in the silence that followed, my heart began to pound. "You don't know," he said at last.

"Don't know what? That he doesn't work here anymore?"

"No, no, he doesn't." He looked away from me, stared out onto his fields.

The pounding in my chest grew louder as though my heart knew the danger before my ears could hear the words.

"He's… He died. I'm so sorry. Phthisis."

"Tuberculosis? When?"

"I'd have to think," he said. "Nineteen-ought-two. Yes. The year the irrigation Reclamation Act was signed. He resigned, said he'd help you farm. Got sick and went to Spokane. I assumed…to be with your family. I think he was in a hospital for a while. I hated to lose him. He was a good worker." He politely didn't ask why I'd never been informed.

I hope I thanked him for his time. I don't remember. He offered me water again, suggested he drive me to the train station when he realized I'd walked. "No, no, the walk will do me good," I said.

My feet knew the way; my mind meandered. Olaf would have been twenty-three when he died. All that time I'd harbored irritation toward him, he was dead.

Waiting for his letters, watching as Louise brought in the packages and mail, had once offered a blend of hope mixed with ache, but now there'd be only ache. I should have tried to contact him sooner. Regret weighted each step I took. Sobs of sorrow made me stop, lean against the gate post. Too late; I was too late.

I'd lost five brothers and sisters to early deaths, all younger than twenty-five. I was living on borrowed time.

I didn't return to Coulee City that afternoon. Instead, I stayed at the Fairview house. I didn't sleep, couldn't concentrate. My eyes swelled with crying. Finally, at dawn I knew what I would do.

The first house I bought was occupied by renters in a growing section of Spokane. Their rents would make the payments. I purchased a second house in the new Alta Vista Estates strictly for investment. I used my Spokane River property as collateral. I'd hold it until the price rose, then sell for a small profit. I'd slowly gain and make money, add to my accounts, that's what I'd do. Build security. I ignored the silent voice reminding me of a different path. It felt right.

But by the next morning, it didn't. There was no need for me to go into debt. This wasn't what living an abundant life meant, was it? What had I been thinking?

"I've been impulsive," I told the real estate agent, catching him before he left for the day. "I want to put both houses back on the market."

"Now?" he said. I nodded. "But you'll lose earnest money. I'll have to charge fees."

"I don't care. Sell them."

"Give yourself time to think this over. You can't go wrong with property," he assured me.

Of course one could. Mama had lost the farm.

"Just sell the rental then," I said, "Even if it's at a loss."

There was something different I needed to invest in as a memorial to my brother. He'd lived a safe and simple life. I needed to fully live my own.

"Where have you been? We've been worried about you," Louise said when I stepped up on the porch.

"I should have called," I said.

"You're not required to apprise us of your whereabouts," Olea said. "But a week—"

"It was rude of me. I'm sorry. I had business to tend to." I chewed on my nail.

"What is it?" Louise said. "You're so pale." She came to sit beside me.

"My brother Olaf died," I said.

Louise gasped. "I'm so sorry." Olea put her arm around my shoulder. "We would have come to be with you. Were there funeral arrangements to make?"

"He died years ago. I...didn't know."

Louise squatted down in front of me. "The brother you hoped to come here to help farm?" I nodded. "Oh, that's so sad, so very sad. What happened?"

I gave her the obituary I'd gotten when I stopped at the newspaper office. I imagined my mother giving the newspaper the information for it. Yet one more child, gone from her life.

"What about one of your other brothers?" Louise asked. "Could you invite them to visit and consider farming it with you?"

"Louise, she needs time to grieve," Olea corrected. "We can fix things later."

But I liked solving a problem rather than dwelling on the sadness. Arthur would be twenty-one. He'd always shown more interest in Ole's carpentry work than in farming. Billy would be fourteen, too young to manage a farm even if he had an interest. Olaf had been the one with soil in his soul.

"I doubt any of the others would be interested," I said.

"Which brother was it again?" Louise asked.

"Olaf," I repeated.

"Why don't you contact your family?" Olea said. Her voice held sorrow. "Let them know you grieve with them."

"They would have seen my letters to Olaf among his things," I said. "It had my address on it. So did the birthday cards I've sent."

"Maybe he didn't keep them," Louise said.

Maybe he hadn't, but someone in the house knew where I lived. No, there'd been no effort to reach me.

I shook my head. I'd been growing new flesh over the cuts of the past, but they still weren't healed. My family, not I, held the key to ending this separation.

"What will you do now?" Louise asked.

I inhaled a deep breath. "I'm going to Finland."

THIRTY-SEVEN

Traveling Mercies

I t's about time," Franklin yelled at me over the phone when I told him I thought we should make the trip.

"It's not necessary to shout," I told him. "I can hear you fine."

"So can our neighbors," Louise said. She gave woolen mittens to children in the winter, so she sat knitting as Franklin spoke. It was eighty degrees outside, but she wore a sweater. Working with wool "keeps my hands warm," she often told me. I'd begun to notice that she was often cold while the rest of us sweltered. Perhaps a sign of aging.

"Sorry," he said and lowered his voice, but old habits die hard, and he soon shouted again. "I'll meet the train on the fifteenth," he shouted. His voice quieted down again on the phone with me. "I'm looking forward to seeing you," he said, "and hearing firsthand about your progress. I intend to see if I can make progress of my own."

His words fell into silence, then I said, "Every man ought to have good intentions." I said good-bye, then hung up.

I dragged the trunk from the attic, ironed shirtwaists, and brushed

Lucy and Lucky's hair from the linen. Franklin and I would be gone no more than four weeks. There were too many demands here at home. I'd contacted the real estate agent and told him to sell the Alta Vista property too. Those were impulsive buys. I'd need to sign papers for that.

Two nights before I was to leave, I passed by Olea's room on the first floor and saw her trunk packed too. I wondered where she was going.

"I had no idea you planned to go to Finland too," I told Olea and Louise. We stood in the living room, Lucky relegated to the back porch. He was happier there anyway, as the house heated up by late afternoon while the porch remained in the shade of maples and elms. Lucy curled on the divan. "I mean, all of us travel abroad? What about this place? Our home?" The air had begun to cool enough that I'd stopped sweating while I packed. I perspired now for other reasons. The scent of coffeecake filled the air, and the sky was magnificent with frothy clouds like shattered silk kissing the coulee ridges.

"The farm takes care of itself," Olea said.

"Yes, but our boarders. There's no time to hire a cook, and the animals—"

"The pastor's wife will look after Lucy," Louise said. "And Lucky can go to… What's their name again, on the farm?" I told her our sharecropper's name. "Yes. And the boarders can eat at the restaurant. The house will be fine."

"We're interested in what might come of your fur ranching plans," Olea said. "My cousin in Norway writes that they've had success in crossing an Icelandic arctic fox with Norwegian reds. They raise the kits on islands. We intend to visit both Norway and Finland. It would be a waste of time not to."

In my conversations about making the trip, Olea and Louise had never once said they planned to go along. I knew they loved to travel. I should have anticipated. "You've never indicated much support for my fur ranching idea," I said.

"That was before I learned that Norwegians were doing it," Olea said. "I'd only heard about the Finns, and frankly, I was a little suspect of that. But Norwegians are a very persistent people. If we can do it, then it can be done elsewhere. We told you that going abroad should have been the first thing you did rather than wasting your time with your trapping period. Now we can all go."

"I always like to travel," Louise said. She watched my face, glanced at Olea, then back to me. "But of course, if you don't want to bother with two old women tagging along, well, I understand that." She glanced back at Olea again, then looked at her hands.

"It's not the bother," I said. "It's… Well, Franklin and I worked the expenses out. I'm paying for this trip. We'll go first to Finland and then visit manufacturing houses in Europe. We only plan to be gone about four weeks."

"It'll take nearly that long by ship to get there," Olea said, disgusted with my naiveté. She exaggerated. "If you're going, you ought to make it worth your time. Three months at a minimum. We've worked everything out," Olea added.

She didn't name her annoyance, and I couldn't find words for mine either. Traveling with them would be an adventure. It always was, and yet I didn't want them along.

I must have scowled, because Louise said, "Let's not be too hasty,

Olea. These are things we didn't consider. Maybe Clara and Franklin, well, maybe they wanted time...together. We might not have thought of that."

"They can be alone all they want except when we're talking furs. This is a business trip for Clara and Franklin, but we have an interest in this too. It'll affect our lives as well. We'll travel as the family we are."

"Then you'll have to make this a family trip without me," I said. "I could as easily end up spending a month or more visiting your relatives or taking a side trip to Oslo that could last a month, as New York did. I spent a winter in Minneapolis because I didn't speak up. I'm speaking up today."

Olea raised one eyebrow. "You appeared perfectly happy to accept my sister's hospitality." She roughly folded a shawl, threw it into her trunk. "We'll take a different ship, do what we want, won't we, Louise?"

"I didn't think about leaving the house with no one in it for so long," Louise said. "What if they forget to come feed Lucky? And I didn't get anyone to look after Lucy." She blinked rapidly in that frightened way she had.

"The pastor's wife," Olea said quietly.

"Lucy won't adapt well to others coming to take care of her. I... I think maybe I'll stay home." She swallowed and tugged on her apron, picking at the tiny embroidered strawberries. "There might be an earthquake to hit us here, like in San Francisco. That's only been two months ago. We can plan another time to go to Norway."

It was such a silly thing to argue over. Maybe if they had told me of their plans earlier, it wouldn't have bothered me. Some of the silver fox pelts raised by the Finns were earning more than a hundred dollars a pelt at the auctions. Olea had a good head for money; maybe that's why she wanted to go along.

If I didn't assert myself with this, I could imagine Olea deciding everything about the ranching operation: where the large pens should go, what the animals should be fed, when the kits should be weaned, which animals to breed. There might not be much demand for ermine yet, but by the time I had the ranching operation down—beginning with fox but moving to mink—there would be. I wasn't interested in importing Norwegian stock; I wanted to do this my own way. The longhaired furs like silver fox had been popular for decades; it was time for the fashion to change, and I could open the door. I felt my heart pound. Despite the uncertainty, I felt...alive.

"I intend to go alone," I said.

Olea sighed loudly. "I thought we were family. We've traveled together before... I simply... Well, perhaps it's time we did do things differently." She straightened a lace doily at the back of the divan, patted it with her long fingers. She didn't look at anyone.

Louise said. "I don't want to travel right now, Olea. My hip... You and Franklin go ahead," she said to me. "We'll make it a foursome another time, won't we, Olea?"

Olea stood quietly for a time, her hands touching the cameo at her neck. Her bearing reminded me of Ida's when Mama and I had returned from New York, anger tensed in a frame as slender as barbed wire and just as dangerous if one didn't know how to get through it.

"Yes, let them go." Olea sighed. "But for heaven's sake, take the time you need. Take three months."

"I can't stay that long. What if I need to sign papers about my properties?"

"Give me your power of attorney then," Olea said. "I can sign for you."

She was my friend. But what if my not wanting the women to come along sharpened Olea's nails on a power of attorney? Still, giving her the power would serve as a backup plan if I did want to stay a little longer, knowing she could handle my affairs.

"Good," I said. I didn't apologize for asking for what I wanted. I didn't back down. "I'd appreciate that. We'll get it signed and recorded in the morning."

Both women waved me off at the start of my journey. The power of attorney niggled at the back of my mind, but by the time the train hit southern Idaho, the changing landscapes, eavesdropping on strangers' stories, and settling in with my book brought me ease. I couldn't help but think of my mother and our journey.

Franklin met me in New York, and we took the train from there to Montreal. "Not a side trip," Franklin said when I protested the delay. "Essential." Montreal hosted the fur fair each year with designers and manufacturers bringing their wares. "I think you ought to see the manufacturing processes, and I want you to meet a few designers. They're very creative and love what they do. It could be a great career for you, Clara. Much less draining than fur ranching and more likely to succeed."

"I appreciate your opinion," I said. "But I'm set on fur ranching; I really am."

The First Nation processing station was a beehive of activity, and I found myself running my hands over the sewn fabrics, looking at the backs to see the thousands of seams, all matched in color and plushness, that made the pelts drape so beautifully. In one room, Indian women used lanolin, salt, and alum to soften the hides. "Used to be they chewed them," Franklin told me. "In their old age, their teeth were nothing but nubbins." Several other women worked on fur hats and muffs. "It takes forty hours for a skilled seamstress to make a single coat," he said as my eyes took in another section of activity.

A scent like leather, not unpleasant, filled the workers' room, and I found I couldn't pass a table without wanting to run my hands over the furs laid out on paper over new designs.

Franklin picked up an unfinished sealskin coat banded with fox and held it for me try on. "I see this worn over a pale blue velvet gown," he said, "to match your eyes." Even without the shoulder pads or buttons and a final cleaning yet to follow, I felt elegant wrapped inside. Maybe even…desired. It was an unfamiliar feeling.

"Much too elegant for the likes of me," I told him and moved on down the tables to watch another seamstress.

"I hadn't realized," I told him as we waited for the cab to return us to the hotel, "how sensual fur is." I know my face grew warm with the use of that word, but I could think of none better. "Soft and warm. It's like wearing fire without being burned."

"Body heat," Franklin said. "Put a fur coat over you at night, you'll see. You've been focused on the business end of things," he said. "And that's not bad," he defended when I started to protest. "But you can't ignore the rest of it. It's why people work with the pelts, why they enjoy coming up with the newest designs. Fur is part of the natural world, the earth itself." My hands still carried the memory of the soft furs I'd handled that day. My shoulders remembered the pleasant weight of the garment he'd draped around my back.

"Let the fullness of this business come in to you, Clara. Be open to it," he said. "You're entitled to the main course of life." I heard more than financial matters being spoken of in the tone of his voice. His words recalled Louise's charge that I ate the way I saw the world, refusing the

main course, spending my time nibbling without taking in true sustenance. But wasn't that required of one in exile, preserving what one
had, carefully rationing it while wandering in the wilderness, hoping to
make one's way home? I put out of my mind the biblical stories of
manna being offered daily in exile, trusting God for provision, with no
preservation but only faith for the future allowed.

"I'm trying to let it in," I said. "I'm here, aren't I?"

The cab arrived. "Good." He pressed his hand on my shoulder and
I allowed it.

Back in New York, we boarded the ship to England. We didn't travel
first class; we occupied separate rooms. Still, in the dining room, as-
sumptions were made when we were introduced because we shared a
last name and it was obvious we traveled together. I didn't correct people. I enjoyed having an escort and I found myself following his advice,
allowing myself to open up to the sights and smells and sounds of what
surrounded me. For entire evenings over dinner, I didn't think of my
family, didn't wonder what they'd say if they knew where I was and
what I was doing, an unmarried woman using *that* money for such
decadent pleasures as fine food and a ship's cabin, becoming a property
owner, and soon a fur rancher too.

Unlike when I'd traveled with Olea and Louise, I set the pace, and
Franklin obliged. If I wanted to be alone to read or write notes back to
Louise and Olea, he left me. If I wanted to talk about business, he
made the time. He'd packed a number of books for reading on board
the *St. Louis,* which took us first to Liverpool. We exchanged titles as
we'd finish and speak of the authors and themes. He was kind to the

servers, gentle with children. But he spoke with confidence at the dining table, told stories that made people lean in to hear him and settle back in laughter at the proper time. In groups, Olaf had been as silent as a mouse. So was I. Others sought Franklin's advice about travel when they learned that he'd crossed the ocean numerous times and felt at home in markets around the world. Maybe Olaf would have found such confidence one day. Maybe I would too, with the proper training.

Franklin walked me to my room, holding my elbow against the movement of the ship. He looked into my eyes as he opened the stateroom door and leaned forward toward my face. I turned away. My heartbeat quickened, though from the inexperience of what might happen next. Uncertainty pulsing? I had no trouble breathing. He wasn't the Forest of my youth. It was an observation I could have done without.

We spent several days in London visiting manufacturing houses. I thought I'd smell leaves and streams lingering on the raw skins as when I'd trapped with the Warrens' help, but the tanning process stripped that all away with sawdust and corncobs tumbling the fur. Franklin patted my gloved hand drawn through his arm as we made our way past the soft gold of fur. This was a new world to me, the facilities bigger than those I'd seen in New York years before.

We shared our dinners in the dining rooms of London's finest. "My treat," Franklin insisted each time. The view of the Thames through floor-to-ceiling windows crossed into tiny squares transported me to Shakespeare's days. I marveled that I was even here.

The day before we left England, Franklin handed me a large box wrapped in a black velvet ribbon.

"What's this?" I asked. I sat a proper distance from him on the settee in his room, always before our dinner, never after.

"Something you ought to have," he said.

I opened it with a flicker of anticipation. I'd never been given a gift from a man who was neither a brother nor stepfather. Out of the box I unfolded a luxurious motor coat made from pelts of white fox with a matching muff.

"Stand up," he said, lifting it from me to place on my shoulders. "I think I chose the correct size."

It felt like a gentle rain falling over me. The collar enthralled my neck, and with both hands I pulled it toward my chin. It smelled of the outdoors, fresh, pure. Franklin stood in front of me and buttoned the coat. It was the length of the reform dress, leaving a good foot of my black skirt hanging beneath it. "We'll be having cooler weather from here on," he said, "and you ought to have fur to ward off the chill." He stood back and gazed at me. "White becomes you, brings out the darkness of your eyes."

His words sounded thick, and his fingers lifted soft curls at my temple. With both hands, he centered the collar so it rose up toward the chignon at the top of my head. "Yes," he repeated. "White fur becomes you, especially with that new hair color." He bent to kiss me. My thoughts jumbled. When our lips parted, he stepped back.

"You'll set the pace of this, Clara. I won't push you."

"I appreciate that." My mind swirled with complications well beyond the innovations of the fur business in Finland. I wished now that Louise and Olea had come along.

Franklin stepped back, rubbed his fingers along my arms, reached back, and gave me the muff. I slipped my hands inside. He didn't apologize, for which I'm grateful, and I had no need to tell him he was the first man who had ever kissed me—save that cheek peck from Forest years before. I felt warm and protected and wondered in that moment if this—not thumping hearts or shortened breaths—was the truer form of love.

THIRTY-EIGHT

Memory Geography

JULY 1906

Cool sunshine brushed my face as summer winds whistled past our ears on the deck of the *Helsingfors* taking us to Hanko, Finland. Franklin didn't tell me until later that our new ship replaced one that had sunk the previous year coming into the gulf.

"They're building a new lighthouse in Bengtskär," he told me as we approached the gulf. "It'll rise up fifty-two meters from a rocky island. We might be able to see it from here." He pointed into the blue horizon dotted with sea gulls.

My eyes scanned the distance. Lighthouses would always make me think of Manistee, Michigan, perhaps my best memory of that city. I wished I had Olea's binoculars along. "You know so much about everything here," I said.

He shrugged. "To know Russia is to know a bit of Finland, and I know a little of Russia." The sea air felt almost warm the closer we got to our destination, and an English-speaking Finn said the port stayed free of ice in the wintertime, making it a desirable passage for both Finns and Russians. "Wealthy people come here for the climate in the summer. And winter too."

I pulled my motor coat tight around me. I liked the admiring looks from fellow travelers. A few even asked to see the coat, and I showed the lining and told them how the manufacturer sliced the leather side and then resewed it to make it supple. I'd gained a sense of competence using the terminology of manufacturing these past weeks. After visiting and listening, I could describe the artistry in what I wore and admire the intricacies of the designs, but I was still a novice.

"If the port rarely freezes, they likely don't need fur coats here," I told Franklin later.

"Russians always need fur coats," Franklin told me. "They may not be interested in your Northwest sable, but they'd be aware if someone became commercially successful in farming it."

"It's my intent to make them notice then," I said. First foxes, then mink.

"Oh, they'll notice you," he said. "I have no doubt."

I was accustomed to Franklin's compliments in the presence of Olea and Louise, but they were different when only my ears heard them. Still, I didn't want to lose myself in this man; it would be dangerous with no certain outcome.

Everywhere we went, we heard about the Finns' decision to grant women the vote and to allow women to stand for public office next year.

A Finn traveler winked at me and said, "We've sent many a countryman to America through the years, so expect them to push for such rights for women there too."

Suffrage had been my mother's cause, not mine.

At the hotel we arranged for a carriage. I commented on how many Russian voices I overheard and that the English used by the serving staff had a Russian accent to it.

"Everyone here is required to know Russian," he told me. "Finland has an uneasy relationship with the Motherland. Russia worries that the Germans might use Sweden to talk Finland into allowing a staging site for a German attack against Russia one day."

"Is that likely?"

He shrugged. "The alliances here are uneasy ones. You have to know the histories and family lineages to be sure not to step on someone's toes. I wouldn't want to be a diplomat in this part of the world. Distant cousins can be as much trouble as siblings," Franklin said.

"You are a diplomat of sorts," I said.

"Trade is different from politics," he noted. "I've kept the same contacts for years now, people Olea and Louise introduced me to, and then those contacts introduced me to others. We make many decisions based on experience over time. I accept the differences of each country's operations, and they accept my expectations and tell me if they can deliver or not. Saves a lot of time."

I knew then I'd always need an intermediary for me if I continued in this trade. I could be blunt with people, but I'd never have the knowledge Franklin had. I looked at the profile of his handsome face as he stared out at the sea. I admired him. I liked learning from him and traveling with him. But I realized that was as far as I ever wanted it to go. Olea and Louise could have come along. I'd deprived them of something they would have enjoyed, and I likely would have discovered what I needed to about Franklin and myself anyway. I'd have to write and apologize.

The second day in Hanko, we took a car to the site of the silver fox farms situated well out in the countryside with the timber and crisp air. I wore my coat, though once we got out of the vehicle, I didn't need it in the balmy breeze. Here my education deepened, and I learned from Kalmar Martensen, our host, that my success would depend on how well I treated my animals. What he told me confirmed that I had the right instincts. Our ranch near Coulee City would be quiet and isolated, no trucks or car noise to stress animals. But I'd have to build covered cages and fence running areas to keep predators out, while also allowing the animals to run freely safe inside, maturing until the fur came into prime. We discussed breeding and birthing needs, space and nutrition. Winter housing requirements. It would be no easy operation.

The foxes disappeared in the underbrush and reappeared for feeding, their bushy tails and bright eyes reminding me of dogs. "Many tons of fish we give them," Kalmar said in quite passable English.

"Fish?"

"We live near the sea, so is easy."

I looked at Franklin. "I'm thinking chickens. And eggs," I said.

"Could work," Kalmar said. We took dinner at noon with Kalmar and his family. The conversation reminded me of the table discussion on the Mica farm, where Olaf and Ole and my mother too spoke of breeding and milking and selling our cows. It was a farmer's life. Kalmar's wife said, "Is your coat one of Tsoukas's designs?"

I couldn't answer, but Franklin did. "No, it's a London designer. We haven't been to Greece yet. We'll go there after Paris. Miss Doré wants to see all aspects of the business."

"You hope to farm fox?" his wife asked.

"To begin with. But what I really want is to breed weasels, for ermine. We have some of the finest in Washington State, though short-tailed."

Kalmar leaned back in his chair. He shook his head. "Can't be done," he said. "Need the canine family to breed. It's why foxes work. Wasted time to try other wild animals. I could sell you breeding stock from here," he offered. "Don't let the woman waste her time, Franklin."

"I don't control her," he said. Then, "How much?"

Kalmar shrugged. "For you, one thousand dollars for the pair."

"A fair price," Franklin said to my surprise. "Will you consider it?" he asked, turning to me.

I knew that a single silver fox pelt could bring in well over one hundred dollars, more than ten times our little Presbyterian church's budget for home and foreign missions. But acquiring the pair would be the least of my expense and worries. Getting the animals back to Washington would be costly, with no guarantee of survival. I wanted to raise game from my own land, not import them.

"I want to try it my way first."

His wife laughed. "You could be Finnish," she said.

Maybe the name Doré was.

"We're this close to Norway," Franklin said. "We could go to Christiania. Oslo. Your relatives came from there, isn't that right?"

I hadn't remembered telling him that. Maybe Olea had. "Why would I do that?"

"Because it's where you began too," he said. We strolled along the wharf at Hanko. "I think visiting Norway would give you a path on your family search," Franklin continued.

I stopped and took a step away from him. Water lapped against the dock where we stood. What had I said or done that invited Franklin to speak of my family? It was more intimate than his kiss, which had neither been repeated nor discussed. "Have I said I'm searching for my family?" I asked.

He looked sheepish. "Memories can flow through blood." He smiled and pulled my hand through his arm and we began walking again.

"My mother left Norway when she was quite young. I can't imagine what I'd gain by walking where she walked as a child."

"The land speaks to people, Clara. It does. Who knows what Norway might have to say to you?"

Franklin put his warm hand over mine as we walked, while memory threads to my family drifted around me like a spider web still being woven.

"I suppose in Norway we could locate the fox operation Olea spoke of and take back information for her," I said.

"We have time. Let's see if we can find where your mother was born. You have a region?"

"On the Hauge farm," I said. "Near Kirkenaer, in Central Grue. Her father died when she was young. Barely two. She doesn't remember him, only her stepfather. How odd," I said, forgetting that Franklin stood beside me to overhear this thought of family. "My mother was raised by a stepfather too. I wonder when she knew?"

We crossed Sweden by train to Oslo. The silver fox operations weren't far from there, and we spent the day discovering only small differences between the management of their farm and the Finns'. Again, though, the need for high-protein food and the oils from fish were identified as important for animal health and quality of pelts. Coulee City was far from a fish source, but maybe there were canneries in Spokane. It would be something I'd have to explore if my plan took wings and flew to the other side of the ocean. The word *if* loomed larger than it had before, as the Norwegian fur ranchers also scoffed at my plans to livetrap and breed weasels.

My mother's birthplace lay north and we took another train to the city of Kirkenaer, arriving at the administrative town along the Glomma River. We headed east to Grue, past the new church built after the terrible fire that had killed over one hundred people years before. The property wasn't known as the Hauge farm anymore, but when I asked locally, people knew where I wanted to go. My nearly pure Norwegian told people I had connection to the area, and they assisted us.

We knocked on the door of the tenant's house. A small building housed pigs we could hear snorting. I thought of Ida stranded in that hog house on Mica Creek, trying to keep the children safe while Bertha lay dying. Ole had built a better building for his hogs than this one appeared to be. I could be grateful for that.

The young farmer and his wife listened to my story. They showed us the house, then urged us to walk the place. "You can't discover where you came from until you've walked about." The tenants' children gathered up eggs, and we heard the clucking of laying hens pecking worms for their young ones. Goat bells tinkled in the distance. As on the Mica Creek farm, the buildings were down in a hollow of sorts, saving open land for crops. Only the denser timber made the land noticeably different. My mother couldn't have remembered this place; she'd been too young, and yet she'd been the one to pick out the farm in Mica Creek. Maybe saving the farm had been, without her even knowing, about preserving something from her past. I wondered how she fared away from it.

Franklin was right. I enjoyed the landscape more than the old house and its sloped lean-to roof, where washtubs leaned against the clapboard. "It reminds me of our Mica Creek farm," I said. "But the surrounding timber, the woods, that makes me think of my property along the Spokane River too. That surprises me," I said.

At the local newspaper office, the editor showed us a copy of the *Morgenbladet* newspaper reporting my grandfather's death in July of 1862.

"Would you like to visit your grandfather's grave site?" Franklin asked.

"There's no need."

"We've come this far. Don't you know, Clara, that moments at a grave site can link you to a place, a people, and a past more than almost anything else?" He patted my shoulder and asked the editor for directions to the cemetery.

I'd never had a man anticipate my needs as Franklin did. It was very disconcerting.

I'd found something on this journey that I truly loved. It was not Franklin nor the furrier trade so much as travel and the nurture that walking in new landscapes gave. Franklin was the perfect companion, giving me room to consider whether I wanted this venture in fur ranching or not, pushing me with his questions while expressing confidence in whatever I decided.

Franklin and I had barely spoken of Louise and Olea as the trip had gone on. I'd sent them a postcard from Norway. (I bought extra stamps to save. I liked the colors and variety and thought placing stamps from various countries into books might fill the winter evenings.) I told them we had stopped to see my mother's home. I even sent a postcard to my mother, writing of Finland's suffrage vote. I didn't give a return address. From Paris I sent Olea and Louise an Eiffel Tower photograph, and from Greece I described our walk through the columns of the Parthenon, how the stones chipped at my leather shoes. They were not unlike the stones between the railroad ties that forced my mother to buy me more than a dozen pair on our trip east. I tried to describe the color of the Aegean Sea. The furriers were charming, I told them. I said nothing about Franklin other than to note his skill in getting me from here to there.

How different this trip would have been with them along. I'd have been looking after Louise, probably contending with Olea over travel details, and I know we wouldn't have taken the time to ride the mules to Delphi. We'd probably have stayed in Norway until winter. No, Franklin was the perfect traveling mate. Curious yet cautious, wise and adventuresome, respectful of the countries we visited, of their citizens and me.

It's what I complimented Franklin on as we steamed back to New York. We carried with us finished garments that he'd place in the retail stores in New York. He also had orders for Chicago's outlets and for Stone's Furs in Detroit. We'd not spoken of the kiss nor had any other intimate conversation, but I knew we needed to.

"I couldn't have asked for a better companion," I told him as I toasted him with my glass of white wine, which we'd taken to the ship's deck following our last dinner. Tomorrow we'd be in New York. A new moon sliced the dark sky, and I could hear the sounds of water shushing up against the ship despite the steam engines pushing us along. The smokestack belched out its inky scent. "You've been the perfect gentleman."

"Not that I think that's a compliment," he said.

"Well, it is. A single woman has to be wary," I told him.

"I don't doubt that. Especially one as lovely as you are, Clara. And you are. Don't protest every compliment you receive," he added as I started to object.

"You took the scare out of traveling for me."

"I suspect your mother did that, didn't she?"

"She was daunting," I said. "She showed me that a woman could be wise enough to raise funds to maintain us as we traveled and have judgment enough to get all the way to New York on foot. But we shouldn't have had to make that trip. If there had been better decisions made before, and after…"

"People make mistakes," he said. "It's not a crime, Clara. Maybe you ought to forgive your parents for that. They were doing the best they could."

"My parents couldn't keep their commitments," I said. "And they turned down an honorable way out."

I wished again my mother could have written of the trek. Maybe she'd have discovered insights about herself, the commitments she made and kept.

Franklin spoke.

"What?" I asked.

"I said it's not only your beauty that attracts, but the mystery and seriousness with which you approach life."

"Mysterious? I'm just…shy," I said. "I lack your wit and ease with people."

"What you lack is confidence, though I don't know why. You're very competent, Clara."

"Only because you and Olea and Louise have sponsored me. I have yet to do things truly on my own."

He turned his back to the railing, leaned against his elbows, still holding his glass by the stem. "We could continue to travel together in the future."

"I hope for that," I said. "I may well take Kalmar up on his offer one day, and I'd want you to be my escort while bringing the foxes back."

"That's not what I mean, Clara. You know that." I did. "I want us to pursue...what we've found here." He pulled a box from his pocket. "It comes with no obligations, but it reminded me of you."

I opened it. "You said I could set the pace," I told him. I held the box in my hand, the diamond ring sparkling in the deck's lights.

"True, but that doesn't keep me from expressing gratitude to you," he said.

"Franklin, I couldn't. It's much—"

"It's not an engagement ring, though I'd be pleased if it were. It's... to commemorate a wonderful journey because you rarely do nice things for yourself."

It fit. I knew it would. I leaned over to kiss him, to see if my heart could open to what I knew he longed for—for me to feel for him what a woman in love should feel, more than the infatuation of Forest. I wanted what he felt to be a bridge to something more between us. His mustache tickled my lips, his breath was sweet, his mouth gentle. Sadly, there were no sparks, no thumping heart this time, as there had been that first night when he'd walked me to the door. Was I prepared to be a spinster all my life because I expected fireworks and frolic? Maybe true love didn't demand one abandon all else for it.

"I like you, Franklin. We're... Well, we're like kin. We share a name," I said. I started to remove the ring.

"Keep it, please," he said. "It's a gift to a friend and fine traveling companion." I nodded. It was lovely. "I'd like more. This trip has shown me that. We could be a successful team."

"We are a successful team," I teased.

He said nothing. He was honest with me, and I needed to reciprocate, but the discussion made me want to chew my nails. "Perhaps I haven't been fair to you, accepting your gift, your time. I surely haven't paid you commensurate with all you've done. The side trip to Norway—"

"Was a highlight for me, to see you pick up stardust that links your family constellation." He brushed at my cheek. "I want to make you want to explore *our* universe."

"It's been the most comforting time. I love to hear you think out loud. I enjoy your banter with other guests. I admire your...felicity with words and languages and the people. I love all of that about you."

"But you don't love me."

"*Love.* Such a multilayered word with rich color, density, coverage."

"Like a good pelt," he said.

I nodded. "Could we see where this journey takes us?"

He smiled, but sadness crinkled at his eyes. " 'The traveler has to knock at every alien door to come to his own, and one has to wander through all the outer worlds to reach the innermost shrine at the end.' Rabindranath Tagore. An Indian poet," he explained.

"I guess I'm wandering through those outer worlds right now, knocking at every alien door."

"What I know is that if one isn't purposeful about affairs of the heart, they may never flower," he said.

Experience entered into this conversation, but I didn't want to know how he might have loved before and lost.

"Consider it, Clara," he continued. "You'll never find anyone who will love you more than I do." He swallowed, his Adam's apple moving in his slender neck. "Promise me you'll consider it. You could stay in Coulee City. You could continue life as you have it, but one day, we'd plan to be together, live and travel together."

"Right now, I want to achieve financial security—or lose it—on my own."

He sighed, turned back toward the sea. "I hadn't thought about love as caught up in some financial endeavor, a sort of currency."

"You invest. You risk. You can't be certain of the outcome."

"Or you double your money," he said. He smiled then. "There is no real security in this world, Clara, save God and love."

"Love is fickle and God distant from me," I told him. "I'll put my trust in the stability of funds. That's what will open those doors to the innermost shrine."

I truly thought it would.

THIRTY-NINE

Finding Home

Home in Coulee City felt right as I walked up the path to the porch. The wide boards had been swept of leaves, and the geraniums were spent-red, splattered into their grassy graves. "Anyone home?" I shouted.

Louise waddled out of the house, wiping her hands in her apron. She hugged me, admired my motor coat, and said we'd have to invest in one of those vehicles to wear it specially one day. "You look healthy and rested, Clara. The trip served you well."

She'd gained weight in the time I'd been gone, or perhaps she'd been slowly gaining it through the years and I hadn't noticed. Her face looked puffy to me and splotches of red that weren't rouge dotted her cheeks and neck. The delivery man carried my trunk inside. "Set it there, please." I pointed toward the alcove under the stairwell. I paid him and he left.

I pulled gloves from my fingers and looked around. I didn't wear the ring, would save it for special occasions. The house smelled of lavender, and I could see small knitted sacks set beside the lamp, another on the mantel, filled with the herb. I squeezed the one on the entry table and inhaled the fragrance. "Where's Olea?" I asked.

"She's…well…she's…" Louise kept wringing her hand in her apron. She turned abruptly, picked up books stacked beside a single chair, and straightened them.

"Is Olea all right?"

"Yes. Well, I believe so."

"Louise?"

"She doesn't live here anymore," she wailed.

"What?"

She collected herself. "How was your trip? Did you have a good time? Did you get new ideas? I love your coat, I simply love it!" She stroked the fur.

"Louise. What's happened?"

"Oh, I don't know." She sat down and took a hanky from her apron pocket and blew her nose. "She came in one day and said she'd found another house, down the street, and that it was time we each had our own place. I…I didn't know what to say. I haven't lived with anyone else since that time—" She stopped. "She asked me to move with her, but I… Well, I'd made a commitment to you. And we have boarders, so I couldn't up and leave them without a cook now, could I?"

I imagined Olea becoming upset about Louise's not moving with her, but what would have made her leave in the first place?

"Did the two of you argue? How soon after I left did this happen?"

If Louise had been running things on her own, that might account for the tired look on her face, the dust where my fingers left an impression when I'd reached for the lavender sachet.

"It wasn't very long after you left, no. Olea has most of the money between the two of us, as I'm sure you know. John Stone may have had the marriage annulled, but he still left her with resources."

"Olea was married? To a Stone?" So that was the reason for the constant tenderness whenever her middle name was mentioned.

"He married her and then left her."

I sat down now and looked around for Lucky and the cat. I didn't see him nor any sign of the cat either. I let Louise continue.

"When they got married, he didn't realize she was…Jewish. His family wasn't happy once they learned that."

"Olea is Jewish?"

She continued to wring her hanky through her fingers. "Let me get you cocoa," I said, to give myself time to consider her revelations. The image of a large candelabra on the Bakkes' hearth in Minneapolis came to mind. It was a menorah!

"Oh, that would be so lovely." She leaned back into the divan, and I saw then that her ankles were swollen and she wore slippers.

I said from the kitchen. "But Olea's a Christian—"

"I know it," Louise said. "She is. Her family is Jewish. She con-verted, but she lets her heritage stand, of course. Being Jewish in the furrier business wasn't a problem, but she is truly faithful. It's so sad she's gone."

The kitchen was in need of a thorough cleaning. Bits of toasted bread caked on the stove. A red sauce was so hardened on the enamel that my fingernail split when I tried to loosen it while I waited for the tea water to boil.

"Are you Jewish?" I asked, standing in the doorway. "Were you?"

"Not really," Louise said.

"She must have felt terribly betrayed by her husband," I said as I turned back to the whistling pot. Moments later I carried the tray out of the kitchen.

"John was quite the charmer," Louise said. "He loved his light Winton motorcar. Your coat would look lovely riding in that. He relished leisure, fine fashion. He was very successful." She sighed. "It's so hard to talk about." She got up and began unpacking my trunk.

"That can wait, Louise. Where's Lucky?" I braced myself for the worst. He was an old dog.

"Lucky's with Olea. I so hope you can talk Olea into coming back. I don't really want to be alone here in the winter when you're out at the farm or on your Spokane River land. And you'll want Lucky for that, won't you?"

"I don't go out there anymore, Louise, remember? Where's Lucy?"

Louise dabbed at her eyes. "She passed on," she said. "I came in here one morning, and she was dead. I dealt with it all alone."

I patted her back. Surely Olea would have helped if she'd known. Louise's hand shook as I refilled her cup.

Olea's move scattered my thinking. Was I still employed by them? If not, I'd need another job. My innovative fur ranching ideas would require more money, for years, before I'd see any real gain. And there'd been secrets kept from me. Olea's marital status, her faith history. How many more secrets might there be among the three of us?

Louise's lip trembled. "Bring her back, Clara. We're a…family."

Olea hadn't been all that pleased with Coulee City. Maybe she'd moved hoping to get Louise back to Spokane, or even New York. But why wouldn't she have bought a house somewhere besides down the street if that was her intent? The trouble between her and me before I left must have festered. *Did she buy the house with my power of attorney? Do I own her house? What's left in my bank account?*

I avoided conflict by refusing to acknowledge it until I absolutely had to; Olea avoided it by going away.

"Tomorrow," I said. "I'll talk to Olea tomorrow and get Lucky back."

"Welcome home," Louise said. She patted the back of my hand.

Within seconds, I watched Louise nod off. I stood to take the cocoa cup from her hand before it spilled. *Welcome home indeed.*

In the morning, cowboys moved cattle through the dusty streets to fading summer pastures, and I knew it wouldn't be long before there'd be the fall rodeo bringing buckaroos from outlying ranches to apply their skills to bronc busting and bull riding.

I tried to decide what I wanted to come out of my meeting with Olea—besides getting Lucky back. Here was a true alien door. I didn't want things to escalate the way the confrontation with my stepfather and mother had. I wanted clarity. My mother would have prayed before a time like this. Maybe if my parents and I had prayed that day, the break would not have happened.

Now I was guilty of fanciful thinking, but I prayed anyway as I tromped down the block to the two-story house Olea had bought. A touring car sat parked in the drive. The porch wasn't nearly as wide as the one at our house on First Street, but it had newer paint that glistened white in the morning sun. The air smelled of bacon as my neighbors prepared their breakfasts.

Olea opened the door before I could lift the knocker. Lucky scampered out past her and wagged his bushy tail, tongue lolling as I bent to hug him. "I knew it must be you. Otherwise Lucky would have barked," Olea said.

She looked the same. She wore her long Victorian skirt that swept the tips of her toes. She'd apparently been looking at a hawk soaring with the lifts and downdrafts along the coulee walls because small binoculars hung at her neck.

"I wondered if you'd come back," she said as she turned her back on me. Lucky and I followed her as I closed the door. My heart started to pound and I took a deep breath. She was a formidable woman.

"Of course I'd be back. Why wouldn't I?" I said. Lucky plopped down on a big pillow beside Olea's reading chair. Then he stood back up and trotted over, nuzzling me with his head beneath my hand. I took a seat at the divan. I scratched his neck as I waited for Olea to respond.

"Oh, I thought you might fall in love with…Europe," she said, "and not want to return to this little part of the world."

"Paris was lively but noisy. And a little smelly too."

"And Greece and Finland?"

"I loved them both."

"What about Norway?"

"I did like Norway. We went to Grue, where my mother was born. Overall, it was a very informative trip."

She put the binoculars to her eyes and looked out the window. "So you made it a pleasure trip anyway, even without us along. Franklin is easy to travel with, isn't he?" she said.

"Yes, he is."

I let the dog groan happy noises as I scratched his belly now. Lucky looked content and well-fed.

"I thought I should look after the dog," she said, turning from the window. "He can be a handful for Louise. His tail could break her hip, I believe."

"You could have done that while you were at the house," I said. "Neither of you would have been disrupted that way."

"I could have."

Would she not say anything about why she'd moved out, bought another house to live in? She took the binoculars from around her neck and set them on a round table. All these furnishings were things I'd never seen before, probably imports she and her sister had acquired. She obviously intended to remain.

"So what did you think of the silver fox operation?" she asked. "The one in Norway."

"How did you know about that?" I asked.

"Franklin wired me. After I'd wired him."

I hadn't been aware they'd corresponded while we traveled, but that wasn't anything strange. Except that Franklin hadn't mentioned it.

"Both ranching operations were...good." *If she doesn't want to talk about what happened to make her move, maybe I won't either.* "It requires a great deal of work, paying attention to the animals' environment and food in order to have a good reproductive rate. They feed the foxes mountains of fish as they're so close to the sea. The owner in Finland offered me a good price on a pair of silver foxes if I decide to start breeding them."

"It would be better to import Arctic foxes from Alaska if you intend to do that," she said.

"I agree. I didn't take him up on it, but I'll either livetrap foxes here or risk my interest in mink. I think the markets will change. There'll be a greater demand for shorter-hair pelts."

"You've come to such a projection after so short a time in the trade?"

"I've had good teachers."

"And Franklin's thoughts?"

"He didn't express an opinion one way or the other. He said I could do what I wanted, that I'm strong-willed enough to make things happen. The Norwegian in me I guess."

"Did he tell you that I sent him a telegram releasing him from working for us?"

Franklin, let go? What was Olea thinking? "No! I mean why? He's worked so well for us for years."

"He worked well for *us*," she said. "Louise and me."

I wasn't one of them; I wasn't. We were not partners and certainly not a family. I found I was short of breath.

My thoughts turned to Franklin. He'd be devastated. I certainly couldn't afford to keep him on at the contracted level he'd had with Olea and Louise. Maybe that was why he'd suggested that the two of us…partner more closely. Maybe he was thinking only of a business operation and nothing personal at all.

Except that we'd spoken of love.

"But why did you do that? You knew this was a temporary trip, so I could learn. You wanted me to go."

"That was before. I've had time to think about a few things these past months. I decided it was time I fully retired. Louise too. We'd almost done so, and then we got caught up again with your youthful interest."

My fault. I've caused the change. I took a deep breath. *I can do this all on my own.*

"Louise isn't well, you know, Clara. Or maybe you haven't noticed."

"She seemed tired," I said, "from taking care of the boarders."

"You have no boarders. Didn't you notice?"

"No. I mean it was quiet last night. I thought they might be on the travel schedule, with both of them working for the railroad."

"The boarders moved out. She doesn't remember things. She's—"

"But then how could you leave her there and move here? Why leave her unprotected, at the mercy of someone like...me?"

"I had no intention of leaving you high and dry with unhappy boarders. I waited until they found other places. But then she wouldn't believe that they weren't coming back, and she wouldn't move. I spent every day with her. Perhaps now that you're here, she'll join me. You'll encourage her, won't you? It would be best."

A distant ache began in my heart, a piercing starting like a pin-prick, then spreading out as wide as the coulee. *She invites Louise to live with her but isn't asking me?* I hadn't thought I'd care.

"What have I done?" I whispered to her. "How have I offended you?"

"I needed time alone, and now I see that Louise is in need of more care. I can do that for her, and that's best done without the distraction of business...or someone less familiar."

"Less familiar? We've been together now for over six years, looking after each other."

"We'll still be neighbors." She looked at the dog. "Lucky can visit between us. He'll get good exercise that way."

"There's nothing going on between Franklin and me," I said, thinking that's what this was all about. "He's loyal to you, as he's always been. More, really. He adores you both."

"Hmm. Irrelevant," she said. "You're free to do what you wish. Work out an arrangement with him, or let him go. But Louise and I are making a change. And sadly, that requires that you make a change too."

She said no more, returned to looking out the window at some unseen bird of flight. I stood; Lucky waited, expectant, his eyes on me. I'd allowed myself to become entangled with them, learned from them, had my dreams wrapped up with them. I'd invested in this friendship, this family. God gives the desolate a family, the Scripture promised. Maybe I wasn't desolate enough to deserve one. It would be all business between us from now on. Nothing more.

"We should finish up details," I said. "Did you need to sign any papers while I was gone?"

"Just the one that completed the Alta Vista sale. That's all settled."

"Thank you. It was good I signed the power of attorney."

She smiled then, a twinkle of the old Olea in her eye. "There was one more item. It was such a good investment I knew you'd want me to make the purchase on your behalf."

"Real estate?"

"No. Transportation. That Ford F Touring Car in the driveway is yours."

I heard the dog's toenails *click-click* along the boardwalk as I fast-walked back. I'd have to learn how to drive the thing. I shouldn't even keep it. It was a luxury purchased without any urging from me that I'd want one. Well, maybe I'd mentioned an auto a time or two, but still. She had no right.

Olea's decisions were based on Franklin, not about Louise's health. There was a jealousy present. I'd invaded a relationship they'd had for years, and though she acted as if it was fine, clearly it wasn't. I'd assumed Olea and Louise would be there to offer moral support for my new venture, that their enthusiasm was genuine. But Olea was independent, had her own resources, and she'd changed her mind because she could. I had let myself forget that, and now I'd pay the price.

"Well, I'm not leaving," Louise said when I returned and encouraged her to do what Olea had suggested. "I like this house and my room in it. It's perfect. It's more than two hundred fifty steps to her outhouse. Why should I leave just because Olea wants me to? We have a ranch to take care of. I help by caring for the boarders. Don't you remember?" She crossed her arms over her chest, tapped her foot.

"It is a lot of work to keep up," I said. Lucky sat now and licked at his hinterland, then yawned and flopped down on the linoleum with a long sigh of contentment. *Share the dog. How can we?*

"I haven't been as good about that as before," Louise said. "I'll do better, Clara." She reminded me of Ida as a child when she'd pulled up a carrot instead of a weed. "We can do this together. Olea will see that we're doing fine, and she'll come back home." She patted my hand, then an adult again, said, "I'd better get breakfast going for the boarders. They surely are quiet this morning. Must be sleeping in."

FORTY

In Service

Like the coloring of the leaves, slowly but inevitably, life began to change. I contacted Franklin and told him how things were here. I couldn't see a way to keep him in my employ as the women no longer required my service as a bookkeeper either. He wrote back, said he'd fill his schedule and now was the time to reach for something more. Would I reconsider his proposal? He included a book of poems by Tagore with his request. In it I found this: "I slept and dreamt that life was joy. I awoke and saw that life was service. I served and understood that service was joy." I quoted it back to him and said I'd be taking care of Louise now; she needed me.

I didn't know how to bridge the gulf between Olea and me, though Louise waited in the middle, ready to help. Olea was civil, even offered to teach me how to drive the car, because she'd read the manual. I could use her help but resisted it. *How dare she?* began my thoughts, though I knew that harboring self-righteousness made me more like Ida than I cared to admit.

Families accommodated, did things for each other that might not be explainable to those outside—or even those inside. What had Franklin told me? *Family* came from that Latin word *famulus,* meaning "servant."

So I became a servant, putting aside what I'd hoped would be a fur ranch one day.

The ad I ran got us new boarders, and I cooked for them myself on days when Louise rested or forgot. Louise couldn't be left alone for very long. I was especially concerned around the stove, as she'd forget the pans were hot and pick them up with her bare palms. Once she even grabbed up my curling iron, forgetting she'd fixed my hair with it. We used as much butter on her burns as in what we ate. It amazed me that nothing bad had happened while I'd been gone with Louise home alone, but maybe Olea had dropped by more than she'd let on.

When I saw the cost of the touring car, I had words with Olea. We stood in her kitchen where I'd been invited to sit for tea, but I preferred to stand instead. "Two thousand dollars? I can't afford that! Especially now that I no longer have employment," I said.

"Well, perhaps I did go overboard," Olea admitted. "But you often mentioned owning an auto. It would make it easier to visit your properties."

"Yes, it would, but at that price? I'm going to take it back," I said, "see how much money I can get for it. And then…I'll buy a Model N. They're only six hundred dollars. I think I can manage that."

"Let me teach you how to drive in the touring car first," Olea said. I thought it might be a way to engage with her without the discontent of her living away from us. So Olea taught me how to drive. It was a despicable affair, really. She didn't know enough herself, but together we figured out how to check the petroleum level, how to move the stick to go faster or slow down. I held tight to the side as we sped down a hill, and Olea shouted, "It says forty-five on that thing!" I'd never gone so fast outside of a train. Louise squealed in the backseat.

I especially loved the gas headlamps that allowed for evening spins in the cool, dry air of the coulee. The Model N didn't have such details, but then it was far less expensive. It was a good investment that brought a little passion and pleasure with it.

The Warren men and I continued our arrangement; I bought their pelts and took the hides to Spokane myself in my Model N. With that sale and the wheat harvest, if rains continued, we'd be all right. The boarders' payments gave us a little more income. I'd spent a great deal of money on the trip, more than I should have, and I had that car now. I'd "hunker down," as I'd heard men say, and do what I must. That's what families did for each other.

Perhaps they overlooked the quirkiness too and the times when one might overstep the bounds.

Snow came, and daily living consumed our time. I shoveled the walkway, ordered books on stamp collecting from the library to occupy me through the winter. Louise now read with a magnifying glass in the mornings, and at night she wrote.

"What are you working on so hard?" I asked one evening.

"Oh, I take little phrases from Scripture in the morning and think about them all day, then at night I write down how God spoke to me through them."

"That's nice," I said as I stuck another stamp into my book.

"Like this one," she continued. " 'Thou shalt love the Lord thy God with all thy heart, and with all thy soul.' Now, I've always thought of that as a command, but it's also a promise that one day I *shall* love God that way. Isn't that lovely? That came out of my day yesterday. And the rest of it is a promise too, that I *shall* love my neighbor as myself, that I can count on that, and not only because it's commanded."

Honour thy father and thy mother came to mind. Maybe that held a promise too. I decided to send a birthday card to my mother. I'd never done that. It was May, and she'd be forty-seven. Love might be more about giving even when nothing was given in return. She could decide on her own if I was worth replying to.

The Fourth of July celebrations saw Louise and me cheering at the races for our favorite horse, though we never bet a dime. Indians camped for the event in the coulee chanted into moonlight while hot breezes flirted with curtains. I checked on Louise before settling in myself for the night. Sometimes as she slept I'd hear the sounds of her snores and be comforted by them.

At the Presbyterian church on Sundays, Olea nodded recognition, then turned away to go back to her home. But she didn't join the Lutheran Danes, so I read hope when I saw her each Sunday.

"We should invite her for dinner," Louise said.

"She doesn't want to be with us," I told her.

"That doesn't matter. We want to be with her. All she can do is say no, and we're strong enough to live through that, aren't we?"

We were, but Olea had chosen to go away; Olea should choose to come back.

The real estate agent I'd had my property-buying fling with contacted me about a small rental house I might want to invest in. I looked at the figures, thought it through, and told him to buy it. The rents would make the payments. Over time, he told me of two or three others, and I invested. The home values increased; I kept the rents low to help young families in Spokane. It was better than fur ranching and, as the drought came, better than wheat farming too.

When Louise began having trouble tying her apron strings with hands that she said "acted like sticks," I sewed an apron for her that went on over her head. It covered both the front and back of her dress, with no ties but big pockets.

"It's a perfect design, Clara," she told me. "You should make several for the Ladies Aid Society bazaar. We're raising money for the Turkish refugees."

It was something I could do, and the satisfaction of making useful things to give away surprised me. I came to cherish our slow and steady life, with just a hint of sadness for the empty chair beside the extra place setting that Louise always put out for Olea. The three of us were like a tree struck by lightning. We gaped at an open wound and yet lived on as though it wasn't even there, though all the world could see.

In February 1908, Franklin surprised us. The drayage firm delivered wood and coal to our door, and Franklin arrived from the train seated beside the driver. He hugged me close when I greeted him, offering the same affection toward Louise.

"I'm inviting Olea," Louise said. "She'll be pleased to see Franklin."

Olea accepted our invitation for dinner while Franklin visited, and it felt like old times with Franklin regaling us about his trips and Olea and Louise blushing to his attention. Louise invited Olea for Easter dinner and again at Christmas. Our family might be fractured, but every now and then it reformed itself into something warm and substantial, just like a carefully crafted fur coat that is split open then resewn to make it lie so perfectly.

Following one of our Franklin dinners, in 1909, after he'd escorted Olea home and Louise had retired for the night, Franklin said, "Louise doesn't look well." We discussed her swollen ankles and the perpetual rosy blotches on her face. "She nodded off several times during dinner," he said.

"It's my cooking," I said. "I've never really gotten the hang of it."

He laughed. "Neither of you is starving. In fact, you look quite perfect. I'll bet the motor coat still fits."

"It does." I winced as I stepped to pick up the dessert plates.

"Are you all right?"

"It's just my foot," I said. "A bunion, the doctor says. I favor the ankle I sprained all those years ago."

"Let me," he said. He rose and took the dishes and put them in the kitchen. I knew of few men who ever stepped inside a kitchen except to eat, let alone pick up after himself if a woman was about. When he returned, he said, "Take your shoes off, and I'll rub your feet for you."

"Oh no, I…"

"I'm practically your brother," he said. "Now just do it."

I sat and unlaced the hooks. "I'm looking after her," I said. "The doctor says it's likely her heart's not working well enough to move everything through her body, so water settles in her feet, maybe her lungs. That all affects her thinking too."

"She has someone good to care for her," he said. He sat down on the stuffed hassock and lifted my foot, careful to keep my skirts chastely near my ankle. The massage felt wonderful, though I worried about my feet bearing smells. "You need someone to take care of you, though. And so do I." His eyes met mine.

"Surely you meet lovely women all the time," I told him. "You could find one willing to look after you."

"It wouldn't be the same," he said. "Did you know that Cleopatra bathed in wine?"

"That's fascinating. No, I didn't know that."

"Picked that tidbit up in Egypt."

"You're full of delightful trivia."

"You see? Who is there that understands what I do better than you?"

"Olea. And Louise," I said. "And dozens you must meet in your travels."

"None as comfortable as you, Clara. I truly mean that. And none with such beautiful feet as you either." He grinned. "I've checked."

"People change," I said. I thanked him and pulled my feet up under my skirts as I sat on the divan. He took a chair, sighed. "If we spent more time together," I said, "you might discover whatever it was I did that made Olea want to separate herself from me."

"There are always strains in families, Clara. The cleavage remains unless someone is willing to risk hurt feelings to bridge the chasm."

"That's why you keep bringing up *us*." I smiled.

"For that, yes, and because I know the three of you would be happier under the same roof. But one of you has to be brave enough to take the first step. Louise would benefit from it, don't you think? Do it for her."

Fur ranching became an idea left on the back of the stove to simmer. Farming of another kind consumed me the rest of the year as we planted our wheat. I made visits to my land along the Spokane River, checked on my rentals driving Louise with Lucky in the backseat. At home in Coulee City, Louise and I planted a big garden. Turning dirt calmed Louise, and I found I liked the weeding, tending, and then the harvest.

We dried fruit, canned beets and beans to have a taste of summer every winter. Louise remained about the same, but I couldn't see myself risking her well-being for the bustle and uncertainties of fur ranching. Gradually I came to accept that I was never going to be the grand success I thought I'd be one day, that I was just an ordinary woman separated from her family of birth, teamed up with a kind older woman who needed me. Could the two of us really be the family God formed in the heart of exile?

The wheat yield in 1912 proved light. None of us ranchers who chatted at the feed mill thought it was a pattern. "It'll be better next year," we told ourselves.

Storm clouds gathered but misted over us instead of dropping the cleansing, soaking rains we so badly needed for our dryland crop. We had more insects each year too, which lowered the yield. The newspapers carried no new information about selling bonds to build the reclamation dam for irrigating our coulee lands. I read that drought spread in the plains states too. We all depended on the rain. Another year like this one, and we'd be unable even to buy seed.

That same year, the train changed its schedule, not coming as often round the Big Bend, as we locals called our little coulee town. Our boarders left, and we found no one to replace them except occasional visitors riding or driving through. I heard from two of the Spokane renters that they were leaving town, their jobs having disappeared. I advertised for others but paid the mortgage for several months without benefit of the rent. It was a great relief to me when I lowered the rent and the homes finally filled up again.

Once or twice a bachelor farmer approached us after church and asked to walk us home. I often let them, fed them, reminded of my brothers. We spoke of crop prices, rainfall, the growing insect problems.

The discourse was safe and friendly and didn't trespass on safe borders; we didn't talk of any alien doors needing to be opened.

I drew from my reserves to buy winter coal and to pay our taxes that year. I had the pelts I bought from the Warrens and made a little at the sale, but my account books showed more going out for doctors' bills too. Louise seemed to like the blond physician despite the fact that she claimed he was "one of those Danes." But in checking the books as I closed out for November 1913, it soon became clear that the pelts, the poor grain yield, and Louise's small income left from the sale of the furrier business would not be enough to keep us solvent. I had to do something different.

I planned to sell the smaller acreage along the Spokane, the one with the orchard. I wouldn't get much gain selling this time of year, but people liked to make a purchase close to Christmas to celebrate in a new home. I hoped for that kind of buyer. Selling the rentals was part of my plan too. I asked Olea if she'd look after Louise while I was gone. "It might be a day or two," I said.

"Of course. If she'll stay here," Olea said.

Louise agreed when I assured her it would be a vacation and I'd be back in a flash.

When I finished my legal business, I drove to the city library to read the latest *New York Times,* which we no longer subscribed to. Wars kept the Balkans busy, the front page announced. I checked the financial section, where extensive commentaries waged about the Sixteenth Amendment and federal income tax becoming law. In New York City, one hundred fifty thousand garment workers went on strike for better working conditions and wages. I wondered if I'd met some of the seamstresses when Franklin and I had been in the city. *Not much comfort in the news,* I thought.

I put the paper back and picked up the latest city directory. My family was the only Estby listed now, all living on Mallon Avenue, Arthur and Billy as carpenters, Ida as a domestic, and Lillian as a dressmaker. My stepfather's name was missing. *Has he found work out of town? Has the printer made an error?* I'd had no return from the cards I'd sent. I flipped to the *D* section to see if any Dorés appeared: one did. Marion Doré, a carpenters' union representative. On a lark, I drove to that office. They'd know if Ole worked out of town. Maybe his absence meant I was to try to see my mother without fear of running into him.

"I'm looking for Marion Doré," I told a chubby-looking man shorter than I.

"Found him," he said. "What can I do for you?"

I wasn't sure what to say. "I…I'm a Doré. My father was from Manistee, Michigan. I always like to see if I'm related to any Dorés I encounter."

"Don't think so. I'm from Minnesota originally."

"I am too. But my name wasn't Doré then, it was Estby."

"We got Estbys here in Spokane," he said.

"Yes. I wonder if you have an Ole Estby on your rolls. What's he working on?"

"He a relative?"

"My stepfather," I said.

He looked on his ledger, his finger running down lists of names. "Well, then I'm sorry for your loss, Miss. Missus."

"My loss?"

"Earlier this year. Accident while roofing a house. Fell and died. He was a good man. Always paid his dues without complaint. You didn't know?" I shook my head. "Oh, I forget. You hail from Michigan."

Maybe they thought I wouldn't care, but I found I did. Ole was stubborn and had sent me away, but he was also the only father I'd ever known. Why hadn't my mother contacted me? Without Ole to enforce my separation, she was free to choose. My eyes started to water, and I excused myself from the carpenters' union office, sat in my car, and cried. *Should I go there? Is this an alien door I should open? Should I walk that way?* I prayed into the sounds of the Spokane Falls, hoping the thundering water could numb the pain from such deep old wounds. Without choosing, I drove and pulled up in front of the Mallon address, hands sweaty beneath white gloves. I pulled the brake. I sat. Did I hear, *Walk this way?* or were those my own wishing words? Wind whipped the elm trees in a swirl and then settled still as stains. I left the car, walked up the stone steps, and knocked on the door. I hoped Mama would be home alone.

Instead, Ida opened the door.

"Clara? Why, Clara, what are you doing here?" Little lines around her eyes suggested she'd aged beyond her years, but she still stood board-straight tall, her embroidered apron colored with stylized Norwegian birds and flowers at the bodice and the hemline.

"I'm fine. I...didn't know about Papa. I just learned. I'm sorry for you all."

A flash of irritation crossed her eyes. "Are you?"

"Yes. I mean I was angry when he sent me away but—"

"He didn't send you away, Clara. You chose to go away...with your dirty money and those women. You abandoned us."

I blinked. That wasn't at all how I'd seen it. Papa said I wasn't an Estby, as no Estby would take the money offered. Mama let him. My family practically applauded! They *sent* me away. How could she not see that?

My throat felt tight, but I spoke. "Taking the money wasn't meant to discount your suffering, Ida," I said. "I know that time in the hog shed must have been horrible."

"It's not about that." She looked away.

"We suffered too, Mama and me while in New York. Everyone suffers. We make do the best we can."

"You did well with your *money.*"

"That money belonged to us," I said, keeping my voice calm, though my hands felt damp and my chest ached. "Mama and I earned it."

She shook her head. She did not invite me in but came out to the porch instead. Wicker rockers sat waiting, but we both stood. *I'm not allowed inside.*

"Papa was right. He got better; he worked until his accident. We're doing fine. We all support each other, Arthur and Billy and now Lillian too. We take care of Mama. The union gave a small life insurance payment. God provides, Clara, without taking dirty money."

A rush of emotion surged up my neck and flushed my face, but I kept my tongue. There was no need to argue. Her wounds ran deep and defined her life even after all these years.

"I just stopped to see how you're doing." I should have kept quiet then, but I added, "I thought with Papa gone Mama might speak again of our walk and—"

"No!" She raised her hand. "It is not talked about. That's what Papa wanted, and that's what we all want too. You're the only one who has trouble with it. We didn't appreciate your postcard from Finland about suffrage. Mama has no more interest in that. I don't think she even signed up to vote last year. They ask for our birth dates; how disgusting." She shivered as though she'd eaten raw liver. "She paints now. It's good for her. Talk of that walk, never."

"Ida," I said, tears brimming in my eyes. "I'm not a terrible person. I only wanted to make my way. I would have helped you, but you wouldn't accept—"

"You could come home now, Clara. We'd welcome you. Take your name back. Doré. That's so…affected, really, isn't it? Let those women make their own way. You've done enough for them. Leave them and their money behind and start over with us. You could get a job here. You could serve your family. We don't mind if you're poor."

"Turn my back on my friends?" *Live with rules of what can be said as though Papa were still alive?*

"It's a small sacrifice to pay for your family."

"I can't leave them, Ida. They gave me a job when I needed one, paid for my schooling, taught me a trade. They nursed me when I was ill. I'm in the furrier business with them. I ranch, own properties. They—"

"No talk of them," she said. "Come home." She reached for my hand.

This was what I'd been waiting for all along, to be invited back. Yet the joy of it escaped me riding on Ida's conditions. This wasn't how the Israelites were called out of exile, was it? They weren't asked to deny the stories of where they'd been and what God had done in their lives. Why, God commanded people to tell their stories to their children.

A bird chirped over Ida's shoulder. "I…can't come home, not the way you want." I couldn't stop the tears. I wiped at them with my fingertips. I reached to hug her and she allowed it, though her arms did not hug back. "I have another family now; I can't leave them," I whispered.

"They're not family, Clara. You've chosen wrongly." She brushed my arms aside, moved past me back into the house. From the other side of the screen door she said, "I won't tell Mama you were here. It would just upset her that you've chosen not to return after you've been welcomed." She turned away, then looked back, squinted. "Your hair looks nice with that shorter style. And the color is good. You look like an Estby now."

I drove home, aware that I did have a family, with its ups and downs, but that family didn't silence me, didn't stand in my way of success or making my own mistakes. Maybe Mama knew the price I would have paid if I'd remained. I would have suffocated inside the silence, watching my tongue, not pursuing what I wanted. I had a freedom Ida never knew, never chose. My mother gave me a gift by sending me out, an expression of confidence that I could make it on my own.

The idea of a shopping spree crossed my mind, but I resisted. The sound of the car engine numbed as I chugged along but soothed too. I knew I had work to do. I needed to bring Olea back home. I needed to move forward on something that could sustain us through the years. I needed to be grateful I'd chosen the road I'd been given, even if I could never be sure where such roads would take me. Maybe I was my mother's daughter after all.

FORTY-ONE

Risk for All

B
oth Olea and Louise were at my house when I arrived. "We had a little problem," Louise said. She sniffed at her lavender sachet, looked away from me.

"She scorched the kitchen," Olea told me.

I looked around them through the door. The kitchen looked fine. I didn't smell smoke.

"My kitchen," Olea said.

"I started to fry the chicken, but then I heard Lucky groan and went to see about him—he's so old, you know—and Olea smelled the smoke and came downstairs. I heard her and noticed the fire then and tried to lift the pan, but I burned myself and threw fiery grease all over the kitchen."

"We got it out," Olea said, "but not before significant damage and the sacrifice of a perfectly good quilt to smother the flames." She clasped her hands in front of her. "I'll be doing carpentry work and painting. I find I like that kind of work, especially now with European imports drying up with war talk. It's as much fun to make furniture as to buy it."

"It's perfect timing then," I said.

"I don't see how," Olea said.

"You'll need a place to stay while you rework the kitchen. I want you to come home, Olea. We do. I'm not sure we ever said that out loud when I got back from Finland and learned you'd bought your house, but I am now. You are my family, you and Louise, and I'd like us to be together."

"What's brought this about?"

"I don't know why you left. Maybe you thought I wanted you to go, or maybe you were offended by my wanting to go to Finland alone, but—"

"But you went with Franklin," Louise said. "Didn't you?"

"Yes. I did. It was selfish of me, and I'm sorry." I took a deep breath. "I just saw my sister," I said. "She invited me to come home and told me I hadn't been sent away, that I'd gone on my own. I don't remember it that way at all. I guess in a way I had, but—"

"So you need Louise and I to be together now that you're going home."

"No! They want me to return but to act as though what I've done these past years has no meaning because…you gave me the start. And they still don't allow my mother to talk about the trip. Apparently she's accepted that, even though my stepfather has passed on."

"I'm sorry," Louise said. "He was a good man."

"You didn't know him, Louise." Olea said, turning to her.

"Didn't I?"

I patted her hand. "But seeing Ida helped me realize I've been dreaming of a reunion that could never be. I'd like to help them, but what Ida wants is for me to forget who has given me strength these past years."

"Oh, you can't forget God," Louise said. "He's the one who's done that."

I looked at her. "Yes, He did, when I listened. But my sister was speaking of you two. I've made a new life, and you're my family now. So please, Olea, come back. Let's live together. I need you because I'm going to do something you and Franklin suggested I do years ago: make up fur fashion designs and have them manufactured. I'm going to sell the other river property and invest it to take care of us."

"You'll make designs?" Olea asked.

"I have a few finished, and I'm thinking of—"

"I thought you should have done that years ago instead of that trapping business or the fur ranching fantasy," Olea said.

"And you were right."

"She got a nice trip to Europe though," Louise said.

"And she almost died of pneumonia too," Olea reminded her.

"But the Warrens looked after me. They were sent just when I needed them," I said. I loved the banter between Olea and Louise, my part in the subject. I'd missed that!

"Lucky you." Olea smiled. "We'll have to plan a trip together, the three of us."

"Yes, we will," I said. "You'll come back and live here? Please do."

"I thought you'd never ask."

We turned the shed into a workplace for Olea and got her house repaired and ready to sell. A hawk circled outside the window higher and higher, and I felt like him, more pleased and satisfied and hopeful than buying property had ever made me. We called Franklin, told him of our plans, and he concurred, helped us define each of our parts in this new venture.

In 1914, when Franklin arrived, we were ready. I'd sold the Spokane River properties to the Washington Water Power Company. It had been the most painful of sales because it meant I was truly giving up the livetrapping future. The water company planned to dam the river, and my orchards and shoreline and even the old building would be under water, only the high timber left. I'd likely never walk the land again. I thought of my mother and the Mica Creek farm. One had to move on.

Olea's house sold. I'd put the rentals in Spokane on the market, and several other properties I'd planned to keep longer to turn a better profit, I released for sale. I wanted to pool our funds for this large investment. We put the farm up for sale too, but I expected it would take a while to sell given the drought. I'd keep the taxes up.

I might sell the ring Franklin gave me to get more cash…but I couldn't let go of it, at least not yet. I twirled it on my finger as we talked.

We all sat at the table after finishing a breakfast of oatmeal and maple syrup. The windows frosted with the February cold made designs that reminded me of my mother's Hardanger lace. Franklin wore a look of anticipation.

"You'll buy high-quality pelts in Montreal, or Russia if you think, but I'd prefer as much come from North American furs," I said.

"The size and coverage is better and the color richer and deeper," Olea reminded him.

He nodded and I continued. "You'll need to secure a contract with tanners and manufacturers in London. Or Paris or Florence or Athens. We'll leave that to you. Have the garments made up where you think best, but I did like what I saw in Montreal and Paris. Bring them back for sale here in the States. Sell them in New York and Chicago."

"Not Spokane?" he said. "Isn't that what you imagined years ago?"

"Maybe, but you were all right: the big markets are where people are, and that's the East, New York. Maybe Chicago and Detroit."

"Clara," Franklin said, "if you now have resources to invest, don't you think you should follow what you'd always wanted to do, ranch wild game?"

"It's sweet of you to remember," I said. I sat back. "This is a better arrangement for our...family. And this yield doesn't depend on vagaries of breeding stock or whether I can locate enough protein within a reasonable distance, nor the years it'll take to see a profit. This is what we think we should do."

"Tensions are running high in Europe," he said. "The Balkans. The Greek president was assassinated. The war could involve us."

That surprised me. "Surely we've found more civilized ways to deal with conflict," I said. We sat thoughtful. Franklin had a better command of European issues.

"Even so, we can contract with Lloyd's to insure the shipments," he said. "That way we won't be out anything if something should happen."

Lucky meandered into the kitchen, shook himself all over. The gray around his muzzle was a sign that all of us were aging.

"Clara has a surprise for you," Olea said. "Go ahead, show him."

This was the real risk, to put out my own work. "I have a few creations," I said. I went to the room where I kept my folder of precious things: the sketches I'd drawn on the walk, the album of stamps I'd collected. The signature page of the distinguished people, including McKinley's, fell out. I laid it aside. He was gone now, assassinated by an anarchist way back in '02, the same year as Olaf's death. I lifted the thin drawing sheets I'd worked on while Louise snored in her chair. Olea showed Franklin her side cabinets, her new interest now with bedside tables over birds.

But they all hovered when I pulled out the first designs, an ermine stole and muff. "I see it over a red broadcloth coat with black velvet lining and a black beaver hat with a veil. This one would be black fox, the scarf and muff with tails." He lifted up two or three others. Ermine caps, "near seal," a man's black sealskin collar on an overcoat. "He'd wear gaiters over black oxfords," I pointed. "And this is my personal favorite, a black velvet mantle edged with white fox." I'd drawn a lattice embroidery of pearl beads and drops to crisscross the cape's back. "The silver tissue turban would have a paradise." I pointed to the feather I'd drawn coming off the model's turban, but Franklin's eyes were on the magnificent cape.

"Do you have more?"

"A few," I said. I felt like I was undressing in front of a window at night with the lights on.

"How much are you willing to invest to have these made up?"

I told him. He whistled. "It should return us triple that."

"Yes. It should."

"I don't have those kinds of funds to match your investments," he said. "I can't even contribute a quarter of that cash."

"You'll be contributing your expertise, the contacts, setting everything up," Olea told him, "making the best deals you can, marketing what we expect will be one of the finest outlays of fur fashion customers have seen since the turn of the century. We've formed a company. Deluxe DDOL Furs, with two Ds for two Dorés and one Olea and Louise. You'll have to escort the finished product back. That will make up your contribution."

"I know exactly who should work on these," he said. "They're stunning, Clara. You could find yourself in demand as a designer. Maybe I should simply take these and sell them. You wouldn't risk so much that way."

"No. We're going all the way. I'm willing to invest ten thousand dollars for our future."

The same as what my mother and I had been promised when we started our walk across the country.

Franklin wrote of his progress. I read his letters while Olea sanded a table in the shed. He'd bought fine pelts; he'd chosen the tanners and dressers and shown my designs to furriers in Paris, whom he said raised their eyebrows at their elegance. "Especially the beaded cape," he wrote. "It will be a smash in Paris and New York."

I worked on others with Olea leaning over my shoulder, commenting now and then. I soon forgot that I didn't know what had caused our rift. Families had their ebb and flow, I decided, not unlike a river. There could be dry periods and floods. What mattered was keeping on the river, not letting old snags pull one under or diverting us to streams that simply dried up and disappeared. That's what had happened with my family: we moved on different rivers. I didn't see how those streams would ever intersect again.

As I walked the fields that summer under blue skies without a hint of rain, I prayed that it wouldn't be another year of wanting. I did miss the green of the Palouse Hills, and I wondered if my mother had missed the Mica Creek farm during that long walk, missed not only the children and Ole, but the land itself. What had given her hope on that trip? Her faith? Her history of persevering, of making things happen? Was she trying to repay Ole for all he'd done, rescuing her from the shame of my existence? Maybe our conversations gave her courage on that journey. Maybe my presence did. But no longer, that was certain.

Franklin sent us postcards with special stamps he'd looked for, which I put into my book. Olea, Louise, and I enjoyed morning walks in Coulee City before the high heat of the day. We took the car out for spins. The new pharmacist in town worked on a poured cement wall around his yard meant to keep the rattlesnakes out, as his young wife deathly feared them. He drew lines in the wet cement to make them look like blocks or bricks.

"Are there snakes here?" Louise asked. "I've never seen any."

"I wonder what he'll do about the gate," I mused. "They'll crawl right under that."

"Maybe I'll offer him a finished board for the gate that can be raised or lowered depending on the season," Olea said.

"What we do for love," I said, thinking that cement wall the sweetest gesture.

When Austrian Archduke Ferdinand and his wife were assassinated in Sarajevo, I read the news report but felt confident it wouldn't affect our transport scheduled for January. I listened to that voice telling me to walk this way and felt sure I was. But one morning I awoke, sweat drenching my cotton gown. I rose and wrote out my telegram, taking it to the operator as soon as daylight showed itself. Franklin was in Paris, and I wanted to remind him to purchase insurance before he shipped.

Then I thought, *How silly. Of course he's already done that.* I walked back home and took a nap.

At harvest that fall, we three women brought dinners of fried chicken, pickled beets, string beans, fresh baked bread, potato salad, and blackberry pies out to the harvesters. Louise commented on my appetite improving, and it had. I enjoyed the taste of the pies and vowed to fix *julekaga* for us for Christmas. My fingernails had even grown out.

Lucky ambled behind us to the fields. I offered to sit in the "dog house"—what the men called the chair on the combine shaded by an awning. A man sat there and sewed tight the ears of the sacks of grain, something every woman could surely do. But the very idea was met with solemn stares. Women couldn't be part of the harvest crew; it was probably considered too much work. We were allowed only to steam over a hot kitchen stove in hundred-degree heat, preparing four meals a day to serve to the men. When he finished with his needle and thread, he stuck the needle into his wooden leg while he prepared the next sack. He pulled the needle out, held it in his hand.

"I bet you can't do that," he said, handing me the needle.

"Sure I can," I said. I took the needle from him and stuck it in his wooden leg myself. He yowled.

"Oh, I'm sorry!" My hands flew to my face. I truly was.

"You were s'posed to stick it in your own leg," he said. "Not my good one."

"Well, you know how silly women are," I told him. "We never get instructions right."

The three of us laughed together when I told Olea and Louise, but I was glad it was only a poke in his leg.

"We feed the world," I told Louise one day as we gathered eggs from the clutch Olea had built in our backyard. Louise wanted to keep the chickens in the basement of the house, but Olea and I demurred.

"I count only six eggs," Louise said. "I don't think that'll be enough to feed the world. Do you think? It's unclear." She sounded so serious, and I laughed and hugged her. What would my life be without her in it? I wondered. I enjoyed the rhythm of this place and was reminded of the peace I'd found growing up on Mica Creek. I missed anew my brothers, sisters, and yes, most of all my mother, but this was the family given to me when I was desolate. I gratefully accepted.

"Fifteenth of January, 1915. Insurance exorbitant. Cargo insured. Not all ready. Getting out. Reach New York, January late. Stop. Franklin Doré." Mr. Raymond read the telegram to me over the phone. "Sounds like everything is all right, Miss Doré."

"Yes, Mr. Raymond." The phrase "exorbitant insurance" bothered me. It would cut into our profits.

"How long has your mister been gone this time?" he asked.

"He's not my mister," I said. "You know that."

"Oh, brother then."

I let that stand. "Where was it sent from?" I asked.

"Oh, let's see. London. The Brits are in the worst of it, I hear. Guess he wants you to meet him in New York."

I didn't hear the telegram that way at all. But when Mr. Raymond delivered the paper copy to me, I did wonder if Franklin could possibly mean for me to come to New York. Maybe "reach" should have been "meet." Commerce was terribly interrupted with the Russians, British, Hungarians, Germans, French, and so many other countries shooting at each other, and I couldn't figure out what it was all about. We read of refugees. It occurred to me that few Europeans would be interested in upgrading their wardrobe of furs until after the conflict was over. Perhaps we'd picked a poor time for this venture.

At least America hadn't entered the war, though the papers suggested that war machinery geared up even here. Billy was of age for enlisting if it came to that. Arthur might be considered too old at twenty-nine. I wouldn't let myself think of that. My mother had lost enough sons and me enough brothers. I'd be glad when Franklin reached our shores and telegraphed or called saying all was well.

"Norway declared her neutrality," Olea said, putting the newspaper down. "But the allies will cut off her trade to be sure we don't support Germany." She tapped her fingers on the paper.

"I'm glad Franklin's getting out and the shipment is on its way."

"With the war," Olea said, "the demand might drop for luxury garments like the ones you've designed, but it could well increase for military use. Fur hats and trim, uniforms."

"Nothing I've designed comes close to being suitable for military function," I said.

"We'll hope for the best," she said.

We women busied ourselves. Louise knitted in between her snoring naps. Olea had made a cradle she carved for the pharmacist's wife expecting in the spring. I sketched more designs and put them away, got out my album of stamps. I organized them by color shadings, almost the way a quilter might piece what was left of her little one's dress or her husband's trousers. Nothing interrupted the growing restlessness.

On a late January morning, Lucky couldn't get up. Olea helped him stand as I entered the living room, the smell of bread baking in the oven. We watched him waddle to the porch. He turned back to look at me peering at him through the diamond-shaped glass in the door, then at the steps, then back at me. I opened the door, pulled my coat around me. "You need help?" I said. I lifted him and carried him down the steps. He wobbled a bit as all fours touched the snow, and I was surprised at how little he weighed. He shuffled to a leafless shrub, watered it without raising his leg, turning the snow yellow. He looked back at me as though apologizing for his lapse in manners, then made his way to lie beneath a tree.

"It's too cold for you out here," I said approaching. He was at least fifteen years old and had marked my life with Olea and Louise. I helped him stand again, and he let me. When he stumbled, I half carried him onto the screened back porch, where he plopped down on his rug. His doleful eyes stared up at me, and he panted as I squatted and stroked him. "We finally get everyone home and on a good, straight path, and you're acting like you might leave us. You stay here and rest," I said. He looked up at me and sighed, closed his eyes and went to sleep.

It's where Olea found us at lunchtime, me lying beside him, stroking the now still fur.

Louise was nearly inconsolable when we told her of Lucky's death. Olea rubbed her back and fixed her tea. "He lived a good long life, Louise. And you fed him like a child. When his time came, he just wanted to lie down and sleep. What better way to end life, right there next to Clara?"

"He wasn't that old," Louise said.

"Old enough," Olea told her. "Come along now, let's have an egg sandwich. Clara made bread this morning. Isn't that nice?"

"I made the bread, you say? It isn't clear."

"You might have," Olea said. "I think you took it from the oven. You did your part."

When Franklin called from New York, I was out building a fire on a spot in the backyard, thawing the ground so I could dig a hole deep enough to bury Lucky. Olea called from the porch. "I'll watch the fire," she said. "Franklin wants to talk with you."

I grieved Lucky's death, maybe even the loss of the routine we'd developed with our four-footed pal. Grief can affect our hearing and our hearts.

"But your telegram didn't say anything about meeting you in New York," I said. "It read 'reach New York.'"

"That was a mistake then," he said. "It was to have read 'meet,' not 'reach.' I wanted you here. That's why we sailed ahead of the cargo."

"But why?"

I didn't really want him chattering about personal affairs on the party line. Olga, the phone company operator, would be listening even now.

"Well, at least you know about the insurance situation."

"Yes, the telegram said the price was exorbitant. The cost of doing business, right?"

"What? No, I said the cargo was *secured*, not insured. It was aboard ship and ready to transport."

"But it is insured," I said. My heart started pounding in alarm. "You did arrange it with Lloyd's, didn't you? You had the money." I could feel my palms grow moist.

"I couldn't," he said. "They make...exceptions during wartime, and the cost... It was too much, Clara. They said themselves that they wouldn't underwrite the policy because everything was too risky."

"You let the cargo ship without insurance?" My throat felt dry. "But we planned for it."

"It would have cost nearly as much as the initial investment," he said. "I didn't have that kind of cash, and I suspect neither did you."

"How much would the insurance have cost us?" I said. "We should have sold—"

He told me and I shivered at the amount. "You're right." I swallowed. "I would have taken the risk too. There wouldn't have been time to sell the diamond ring. But we should have been consulted." *Could I have come up with more money quickly enough?*

"The phone lines are spotty for getting through, Clara." He had a reassuring voice now. "Most of the ships have made it fine. America isn't in the war. And I agree. I ought to have wired you, but I thought that if you'd been with me, you would have done the same. That's how I evaluated it, by asking what Sharon would do."

"Who is Sharon?" I said.

"What? I meant I asked myself what would Clara do."

"And you thought I'd risk the shipment?"

"I did," he said.

"Is the cargo on an American ship?" I held my breath. It would be the safest.

"No. British." he said. "The Brits have lost only a few ships, and those farther south. I just hoped you'd be here so we could talk in person. And so that, well, so that you could meet my wife. I hoped you could get to know each other on a train ride out west."

Franklin's married. I wanted to learn of the trip, everything that he hadn't been able to put into letters or that phone call. *Franklin is married.* I wanted to know about the production of the designs. *Franklin. Married.*

I wanted him to be happy. I tried not to think that he might have been distracted, and that was why he chose to let the cargo be transported uninsured. We had several thousand dollars invested, and not to cover it seemed foolish. And yet, the price… Insurance wasn't always considered necessary by our neighbors. I wondered what Sharon *had* thought.

I heated my curling iron. Things would change yet again. I'd enjoyed knowing that someone special thought about me when I wasn't there. I had looked forward to Franklin's letters, his calls. Because I so seldom saw him, he proved more angelic in my eyes than he probably was. "He was your held-out hope," I said to the image in the mirror. I felt the tears come—hard, wrenching sobs that I hoped Louise and Olea couldn't hear. I set the curling iron down and stood at the window, my chest aching with an uncertain future. I was not alone, not with Louise and Olea outside my bedroom door playing Chinese checkers. Louise had to be told the rules over and over, but Olea didn't seem to mind. They were special in each other's hearts, shared a common history as cousins. I had no one with whom I shared an uncommon past— no one except my mother and our walk, but I was no longer special in her eyes. My shared "common" past with Louise and Olea would have to be memory enough.

My mother used to say that each of us is unique in God's eyes, that God offered a fullness of life if we but allowed it, even if no one else on this earth did. *I have loved thee with an everlasting love.* I remembered the scripture from Jeremiah.

"Women friends fill up a certain space in our hearts," my mother told me following a presentation in Omaha, "and romantic love fills another. Family, though, has a special chamber that expands and expands." She'd widened her hands to show me how large a family place could be. "There's room for sunsets and rainbows and shiny rocks that remind us of our strengths, for dogs and horses and cats too. Room for the giggles of toddlers you don't even know. And over all is God's love, which flows through all the chambers, seeping into cracks and filling up the empty spaces until you're so full you almost cannot breathe. It's God who shines in the faces of all those other people looking back at you. You don't really need Forest Stapleton or anyone else."

Now, years later, I had to accept that at thirty-eight years of age, it was unlikely I'd ever find that special spark of romantic love. Franklin had come as close as any, and now he lit another woman's life.

Franklin's second call came a week later. He and Sharon were heading west as soon as the shipment arrived and he'd placed the garments in the retail shops in New York. He'd make deliveries along the way in Chicago and Detroit, Minneapolis too. Once here, we could celebrate and confer about our affairs.

I tried to imagine what Sharon looked like. He said she was French, and he pronounced her name with emphasis on the second half, "share-own." I wondered where he'd met her and how apparently effortlessly he'd brought her into his life. He might have been lonelier than I imagined to have taken a wife he'd known for such a short time.

Or maybe he'd known her for a long time. I'd had a chance with Franklin, and I'd turned it down. I felt a little sorry for myself, but I deserved this. I hadn't taken the risk of the heart. Only in business had I ventured into the unknown.

I blew my nose and lifted my chin. It was what a Doré did.

Then the third call, at three in the morning.

Franklin's voice cracked. "She's gone," he said.

"What! Who? Sharon's gone?"

"No," he said. "The ship. It went down and—"

"What! No! No, don't tell me that! Don't say that."

"What is it?" Olea asked, stepping out from her bedroom, the kitchen phone having awakened her. I shushed her.

"January 27," he wailed. "I don't know what she was doing in those waters, but the Germans sank her on January 27. No lives were lost, and they didn't even try to save the cargo. Ours wasn't the only cargo lost."

"The garments? They're...gone? Nothing was salvaged?" I thought of the beaded cape.

"Nothing," he said. "If it had been, the Germans would have taken it."

"Are you certain? Are you?"

"I am. I'm...so sorry. I..."

"I'm ruined," I told him, sinking onto the chair. "We're ruined."

Franklin had been right those years before: only God and love last, with the latter having a statute of limitations.

FORTY-TWO

Necessary Alterations

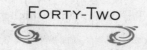

Sharon, tall and slender with eyes as dark as good earth, was gracious when they arrived in Coulee City after the disaster. That's what I called my investment gone so wrong. She told me how much Franklin cared for me. "He is like a brother to you, *oui*?"

"Yes," I told her. "A very fine brother."

"This is good then. I have a new family with a sister-in-law and aunties. A family all into one."

We sat in the kitchen going over our accounts. Franklin's face was drawn as he talked about receiving the news, how he'd hated to call me. He apologized again and took my hand in his. Sharon sat beside him. "I wouldn't have done anything to hurt you; you know that. We were partners."

"We were." I pulled my hand from beneath his. "DDOL, gone. What will you do now?"

"We've talked about it." He turned to his wife. "I think we'll settle in Montreal. I can get contracts from there. I'll still be in the business. And you? Would you consider more designing?"

"I suspect military designs will be of greater importance now."

"I love what you did," Sharon said with her French accent. "The clothes were magnificent."

"You saw the coats before they shipped?" I felt a twinge of envy.

She nodded. "Fur as soft as a baby's bottom. Supple and such beautiful lines. Franklin picked skillful tailors. And the pearl cape"—she kissed her fingers—"magnificent!"

"I don't think I'll pursue design," I said. "I'm going to get steady work, with a paycheck. Something we can count on. In time, I might reinvest in property. It financed this…adventure." I tried to be philosophical about this great loss, remembered my mother's attitude that December in New York.

"It was circumstances, the way things happen. You do what your heart tells you," Franklin said. "You understand that, don't you?"

I nodded, and I knew he spoke not only of furs but of the love of his life now sitting beside him, a gold ring on her finger. I'd made a different choice years ago not to pursue that life.

We moved into the living room. Franklin and Sharon sat on the settee, one Olea had imported and kept. We three women of the house sat in high-back chairs across from them. I felt like my aunt Hannah, though I was only thirty-eight. Somehow I'd become the older generation that my younger brothers and sisters and I had giggled over when they came to visit, smelling of cabbage or pulling on their heavy socks.

"Do you have a big family?" Olea asked Sharon.

"Oh no. Only me now. My parents are both gone. I am without brothers or sisters. And my first husband, he has died too."

"How did you two meet?" Louise asked. "I love romantic stories."

Sharon cuddled up against Franklin's shoulder. "She's a model," Franklin said. "I met her on the runway at the Montreal fair."

"He was the tall American who always arrives late," she said. "This time I bump into him, and *voilà*, it is love at the first seeing."

"It was that," he said.

As much as I struggled with the business loss and my own emotional disjoining from Franklin, I found I liked Sharon. I enjoyed seeing my friend's eyes shine when he looked at her. We'd find a way to accommodate, to alter our relationship. When they left, I became another shoulder for Franklin to hug, just like Olea and Louise; Sharon's was another cheek to kiss. I'd accept it and be grateful. I wouldn't become embittered like Ida, letting past disappointments or mistakes define my future.

I worked as in a daze, forgetful like Louise, unable to stay focused. I had no real goal, no real plan except to survive. Louise complained that I'd stopped filling my plate again, picked at my food "like a chicken."

There was nothing to keep us in Coulee City, I decided. Farm auction signs sprang up like tares among the wheat. In February, a cattleman expressed interest in our wheat land, and I told him to make me an offer. It was less than I'd hoped for, but once the house sold, we'd have enough to buy a place in Spokane, which is where I felt we needed to go.

Olea said I chastised myself too harshly about the grandeur of the plan, the impact of the insurance and the war. "People make judgments. They're good or bad. Seeking wisdom is like that. Look at us, with you and your mother's wager," she said. "Five of us offered funds in 1895 to set up the walk, and one year later, everyone's pot was less full. But we found a way to come back, at least a little, and then we could help you. You'll rise again, Clara. We'll rise together."

I looked at her, this resilient woman who had endured loss she rarely spoke of, hurts over faith too deep to share with friends.

"I'm not the prettiest woman—"

"That's not true," Louise said. "You're lovely!"

"Please." I held up my hand to stop her. "I have to say this or I won't. I'm not the most attractive woman. I know that. I'm not particularly talented. Oh yes"—I rushed on to prevent another Louise interruption—"I know I've created some designs that were well-received, but those lie at the bottom of the ocean now. I have no ability to talk to people, make them feel warm and welcome the way you do, Louise, and I'm certainly not relying on my faith the way you two do. I told myself I listened for God's direction, but it's not true. I go on about things my own way, as independent as...well, you know." I brushed a strand of hair behind my ear. "The one extraordinary thing I did in my life I can't talk about without pushing my family further from me, because it was a failure in their eyes."

I could feel the emotion welling up, threatening to choke my words. "The one thing I thought I did well—manage my money, make something of myself financially, be a successful businesswoman..." I scoffed the way Olea did when she was disgusted with something. "I've now proven that was a sham as well. I've failed at everything." My voice broke. "And I've taken your confidence in me down too. I've...failed, and I'm sorry, so very, very sorry."

The clock ticked into my terrible ache.

"May we speak now?" Olea asked.

I nodded.

"You've left out the greatest gift," Louise said. I looked up at her, took the handkerchief she handed me as she slipped her arm around my shoulders. "You have a servant's heart," she said. "You give to your family."

"My family won't even claim me," I said, "unless I abandon you."

"This family. Us. Our family."

"But I've lost the money you invested, all the money I invested too. How is that serving you?"

Olea said, "You've looked after us from the time we met you, helping with our books, giving us new interests at a time in our lives when we'd begun thinking we were, well, old. And most of all, you forgave us for not rescuing you in New York."

She'd once said I kept them in a business they'd tried to get out of. Time had changed the tune.

"But it was you who took care of me, sending me to school, giving me a roof over my head, providing me with a job, granting me money—"

"Which you'd earned," Louise insisted. "Didn't she, Olea? It isn't clear."

"It isn't clear," I said. "You let me become involved in your fur industry, introduced me to Franklin," I rushed on. "What did I ever do for you?"

"You let us," Louise said. "You let us give to you."

I sat stunned.

"I'd add another gift," Olea said. She came to sit in front of me on the big round hassock. "You know how to evaluate a situation, take in new information, and start again. That's no small feat. And that's exactly what we'll do. We'll go to Spokane and we'll get jobs."

"I'll need to sell the car."

"If you wish. But we can still work. We're not so old. Louise is right. You've taught us that. We're a family of new beginners." She patted my hand. "Clara, the best is yet to be."

"Is it?" Louise asked. "It's unclear."

But it wasn't.

"You'll come back," Louise said as I boarded the train in June 1915. I knew she wasn't talking about my business acumen. Here I was: nearly as penniless as my parents had been when the farm foreclosed. The pharmacist purchased my car for nearly what I'd paid for it, so we had a little cash, and the women insisted I keep Franklin's ring "until we're desperate."

"Yes," I said. "As soon as I have employment, I'll come back. We'll move, and things will get better."

As the train rumbled across the tracks, I thought of how I'd gotten here, my risk taken. I'd tried to control everything, but of course, no humans control the weather or "acts of war" or, I was learning, much of anything else. I leaned back on the seat, closed my eyes, tried to hear the Voice I hadn't heard for so long whispering to me, *This is the way, walk ye in it.*

At the newspaper office in Spokane, I searched the help-wanted ads. No openings were posted for any accounting work, furrier work, or even ranch management. I chose a job waiting tables at the Davenport Hotel, a grand facility that had opened the year before. I'd apply and see if my previous years of domestic service would meet requirements. Of course, they might want younger people now, but a mature woman could be an advantage in handling disgruntled customers.

The city directory lay next to the *Spokane Daily Chronicle.* Because I couldn't resist, I found the Estby page. *Helga, Arthur, Agnes, William, Ida, Lillian.* All still lived on Mallon Avenue. I wondered who Agnes was. Maybe Arthur or Billy had married.

Spokane felt like an eastern city to me as I walked toward the Davenport Hotel. New construction promised prosperity. Washington women had earned the right to vote in 1910, and there were parks with benches to sit on that I attributed to their influence. The Huttons had poured much of their $150 million silver, lead, and zinc strike into Spokane, especially helping with orphaned children. The Colville and Spokane Indians I met walking on the street stood taller. Fewer leaves gathered in the door wells, and the streets looked cleaner to me than I remembered. The Church of St. Joseph, grown from a carpenter's shop and a brick structure when I'd left, had become the Our Lady of Lourdes Cathedral, a building as imposing and intricate as any I'd seen in Europe.

I passed a furrier. I'd need to bring my motor coat here not for summer storage, but to sell.

The Davenport Hotel rose up several stories between Sprague and First Street, and the elegant lobby was as astonishing as the Waldorf-Astoria's, though much newer. I didn't swirl around like a country bumpkin beneath the domed ceiling nor stare too long at the intricate wrought-iron railings that defined the balcony, but I considered it. The thick Persian carpets, large potted plants, and English furniture softened the noise of a very busy place. Men and women in fine fashion, many wearing furs, sauntered after bellboys carrying stacks of luggage like layered cakes. The men behind the desk wore ties and vests and boutonnieres, while the scent of fresh croissants floated like a melody from the kitchen.

This is what my life had come to.

I turned around, entered the more appropriate service entrance.

I found a house for us to rent on Fairview, the same street Olea's home had been on, just down the block. She'd sold it to enter our adventure with my designs. From that quiet street I walked to the streetcar stop and began my life as a waitress at the Davenport Hotel. After three months, both Louise and Olea were hired as domestics at a smaller hotel down the street, changing sheets and washing towels. It troubled me to see them working so hard, but unexpectedly, Louise perked up with steady, routine tasks. Olea could encourage her and urged her to rest at various times through the day. It kept Louise from thinking about the garden she no longer tended.

On the streetcar, we made a game of looking at the people, guessing where they hurried to or what happened in their day to make them laugh or scowl. When I ate my lunch outside, the sun warm on my face, I wondered what I'd do if I saw Arthur or Billy or Lillian, or if I'd even recognize them. Lillian had been twelve, writing in a diary, when I'd seen her last. Maybe I'd find out where Lillian worked and take an order to her, have a dress made for Louise when I had enough saved up.

While elegant, the Davenport didn't pay waitresses all that well. But a meal was included, and I liked working among the other servers. I enjoyed the finery of the hotel and its well-portioned guests. The kitchen help told jokes, and I often took my lunch with them, remembering the hotel in Minneapolis where the reporter had found us laughing in the kitchen. Even the Deer Park Egg Farm delivery man sometimes sat down for coffee with us. His presence made me briefly long for my idea of the fur ranch. Eggs would be good food for captive animals, a fine source of protein.

Once I even brought water to the table of a man who looked familiar, and I startled when I realized it was Forest Stapleton seated next to a woman I assumed to be his wife. He was dressed as a fine businessman, but the cuffs of his coat looked frayed. He wore a puzzled expression when I said, "Good afternoon." He stared at my face and didn't answer when I asked what beverage he might like. His wife poked his side and said more loudly than necessary, "It's not polite to stare, especially at the waitresses."

"Yes. Coffee. With cream and sugar. Don't I know you?" He stared again as he handed me the menu.

"How could you, Forest? Goodness. She's the help!" his wife said, grinding out the word *help*.

"You're right, my dear." I knew he recognized me. "How ever would I know a serving girl, not even from my youth?" He looked away.

I took her order, curtsied, and left, expressing silent thanks to my mother that she had offered me a different path from where my fantasy of life with Forest Stapleton might have taken me.

I put aside a little money each month in the precious packet that held the news clippings of the walk. The hotel work proved tiring, and I slept well but had little time for card playing, stamp collecting, or even trying my hand again at designing. Walks brought me by the Spokane River and the falls, and the views of the Twin Sisters mountains in the distance gave me riches.

Olea said I became more and more frugal. I'd be alone before long. My two friends were in their sixties and I'd likely outlive them, so I needed to prepare for what lay ahead. I found it difficult to accept Olea's contributions to the household rent, but each of us contributed. That's what family did.

Franklin continued to write to us all. I read the letters out loud. He and Sharon had settled in Montreal, and he'd acquired new work in the furrier field that still required him to travel. He encouraged me to offer up new designs. He sold the ones that had been made up as garments before and made certain I received the proceeds. *If you come to Montreal, you could see them on the models at the fair next spring. The seamstresses in Paris plan to replicate the latticework cape. Bring more*

designs with you. You could keep a little finger in the business without any
risk at all, except perhaps becoming known as a fine designer.

I had no money to go to Montreal, barely enough to take the streetcar across town.

Sharon always added a message or two in her tiny script. This time
she told of the weather and the beauty of the city. "You must come
visit," she wrote. "Franklin says you are destined to travel."

"She's so much like you," Olea said after we read the last letter
aloud. "You could be sisters."

"Clara has a sister?" Louise asked.

"We have the same name."

"Your name is Sharon?"

"Her last name, Louise," Olea said. "Doré. I didn't say Clara has a
sister, though she does. I said Sharon and Clara were so much alike they
could be sisters. That tiny script, the same tall stature, that baby-fine
hair."

"And they both love Franklin," Louise said.

"But in different ways," I told her. "My hair has a bit of gray in it,"
I said. I'd long ago let the blond grow out. "Sharon's is black as mink."

"What about your other sisters?" Louise asked. "What color is their
hair?"

"They're blondes," I said. "They're too young yet to have gray twin-
ing through their chignons."

"Maybe you ought to see for sure," Olea said.

FORTY-THREE

Accounting

Olea discovered the Unity Church of Truth on Sixth and Jefferson with an assistant pastor named Emma Wells. "The first woman pastor in Spokane," Olea said. "It's good to know the faith is expanding to allow women to be of greater service." Though Emma Wells did not preach, she taught, and there was a calm about her as she did. She was gentle with Louise, so interested in what anyone had to say that I found hopefulness in her presence.

On Mother's Day I thought of contacting my mother. It was her birthday month as well. Now that I had no "dirty money" behind me, perhaps I'd be seen as one of them again.

I talked with Reverend Wells about it, and she asked me one day if money was really what the separation had been about. "The real story is rarely about what the story is about," she said. "There's always some underlying theme, with guilt and the lack of grace the main characters." I'd made an appointment to talk with her following a service when I couldn't hold back the tears. The sermon had been about the Prodigal Son.

"Louise said this curious thing one time," I said, "about how I act as though I don't deserve a full plate. Something about how I leave no time for real nourishment. I'm always busy working, looking at my schedule, keeping tidy ledger notes," I said. "Silly, don't you think?"

"It doesn't matter what I think," Reverend Wells said.

"But could that be? Could my desire to do things my own way be what I feed on?"

"It could. Or it could be what keeps you from a nourished spirit. Many of us don't think we deserve the goodness of life. We think suffering is our lot. We forget that like the Prodigal Son we are always welcomed back by God. *Prodigal* even means 'given in abundance.' Did you know that?"

"No," I said. "I thought it meant 'wayward' and 'wasteful.'"

"You're focused on how the boy behaved, not on how the father loved him."

"I attempted to reconcile," I defended. "I visited my sister."

"And you've forgiven your mother? Your sister? Forgiveness is a choice, Clara. We're commanded to forgive." I wondered if Louise's corollary about commands as promises fit with forgiveness. "It's for our own good," Reverend Wells added. "Not just for the one who is separated from us."

I rolled the Reverend's words over in my mind as I took the streetcar home. I'd accepted Ida's version of my mother, but I hadn't seen her for myself for nearly twenty years. As an opening perhaps I'd take to my mother my packet with the newspaper clippings, the signatures, those few sketches I'd made. Maybe seeing the old articles would encourage her to write the story down in secret if she hadn't already; maybe it would let her see how important the walk had been for me and for her and for other women too.

Or maybe the articles would open old wounds, as Ida suggested, where flesh had already grown over and was best left alone.

We'd lived on Fairview over a year when I learned of an opening for a clerk at a finance company, the Merchants Rating & Adjustment firm located in the realty building near Riverside and Main. I applied, and though I was a little disconcerted by the work they did—collecting from people who could not pay their debts—it paid so much better than the serving job, and physically, it wouldn't drain me. At least I hoped it wouldn't.

"You won't be asked to make collections," Mr. Oehler, the manager told me. "That task is reserved for men. It's not the sort of thing a woman could handle. But I need a clerk, a good stenographer, and you've had classes at Blair Business College, I see."

"Some years ago, but yes."

"And what have you been doing since then?"

I cleared my throat. *If I tell him I've been destitute, will that disqualify me?* "Working in the furrier industry," I said. "Assisting businesswomen from New York who moved here. I kept their accounts for many years."

"That's good. You have business experience. You've never been sent to collections?" I shook my head. "No foreclosures in your past?"

"Not in my past, no," I said.

"And right now you're…?"

"A waitress at the Davenport." He frowned. "To supplement my other work," I explained. "I like to pay cash for everything."

"That's good. You have a family?"

"I'm not married."

"Well, I know that. I wouldn't interview a married woman. Married women belong in the home. I meant, will anyone be distressed if you're asked to work late?"

"I live with two friends," I said. "If I'm needed to work late, I can arrange that." It was good to consider that I had others who might "be distressed" over me.

"Very well. I think you'll find our industry quite intriguing, Miss Doré. We're good for this country. We help people be accountable and thus become good citizens. Their lives have less pressure when they pay their bills on time. It's good they learn that."

" 'Nothing strengthens the judgment and quickens the conscience like individual responsibility,' " I quoted.

"That's good," he said. "Very good."

"A suffragette said it years ago." He might as well know that I could be outspoken.

"Are you one of that ilk?" he asked.

I had not yet registered to vote. "I believe individuals ought to have the right to pursue their dreams and live with the consequences of their decisions, whether men or women." *I sound like my mother.* "If that makes me of that ilk, then I guess I am."

He grinned. "My wife says the same thing." He wagged his finger at me. "She'll be pleased to know I'll be kept in line during the day."

And so our lives went forward one step after the other.

Louise became neither better nor any worse but continued her daily devotional ritual, finding new insights every day. The three of us shared the household tasks, took occasional weekend camping trips to

Coeur d'Alene Lake, and sometimes rode the train back to Coulee City
to visit the town and tell our old friends hello. We attended the big
rodeo in the fall, sang Christmas carols in December, and watched with
interest the smaller fur auction in January just to see how things had
changed.

Steady work gave me confidence, and I found I liked the duties,
keeping track of numbers and accounts, taking dictation, and having
my suggested wording be well-received by my employer. I looked forward to the evenings, reading and listening to the new radio Olea had
purchased. I thought about contacting my other family. I really did.
But I couldn't find the steps to take me to their door.

America entered the war then, in the summer of 1917, and we each
involved ourselves in the women's clubs raising money for refugees in
Europe. Olea attended suffrage ratification meetings and told me that
four women were arrested in front of the White House for picketing in
support of the suffrage vote—Washington women had the vote, but
only fourteen other states had adopted it. The three of us went to see
The Butcher Boy with Buster Keaton. In all the shopping, traipsing
around Spokane, and riding the streetcar, I never once caught a glimpse
of my mother or sisters or brothers.

"I wish there was a way to get a little more money so we could purchase a rental," I told Olea. I put my colored stamps into the book,
having solicited neighbors and office mates to share their canceled
stamps with me.

"What would you do with it? We're comfortable," Olea said.

"Enough is as good as a feast," I said.

"Well, yes it is," Olea agreed.

"I wish we could own this house we live in so no one could evict us.
I wish we could buy a few other properties where rent would make the

payments. We could keep the rents low, for young couples with families, but those would be good investments. You have to keep making money grow," I said.

"You never rest, Clara," Olea said, but she smiled.

"I'm still young," I told her. "I'd like to travel. We never did get the trip all of us hoped to make."

"No, we didn't."

"Even Louise last week told me that the scriptural phrase 'commit thy works unto the Lord' is yet another command that turns out to be a promise as well, that one day we'll all commit."

"The rest of that Proverb is 'and thy thoughts shall be established.'"

"I guess if we're to take another trip one day or have funds to help out others, we'll have to commit," I said. I put the stamp folder into my packet with the articles and the sketch of the Dale Creek trestle I'd made those years before. I looked over the signatures again. "It really is amazing that we got these signatures," I said. "The Governor of Idaho. President-elect McKinley. Mama got Mr. Depew to sign it too. He said he'd buy the first book, which, of course, we never wrote." I proclaimed, as Mr. Depew had: "'The first step toward getting anywhere is to decide you're not going to stay where you are.' He told us that when my mother and I sat in his office looking at his glass cases of collections and begging for train fare."

Olea winced. "I'm so sorry you had to ask for help like that. If we had been there—"

"I didn't mean that, really. It's all forgiven, truly."

She nodded. She too wished more than once she'd done something other than what she had.

"What sorts of collections did Mr. Depew have?" Louise asked, rescuing us from further painful reminiscence.

"Let me think. Something that belonged to President Lincoln, a coffee cup, I think. A pen from General Grant. Oh, and a letter supposedly written by Shakespeare to his publisher."

"Depew was a senator for a while, you know. He must like singular memorabilia," Olea said.

"Apparently," I agreed.

I looked at the signatures. I looked at Olea.

"Do you suppose," I said, my throat dry, "do you suppose he might be interested in purchasing *famous* signatures? From a remarkable walk?" I waved the list. "Like these?"

Olea grinned. "It wouldn't hurt to commit to trying."

I might still be able to hang on to my ring.

Mr. Depew paid us well for the signatures. He planned to have them framed and hang them in his office with a tiny brass plate saying they came from "The Women Trekkers of 1896: Spokane to New York City."

"You can do what you want now with the money," Louise said when I told them. "You don't have to work at Merchants."

"I like my employment," I said. "It's honest work, and I do it well."

"Then you can take a trip, go to Montreal as Franklin's always asking you to do," Olea said.

"The money belongs to all of us," I said. "I'll give some away. Louise, you get a shopping trip. And Olea?"

"Until we have universal suffrage, there's still work to do."

"We'll make a contribution to suffrage ratification and to the refugee fund too. And I'll find a way to give some to my mother." I wasn't sure how. "Maybe through the carpenters' union. I'll ask Marion Doré to make sure she gets it. She need never know."

And one day, when I heard the Voice say, *This is the way,* I'd take a step toward reconciliation, a word Reverend Emma Wells said meant "to regain." Perhaps my mother had nothing to regain in seeing me again, but I did.

I invested the remaining money in what had nurtured me as a child: land.

I bought a house on Cleveland, a block from Fairview, with a nice backyard (and a close-by privy) and inside plumbing too, and we three moved into it. I believe that house helped us weather the terrible flu epidemic that swept across the country in 1918. None of us got sick; we were healthy enough to help our neighbors who suffered.

When the house next to ours became available, I purchased it as well. "I'll rent it out to young families," I told Olea, "and keep the rent low." The upkeep and management of renters occupied me on Saturdays, and Olea enjoyed the work of repairing porch steps and painting fences while Louise bought material she turned into slipcovers and drapes. The real estate agent came to dinner often with new properties to invest in, and so I did, buying and selling, accepting an occasional loss but mostly modest gain.

In the new decade, with hemlines and hairstyles much shorter, we planned a trip—we added Franklin and Sharon—traveling to Paris and Sorrento and later to Norway, where Louise and Olea visited relatives. Franklin, Sharon, and I took a boat ride on one of the sparkling lakes near the women's family home, and we returned refreshed from seeing other lives and ways. We even bought a settee and rocker from France and had it shipped back to Spokane. Olea said her sister would be proud that we found such a bargain.

Small goals accomplished with and for family were worthy, I decided.

Then one June day in 1924, I read the Spokane paper as I usually did and found a story that told me I had steps to take. The Voice I couldn't hear but felt said, *This is the way, walk ye in it.* Walking. I'd spent my life walking toward goals and then away from them. Unlike my numbers and columns, this journey I couldn't control. I swallowed. Would she acknowledge my existence, allow me back into their lives without requiring I set aside my friends? It was time to find out.

I approached my mother's house and paused. This fine structure would have been Ole's satisfaction, that and taking care of his family without the world knowing that his wife had defied him. That was all he really wanted. I could forgive him for not taking the money but not for diminishing what we'd done those years ago, denying how we'd accomplished something remarkable, refusing her the comfort of that story. But he was gone now; hanging on to resentment hurt only me. And my mother had lost another child, her sixth. I wanted to grieve with her.

I took a deep breath. I knocked on the door. Ida opened it.

"Oh," she said, her eyes as big as biscuits.

"Who is it?" I heard my mother speak from another room, her voice a sigh from the past. "Has someone brought another casserole?"

My mother entered from the kitchen, wiping her hands on her apron.

There she stood, white hair, eyes with lines, skin drawn tight against that strong face and chin, glasses slipping on her nose. She pushed them up. She was still a handsome woman, shoulders straight as railroad ties. She no longer looked defeated, just profoundly sad.

She stepped next to Ida, stopped. "Clara?"

I am five years old, aching for her arms to comfort me when I've scraped

*my knee; I am fifteen, angry that she's told me I must leave the farm and go
to work to serve the family but still longing for her words of reassurance; I
am eighteen and she has taken me from love to walk across the continent,
propelling me to life.*

*I am a young woman standing at the edge of the Dale Creek trestle. My
mother is across the chasm looking back.*

*I am a forty-seven-year-old child, walking this way and that, aching
for my mother to call me home.*

My heart was pounding, pounding. *She has not put her arms out.
Should I reach out to her? Can I withstand the pain if she steps back?*

I am her daughter. She is the mother who started me on this walk.

I stepped forward.

PART THREE

Reunion

Forty-Four

Out of Exile

lara?" Mama repeated. "You've come home."
I put my arms up and she walked into them, the daughter giving comfort to her mother, but she reached her arms around
me too. I felt the bones in her back, her spine built of pearls, delicate but
strong.

Tears streaked the powder on my face. *She isn't sending me away.*
"Oh, Clara. You've come home, when we needed you." We held each
other, seemingly alone in the room, the longing slipping away, my soul
filling up.

"Look what the cat dragged in," Bill said then, coming from the
other room. At least I assumed it was my brother Bill. It wasn't spoken
cruelly but was Bill's way of broaching awkwardness, I decided.

"Better than a mouse, I hope," I said releasing Mama. "Though I
eat more, Billy. Do you even have a cat?" I asked.

"Not much more," he commented. "You always were thin, as I remember." Bill patted his own stomach, flat as an iron. "Can't say the

same for myself." Self-deprecating. That was a Norwegian man for you, I thought.

"Your carpentry work keeps you fit," I said.

"Meat cutting," Bill said. "I stopped carpentry a few years back. Lost the lust for it after Papa... Well." He lifted his palms, dropped them.

Lillian said, "I was seven or eight when I last saw you." I nodded. *A beautiful woman.*

"Though one day I walked by as you sat on the steps, writing in your diary with your friend...Marcia. You might have been eleven or twelve."

Lillian's brow furrowed. "Yes. Years ago," she said. A man came up behind her and put his arm around her shoulder. "My husband," she said.

"You're old enough to be married," I said.

"Of course." She smiled. A warm and direct gaze met mine.

"You were always lovely and still are," I said. "Ida," I turned to her. "It's good to see you." I didn't add "again," not certain if my mother had ever known of our encounters those years before.

"Would you like coffee?" Ida asked, and when I nodded, she left the room.

Maybe that's what was necessary now as we gathered our bearings. These mundane words, spoken like garden tools making room for bulbs, people setting themselves into this surprise, forming a new planting to bloom in the future. Maybe Mama wouldn't ever speak of the day I'd left or of the intervening years between.

"I came because I read in the paper, about Arthur," I said. "I'm so very sorry."

A woman stood beside Mama, a child huddled behind her. I wondered if it was Agnes, the name I'd read in the directory. A toddler sat on the rag rug picking at loose threads. "We haven't met," I said. I put my hand out. "I'm Arthur's sister Clara, and I'm so sorry that he's left us all."

The woman's eyes pooled with tears. "Agnes," she said. She patted her daughter's shoulder and pulled the girl to stand in front of her, arms soft on the child's shoulders. "This is Thelma. And that's Roland, our son." He had a small piece of Hardanger lace pinned to the front of his shirt. Her voice broke, and I watched as Mama moved to stand beside her, handing her a tissue. I stared at the lace piece.

"It was Arthur's," Agnes said in explanation. "I have no idea why he kept it. You're the sister Arthur wouldn't talk about."

I winced. What despicable crime might she think I'd committed?

"I've been gone a long time."

"Well, come in, sit down," Mama said. "Lillian, help your sister. You'll stay for lunch, won't you? People have been so generous, bringing food. Meningitis," she said then. "As bad as diphtheria, tuberculosis… Poor Arthur. Survived the flu and then…so very sudden." Her eyes pooled again with grief.

"I'd be pleased to, but I don't want to disrupt." I looked at Agnes. "I came…to pay my respects. To witness to our loss."

"Hardly your loss," Ida said, holding the tray with coffee on it. "You haven't seen him in more than twenty years."

"Ida," Mama said.

"To me he'll always be that young man who loved horses and dogs—"

"And cats," Thelma said. The child's lip trembled. "We had to leave our cat. Grandma and Aunt Ida say there's no room here."

"Hush," her mother cautioned.

"I've...rental property," I said. "You're welcome to it, and a cat would be fine. Your family could stay until—"

"They don't need charity," Ida said. "They need family around them, and that's what they'll have living here. We can take care of you, can't we, Thelma?" She set the tray down and with one hand hugged the child, a gesture genuine and warm. Thelma hugged her back. "We'll find ourselves an alley cat to feed. He'll be an outdoor cat. Take care of those mice." Thelma nodded her head, wiped at her eyes.

I wished I hadn't made the offer of the property. It sounded crass— or worse, boastful that I had something like that to give. Ida was right. They needed family now to ease the pain. All the money in the world could not relieve that. Money never could.

"The service will be Thursday, in Wilbur," Agnes said. "That's where we live. Lived. I'm not sure what we'll do..."

"You'll let us take care of you," Mama said. "It'll be good to have the voice of children echo in these walls for however long you need. You're doing us a favor by joining us. That's what families are for."

Agnes dabbed at her eyes, and Mama nodded once in that firm way she had that indicated, *Well, that's settled.* "I'll get us cookies." She left the room.

"So," Bill said. "What have you been doing all these years? Been in jail?" He grinned.

"Not the kind with walls," I said. "I haven't really been held hostage except by my own doing." He frowned. "I've ranched, out at Coulee City."

"You, a farmer?"

"Yes, and then I trapped for a while, got involved in the fur trade."

"Wouldn't have pictured you doing anything like trapping. Not exactly a woman's task, that."

"No, but I learned to do it. Not all that well, but adequate."

"Wait," Mama called from the kitchen. She stuck her head out through the door opening. "Wait until we're out there so we can catch up too."

I asked Bill what made him decide to become a butcher.

"Oh, I fell into it mostly. A friend told me about the work, and it pays good. Always thought it odd to call it butchering when it requires such precision." He shrugged. I wondered if he'd been in the war, then saw a photograph on the mantel of him in a uniform. "I still like music," he said. "I took up the violin."

"Did you?"

"We go to concerts now. Mother enjoys them. We heard Rubinstein play."

"I love the concerts," Mama said, entering with food she set on the dining room table. She straightened the lace doily in the center. "They remind me of the concert halls when we were in New York and—"

"Now, Mother," Bill warned. He wagged his finger. "None of that."

"We don't need to hear about New York," Ida agreed, dragging the name out as though it was scum. Ida cast a frowning glance at me. So the rule still stood: no talking of anything related to our journey, our time of perseverance, of pain and disappointment. Mama wasn't to draw nurture from that journey in front of them, not even as she faced the death of yet another son.

"Bill's quite good on the violin," Mama said skipping over her chastisement. "Here, fresh *sandbakkels*. Sit, all of you." We did. "Tell us about what you've done, Clara. Did I hear fur trapping? Goodness, what a job that would be."

I told them of my work at Merchants, my flirtation with designs, my association with Franklin. I didn't mention his last name. "And I continue to care for and live with my two friends." Ida fidgeted on her chair at the mention of them. I watched Mama's face. "They stood with me through the drought and when some of my business ventures turned sour."

"You had misfortune?" Mama asked.

"Despite all that money they gave you?" Ida said.

"Trials come to everyone," I said. "Whether you have money or not."

My mother nodded. "It does. And love and faith see us through."

"That's from your book, Grandma," Thelma said.

She is *writing her book.*

"The book you like me to read to you," Mama said as I held my breath. "Yes, I read that one to all my children. Your father loved that book too." Her eyes teared again.

"I considered fur ranching," I continued. "I went to Finland and Norway to see their operations."

"I heard there's a farm south of here trying to raise mink and fox," Billy said. "A wild scheme, if you ask me."

"I didn't know," I said. So someone else had taken on the mantle.

I was grateful to be speaking of safe things while grief settled on each person's shoulders. I wished I could find words to keep their hearts from breaking further, but I didn't know what to say.

"Norway," Agnes said. "Arthur always said he wanted to go there one day."

Maybe mundane things give way to deeper healing. "We visited Grandfather's grave, in Grue," I said. My mother jerked her head up. "Yes. And walked at the Hauge farm. It's pretty there. Parts of this state remind me of Norway, with its towering trees and streams and mountain peaks. We stayed in Oslo. The river... So deep and winding right through town, just like here."

"I was Thelma's age when I left there," Mama said. She looked at

Thelma. "My mother remarried, but not before she sent me to an English-speaking school. That was so wise of her, and I know they sacrificed to pay for it." She looked thoughtful. "It's funny, but I never felt at home in Michigan or Minnesota. Cyclones, prairie fires. But there's something comforting about Mica Creek and Spokane. Now that you say it, I do see the resemblance to Norway. Maybe our feet find the way along our ancestors' paths without our even knowing. It's good to walk them now and then."

Ida opened her mouth as though to protest the very word *walk,* looked confused, didn't speak.

"I was glad I went there," I said. "I find I like to travel. Maybe we could go there together one day."

"Clara…" Ida's voice held warning. Vigilant, that was how I'd describe my sister, vigilant in holding resentment close as a fur coat. But she must have decided that not all travel discussion could be silenced because she didn't stop me as I continued.

"I traveled to Montreal, Paris, London, even Greece. And then I spent a little time in Minneapolis and Manistee, Michigan, too."

My mother's hand shook a little, and the ice clinked in the glass as she brought it to her lips.

"What's in Michigan to see?" Lillian asked.

"A lighthouse. Timber. I walked where Ole worked and where Mother and Grandmother lived," I said, looking at my mother. "I found I didn't leave anything there I need to go back for. And besides, coming home is always best."

"It always is," Mama said. She covered my hand with her own. "It always is."

I didn't attend Arthur's funeral. It would detract from what Agnes needed then, which was all the Estby support geared toward her and nothing unpredictable coming from my presence. I planned to visit the cemetery later to lay flowers on Arthur's grave, and Ole's and the others.

Both Olea and Louise eagerly heard my story of the visit, and I saw relief when I told them how much I appreciated having them as a family to come home to.

"We're a pair," Louise said.

"There are three of us," Olea corrected.

"That's right. We're a triplet. They say good things come in threes."

"It's trouble that comes in threes," Olea said.

"Maybe. But this triplet's been good for each of us, hasn't it?"

"Indeed," I said.

"And your mother forgave you?" Olea asked. "For your association with us?"

"I believe she did," I said. "Though not in those words. We crossed a bridge, though. We'll see how things go once we're on the same side for a time."

I lit a candle and reminded Louise not to move it. Then I slipped an apron over my head and started supper.

No one had said, "I forgive you." No one had asked. It wasn't needed. Love would rebuild like bricks raising a cathedral.

I waited until a Saturday, when I was sure Ida would be at the Hutton Settlement House where she volunteered and Lillian would be working at the millinery on Sprague. Bill said he worked Saturdays until noon. I called on my mother in the morning. I carried a package with me. If Mama was alone, I'd speak with her there; if Bill or Agnes and the children were around, I had other plans.

"Well, howdy, Clara," Bill said when I stepped inside. He wasn't exactly warm, but he was cordial. "What brings you this way?"

"It's a lovely day. I thought I'd see if Mama might let me take her out to lunch."

"Clara!" Mama said. "Come in. Did you say lunch?"

"I wondered if you'd like to join me for an outing."

"Oh, I can fix us a bite right here. No need for you to spend your money."

"I'd like to," I said. "They make lovely cream puffs at the Davenport."

"Go," Bill told his mother. "Bring me one."

"Can I come too?" Thelma asked. The child wore a big red hair ribbon, and Mama touched it when she put her hand to the back of the girl's head.

"If Clara doesn't mind," Mama said.

"I'd like that," I said. "If it's all right with your mother."

"Maybe another time," Agnes said. She pulled the girl to her as though I might be carrying disease. Who knew what Ida had said. But maybe she wanted her child near to help her face her loss. I decided to look at it that way.

"I'll look forward to that. Maybe we can all go to the Davenport together one day."

"Too rich for my blood," Bill said.

"She was inviting us girls," Mama said.

Bill grunted, but he didn't look displeased.

We walked beneath a canopy of trees along Riverfront. As in the past, my mother set the pace; this time I lessened my stride to remain beside her. Silence marked our steps though it was a pleasant calm. Mama asked about my work, and I told her what I did at the bank. "Well, that's a good job," she said. "You were always good with numbers."

"I was," I said. "But it didn't keep me from making financial mistakes."

"Oh?"

I told her then of our venture with the furs and how we might have made a profit to provide for ourselves and our family in later days, but the war had come. We couldn't afford insurance. "I lost ten thousand dollars," I said.

"Oh, Clara."

"I learned a great deal about how little we really control despite how hard we plan. In hindsight, insurance would have been a good investment, but it was so expensive that even Lloyd's didn't want to insure the shipment."

"Hindsight," Mama said. "Such a fine binocular into history, so crystal-clear. But you've recovered."

I cleared my throat. "Yes, I recovered. With friends and good fortune too."

"Providence provides," Mama said, and I agreed.

At the restaurant, Mama ordered a beef sandwich with mayonnaise and onions. I ordered tomato soup and asked for extra cream puffs to take with us, enough for Bill, Agnes, the children, and all the rest when they got home from work.

"You have a package you've carried with you," Mama said.

I pushed the large square box toward her. "It's for you."

Mama looked pleased as she pulled the strings and lifted out the slender book. She opened the cover and gasped. "Where did you get these?"

"I hid them for a time," I said. "Behind the cabinet in the kitchen at Mica Creek. It's what I took with me...that day. Since then, as I traveled, I've stopped at newspaper offices and got copies of the interviews, a few of the photographs we sold. Not all of them."

"The Minneapolis articles," she said. Her shoulder rounded over the packet as though we might be arrested for looking at bad pictures.

"I thought... Well, I know Ida and Bill and maybe Lillian too don't want you talking about the trip, but it was the defining event of my life," I said. "Everything began with that journey. It's something that belongs to you and me, if not to the world. I wanted you to know I will forever treasure those months we had, despite what happened while we were gone and what happened afterward. If I could bring them back—"

"I know, I know," Mama said.

"I made a list of the signers, but the actual signatures, those I sold to Chauncey Depew. Remember him?" She nodded. "He loved memorabilia. I have the money for you, from that sale," I said.

"Oh no, Clara, that's yours to keep. You have 'occupied' well." I looked puzzled. "We should use what we're given and invest it. You have. Besides, the union pension said they'd found additional payments meant for me after Ole died, so I'm fine, with what the children share. Maybe you can help Ida one day, after I'm gone. But you're the one who saved the signatures, so you keep that money for your family."

"My family? You're my family."

"Your friends are too, Clara. They've stood with you as mine did for me."

"If only Ole had accepted the money." I sighed. "None of this separation would have happened."

Mama sat silent for a time. "When I became pregnant with you, the Dorés offered my family money. They gave it to Ole to help us make the move to Minnesota. I think he always regretted that. He wanted to do things on his own."

Dirty money. I wondered if he thought of the Dorés' funds that way.

"After Bertha and Johnny…died," Mama continued, "and we lost the farm, they tended me, Clara—Ole and my children. They brought me back to myself in time. They reminded me once again that all things are possible, even keeping silent about a special time in my life. Our lives, if that's what it took to keep my children as close to me as I could." I didn't say it was the least they could do after beating her down. The server brought our cream puffs. "After Ole died, I thought I'd contact you. I saved the cards you sent. But the others would have seen my seeking you out as a betrayal to them, to Ole too, I think. I chose," she said. "I hope you can forgive me."

"Honour thy father and thy mother," I said. "That's all I wanted to do. I'll always be Clara regardless of the last name I pick. I'll always belong to you—if you'll have me."

Mama wiped at her cheeks. She sniffed, reached for her hand-kerchief.

"You'd had a terrible grief, to the bone," I said.

"But I shouldn't have let them send you away."

"I couldn't have stayed, Mama. I know that now. I thought maybe you'd write the book for yourself, for your grandchildren to have one day. What we did, it was nothing to be ashamed of. You were doing what you thought best in serving your family. That's what I did that day I left too. I didn't really understand then about sacrifice, but I do now. I understand why you've kept silent, why you did back then."

Mama inhaled, took a sip of her lemonade. "After Ole died, I went back to the suffrage meetings. I never told the girls. I was careful, but I

loved the time with those women. I did talk about the trip then, I did."
She nodded her head. "Maybe I wasn't honoring Ole's death by doing
that, but he was gone and my memories weren't." She leaned toward
me, whispered. "I started writing things down. I have many, many
pages. I work on it late at night in my painting room. They never bother
me there. Once, when I wrote of our crossing at the Dale trestle, Thelma
came in to play in my upstairs room. She likes to do that. Such a sweet
child who so misses her father, just as I did at her age. I was so enthused
from remembering that I put my pen down on the yellow pages and
looked up and said to her, 'Thelma, don't ever forget my story.'

"'I won't, Grandma,' she said, and she hadn't a clue what I was
talking about. But maybe one day she'll get curious. Then the pages
will be there in the bottom of my trunk. And this scrapbook of yours,
that'll be there too." She reached for my hand and held it. "What a
treasure! What a treasure!" She turned the pages, let her fingers scroll
down the articles. "Oh, a dried sunflower. Yes. I'd forgotten that." She
read further. "Oh, and when the Indians in Utah looked inside our bags
that time and we had to show them what that curling iron was for, remember that?" We laughed. "The tramp and your pepper-box gun and
how the papers called our bicycle outfits Weary Waggles after the comic
hobo!" She laughed outright then. "Oh, and here's the mention of our
modeling in Chicago and all the shoes and hats we went through!"

Her face lit up and I realized how much I'd missed talking of that
trip. Olea and Louise listened, but it was nothing like the shared experience with one who'd participated. She read more, then said, "There's
nothing wrong with remembering our story, is there, Clara?"

"Not a thing," I told her. "It's how we remember what it means to
be strong. You did it for your family, Mama. You served them as best
you knew how."

"Just as my mother served me when she found Ole for me to marry."

"And me, when you made me leave my fantasy of Forest Stapleton to find a new life."

Mama leaned back, closed the book, her eyes shining with happy tears. "Visiting all those places. Being lost. That trestle. Meeting Mary Bryan, the McKinleys. All of it. It was quite a grand adventure, wasn't it, Clara?"

"It was."

"We kept those reporters entertained that evening in Minneapolis. We laughed through our tears. But that's what living looks like, I guess."

"*You* kept them entertained, Mother," I said. This was what I had to give her, a shared memory that nourished and transformed, and she received it. "Every evening that you stood on a stage and spoke, you amazed people. You were a marvel all across the country. I am so proud of you." I put aside the rightness or wrongness of what had happened those years before and just met my mother where she was.

"Are you?" Mama blinked back tears. She reached for my hand. "Well, you amazed them too," she said. "You were quite the trooper, my daughter. Such good wisdom shown, every step of the way."

I leaned back and grinned. "Oh, Mama, I was just along for the walk."

Epilogue

They'd made the arrangements before they had to. Ida accepted Clara's invitation to live with her in the house Clara owned on West Eighth. It was a Tudor duplex, and Bill and his wife, Margaret, already rented the upstairs. Clara and Ida would share the lower level.

Clara had lived alone these past four years in the Cleveland house, and during that time, Ida accepted her invitations to tea. They'd found an uneasy peace, simply never talking about "that time." Olea died in 1935 and Louise in 1938. Emma Wells presided over the services for both women, held in their home on Cleveland, and led the graveside services for them as well at Fairmont Cemetery. The two women were buried side by side, and there was an additional plot purchased for Clara. She didn't assume her family would want her buried with them at Mica Creek.

But now Clara would live again with her sister and brother. Their mother would be buried later in the week, forty-six years after she'd committed to the walk that changed all their lives.

Clara remembered Helga's words about her writing the story down. They'd talked about it now and then when they had lunch together and once when Clara joined her at the Mica Creek cemetery on the anniversary of Ole's death. Helga had continued to write, though she told no one.

Clara was glad she came to the cemetery to honor Ole. He'd been there for her mother in the beginning and cared for her through the years, not in ways Clara wanted for her, but it was really not her business how others worked out their affairs. John Doré gave Clara life, but it was Ole and her mother who gave her the family of her youth; and now, as she grew older.

After Lillian gave birth to her daughter, Norma Fay, Helga and her daughters would often get together at Lillian's house on Shannon Avenue so Lillian wouldn't have to take the streetcar with the child. Clara would pick up pastries with maraschino cherries on top and ride with them on a cardboard tray on her lap to where Lillian lived. Clara took a special liking to her nieces and nephew—and even great-nieces, after Thelma married. In later years, Clara discovered she had a creative bent in poetry and sent Norma Fay little poems. When she forgot Norma Fay's birthday one year she penned:

I bethought me of my promise
To teach our Norma Fay
That nickels make the dollars,
As she trudges down life's way.

So here you'll find another—
I have sent one on before—
And I must wait for orders,
Ere I can send you more.

And lest I should forget,
When I'm told another time,

I send along as penance,
This little, shiny dime.

She signed it "With Love from Clara to Norma Fay" and always included a coin or two or a colorful stamp. Norma Fay liked to hear the stories of the countries the stamps came from. Clara hoped the poems spoke of frugality and put personal responsibility at the forefront of any young person's mind. Her work at Merchants reminded Clara of what can happen when people overextend themselves or neglect their bills. Sadly, the collection agency thrived because of people who never learned that important lesson.

Before her mother's death, Clara had been preparing to join Franklin on a trip to Europe, as they'd done so many times since Clara had reconciled with her family and since Sharon's surprising death in 1929. That's what Clara called her slow weaving of threads back into her family quilt: reconciliation. "To reestablish friendship," her dictionary read.

Bill made little comments about her "traveling" with a man when she packed her trunks and headed east. She supposed he thought she was a courtesan, but she and Franklin were good friends who grieved Sharon's death together and enjoyed sitting by the Aegean, watching feral cats and fishermen at their trade.

That morning in April, however, Clara canceled her plans with Franklin and made the sad journey by streetcar to the house on Mallon to help sort through her mother's things. Clara hoped to take her mother's manuscript for safekeeping. Maybe after Ida and Bill passed away, it could be published. Surely her sisters wouldn't want it if they even knew of its existence. Clara didn't know how her mother's personal effects would be divided, but she'd ask for the scrapbook too and maybe one of her mother's Hardanger lace tablecloths and a quilt or a painting. She'd loved how her mother used color in her floral paintings.

When she arrived on Mallon Avenue, a presentiment silence greeted Clara. She went up to her mother's room, but her sisters weren't there. The trunk was gone. She heard voices in the backyard and looked out through the upstairs window, pulling the lace curtain back. She smelled smoke. They were likely burning trash to clean things up before people visited after the service later in the week. Margaret, Bill's wife, stood off to the side and looked on while Ida and Lillian leaned over a smoky barrel. Bill wasn't there.

Clara saw her mother's trunk beside the barrel.

The manuscript! Her heart pounded. She ran down the steps, nearly tripping on a loose tread. She swung around the banister, out through the kitchen, the glasses on her neck holder bouncing as she ran.

"Good riddance to that," Clara heard Ida say. She stopped short. "I can't believe Mama wrote that horrible story down after Papa begged her not to." Clara watched as Ida tossed the last of a pile of yellow foolscap into the flames.

"What…what are you burning?"

"Mother's story," Ida said, turning. "She wrote about that terrible, terrible time. Who would want to know what you two did back then? It's not right. It was private and painful, and Papa said never to speak of it, ever. Bill doesn't want it talked about. Lillian doesn't. I certainly don't. And you, Clara? Do you want it talked about?"

Clara stood speechless. Then, "It was her story."

"Just an old woman's reminiscing," Ida said. "And she had no right to any joy from that time, no right at all."

Ida turned back to the fire and Lillian gave Clara a hopeless look. With a stick, Ida poked the pages free to be thoroughly licked by flames.

She'd come too late!

At least her mother had had the joy of writing the story for herself. She had perhaps found comfort in remembering how her life changed by setting forth on that long-ago walk. Maybe she wrote down how she was acknowledged with an occasional smile and head nod by suffragette women when she met them later on the streets of Spokane. Honored by strangers though not by her family. Maybe she had written about Clara; she was sure her mother would have. And she'd have written of her grief, her losses, and the things that mattered most to her—family.

The scrapbook! Clara looked around. It was the only other evidence of what they'd done together. Her sisters might have burned it first. She looked at the trunk. *Empty!* Maybe her mother had hidden it separately from the manuscript. She sped by Margaret toward her mother's room, when Bill's wife reached out and touched her sleeve. Clara stopped. Margaret put her finger to her lips for silence. She moved her eyes toward a box resting on the porch.

With Ida and Lillian engaged in watching the flames devour their mother's story, Margaret spoke quietly to Clara as they moved to the steps. "I thought Thelma or maybe Norma Fay might want some of Mother Helga's lesser things one day. *The Lamplighter* book your mother read to Thelma, a few other trinkets." She moved aside one of Helga's quilts, the one with squares from the reform dress. Beneath it Clara saw two little red shoes Helga had brought with her from Norway, and Clara could see the edge of the scrapbook. Margaret looked into Clara's eyes, patted Clara's shoulder. "I'll keep them safe," she said. "You never know what stories will interest children when they're older." Then she pulled an envelope from the book with Clara's name on it, and handed it to Clara. "Your mother must have meant for you to have this," Margaret said.

Clara held the envelope, opened it. Inside was a piece of Hardanger lace, not yellowed though it was old. Clara recognized it as the piece of the heart her mother had carried on their walk. No note, but Clara knew: Helga had made certain Clara would always hold a piece of her mother's heart.

AUTHOR'S NOTES AND ACKNOWLEDGMENTS

This story could not have been written without Margaret Estby's careful saving of the scrapbook bearing bits of history of a grand walk across the continent in 1896. Margaret kept the secret until her husband, Bill, died, knowing that he too harbored resentment from that time of quarantine and loss.

The memories also would have been lost without Thelma Estby Portch's choice to dance with her grandmother through the stories. She didn't know what story her grandmother Helga wanted her to take care of, but years later, Margaret gave Thelma the scrapbook, and at last, Thelma knew the story that had meant so much to her grandmother. Darillyn Bahr Flones, great-niece of Clara, first wrote the story for a school paper in 1979. In 1984, Doug Bahr, Helga's great-great-grandson, chose to write an essay on Washington history for a contest. He based the piece on the clippings and interviews with his grandma Thelma.

Linda Lawrence Hunt's rag-rug history, which pieced together fragments of newspaper accounts, social history, and descendants' memories also kept the story alive. She filled in many of the missing pieces about the walk, Helga's life, and the social context in which the walk was made. Her award-winning account, *Bold Spirit: Helga Estby's Forgotten Walk Across Victorian America* (Random House, 2003), celebrated the often-overlooked stories of women's journeys and applauded the extraordinary trek this mother and daughter made in service to their family. It was when reading this book prior to publication that I had the privilege of meeting Linda Hunt and her husband, Jim, both professors then at Whitworth University in Spokane, Washington. Jim had been the judge in that essay contest and first alerted Linda to Doug Bahr's captivating account.

The book fascinated me, especially a brief reference stating that after their return, Clara changed her name and separated herself from the family for many years. I wanted to know what happened to Clara, how the journey might have affected her. As I began to research Clara's life, I wondered how she'd found a way to go on to business school while the Estby family perched on the cliff of foreclosure. Why did she change her name when she did and why to the name she chose? Where was she those twenty-plus years, and how might she have felt separated from her family?

I've often said that like good scientists, writers find something strange and then want to thoroughly explore it. Biography is one path to exploration. It tells us what and when and who; social history sets the context, and in this case, *Bold Spirit* set the stage for understanding the power of story and grief and what happens when one attempts to silence both. As Shakespeare so wisely noted in *Macbeth:* "Give sorrow words; the grief that does not speak, whispers the o'er-fraught heart and bids it break." Without the witness, grief sinks us into depths only love can pull us from. But neither Helga's biography or social history can tell us why the family separated as it did. Only fiction allows us to explore the truths and turmoil inside the landscapes of Clara's heart and soul, about whom the present-day family knew so little and who was described by one descendant as having "abandoned" the family.

So with the blessings of descendants Mary Kay Irwin, Dorothy

Bahr, Stephen Portch, and Norma Fay Lee, and with Linda Hunt's encouragement and shared research, I began my pursuit to discover the what and why of the daughter's story.

My journey took me to Olea Stone (sometimes called Steen) Ammundsen and Louise Gubner, the latter in partnership with Clara while they lived in Coulee City, according to the 1910 census. Olea lived down the street. Both Olea and Louise came from Norway and held links to the New York furrier industry prior to their arrival in the Spokane area around 1900, about the time the Estbys struggled with the final throes of foreclosure. This linkage to the New York fashion industry let me find them in New York in 1897 (when Louise changed her name from Gulbrandson to Gubner), and so I speculated how they might have found their way into Clara's life. I wondered if they might have had something to do with the "eastern parties" in the fashion industry who sponsored the original walk and whether disagreement tied to that journey ultimately caused the family severing. One family story indicated there were "two Norwegian women who helped Clara go to school" and finding their names linked through property and census records gave me license to make those women be Olea and Louise.

Records of deeds and mortgages reveal that Clara had funds as early as 1901 and began buying and selling property shortly after that. She owned more than twenty separate pieces of property and farms or ranches throughout her life. That she paid cash for many of the properties (the Spokane River farm, for one) proves she had funds, though the source I provided is speculation. Half and quarter sections were also owned by Clara in 1911, quite a feat for a single woman of the time. Clara owned several houses in Spokane proper. Somehow she acquired funds even after a financial failing that forced her to take a job as a waitress.

Whether Clara and her friends lost thousands in a risky venture affected by the war is unknown, but returning to Spokane and taking a position as a waitress suggests that Clara was starting over. Olea did have Clara's power of attorney, a sign of great trust between the women who shared housing in Spokane, lived on Fairview and Cleveland, and purchased burial plots together. The three women looked after each other as family.

There is no evidence that Chauncey Depew, who was a senator from New York and who did help the women return to Spokane, ever purchased the signatures. But in a twist of fate, a descendant of Helga's did marry a great-nephew of Chauncey Depew, linking the Estbys with the Depews in yet another intriguing way.

John Doré is a speculated character. However, there was a Doré in Manistee, Michigan, around the time of Clara's birth, and Clara Doré was the mother of a male Doré in that census; I named him John.

Clara began working for Merchants Rating & Adjustment Company in 1917, a position she held until her death from cancer in 1950. Her niece Thelma and Thelma's husband brought Clara a bouquet during her illness, and Clara told them it was the first time she'd ever received flowers in her life. They greatly cheered her.

The women attended the Unity Church in Spokane, and when Olea died in 1935, the Reverend Emma Wells did perform the service at the Cleveland home. Louise died three years later. After Helga died, Clara and Ida shared the home Clara owned on Eighth Street in Spokane along with Bill and Margaret, who paid their rent to Clara.

Family stories record that Clara traveled with a man to Europe and enjoyed imported European furniture. The Bahrs and Portches look after exquisite settees and chairs Clara gave them. She enjoyed stamp collecting, wore fine jewelry (Norma Fay has Clara's ring and Helga's red shoes), and knew of fashion, though she dressed modestly and fussed often with her hair. She rode the streetcar across town to pick up special pastries and share lunch with her sister Lillian and niece. Norma

Fay Lee, now in her eighties, recalls never hearing of the story of the walk until she was an adult. She and her husband of sixty-plus years began their marriage in a rental owned by Clara.

The burial plot Clara purchased next to Olea and Louise was never used by Clara. When she died in 1950, Clara's surviving siblings (Bill, Ida, and Lillian) had her buried in the Estby plot at Mica Creek. The unused burial plot with Clara's friends was sold back to the cemetery by Norma Fay in 1998. Ida was the last of the Estby children to die, at the age of ninety-nine.

While I discovered much about Clara, where she went and who she was with, I had to speculate about where she got the money to buy property, what she might have been doing in Coulee City, and who this man was she traveled with. One descendant reported his mother saying that Clara had been a courtesan and then corrected herself, saying she "traveled" often to Europe with a man.

Descendants reported that Ole was adamant about Helga not making presentations about the walk after they returned and that he forbade her to write the book or even speak of the journey. Knowing that the daughters burned the manuscript Helga wrote after her husband's death, and knowing that even her son held resentment for her having left them to make the walk, it seemed feasible that Ole might well have seen the source of Clara's funds—if they did come from "eastern parties"—as unacceptable. Helga was a guilt-ridden and shattered woman after their return, and her ability to resist the flood of grief, anger, and demands of her husband and children would have been negligible. Some answers will never be known, but I've tried to uncover the truth as revealed by the facts and stories as best I can.

Whether Clara was involved in the fur industry is speculation, though Olea and Louise's involvement is based on fact. Fur farms were in operation in Finland and Norway as portrayed. Washington State's involvement in the fur-ranching industry did not occur until the 1920s. News accounts of the famous walk mention Clara's plan to sketch for the proposed book, and Helga was an artist who painted in later years, so it seemed feasible that Clara might have created fashion designs and been successful with it.

Ida never married. She lived out her life with Clara, the sisters coming to a comfortable truce. The great-nieces and -nephews of Clara recall visiting both women and said that Ida seemed more ready for playful, energetic children than Clara was, but that both women made them feel important and welcomed as treasured members of the family. Norma Fay held a special place in Clara's heart, as evidenced by the numerous poems Clara wrote to her and the frequent trips Clara made by streetcar carrying the pastries with maraschino cherries on top on her lap.

The details that lend authenticity to any historical novel often come from people who are passionate beyond that of an individual author. Several such passionate and generous people assisted me in creating this story.

Descendants Harold Portch, Dorothy and Daryll Bahr, and Mary Kay Irwin (Dorothy and Mary Kay are daughters of Thelma Estby Portch), and Norma Fay Lee, Lillian's daughter, met with me in Spokane, answered questions, offered possibilities and, like me, were surprised by the discoveries of Clara's property acquisitions, her living in Coulee City, and her affiliation with the New York women. Dorothy and Mary Kay met with me and Linda Hunt at the little café where Helga often liked to eat pastries with maraschino cherries on top. Their willingness to answer questions and speculate was invaluable. Harold Portch's warm welcome in his home, Stephen Portch's conversations with me by phone, and Daryll Bahr's sharing photographs of the furniture Clara loved as well as family portraits and remembrances were all greatly appreciated. The kindness and generosity of these descendants, including the best chocolate dessert ever, reflected that same care I imagined in the lives of Helga, Ole, Clara, and the Estby family when they were not dealing with devastating losses.

I was blessed with access to a family history, "The Descendants of Kari Henriksdatter Furuberget Bing, the Mother of Helga Estby," by an unnamed descendant. It included the copy of Helga's article responding to a *New York Times* piece about unions. She wrote about her trip to the silver mines of Idaho. The article was printed in Norwegian in the newspapers in Chicago, Minneapolis, and St. Paul in February 1897 (translated by Tove Dahl Johansen). This family history also verifies that Clara was born to an unknown father, not Ole Estby.

Penny Hutten, coauthor with Don Popejoy of *Early Spokane* and the director of the Westerners International organization in Spokane, Washington, provided numerous details of early life in Spokane, news articles related to furriers, contacts for clarifying burial information, and even details such as who supplied the eggs for the Davenport Hotel. Penny's enthusiasm for this story and her willingness to assist with my many questions were invaluable. Her knowledge of early Spokane was priceless.

Evelyn Fricke, coordinator of the Rockford Museum near Mica Creek, is a treasure, sharing exhibit information about the Estby family and speculating with me about Clara and her relationship with her family. Linda Jones, another Rockford soul passionate about history, provided photographs and gave directions to Linda Hunt and me so we could locate the hog house the Joneses had moved from their farm, which had once been owned by Ole and Helga. This hog house, built by a careful craftsman, might well have been the place that Ida, Johnny, Arthur, Billy, and Lillian huddled in that cold spring of 1897 while Bertha lay dying in the house with her father and brother Olaf, and while Helga and Clara desperately tried to raise money to return home.

The passages about the fur business drew from the generosity and speculation of Teresa Platt of the Fur Commission (California); Dale Thiesen, Director of American Legend Fur Auction (Seattle); and Howard Noseworthy, Director of Planning for Fur Harvesters Auction Inc. (Ontario, Canada). Any inaccuracies belong to me, but their willingness to suggest the process that might have been in place in the early 1900s, and the hours spent with me at their facilities, provided authenticity to what might have been Clara's, Olea's, and Louise's roles in the furrier industry. Teresa read sections of the manuscript for accuracy, tracked down prices of pelts, and gave of her time. I am deeply grateful to her.

Franklin Doré's character grew out of their discussions that women in the industry would have had a male to act as their agent and to enter the auction houses, as women would likely not have been allowed. Teresa especially went beyond the call and was instrumental in locating the New York verification of Louise's name change in 1897. She also provided two resource books, including R. Turner Wilcox's *The Mode in Furs: The History of Furred Costume of the World from the Earliest Times to the Present,* which provided me with Clara's design for the beads-and-drops cape.

Several archivists provided copies of news accounts written about the walk, including the most extensive articles by the Minneapolis and St. Paul newspapers that included reference to the letter from the mayor of Spokane, the signatures Helga and Clara collected, and the many prestigious people they met, including the McKinleys and the Bryans.

Library archivists Riva Dean (Northwest Librarian, Spokane Public Library), Mark O'English (University Archivist, Manuscripts, Archives, & Special Collections, Washington State University in Pullman, Washington), Brigid Clift (Regional Branch Archivist, Washington State Archives in Ellensburg, Washington), and Amber Paranick (Library of Congress Serial and Government Publications Division) each located valued information, especially access to an unpublished manuscript written by Leslie Edwin Lillquist about the Big Bend country, early Coulee City, which allowed me to create a world for Clara and her acquired family there. Judy Harmon of the Sherman Public School Library in Moro again proved helpful in connecting me to a variety of library sources.

Sandra Gourdin of the Bureau of Land Management located essential maps and directed me to the land grant information for Clara's purchase of property along the Spokane River, and Alan Christianson of Western Rivers Conservancy made references for information about early fur farming that I appreciated. Lynn Wells, Spokane historian, provided details of Clara's river properties and the LaPray bridge. A morning spent with Spokane County's search of deeds located the variety of properties Clara bought in Spokane and helped me find the first mention of Olea Ammundsen. Mary Kay Irwin spent hours there and located the trail of many purchases made by Clara and the power of attorney granted to Olea, then generously gave the information to me, saying she could hardly wait to see what I would tell her about what Clara had been doing with that property. Her confidence is humbling.

Author and artist Mary Anne Radmacher created the idea Louise used to further her understanding of Scripture through Mary Anne's "Wear the Word paraPHRASE" online writing class I was privileged to take.

I must thank again Linda and Jim Hunt, who opened their home to me while I researched, shared reference material with me, and introduced me to the Estby descendants who helped make Clara's life come alive. Thank you for making room for this story in your lives.

The team at WaterBrook Multnomah Publishing Group continues to amaze me with their support. Special gratitude goes to editors Erin Healy, Shannon Marchese, Laura Wright, and all those behind the scenes who bring this book into the hands of others.

Finally, but not least, my home team deserves accolades: my husband, Jerry, map maker and cook, listener and speculator of story structure and meaning, I could not do this without you. My prayer team, Carol, Judy, Susan, Loris, and Gabby; friends Sandy, Kay, Blair, and Nancy; and my stepson, Matt, and stepdaughter, Kathleen, all sent happy thoughts and prayers through the writing process. I am grateful to them. And finally, to the readers who continue to read my stories and allow them to nurture their days: You all help me listen to the Voice saying, "This is the way, walk in it." My deepest thank-you.

Robert McKee, in his book *Story,* writes that there is truth in fiction when one can answer this question: do you believe it? If the writer and/or the reader believe it, then a piece of truth has been revealed. I hope you find it so in my accounting of *The Daughter's Walk.*

Visit Jane at www.jkbooks.com to sign up for her *Story Sparks* newsletter and to read her blogs. If you're part of a book group, consider asking Jane to join you by speakerphone for a discussion of *The Daughter's Walk.* Jane can also be reached at her Web site. To schedule bookstore events, contact Lynette Kittle at lkittle@randomhouse.com.

READERS GUIDE

1. Clara says she doesn't want to go on this trip her mother has arranged to walk from Spokane to New York City. Why do you think she didn't simply say she wouldn't go? Why do you think she agreed?

2. Why did Helga want to make the walk to New York? Were her stated reasons her real reasons?

3. Marcel Proust writes, "The real voyage of discovery consists not in seeking new landscapes but in seeing with new eyes." At what point did Clara begin to see her mother with new eyes? When did she see herself differently?

4. Clara is critical of her mother's poor planning, her side trips, and her trust in the sponsors. Yet later on, she accepts money from the very people who were part of the disastrous outcome of the journey. What allowed Clara to accept their assistance? Do you think the money was "dirty money"? Should Clara have given it back?

5. Did Clara get sent into exile, or did she exile herself by her choices?

6. Can one make gains, "occupy," and expand gifts and talents financially or emotionally without some risk? Did Clara find a way to invest in her life without risk? Why did she resist Franklin's attempts to court her? Did she see life as Louise said she did, as though she "didn't deserve a full plate"? Why or why not?

7. What was Clara seeking when she went to Manistee, Michigan? Did she find it? How did the conversation with John Doré affect her understanding of family, if at all?

8. Ida is portrayed as an angry woman, and yet her mother tells Clara she is grateful to her children, including Ida, despite their insistence that she never speak about the walk to New York. In later life, Ida and Clara live together. What do you know about Ida and Clara that makes this end possible? Is it realistic? What had to change for Ida to accept Clara back into her definition of *family*?

9. Why is it so difficult at times to hear the Voice telling us, *This is the way, walk in it*? Did Clara listen to that voice through the years? When didn't she? And what were the consequences?

10. Acts of living contain risk, and risking for family can bring both great joy and great sorrow. How did Clara deal with her times of overt family rejection such as Ida's and her stepfather's rebuffs? How did her mother deal with it? Did the two women follow similar paths, or were their journeys very different from each other? In what ways?

11. Franklin tells Clara that *family* means "servant." Do you agree with this statement? Who was Clara's family? With biological families often spread around the country, how do you define *family* today?

12. What did Clara eventually regain by reconciling with her family of origin?

13. What are your thoughts about the silencing Ole imposed on Helga? Do you agree with Clara that we are asked to "tell the stories" and that they each belong to us?

14. Are there stories within your family that have been silenced?
    Do you see ways in which the silencing has harmed or strength-
    ened the people involved?

15. What prevents you from writing your story down?